JUST TRY ME

By Paxton Quigley

GROVE ISLE PRESS

TO MY SENSEI

The Apocrypha,
Written in the First Century B.C.
The Story of Judith

"...She went up to the bedpost near Holofernes' bed, and took down his sword that hung there. She came close to his bed, and said, "Give me strength today, O Lord Our God of Israel!" Then she struck his neck twice with all of her might, and cut off his head. Next she rolled his body off the bed and pulled down the canopy from the posts. Soon afterward she went out and gave Holofernes' head to her maid, who placed it in her food bag. Then the two of them went out together and went up to the gate to Bethulia...When the people heard her voice, they hurried down to the town... "Priase God, who has not withdrawn his mercy from the house of Israel, but has destroyed our enemies by my hand this very night!" Then she pulled the head out of the bag and showed it to them and said, "See here the head of Holofernes, the commander of the Assyrian Army and here is the canopy beneath which he lay in his drunken stupor. The Lord has struck him down by the hand of a woman."

From: The New Oxford Annotated Bible with the Apocrypha.

PROLOGUE

Officer Jonathan Gondo really needed that cup of coffee. The Palo Alto Police Department's recruitment propaganda—four days on, four days off, eleven hour shifts—sure sounded good at first, but no one told him about the endless tedium of the night shifts. Every cop on the force knew that the Happy Donuts on El Camino was the only place that served up caffeine fixes twenty-four- seven, which is exactly where Gondo had purchased his final cup of java. He was carefully sipping the steaming brew as he walked back to his patrol car when the well-dressed gentleman approached him to ask directions. Gondo didn't hear where exactly the man wanted to go. It all happened too quickly.

And now Officer Gondo, stripped down to his tighty whities, his neck snapped almost in two, was folded awkwardly into the trunk of his squad car, which was parked toward the back of the parking lot of the Bridgeway Church on Middlefield Road. The gentleman, somewhat less resplendent in the patrolman's uniform, sat in the driver's seat studying a photo on the screen of his smartphone. He scrolled down from the photo to re-read the page he'd already pretty well memorized.

Sale of Tru-Youth to French Conglomerate for $550,000,000 Puts Founder Justine Baron on List of Silicon Valley's Multimillionaires Under Thirty-five

Age 32

5'7" approx 120lbs

Shoulder length blonde hair (last known photo, recent)

Daughter of Lise Baron, NYC fashion mogul and philanthropist

Co-founder and President of Tru-Youth Cosmeteuticals, Inc., Sand Hill Road, Palo Alto

Romantically linked to photographer Scott Reddington (travels a lot, rarely present)

4577 Edgewood Drive, Palo Alto

Home equipped with state-of-the-art alarm system

The smartphone rang. "Yeah," he said abruptly. "It's under control. I'm officially a twenty-four-year-old Palo Alto patrolman now. Don't worry, I did my research. Nobody's gonna miss him."

CHAPTER 1

Justine Baron left the office the same way she had every weekday, and most weekends, for the past seven years. There'd been no farewell party, no Mylar balloons, champagne toasts, no tears. Driving her Tesla out the Sand Hill Road parking lot for the last time, she did a quick check of her own emotions. Sadness? No, maybe what she felt could be better described as nostalgia, but that didn't quite cover it either. Pride? A little. Or maybe more than a little.

She'd founded TruYouth nine years earlier. Senior year at Stanford. Sheer luck and determination, and the genius and tenacity of her two Israeli partners. The luck part came when she met them during her junior year. They were grad students from Tel Aviv working on their PhD in biochemistry, she an undergrad from the Upper East Side of Manhattan majoring in Management Science, Stanfordese for marketing and business. The three had clicked the moment they met, and together they developed a formula that would revolutionize the cosmetics anti-aging industry.

Just that afternoon they had closed the sale of their company to a French luxury goods conglomerate. Of course she was proud. Elated. Rich in her own right. Finally.

So much to look forward to. So why the butterflies fluttering about her gut? Justine knew why, but she was unwilling to admit that after thirty-two years of setting goals and working to achieve them she was now allowing herself to indulge. Or at least partake in one of the two indulgences she'd denied herself since college. Without the constraint of the work ethic her mother had drilled into her since Justine started kindergarten, she was now free to play. With boys. Okay, men. One man in particular. She'd had her share of hook-ups and two or three—depending on how she counted them—serious relationships with boys and men. She and Danisha had discussed and dissected *every* detail of *every* sexual encounter like tweens at summer camp, laughing at their own girlish behavior and innocence. That innocence was long gone, but their girlishness continued unabated. Danisha would get the reasons for the butterflies.

"Call Danisha," Justine said, pushing the phone icon on her steering wheel.

Danisha picked up on the first ring. "Can't talk. About to start pinning a dress on Jennifer Lawrence."

"Quick question." Justine interrupted, "This giddy feeling in my stomach. Does that come with the truckload of money I just made?"

"No silly. That's your date with Scott."

"Well, that's stupid. I've had plenty of dates with Scott. Never felt like this."

"Sex gets hotter and hotter?"

"Yep."

"And you still want to have conversations with him? Travel with him?"

"Yep."

"Sorry to be the bearer of such devastating news, but you might just be falling in love. Later. Love you."

Waiting at the light on University Avenue, she caught herself fantasizing about Scott's naked body, running her hands over his long, lean muscles. Scott would be at her place in forty minutes. *Shit*, she thought, checking her ETA on the GPS, that only gave her twenty minutes to get ready and she *had* to look perfect when he walked in the front door. She'd splurged on a crimson Alaia dress and a pair of strappy Louboutins specifically for this occasion. Their last night together before he left on his next assignment. He was always traipsing off to some far-away exotic locale with no wifi or cell service. This time it was Namibia, photographing cheetahs for a Nat Geo cover story.

They'd met on an Extreme Sports climbing expedition in Yosemite. Justine's Israeli business partners had brought her, without them the group would've never accepted her as a guest, much less a member. The partners vouched for her skills in *Krav Maga*, the Israeli martial art, which she'd started studying back in high school in New York City.

That day at Yosemite, Justine was the newbie in the group—her mother called them daredevils, "Evel Knevil on steroids," of which Scott was a charter member. The group didn't call themselves anything as they were too preoccupied with scaling steep rock faces, hang gliding over the Central Valley, body-boarding in the death eddies of the Pacific, bungee-jumping or parachuting off bridges or any machine that could take them high enough to achieve that adrenaline rush that comes with daring to glimpse the shadow of death, protected only by their superb physical conditioning and lightning reflexes.

Justine and Scott were the only civilians in their Northern California group. The sport, known formally as Extreme Sports, was, for the most part, dominated by former American military men, and probably a few military women. Though Justine had yet to meet one. She did meet former SEALs, Delta, Air Force Power Rescue, Green Berets and even a SPETNAZ from Russia. Justine's group had no Russians, but they did have plenty of Israelis.

"How's it feel to be the only woman here?" Scott had asked her.

"I hadn't noticed," Justine lied. She knew the question was both a come-on and a challenge. Any trepidation she'd felt at the prospect of scaling the rest of Elektra swiftly morphed into adrenaline. She didn't have to struggle too hard to keep up with Scott, and being just a few feet behind him gave her the sweetest view of his perfect ass.

It wasn't long before they'd started spending all their free time together. But as Justine was also preparing to sell her business, that time was limited.

Now, standing at her front door, she disarmed the alarm, unlocked the door and ran up the stairs to her bedroom. After dumping the contents of her purse on the bed; three iPhones, one iPad, and one overstuffed cosmetics case, she hit the Rihanna playlist on her Sonos, then stripped off her clothes and headed for the shower.

She was lathering shampoo into her hair when she felt it. Something was not right. Suddenly she knew she wasn't alone.

CHAPTER 2

She could barely make out the outline of a body on the other side of the shower door. It was tall—probably male? Definitely moving. *Shit. Is he taking his clothes off?* She looked around frantically for some kind of weapon. A razor, a full glass bottle of shampoo, anything heavy enough to smash over his head.

"I have a gun!" she called out loudly but calmly.

"You have a gun?"

It was Scott. "What the fucking fuck?" she screamed, kicking the door open.

"I didn't get your text until I was at your front door! Which was un-locked, by the way."

"You scared the fuck out of me!" she said, smacking his chest with her fists.

"I certainly hope not," he responded, amused. "When I heard your shower running, how could I resist?"

Justine softened and laughed along with him. "I'm so happy that you didn't resist, since I *can't* resist," she said, pulling him towards her. "Come on in. Get wet with me."

"I'd like to get you wet in another way," he said, resisting her. "Come, my lovely turbaned goddess. You're clean enough. Let me dry you off. Then we can do all sorts of fun things. In the bed things, on the floor…"

They'd both fallen into the first stages of sleep, after what seemed like minutes but was actually hours of lovemaking, when Justine was startled awake by the chime of her front doorbell. She glanced at the time on the TV cable box. Two A.M. The doorbell chimed again.

Scott roused. "They'll get tired and leave," he whispered. "Go back to sleep. I gotta be at the airport in a few hours. My flight leaves at ten."

The doorbell rang again. And again. And again.

Justine reached over to her nightstand for the remote control, turned on the security monitor on her TV. "It's a cop."

"He must have the wrong house. Ignore it."

The doorbell continued to chime incessantly. Scott groaned.

"What if it's some kind of emergency?" Justine said. She sat up and almost made it out of the bed before Scott pulled her back under the covers.

"Fuck the police! What's an emergency is *me* wanting to fuck you again before I have to leave."

"Oh for the love, stop with the fucking doorbell already." The sound was unbearable. "I'm gonna go downstairs and check this out."

"Seriously?"

"Seriously. And no playing with yourself while I'm gone."

Scott grasped her hand and said, "I'd rather play with you."

Justine whacked him with her pillow again and got up. Hastily pulling on her white silk Le Perla bathrobe, she hurried down the stairs towards the incessant chiming of the doorbell.

Now she heard also heard a fist pounding on the door. She turned the deadbolt and opened the door a crack, just enough to get a look at her impatient visitor. He was indeed a cop.

"Hello, officer. What's going on?"

The officer tipped his hat to her. "Sorry to disturb you, Ms. Baron. I'm Officer Gondo. Palo Alto PD. We have a dangerous sex offender on the loose. He escaped from police custody a few hours ago and was last seen in your neighborhood."

"Okay, so why are you *here?*"

"We're concerned for your safety. He knows what you look like. Because of all the publicity about your company. All the pictures. You fit the profile of all his victims."

Justine gulped. "Well thank you, but…"

"No buts," he said drawing his weapon before abruptly pushing Justine aside and forced his way into the foyer. He aimed the gun toward the top of the staircase.

"Stop! Police!"

Justine looked up to see Scott, wearing nothing but his boxers, standing on the stairs.

"Me?" Scott asked, incredulous.

"Yeah you, asshole. That– Ms. Baron—is our man. Now you, pervert, walk here. Slowly."

Scott, his hands steady above his head, obeyed.

"Him?" Justine wanted to laugh, but the look on the officer's face told her he was not joking. "No! You've got it all wrong," she protested. "He's my boyfriend!"

The officer ignored her, kept his eyes on Scott. "On the floor! Face down!"

Scott had covered enough political demonstrations in his day to know the police brutality drill. He followed the order.

"He's a fucking National Geographic photographer, not a rapist." Justine was livid.

The cop glared at her. "No. He's definitely the escaped prisoner."

"He's been with me all night. Stop that. Leave him alone and go find the real rapist, goddamnit."

"Shut up or I'll arrest you for obstruction of justice."

"Do as he says, Justine. We can easily straighten this out." She wanted to object, but the tone of Scott's voice calmed her.

The cop aimed his pistol directly at Scott's head, then shoved a knee into his back, knocking the wind out of him. Justine screamed furiously, "NO!" and rushed to protect her lover. The cop grabbed her hair and spun her to the floor.

"Oh no you don't," Scott yelled, attempting to get up to protect her. But the cop was fast. Grasping the back of Scott's head, he smashed his forehead on the marble floor. "Now he's asleep. He'll be fine right there until I'm ready to deal with him."

Justine looked up at her attacker as he pointed his pistol at her face. "Move and you're dead."

CHAPTER 3

Justine sat on the cold hallway floor frozen in fear.

"On your face and spread-eagle like your boyfriend!"

Angry, but also frightened, she meekly complied with his orders. He holstered his gun and took a pair of handcuffs from his belt, snapped one cuff on her right wrist, yanked both arms behind her and cuffed them together.

She whimpered, but tried to get up.

"Shut up! And don't fucking move," he barked at her. Taking a second set of cuffs from his belt, he stepped over to the unconscious Scott and snapped a cuff onto one of his wrists. Then he dragged him the few inches to the wrought iron stair railing, looped the cuff's chain around a post, and secured Scott's other wrist. The cop then pulled a folding knife from his front pocket, sliced through Scott's silk boxers, and, with the precision of a psychotic Boy Scout, knotted them in a gag around Scott's mouth.

Justine's eyes bulged in terror as the policeman stomped back towards her, grabbed her hair and pulled her to her feet. "Upstairs, bitch," he growled as he pulled out his gun and rammed it into her ribs.

"You're not a real cop," she hissed, then spat in his face.

He wiped the spit off his cheek and spread it on her mouth, then laughed as he tightly held her jaw. "For a big CEO, you're just another stupid bitch! But this here?" he said, as if talking to a child, "this is a real gun! So you're gonna' to do exactly as I say. You get it?" He turned and pointed his pistol between Scott's legs, "Or I'll blow his balls off!"

"What do you *want?*"

"Get up. I wanna see your pretty bedroom," he said snidely with a crooked smile. Justine ascended the steps as slowly as she could with the muzzle of his gun pressed to her spine. As soon as he saw the bedroom the guy grabbed the back of Justine's neck and shoved her onto her bed. "On your back, bitch, just like you were for him!"

She lay back on the bed with her arms bound painfully beneath her. She was breathing hard. She took a deep breath, trying to steady her nerves, regaining her "confidence." Looking directly at the man's face, she carefully studied his every feature. If she ever had the chance to identify him, she wanted to remember.

He holstered his gun, pulled four thick plastic zip ties from his pocket, spread her legs and zip-tied each of her ankles to the lower mattress handles, then un-cuffed her wrists and zip-tied each one to the upper mattress handles. "There ya' go," he snickered. "Spread-eagled, just like you do with your boyfriend. But now it's *my* turn."

Justine's robe was loose but still knotted at the waist. The man laughed as he opened his folding knife and slit her belt. The razor-sharp blade cut through the silk like it was butter. Then he flipped open her robe with the back of the blade to expose her breasts, and gently licked each of her nipples. The smell of his sour breath made her want to gag, but somehow her nipples hardened. Pulling her robe further open, he ran the tip of his knife around her breasts, down her belly, and finally around her clitoris. Justine kept her eyes on his crooked yellowish teeth and cartoonish grin until she couldn't stand it any longer. She held her breath and squeezed her eyes shut, trying not to picture the blade penetrating and cutting the most sensitive parts of her body.

A cell phone vibrated. Cursing, he folded his knife, then pulled a phone from a back pocket. "Yeah. I'll send you a video," he said, keeping his eyes on Justine's exposed crotch. Then he pointed the phone at her tear-streaked face, then down to her breasts with their erect nipples, and then between her spread legs, still damp with Scott's lovemaking.

The male voice on the other end of the call spoke in a language Justine couldn't understand. Her captor sneered, "She's been fucked a lot so one more time won't make a difference."

The voice on the other end grew louder. Whoever he was, he sure was angry.

"If you don't want me to fuck her, you're gonna have to pay me double."

He put the phone back in his pocket, and then gave Justine a sharp whack between her legs. "I don't like sloppy seconds, anyway," he said. He walked to the door continuing his tirade, "I'm gonna make your boyfriend watch me fuck you up the ass!"

Justine could hear him stomping down the stairs. Frantically twisting her body, she wriggled her zip-tied right hand until she could get it under Scott's pillow, and feel for the edge of his Leatherman folding knife. After years in the field, it had become habit for him; Scott never slept without it. She used to tease him mercilessly about it. Never again.

With the tip of her middle finger she could just touch the handle. *Come on little knife, just one tiny centimeter and we'll be together.* She stretched her arm further, pushing down on the mattress. *That's it, almost there.* And she had it! She unfolded the knife blade with one hand, reversed her grip, and cut through the zip tie holding her wrist, and then reached over and cut the zip tie that was binding her other hand. Then she sat up and quickly cut her ankles free.

She leaped off the bed and tip-toed over to her second closet, which the previous owner had built as a safe room, in case of home invasion. She had actually laughed when the realtor touted this high tech security feature. But she wasn't laughing now. Now she was grateful that the tech billionaire that built the house had a serious case of paranoia.

Justine quietly closed the safe-room door and locked it as she reached for the secure landline phone on the wall which automatically connected her to the Palo Alto police dispatcher, she didn't have to push a button.

"Are you Ms. Baron on Edgewood Drive?" said the voice on the magic phone.

"Yes. He's dressed like a cop. He just tried to rape me. He's still downstairs right now about to kill my boyfriend."

"Try to remain calm Ms. Baron. Help is on the way."

"Open up, you fucking bitch, or I'm gonna go downstairs and blow the balls off your pretty boyfriend!"

"Do *not* open the door," the dispatcher warned her. Her voice was stern, but calm. "Stay where you are or you'll both be dead."

CHAPTER 4

Lily Marshall picked up on the first ring. She'd always been a light sleeper.

"We just got an alert on one of our VIPs."

"Must be serious if you're calling me at," she took the phone from her ear to look at the screen, "2:45 AM."

"Home invasion. Justine Baron on Edgewood Drive. Intruder. Armed and violent. Dressed as a cop."

"When?"

"In progress now."

"She was raped?" Sergeant Marshall.

"Unclear," the dispatcher responded. "She says attempted. I've texted you the location. Get over there immediately."

"I'm going solo?" Sergeant Marshall asked as she pulled on her jeans and t-shirt.

"Johnson's on back-up."

"Okay, I'm on it."

Marshall strapped her Glock Nineteen and Taser to her belt. She remembered Justine Baron. They had met three years earlier at a fundraising event for after-school recreation centers sponsored by local law enforcement. Marshall had already known about Justine, her business as well as her personal life. Almost everyone in Palo Alto did. It seemed like every month or two some local business journal or newspaper ran a story about her: Justine Baron, the beautiful blonde Stanford grad who'd worked her way to the top of Silicon Valley's macho-frat-boy business community; Justine Baron, the beautiful, sophisticated young New

Yorker who was infusing the one-note Valley with her East Coast intellect and culture; Justine Baron, the statuesque Founder of *TruYouth,* Silicon Valley's great non-tech success story. Every article Marshall had seen about Justine—and she'd seen plenty—included at least two flattering photographs, as if the editors needed to prove their claims about Ms. Baron's looks.

As soon as she'd met her, Sergeant Marshall understood all the hype. Justine was the real thing. Women admired her beauty and success; men admired her beauty and her body. Lily Marshall could appreciate everything Justine had accomplished, but she was more concerned about her safety. Anyone that rich and beautiful was a potential target.

CHAPTER 5

"I can't just leave him out there," Justine said, knowing all too well that opening the door would be her last mistake.

"Help is on the way, Ms. Baron" the dispatcher reassured her. "Try to remain calm."

Easy for you to say, Justine thought as Gondo—or whatever his real name was—continued his furious pounding and screaming from the other side of the steel door.

"Our records indicate that your safe room is equipped with a security monitor," the dispatcher continued.

"It is? How do I find that?"

"Look for a TV screen. Probably on the wall beside the phone."

I should've paid attention to that realtor, Justine thought as she pushed the power button on what she had thought was yet another built-in television. On the screen she could see a shot of every room in the house. She tapped on the images from her entry hall, and through that camera's wide-angle lens she could see Scott, still-dazed and cuffed to the post. Suddenly Gondo entered the frame and deftly released one of Scott's hands to release the cuff's chain from the rail, and then re-cuffed his wrists behind his back. He then grabbed Scott by his hair and began to drag him up the stairs.

"Scott's still alive!" Justine told the dispatcher. "I think. Where the fuck is he taking him?"

"Look what I found!" the man who called himself Gondo sang in a whiney, childish falsetto. He was back in the bedroom, outside the safe room door. Justine switched the camera feed on the security monitor. She could see Scott, conscious now, his head bloody, on his knees.

The man pointed his weapon at the handle of the safe room's door and pulled the trigger. Justine shrieked. The steel door not only remained intact, it shattered the bullet. Hot copper and lead fragments ricocheted back into the man's hand. Blood spurted from his wounds like floodwater from a busted dam. Desperate to stop the bleeding and screaming with rage, he dropped his pistol and let go of Scott's hair.

Even with his hands cuffed behind him, Scott was able to fall backward on top of the pistol. When the man tried to yank him off of it, Scott started kicking with a force that surprised even Justine. Through the security system's speakers she could hear Scott's muffled grunts—he was still gagged—and the gunman's undecipherable swearing. Then she heard the sirens.

The attacker let out one final curse as he ran out the room.

Justine waited for a long moment, upset for being so afraid, then unlocked the safe room door and removed the gag out from Scott's mouth. "I'm sorry. I'm so sorry. I can't believe I left you with him," she mumbled almost incoherently as she kissed his bloodied face.

Scott turned his face away from her kisses and said sternly, "Get the gun!" as he rolled off of it. Blood seeped from a wound on his back.

"Oh my God, he shot you?" Justine said, shocked.

"No. That thing has sharp corners. Must've cut me."

Justine tentatively picked up the pistol. "I don't know how to use it," she said.

"If he comes back, point it at him and pull the fucking trigger."

Justine gripped the pistol, slippery with blood from that creep's hand and her lover's back, stood up and walked over to the bedroom door. She looked down the hallway. Nothing. She listened. Nothing. She closed and locked the door, then went back to sit beside Scott.

Suddenly she heard footsteps running up the outside stairs.

Holding her breath, she aimed the bloody gun at the door and pulled the trigger. The sound of the explosion startled her. She screamed. The blast continued to ring in her ears. She shook her head back and forth, but the noise didn't stop.

"Police! Drop your weapon!" Justine swore she heard a female voice intermingled with the ringing in her ears.

Scott leaned against Justine to get her attention. "Drop the gun, baby. We're safe now."

The weapon fell from her hands and landed on the rug with a soft thud.

Scott yelled, "In here. She already dropped the gun! She only fired because she thought you were the guy coming back to finish us off."

They heard a sharp thud as the door swung open. A pistol muzzle nudged its way around the doorjamb as a woman's voice shouted, "Hands in the air!"

Still trembling with fear, Justine complied.

"Detective Lily Marshall. Santa Clara County Victim Assistance." She flashed her shield as she entered the room. "Justine Baron?" she said, keeping her eyes and her weapon firmly trained on Scott.

"Yes. Yes. I'm Justine Baron. This is my boyfriend, Scott Reddington. Can you put that thing down please?"

Detective Marshall ignored the request. "Slowly roll away from me and let me see your hands," she said to Scott. He obeyed.

Marshall stepped over to the pistol on the floor and kicked it out of reach. "I'm securing your gun so you don't shoot at me again."

"It's *not* my gun!" Justine sobbed. "I hate guns! Can you please untie my boyfriend?"

"I'm sorry, but I can't do that until my backup arrives. Though I can probably do something to help him feel a little less, um, exposed." She scanned the room, then grabbed a throw from the foot of the bed and placed it over Scott's naked lap. "The detectives will need to take your statements separately, but I'll stay with you," she said with a reassuring nod to Justine.

"Can I, um, can we at least sit on the bed, or in a chair while we wait?" Scott asked, trying not to sound annoyed.

Detective Marshall nodded. Justine helped Scott stand and walked him the few steps to the edge of the bed.

"I probably shouldn't tell you this in uber-PC Palo Alto," the woman said to Justine as she wrapped the edges of the comforter from the bed around Justine's shoulders, "but you need to buy a gun and learn to shoot."

"Her with a gun? Hell no!" Scott exclaimed. "She'll shoot me going to the bathroom at night!"

"Not if she knew how to handle one. Ms. Baron, you've suffered a devastating attack. You were lucky this time. But your stalker is still out there. He's probably going to come back to finish what he started."

"Couldn't I just get a dog? Like one of those seemingly super vicious but actually super cuddly pit bulls?"

"You could try that. They poop a lot, you know."

"But Jewish girls from my neighborhood don't play with guns," Justine stated emphatically. She tried to imagine her mother's reaction if she told her she was going to buy a gun. "I'm the poster child for the anti-NRA movement. I despise guns. Hell, I almost shot *you*!"

Lily Marshall laughed. "You missed me by a mile. Though you certainly got my attention. But seriously, you should learn to defend yourself. I could teach you to shoot a pistol effectively in one afternoon."

"You?"

"Me. I could take you to a shooting range. Teach you the basics. If you have a knack for it and want to continue I'll send you to my teacher. He's very Zen."

"All of a sudden you sound more like a California girl," Scott quipped.

"A Zen shooting instructor? Isn't that a contradiction in terms?" Justine laughed.

"Absolutely. Everything about this guy is a contradiction. He's an ex-spook that developed…"

"Spook?" Justine interjected.

"Spy," said Scott, with a tinge of impatience in his voice.

"Very good. Yes, he was Special Ops in the early days of Desert Storm, then CIA, Special Activities Division. Anyway, he developed a system he calls *Zen and the Art of the Pistol*. But he chooses his students, they don't choose him."

"Sounds a bit too cloak and dagger for me," Justine said.

"Well, you're going to need protection. That part's obvious. You could hire an executive protection company. They'd charge you at least half a million a year, and you'd have different bodyguards, all huge guys with huge guns, with you twenty-four-seven. You'd have zero privacy. And most of them would get the hots for you. You're better off learning to protect yourself."

"With guns?"

"Among other things. Like I said, my teacher doesn't accept just anyone. But you, I don't know. You're not just anyone."

"You just met me and you can say that?"

"Actually we've met before. At a luncheon for the East Palo Alto Boys and Girls Club. Don't worry, I don't expect you to remember me. But I remembered you. You struck me immediately as strong and determined, so I was impressed."

"Um, thank you?"

Detective Marshall smiled. "Sorry, didn't mean to put you on the spot like that. Anyway, I really think you should consider this. *If* he takes your case, he would teach you to become your own bodyguard, and then he would help you hunt down your stalker. So far his record stands at clients: 99, stalkers: zip."

"You should consider this Jus," said Scott. "Detective, how much would he charge her?"

She thought for a moment before replying. "I can't say exactly. He's taught lots of women in danger and not charged them a penny, but you have money. He would most likely charge you something. I'm sure he'd be fair. He doesn't do this for the money." Lily glanced over at Scott. "Or you could just marry a big strong protective man, a guy with big guns of his own. But you still couldn't stay here. It's not safe for you anymore."

Before Justine could respond two plainclothes detectives arrived. Marshall briefed them on the current situation. One of them went downstairs to inspect the property while the other freed Scott from his shackles and dragged him to another room to take his statement.

"So, Ms. Baron," Detective Marshall said, ready to take up the conversation again.

"Justine. Ms. Baron is my mother."

"In that case you'll have to call me Lily." She handed a card to Justine. "Call me. Any time. I can teach you how to shoot a gun. We could start later in the day. After I get a nap, that is."

Justine took her card and looked at it. "I don't know if I can do this," she said.

Lily smiled. "You won't know until you try. But you saved yourself tonight, didn't you? Got yourself free?" Justine nodded. "That was no accident. You weren't the quick and easy victim this guy thought you'd be. You used your brain. You took action. If you hadn't, we wouldn't be here talking right now. I'd be watching the EMTs carry your bodies out on stretchers. Imagine that…"

CHAPTER 6

Danisha Howard was a busy woman. The tall, leggy, light-skinned, brown-eyed beauty was one of the most sought-after costume designers in Hollywood. She always had at least three projects going, so her phone rarely stopped ringing. As a black woman in a white man's world, she'd had to work harder and smarter than everyone else to get to the top of her game, to put up with the indignities of making less for better work, the slaps on her ass, a hand on her inner thigh during a business meeting lunch, the crass remarks. Unlike many other attractive and successful women in her business, Danisha never had to sleep with anyone to get ahead. She got there on the strength of her talent and work ethic.

Saturday mornings she set aside for taking care of herself. She followed her long-established schedule with military precision. Wake up at 6:30, drink one eight-ounce glass of hot water with the juice of one whole lemon, work out for ninety-minutes in her home gym, meditate, shower. She had designed the workout/meditation room in her Malibu home to take advantage of the indirect morning light and spectacular view of the Pacific Ocean. She'd come a long way from her mother's small two-bedroom apartment on Chicago's Southside.

No one could interrupt Danisha's Saturday morning routine; it was what kept her sane in the insanity of the entertainment business. No one except her *bff*, Justine.

Danisha had just stepped onto the treadmill when her cell phone buzzed. Seeing the caller ID, she answered on the first ring. "Took you long enough to call. I want a full report on your sizzling hot date last night with Mr. Perfect."

But Justine didn't hear a word Danisha said. She didn't even say hello, went straight into an hysterical rant that Danisha couldn't quite decipher.

"Woa, take a breath, girl. What the fuck happened last night? If he upset you, I swear I'll kill him."

"Oh…Dani. I can't even…it's so, you won't believe it, but it's true…"

"Justine, I won't believe *what?* Use your words."

"I was tied up and almost raped. He knocked Scott out and handcuffed him, then dragged me upstairs. Did you know I had a panic room?"

"Like in the Jodi Foster movie?"

"Yes!"

"In the second closet?"

"Yes!"

"I told you that room would come in handy one day. Now tell me, slowly. What the fuck happened?"

Justine could barely get her story out. When she finally finished giving Danisha as many details as she could recall, she said, "This guy—this motherfucker—he's not done with me. He's gonna' come back to find me, then rape me, murder me. I've got to move out. And Scott, the son of a bitch, he just left for the assignment in Africa. He left me here. Alone. I'm freaking out. Also, I'm pissed. This is the first time I've ever been scared. Of anything. That creep could come back and murder me tonight."

"Listen to me! Get in your car and drive here right away. You can stay with me."

"No. I'm not running away. I'm going to get a gun."

"A gun? What about the police? They'll protect you."

"Protect me? No, they won't. You don't understand. It was a cop who told me that I have to protect myself. She even offered to teach me to how to shoot. I'm thinking about taking her up on that offer."

"What? When?"

"This afternoon."

"No. No. *Hell No.* No guns."

Danisha hated guns. And with good reason. She knew guns. Her mother had grown up on Chicago's South Side, where guns and bullets ruled the streets and too many boys and young men ended up either in jail or dead. A few years ago Danisha's cousins' next-door neighbor, a seven-year-old girl, had been killed in a drive-by shooting. The collateral damage of the city's gang wars was staggering.

"Right now you just need to calm down," Danisha responded with genuine concern.

"You're right. I'll try. Love you. So much. I'll call you later when I figure it out."

Danisha stared at the screen of her iPhone, wondering what to do next. In her mind she could clearly see Justine tied up, at the mercy of some mad man pointing a gun at her head. It was too upsetting. And the idea of Justine with a gun was almost as upsetting. Guns were never an answer. But what was?

CHAPTER 7

Justine opened her guestroom window and lit up a pre-roll. She hadn't smoked weed since college, had only recently decided to start again, on Scott's suggestion, once she was no longer a corporate executive. Scott always kept a few tubes and vape pen at her place whenever he visited his dispensary in Mountain View. She never thought she'd be so grateful for medical marijuana. Who knew it actually worked as anti-anxiety med? Justine always thought it was only good for activities like video games and sex.

Scott had left a half hour earlier. Neither of them could even peep into the master bedroom suite, much less sleep in it once the cops had cleared out. She dreaded the lonely night ahead of her. All the Purple Kush in California couldn't get her calm enough to sleep alone in the nightmare that was once her bedroom. But she knew she'd have to deal with her new reality sooner or later. Having always been the sooner rather than later type, she took a deep hit off the joint and willed her dread away. Within seconds she felt better. Mellow. But she was still pissed at Scott. Sure he couldn't cancel his assignment, but couldn't he have *maybe* postponed for just one fucking day?

The Kush proved to be a great motivator. Justine decided to face her demons, go find her phone and text her mother.

Emergency. Must talk immediately. Call me.

Lise Baron, fashion industry mogul, jetsetter, and mentor to cutting-edge designers everywhere, always responded to texts.

Justine's phone rang seconds later.

"What's wrong?" Lise cried out. "Are you in the hospital? Is this because of your stupid extremist sport?"

"Its *extreme* sports—not extremist." *Why does her mind always go straight to the edge?* "No hospital. No sports. I'm afraid it's pretty bad news. I need your help." Justine didn't want to alarm her mother, so she told her story in the most calm and measured manner possible.

"Oh my God," Lise screeched when she heard the word *gun*. "You've gotta' get out of there!"

"I'm not going anywhere, Lise. Weren't you the one who taught me to never run away from my problems?"

"Then at least hire a private agency to protect you twenty-four seven. That's what the celebrities do in New York. I bet they even do it in LA."

"I'm actually thinking of getting a gun."

"Are you insane? Guns kill people!"

"I know that Lise. I had one pointed at my head just a few hours ago."

"You'll shoot your foot off! Don't get a gun."

"The cop who came last night, she's with some special victim's unit out here. She made a lot of sense. Offered to teach me how to shoot."

"Okay, listen," Lise said sternly. "I've got another option for you. I know two women who can find this scumbag and do whatever you want them to do to him. I'll hire them."

"Hire them? Who are they?"

"They're dominatrices."

"I beg your pardon?"

"Now don't get upset. They're professional dominatrices. And more. You know I know a lot of people. These women are really good. I'm hanging up and calling them right now. They'll fix this."

Before Justine could utter a word of protest, Lise had hung up.

Out of curiosity, Justine opened her laptop and did a Google search for the highest rated executive protection agency in Silicon Valley. She called the number listed and started asking questions. The first few answers made her understand that Lily Marshall was right. If she hired any agency she could say *au revoir* to her privacy and independence, along with at least half a million dollars a year. For the rest of her life.

She opened a Word document and started writing a list of pros and cons. Police and bodyguards were trained to protect and they carried guns. That was it. Lily seemed confident that she could teach Justine to use a gun responsibly to protect herself.

Her next step was now obvious. She found Lily's card, punched in her number and arranged to meet her two hours later.

"Good afternoon, Detective. I must say I like the service in this town. How many girls get to hang out with their own personal cop?"

"Only one. Except today I'm not a cop, I'm your, let's call me pre-liminary instructor. Hop in and buckle up."

Justine was happy to let someone else take charge for a change. The more she thought about the offer Detective Marshall—or rather Lily, as she now called her—had made just a few hours earlier, the more she liked the idea. Growing up in New York City Justine had never so much as seen a real gun, except in Police holsters, until last night. Now she was on her way to a shooting range with a law enforcement officer from Palo Alto.

Lily suggested they take her Dodge Charger Pursuit, disguised as a civilian sedan because of the way its All Wheel Drive handled the winding backcountry roads that led to Skyline Drive. "While we're at it, I might as well teach you a few evasive-driving techniques," she told Justine.

"Seriously? I need to know *that* to use a gun?"

"All part of the self-defense package. Whoever was after you, they're not gonna' stop after one minor setback." As she drove, Lily demon-strated various grips on the steering wheel, downshifting to slow down instead of using the brake going into curves, and then accelerating around corners for better traction, and practicing something she called "brake and evade" around or over fallen rocks on or off the road.

"This is awesome!" Justine said after her first turn at the wheel. "Even the ride up to the lesson is fun."

"Later on I can teach you how to do drive-by-shooting and ram cars. I want you to learn as many ways as possible to defend yourself, and, if necessary, defend your friends."

"Maybe just one thing at a time? This is kind of overwhelming."

Lily smiled at Justine. "Okay, good point. You're a strong, savvy, woman. I really want you to stay that way. You've already proven that you're not gonna be anyone's easy victim," she responded.

"Did I tell you I studied *Krav Maga* when I was a kid?"

"Nope. You did not tell me that."

"I was pretty good, too. My mom made sure I studied with the top Israeli guy. One of these days I'll have to tell you all about my mom. If you think I'm tough, I'm a rose petal compared to her."

"That's totally bad-ass. If you already know the basic *Krav Maga* techniques, you could totally become a full-fledged bodyguard."

"Now we're getting ahead of ourselves," Justine said, only half joking.

"Are we, though? Justine, I think you're ready. I can start to train you not just to shoot a gun, but also to know that a gun just might be your greatest friend."

"You're really taking the whole *To Protect and Serve* thing to a whole new level! But please don't expect much from me. The first time I ever touched a gun was last night, and you saw how great my aim was."

"True. But that was last night. From now on, anyone trying to get up your stairs uninvited will be dead meat."

CHAPTER 8

When Lily pulled into the parking lot of the Los Altos Rod and Gun Club, Justine noticed two men waiting outside. "Those are our range masters," Lily explained with a knowing smile. "They're expecting us."

"Now I'm starting to get scared," Justine said out loud, though in her brain she was thinking, *Why am I here? Why am I here? These people have guns!*

"If you have the dexterity to apply a makeup concealer, you can shoot a pistol. And I know you're wearing concealer because you look too perfect after what you went through last night."

"At makeup I'm most definitely a pro. But concealer never killed anyone."

"I just realized how you're going to pay me. You're going to teach me how to do my makeup."

Justine agreed, happily. "Our next date is at Saks."

The two range masters welcomed them and took Lily's gear, two aluminum cases with what looked like serious combination locks, from the back of the car. "We have rattlesnakes up here so I hope they won't try to mate with your boots," teased the older of the two men, with a nod to Justine's python boots.

"I'll keep those critters at bay to start and by the end of her lesson my friend here will shoot their heads off," grinned Lily as she strode to one of the shooting tables. Right behind her, walking at a much slower pace was a still uneasy Justine.

Lily stopped at one of the tables and chose eye and ear protection for Justine. The range masters placed the cases on the wooden table, which

Lily then unlocked. When she opened them Justine saw an array of guns that looked like they belonged on the set of a Quentin Tarantino movie. "The method I'm about to teach you is called *Zen and the Art of the Pistol*," Lily stated matter-of-factly.

"Seriously?"

"Seriously. First, we have basic gun safety rules. One, treat every gun as if it is loaded. Two, never point a gun at anything you don't intend to destroy. And three, keep your finger off the trigger until you're ready to shoot," explained Lily as she pulled out boxes of ammunition.

"The size of the bullet is the caliber."

"I've watched more than a few episodes of Law and Order. I know what a caliber is."

"Excellent. Let's continue then," Lily exclaimed. She picked up a single small bullet and held it between her thumb and forefinger. "The smallest —and most popular caliber—is the point twenty-two. Too small for self-defense, but just small enough and light enough to carry concealed in a small purse or in the pocket of a blazer. On the negative side, it has low intimidation value. The only people who really rely on it as a primary weapon are assassins who have to zero in on a close shot to the head!

"There are other calibers," Lily continued, picking up each bullet in her show-and-tell.

Justine's head was spinning. So many bullets, so many choices. "Which is the best for women...for me?"

"The rule of thumb is shoot the biggest bullet you can handle with speed and accuracy. For self-defense, the best range is between a thirty-two to a forty-five caliber bullet. That goes for both women and men.

Lily picked up an enormous handgun. "This is the three-fifty-seven Smith & Wesson with a six-inch barrel. And yes, size matters," Lily hooted. "The longer the barrel, the more accurate the gun will shoot at distances over seven yards. But, it turns out the size of the grip may be the single most important element. You want the strongest point of your index finger," Lily pointed to the middle of the pad of her own finger, "right here, to be on the trigger. If the grip is too big, you'll be pulling with your fingertips, which is difficult to do, or you'll jerk the gun off the target."

"So it's finger size, not hand size that matters?"

"It's both. But you can always buy different sized grips for any gun. If you can't get the perfect grip, you've gotta get a different gun."

"Got it."

"Because this is your first lesson I'm gonna start you off with dummy rounds in a twenty-two revolver. It has almost no recoil, no kick, so it's the easiest to shoot, especially for beginners. Then we'll go to live ammo in the twenty-two. The last gun you'll shoot today will be the Glock nine millimeter semi-automatic pistol, which will be your so-called "carry gun" once you can legally carry a gun in a holster."

"I'm not exactly a holster type of girl?"

"No problem. You can buy a *Pax*. They're gorgeous."

"I thought a *Pax* was the name of a high end vaporizer."

"It might be, but first it was the name of a high end hand-bag specially designed to conceal a handgun of any size."

"Ooh, I love purses. Do they sell them at Saks?" Justine asked, only half kidding.

"Gun stores and Internet. But you're still taking *me* to Saks," Lily said with a wink.

Justine's first lesson lasted three hours, though she could've sworn less than an hour had passed when Lily said it was time to go.

"But we only just started!" Justine protested.

"You've already caught the bug. Or maybe it's caught you. Look what you did to the target!"

Indeed, even with Lily's 9mm *Glock*, Justine had landed most of her shots in what Lily called "the center of mass," the area surrounding the heart and lungs of the human silhouette paper target.

"Not bad, eh?" Justine said proudly.

"Not bad at all. You must've had a fantastic teacher," Lily laughed.

By the time they packed up Lily's gear and had it loaded into her car, they'd passed the entire afternoon together. Justine felt both exhausted and exhilarated. She happily admitted that, for her, the day was a surprising success. "I had no idea that learning to shoot guns would be so easy, and so much fun."

Lily got a kick out of Justine's enthusiasm. "It's not! Most cops need a solid forty hours of instruction. The man that taught me developed his own method, a combination of the best education theories out of Stanford and Harvard, mixed with a scoop of Eastern philosophy and martial arts. I taught you to shoot the way he taught me, so it seems easy."

"Anyway, guns alone won't cut it. You also have to learn unarmed combat techniques."

"Will that be our next lesson?" Justine was excited at the idea of learning more.

"Well, with a little bit of luck you will be studying with my teacher. He started off with white belts in thirty styles of martial arts but earned black belts in nine of them before creating his own martial science system."

"Isn't that overdoing it a bit?"

"Not at all. Each style has strengths as well as weaknesses. My teacher spent his first few years of life in an orphanage in Japan, so he calls his original fighting techniques *orphanage-fu*. No rules, no mercy and you never quit or it will just get worse. His mother was a nurse, but his father abandoned them when he was two. They lived in the bombed out ruins left over from World War Two and ate from the garbage cans of restaurants until the snows came. She put him in an orphanage, thinking he would be safe and then ended up in a shoddy Geisha house on the wrong side of Kyoto to pay the orphanage to take care of him."

"This sounds like a horror story," Justine said, thinking of the poor baby, alone and hungry in Japan.

"It would've been, and I guess in many ways it was. But he got lucky. An American Navy couple adopted him when he was five. The orphanage was glad to get rid of him because he was always running away to try to find his mother.

"No way!"

"I know, right? I promise I *couldn't* make this shit up, even though it sounds like a spy novel. Anyway, the American couple brought him back to Virginia. He spent the rest of his childhood in the shadows of Langley since the Navy was his new father's cover for the CIA. He learned I don't know how many languages. Traveled all over the world, and heard every intelligence story ever told, right from the source in most cases."

"Wow. And I thought my adoption story was juicy."

"You were adopted?"

"Yeah, by a successful businesswoman in New York. Through a Jewish adoption agency. No orphanages. No prostitutes. If I ever suffered, I don't ever remember it."

"Well then, you two will still have a lot in common. Like you, he also went to Stanford."

"So how did you meet him?" Justine asked with genuine curiosity.

Lily hesitated, not sure that she wanted to tell so much of her own story, but decided that she could tell Justine a few details. "Well, after college, I joined the Army. At first I was MP—Military Police, then got transferred to a Military Close Protection team. MCP are specially trained security detail for VPs in various countries. I met him there. He trained me."

"Desert Storm?" Justine asked.

"Around then, a couple years in. Anyway, long story short, I got my discharge, came home to Palo Alto, joined the police force. They put me on the Dignitary Protection Team, because of my military background."

"Dignitaries in Palo Alto?" Justine asked, incredulous.

"Hell yeah. That University pulls some major weight. I guarded some heavy duty guys."

"Who?"

"You know I can't talk about it."

"Am I a dignitary?"

"Yes ma'am, you sure are. It was all set up by your lawyers."

"That's good," Justine said playfully. "Now, when will I get to meet your teacher?"

"I already texted him my recommendation and he agreed to meet you. You are now officially a beginning white belt."

"What does that mean?" Justine was a bundle of confusion and excitement.

"You'll find out soon enough. You're to meet at *Nepenthe* in Big Sur, tomorrow at 19:30."

"Tomorrow? Oh. Oh! How will I recognize him? What does he look like?"

"I have no idea."

"I beg your pardon?"

"For now you just need to understand that our teacher has a thousand faces. I do know that he's at least half Japanese, but depending on his clothes he can look Hispanic, Middle Eastern, Asian, Indian, almost any ethnicity, except WASP. Though to be perfectly honest I wouldn't put that past him. He uses the whole bag of CIA tricks; wigs, latex masks, and contact lenses. He can even change his body type from fat to thin. I never know what to expect."

"So I'll be meeting a strange man, probably in disguise, in a bar fifty miles from my house. Not my normal style," Justine said uneasily.

Lily hesitated. "You'll have to pick up a car at San Jose Airport."

"Are you going to take me there?"

"No. You drive yourself and leave your car at the airport."

"Do I at least get to know his name?"

Lily hesitated again. "Even I don't know his real name, but you can call him Don. Now, before I take you home, you have a debt to pay. We're going to Saks!"

Justine laughed out loud. "Game on! Bring on the beginning white belt in makeup!"

CHAPTER 9

There are three different types of people that live in New York City: Authentic Cognoscenti, Pretentious Downtowners, and Everyone Else. The first are the trendsetters, the visionaries, designers of people, places and things, innovators of style and substance. Members of the second group see themselves as members of the first. They refuse to venture above Fourteenth Street, preferring to be seen at the freshest downtown hot spots—bars, restaurants, hotels, and art galleries in Soho, Nolita, Tribeca or the West Village, but preferably adjacent to the Highline. Invariably, they will abandon these venues as soon as they discover Everyone Else has caught on to the trend and followed them there. Members of the first group are exceedingly rare. They don't follow anyone. They lead.

Anyone that knew her, or knew of her, or that had read any of the numerous articles about her various companies in the fashion and media industries, or seen her feminist philanthropy's viral video clips about the scourge of date rape, domestic violence, or international sex-slavery, knew that Lise Baron was the real deal, a true leader.

Lise still lived in the same apartment she'd owned since Justine was a baby, a duplex in The Century, one of the city's first Art Deco buildings, overlooking Central Park West. Over the years she had invested in buildings downtown, primarily in SoHo and Tribeca. In the mid-nineties she started buying properties near a crumbling relic of an elevated rail line overlooking the Hudson River. A few years later she helped raise millions of dollars for the Friends of The Highline, the organization that lobbied the city for the right to transform the elevated tracks into a verdant public promenade, similar to the *Promenade Plan-*

tée in Paris. Lise personally convinced many of her closest friends—celebrity chefs, hedge fund billionaires, and real housewives from all the cities—to build on its perimeter restaurants, architecturally important office and condominium buildings, boutiques and art galleries. But when she had to take her most important clients or colleagues to lunch, when she needed to discuss serious issues over an excellent meal, she wouldn't even consider going to one of her favorite eateries on the Highline. On those occasions—and every Wednesday—Lise Baron would go to her favorite restaurant in Manhattan, Michael's on West Fifty-fifth Street.

Michael's was the type of place that, due to its central Midtown location, haute California cuisine, clubby atmosphere, and perfect service, attracted media executives, network news personalities, film producers, superstar actors, athletes and models. Ordinary civilians had to book a table at least a month in advance, and then they'd most likely be relegated to a table near the kitchen. The owners made sure that whenever she needed it Lise had her table just adjacent to the large bay window. That way people saw her when they came in or departed. Those who knew her always stopped at her table for a brief chat.

She told Eniko and Iya, the twenty-three-year-old model-slash-dominatrices, or *dommes*, in the jargon of their world, to meet her there at one. It had taken Lise the better part of three days to track them down, and they'd apologized profusely when they finally responded to her texts, emails, and tweets. Their previous assignment had them in Asunción, Paraguay taking care of a slimy Russian oligarch. Lise accepted their explanation for their delayed reply without further questions. She had no interest in the sordid details of that adventure. With Eniko and Iya, the details were always sordid, but they were the only people Lise trusted to find and "take care" of the scumbag that attacked her daughter.

Lise arrived at Michael's a few minutes before one. Michael himself greeted her, and led her to her usual table. At precisely one o'clock the din of the crowded room suddenly softened, and Liz knew that her guests had arrived. Heads turned as Michael escorted the two young women to her table. Both were wearing pastel silk dresses that moved gracefully with each step they took. They walked with the confident air of those that never wait in line for a nightclub. Both had long legs, and in their Manolo stilettos they were easily six feet tall. Neither wore earrings, necklaces, or rings to distract from their natural beauty and femininity. Yet somehow they exuded an air of wealth, like women whose jewels were so valuable they kept them in a safe.

Iya, with her short blonde hair and yoga-toned body, was born and raised in Kiev. Her thick blond locks fell over her shoulders in shiny waves. Her stature, along with her pouty rose lips, reminded Lise of a young Brigitte Bardot. Eniko radiated class, even though she said she came from a dirty manufacturing town with an unpronounceable name. Lise thought Eniko was the prettier and sexier of the two. Both Eniko and Iya were Ukrainian, and they shared the four characteristics that Lise had come to associate with young Russian women in New York; gorgeous, blonde, extremely ambitious, and devilishly cunning.

"Welcome back to civilization girls," Lise said as she stood to greet them, giving each three kisses, one on each cheek and one on the lips. "Sit, please. Prosecco's on the way. Hydrate first," she ordered with a nod to the waiter, who poured Pellegrino into their water glasses.

Eniko set her purse on the table beside Lise's bread plate.

"Cute new bag," said Lise, reaching to inspect it.

Eniko tried to hide a look of concern. "Careful. My Makarov pistol is in that bag. Iya has one, too."

"Is that legal?" Eniko didn't offer an answer, but Lise hadn't actually expected one. "You have to go to California right away. Justine needs your help."

Over the next ten minutes she filled them in on the details of her daughter's terrifying encounter and offered them three thousand dollars, plus expenses of course, to take care of it.

Eniko and Iya listened carefully, their eyes locked on Lise. After hearing her offer, they turned to face one another and quietly exchanged a few words in Ukrainian.

"Okay," Iya said to Lise. "But we want three thousand. Each. Per day. We're worth it."

Lise tried to mask her reaction to the demand. "That's an extraordinary amount of cash," she said coolly.

"Yes. We live life on the edge. You know this."

Lise had heard their story. She understood that for these two, beauty and grace had been both a blessing and a curse.

Eniko and Iya grew up in dingy, industrial cities. The two very pretty girls had met at the age of eleven when they were sent away to the same live-in facility outside St. Petersburg, ostensibly to train for a career as "models" in Russia's burgeoning high fashion industry. For the next two years they were taught how to walk, talk, and dress. They learned English, French, and Italian. Then, the rapes began when they turned twelve. Every night two of their male instructors, agents of the state, came into their small, dank room and took turns with them. One man held Eniko down while the other raped Iya. Then they switched places and started again. The abuse continued, with new instructors and new associates, daily, for more than two years, until they started menstruating. They were both fourteen.

After that, their lessons changed, but the forced sex continued. They were sent to a different facility outside Moscow, where agents of *SPETNAZ*, the Russian equivalent of the US Navy SEALs, taught them the *Systema* martial arts combat technique. They also learned how to handle weapons, and, for the purposes of protecting their motherland from the imperialist United States, how to use their sexuality to extract economic and military secrets from targeted men and women.

Lise understood that their training amounted to the equivalent of PhDs in subterfuge, sex, pleasure, and pain. Eniko and Iya finally managed to break away from their Russian captives when Iya "neutralized" their Russian handlers. Knowing that their training had many practical applications, on the dark as well as the lighter side of the beauty industry, they both secured modeling contracts, first in Milan and then in New York, where they first discovered the underground—but legal—world of role play dungeons. Within a month they decided to go into business for themselves. The lucrative business of giving pleasure by inflicting pain on men and on women.

Lise had hired Eniko and Iya to model a line of bathing suits one of her companies was marketing, and met them in Miami on the set of a shoot for a European magazine. They spent lots of time together over the three-day shoot, hanging out at Zuma, one of Miami's finest restaurants, and dancing all night at the clubs in South Beach. Eniko and Iya knew how to party—they could easily down eight tequilas, always had the best weed, and were eager to experiment.

At the age of fifty-two, Lise still loved sex. Spending time with the girls made her feel even sexier. When they all returned to New York, Lise continued to hang out with the Ukrainian beauties.

Just six weeks before, over drinks at the Aviary, on the 35th floor in the Mandarin Oriental on Columbus Circle, Lise casually mentioned a problem she was having with Philippe, a Parisian playboy she'd been seeing. "I'm pretty sure he stole my secret stash of emergency cash," she told them.

"How much cash?' Iya asked.

"Fifty thousand dollars," Lise answered, reluctantly. "I kept it in a large envelope at the back of my lingerie drawer."

"When?" Iya asked.

"This morning. The envelope was there last night and this morning when I left to get croissants at the Epicurean. He was still asleep. I was gone at most fifteen minutes. We ate, we fucked, and he left. Then when I was getting dressed I noticed the envelope was gone."

"That dick." Iya's face went dark with anger, though Lise suspected that the stronger motivation was excitement.

Seeing her friend's reaction, Eniko exclaimed, "We can certainly help you."

"We will provide dominatrix service," said Iya, smiling like the president of a high school debate team. Then, with a methodical calmness that gave Lise an equal dose of hope and the creeps, Iya told Lise all about their *other* business.

The moment Lise understood that the girls could help her "take care" of Philippe, she knew what she had to do to get her money back. She sent him a text suggesting they spend the following night together at his place. He texted back a smiley face and thumbs up emoji. To pique his curiosity Lise sent a follow up text saying, *surprise plan for you,* and added a sexy-lady *emoji*.

"So we get to meet this asshole tomorrow night?" Eniko asked once Lise put down her phone.

"Yep. I'll text you his name and address. I'll make sure the doorman is expecting you at nine."

CHAPTER 10

It was exactly eight when she walked into Philippe's lobby the next evening. The doorman took her bag and walked her to the elevator.

"Gracias, Mario. By the way, we're expecting guests," she said with a conspiratorial wink. "Two models in town for fashion week. Leggy girls with foreign accents. Don't bother calling us, just send them up," she said, slipping a one-hundred dollar bill into his palm.

Eniko and Iya arrived exactly one hour later. Iya wore a black leather trench coat and Louboutin stilettos. Eniko wore a black Chanel moto jacket and Jimmy Choo stilettos. Both women carried large Chanel tote bags. Mario walked them to the elevator and pressed the button for the twenty-seventh floor.

Philippe's front door was ajar. Once inside the apartment they followed the sound of Lise's moaning to the master bedroom, stood in the doorway and watched as Lise rolled Philippe onto his back, straddled him, and screamed in orgasmic pleasure.

"We could learn a lot from a woman like you," Eniko said once Lise had finished coming.

"Hey girls!" Lise exclaimed, trying to regain her composure. "I'm so glad you could make it. You can finally meet my Philippe."

Philippe's eye's locked on the two figures in his doorway. "What's this?" he asked, smiling. Lise could tell from the greedy look in his eyes that the girls' plan would work.

"I got you a present," Lise said with a touch of mischief. She climbed off of him, slipped on her black silk kimono, and walked over to the girls. "This is Francoise," she said, placing an arm around Iya, "and this beauty is Monique." Then she took both women by the hand and led them to the bed.

They kissed Philippe's cheeks then did the same for Lise. The harsh reality of the plan was setting in, and Lise had a brief moment of doubt. No one had ever made her come like Philippe could. If she went through with this scheme, she might never again experience such ecstasy.

Before she could say anything, Philippe was beside her, whispering, "Now I know you love me." He gently caressed her cheeks. "And you know how much I love your sweet tight pussy, *mon trésor.*"

He didn't say *I love you;* he said he loved her pussy. She already knew that. He'd told her so many times it had become a cliché. Lise detested clichés. Taking his right hand, the hand that had just played her clitoris like a maestro conducting a symphony, she looked up at him and softly kissed each of his long, graceful fingers.

Lise looked right into his glistening eyes. "I wanted to show you how much."

"Exquisite surprise, *mon amour.* Now let us celebrate this occasion with a drink. Come, come," Philippe said as he led the women to the living room.

Philippe prepared tequila shots while Eniko and Iya stood at the floor to ceiling windows making a fuss over the views; the Empire State Building to the south, the East River to the east, and, over a beautifully landscaped terrace, all of upper Manhattan to the north.

"Philippe, why don't you take the girls back to your bedroom?" Lise suggested. He nodded, and, carrying a silver tray with a shaker of salt, four crystal shot glasses and a bottle of tequila, went back to the bedroom. "This is the finest, most expensive tequila. *Herradura, Seleccion Supreme,*" Lise heard him say to the girls. *Ugh, he sounds like a fucking spokesman. He thinks he's the Most Interesting Man in the World.*

But somehow his sexual talents stayed with her. She tried not to think about his body and the oh-my-god explosive fire he'd just set in hers. Memories of sexual escapades past flashed through her mind; fucking him on the roof of his building during the July Fourth fireworks display, in the bathroom at the Plaza Hotel, in the Dior dressing room at Bergdorf Goodman.

She stood in the bedroom doorway and watched as the action began.

Eniko kneeled on the bed, slid one of the straps of her silk slip dress down her shoulder to uncover her breasts and sprinkled salt above her left nipple. "Who wants the first body shot? Come and get it, Philippe," she said with a sexual authority that was difficult to deny.

"Yes, Philippe," cooed Iya. "You go first."

He eagerly complied. He licked Eniko's nipple, then the salt, then he downed his first shot of tequila.

"Now your turn, Francoise," Eniko said to Iya. She leaned in to kiss Eniko's breast, then swirled her tongue over the salt before downing the tequila shot Philippe handed her.

Lise held back.

Now it's your turn, Lise," Eniko giggled as she drizzled more salt on her breast. "You gotta do it, too."

Philippe gently pushed Lise closer to Eniko.

Lise tried to focus on Eniko's pert nipple. She'd never touched a woman's breast, let alone licked one. Eniko sprinkled salt on her own breast. Lise hesitated until Eniko grasped her head and whispered, "Kiss me, *Embrases-moi*. Yes, yes, *Cherie*, like that."

Lise squirmed, a teeny bit annoyed at the sudden French endearments. Now Philippe would think she'd been intimate with these two all along, or worse, he'd expect this treatment all the time. She glanced up at Eniko, who shot her a look that said *get with the program bitch, we're putting on a show*. Lise succumbed. She licked the salt off Eniko's moist breast, and then threw back a tequila shot, surprised at surge of heat she felt between her legs.

Iya, kneeling beside Lise, went next. Then Eniko refilled all the glasses, raised hers in the air, and shouted, "*À votre santé!*"

They repeated the ritual, without the salt. Lise stopped after the third, and sat back to watch. Iya took off Philippe's shirt and unzipped his pants and ran her fingers along his hard penis. He glanced at Lise, smiling appreciatively. Unwittingly, she returned his smile.

For Lise, it was watching a movie on fast forward. Eniko lay back on the Pratesi sheets. Iya followed. They began kissing each other on the lips, groaning softly. Eniko reached under Iya's dress and stroked her. Iya threw her head back, then hastily pulled her dress off over her head. Lise again felt a tingling all over her skin as she watched Eniko slide her hand into Iya's thong and gently massage her clitoris, like she was petting a kitten. Iya shuttered and let out a scream.

"Hey, I want some of that," Philippe demanded. He joined the two women in his bed, kissing Iya as she rubbed his throbbing dick.

Yep, you'll get some of that. Lise slowly backed out to the doorway.

"Philippe, come, play our favorite game," Iya suggested seductively.

"*Mais, bien sur!* I'm game for *everything.*"

"Good, good, *mon chaton*," Iya said gleefully. She reached for her stilettos, and, in a sort of reverse striptease dance, put them on her feet, and then strutted across the room to the bag she'd placed on the chair and bent over it, knowing that Philippe's eyes would be locked on her ass. She put on a pair of black leather gloves and threw another pair to Eniko. Next she took out four coils of parachute cord with wide sheepskin straps. Then she brought the other bag to Eniko, who, straddling Philippe, took it and pulled out the hardware.

Iya slipped onto the bed and positioned her smooth pussy over Philippe's face. Then she began to explain the rules of their game.

"We're goin' to get you so fucked up. We're goin' to suck your dick dry. We're going to sit on your face. And then Francoise and I are going to make love to each other and you're the lucky boy who'll watch us while you jerk off. Sounds real good to us. What about you, *mon matou*? You are a tiger, no? With that glorious cock."

"Yes, go on, yes!" he blurted out in carnal amazement. "Yes, I want it all. You can even hurt me, but not too bad. I like that. Just gimme' another shot of tequila."

"No more tequila for you," said Iya, knowing that alcohol would increase his tolerance for pain.

Lise was riveted. This show was better than any of the X-rated movies she'd ever seen. Iya and Eniko were like a dominatrix SWAT team. For a moment Lise worried that if they killed Philippe she'd be an accessory. After all, she really didn't know them that well. But she couldn't stop watching.

Eniko licked the shaft of Philippe's huge, throbbing cock, then took the whole thing in her mouth while Iya glided her pussy across on his face. Philippe groaned. Iya and Eniko moaned and sighed.

Just when he was ready to come, the women, without saying a word, suddenly twisted themselves around like gymnasts, both landing on Philippe's shoulders, and quickly tied his hands to the bed-posts with the parachute cords.

"What the fuck are you two doing to me?"

"I told you we were going to fuck you up, didn't I?" Eniko grabbed his ankles and Iya spread his legs. Philippe struggled. Eniko tied his body to the bed with a piece of rope to keep him from falling off. Lise felt a twinge of pity as she watched him lying there, helpless, his erect dick standing tall like a flagpole in Marseille. He whimpered. Iya started sucking his cock. He quieted down.

Eniko pulled a flogger from her bag, and, standing at the foot of the bed, began swatting Philippe. Gently.

He moaned. "Yes, keep going. Yes."

Lise was stunned. *He likes this? Who the fuck is he?*

Eniko flogged him harder. He groaned. Her strokes grew increasingly harsh. His groans started to sound less contented.

"Safe word!" he cried.

Eniko hit him harder. And harder.

"Where's the fifty thousand dollars?" she demanded.

"What fifty thousand dollars?"

"The money you stole from Lise's apartment yesterday."

"What? I don't know anything about that!" he shouted. Now he was angry. Or scared. Lise couldn't tell for sure with all that rope.

"No? Nothing? Are you sure, Philippe?" asked Iya with a sweetness that could rot a tiger's tooth. She took a whip from her bag and cracked it over his arms and chest. Her whip made a much fiercer, much scarier sound than the swoosh of Eniko's flogger.

"Hey, hey, I thought you two were here for fun. I'm not a thief! I took no one's money! Look around you, I'm rich. I don't need to steal."

"You're a liar!" Iya screamed as she whipped him harder and faster.

Philippe started to squeal and sob. He wasn't enjoying the game any more.

Eniko opened one of his bedside drawers. "Well, lookie, lookie at what we have here," Eniko she, holding a small plastic baggie. She examined its contents. "Hmmm, looks like some tabs of acid," she said like a prosecutor on a cheesy seventies cop show. "And look—here's some GHB....and GBL....and oh, lucky us...he's got some ketamine, too. And Lise, I bet you didn't know this...he also has Viagra! Let's give him a double dose." She set two blue pills on the nightstand. "Okay Philippe? Then you will have an erection lasting more than four hours!" She reached for her bag again and pulled out a giant black dildo and another ominous-looking phallic contraption.

Iya whipped him even harder, then stopped when she noticed his dick had gone soft. "Eniko, suck his limp dick. It's pitiful."

Eniko obeyed, but Philippe's cock refused.

"He definitely needs his Viagra, poor little kitten." Iya said.

Eniko started laughing. "Ohhh, poor Philippe can't get a hard-on." She used the heel of her stiletto to crush the blue pills, licked her index finger, dabbed it into the powdered Viagra, and then shoved her finger up Philippe's ass. "It works faster this way."

She was right. Within fifteen seconds Philippe's pitiful limp dick had swelled into a rigid red rod.

Lise couldn't take it. She turned away.

Eniko, still holding the flogger, took a paddle from her bag. "Which one would you prefer, Philippe, the flogger or the paddle? The paddle hurts more than the flogger, but you knew that. Right?"

She swatted him with the paddle, hard.

He screamed.

"Where is the money, Philippe?" she said as she flogged his engorged cock.

Traumatized by the violence and noise, Lise, ran toward him. But, Iya stopped her.

"Philippe, did you steal my money?" Lise asked.

He wouldn't look at her. "No, no," he pleaded. "Get them off of me!"

Eniko flogged him again. Welts began appearing on his legs and stomach.

Philippe sobbed. Eniko hit him harder.

He was done. "It's there…in the closet…in the safe."

"The combination. The combination, please," Eniko said, raising her flogger.

"Two. Nine. Six. Eight."

"Merci monsieur," she responded. Then, to Lise she said, "Get your money."

Lise went to the closet and opened Philippe's safe. The first thing she saw was a white envelope. *Her* white envelope, with *her* name and address engraved on the back flap. She opened it. Saw the thick stack of cash. Still sealed. Fifty thousand dollars. It was all there.

She was just about to close the safe when she saw the ring. An emerald, at least six carats, encircled with diamonds. And a diamond bracelet. And stacks and stacks of hundred-dollar bills, rolled and wrapped. She picked up the ring. It looked so familiar. Just like the one she'd noticed on the woman sitting next to her at the St. Jude's Children's Hospital Gala a month ago. *Could it be hers? Was he doing this to other rich, naive women?*

Lise stormed out of the closet to find Eniko moving on to the next phase of their project. From a small metal box she'd fished from her bag, Eniko took a syringe and a glass bottle filled with a clear liquid. With the skill of a surgical nurse, she filled the syringe with the substance from the bottle, rolled him over on his side and slowly injected the liquid into his anus.

"You go to sleep now, *chaton*. When you wake up you won't remember any of this."

He was asleep within ten seconds. "Don't worry," Iya said, taking Lise's hand like a big sister. "He'll be fine in a few hours. For us, mission accomplished. Time to go."

Eniko handed out green rubber gloves, which she pulled from a pocket in the tote bag.

"Holy Ritchie Petrie, who are you two with that bag, Mary Poppins?" Lise cried. Iya and Eniko just stared at her. "Really? You never saw Mary Poppins? You really did have a deprived childhood. What else is in that bag?"

Eniko snapped, "This is not the time for packing lessons. Start cleaning."

In less than three minutes, Iya and Eniko had untied all of Philippe's bonds, lifted him off the bed picked and carefully set him on the carpet.

Iya sprayed his wounds with antiseptic. He didn't stir.

Together they stripped the bed, packed the soiled sheets in one of their totes, and then remade the bed with fresh sheets Lise had brought from the linen closet. Then the two girls picked up Philippe and laid him back in bed. Five minutes later not one trace of their presence remained in the entire apartment.

Lise gazed at Philippe one last time. He looked different. Like he had nothing inside him. No heart, no blood, not even a thought. Like he was lying in a coffin.

"He's dead," she said without a trace of affect.

"He's fine." Eniko pulled Lise away from the bed. "Don't take pity on a monster. That dose was nothing compared to what he was doing to innocent women."

Iya put her arm around Lise's shoulder and warmly kissed her cheek. "Please, darling, don't touch him. You don't want to leave any finger-prints. We already cleaned him up."

Eniko kissed Lise on her other cheek. "It's time to go now *kroshka*."

"No pain, no gain. He told me that. Stupid Frenchman. It's a fuck-ing advertising campaign!" Lise yelled as walked out of that bedroom for the last time. "What a fuckin moron asshole fuck face he is."

"Yes," said Iya as they walked with all their gear to the front door. She and Eniko left first, as planned. Lise quickly changed back into her sweater and pants and waited five minutes before turning off the lights and gently closing the front door behind her.

CHAPTER 11

Only six weeks had passed since Eniko and Iya helped Lise retrieve her stolen money, yet Lise knew she was so much more than a six weeks wiser. Her two beautiful lunch guests had taught her invaluable lessons; never again would she allow herself—or her daughter—to be a victim.

"I never paid you for that night," Lise said to the girls.

"What night?" Iya asked.

"With fuck face Frenchman," Lise said.

"That one was on the house," Eniko laughed.

Lise knew enough about business to know that nothing is ever on the house. "I appreciate that, but nevertheless…" she said as she slid a white envelope over to Eniko. "Put this with your Makarovs."

The waiter brought a bottle of Prosecco and bucket of ice to the table. "Compliments of Michael," he said as he poured sparkling wine into each glass.

Lise raised her glass. Eniko and Iya did the same. "No fear!" Lise said. They all sipped. "I'm used to having power and money. Getting my way. Yet I let a man turn me into a victim. Because I was afraid. Thank you for, well, everything." The girls raised their glasses and drank again.

"I have complete confidence in your abilities to deal with any situation," Lise continued. "Justine's situation is bad. She needs your help now."

"And she'll have it," Eniko said. "For six thousand dollars a day. Life before."

"Each," Iya chimed in. "Plus expenses."

"I'll pay you whatever it costs. This is my daughter we're talking about. I'm taking your word that you'll get this beast."

CHAPTER 12

State Highway One runs almost the entire length of California. In some parts of the state it was called the Pacific Coast Highway. In others it's the Shoreline Highway, and others just call it the Coast. In Sonoma, Monterey, and other northern counties it's known simply as One. Driving south on that road, Justine felt like she could fly. The car she picked up at the San Jose airport, a brand spanking new Porsche Carrera GT that someone else had paid for, hugged the curves of the storied road, which snaked from one spectacular vista to another. Sheer cliffs tumbled down to the Pacific Ocean to her right and towered up to her left as she rounded a blind corner. Slamming on her brakes, she turned sharp into the oncoming lane, then counterturned and accelerated around a fallen boulder—a perfect brake-and-evade maneuver. *Thank you Lily Marshall.*

Justine sang along as her girl Bey belted *You must not know 'bout me/ You must not know 'bout me* through the thousand-watt sixteen-speaker Burmester surround-sound system. The Porsche's engine growled with the throaty purr of perfection through more devilish twists. For one brief moment Justine felt pure effortless bliss.

But doubts ultimately found their way into her head. She'd spent three consecutive afternoons with Lily Marshall—at the shooting range as well as at the cosmetics counter at Saks Fifth Avenue—and Justine had become as comfortable and confident with a Glock as Lily was with a Dior eye shadow palette. Lily had taught Justine how to drive high performance cars and shoot high performance guns and now Justine was on her way to meet some mysterious high performance security dude at a bar in Big Sur. Was she crazy? She'd known Lily for less than a week, and they bonded like long lost friends, but what if Lily was in cahoots with this Don guy? What if they were both assassins, part of a huge conspiracy to kidnap her? Then again, why would they do that? She had to stop the negative thoughts. Time to call Danisha.

She pulled over to a scenic overlook, closed her eyes and visualized Dani's phone number. It was yet another trick Lily had taught her after advising her to clear her phone daily and store nothing in its memory.

"Hey, Dani, I'm in a rented Porsche to meet a serial killer. Wanted you to be the first to know!" Justine said, laughing.

"What the fuck, girl? Where are you now?"

"I have a new cop friend, Lily. She taught me how to shoot. For the past three days."

"Oh no you didn't!"

"Oh yes I did! And I was fucking awesome!"

"Jus! Guns? Sheee-it!"

"Anyway, Lily set me up with this guy. Supposedly he's the baddest bad-ass bodyguard—or security agent, or whatever—in the world. Either that or he's a serial killer. I'm meeting him at that place in Big Sur, Nepenthe. So, I thought you should know in case I disappear."

"What's his name? I'm gonna Google him."

"Are you kidding? I don't even know what he looks like! Lily calls him Don, but who knows? It's all super hush-hush top secret shit."

"So…you're going to meet a man with no name and no face at a bar in fucking Big Sur, a restaurant named after a carnivorous plant?" Dani sounded exasperated.

"Wait, what?"

"Did you sleep through biology, girl? Nepenthe plants are kinda like Venus Flytraps. They eat flesh. There's a metaphor here, I'm sure."

"This isn't helping."

"Okay fine. You're gonna do what you're gonna do. I know you. Unstoppable Baron. Tell me you're wearing your Jewish good luck charm at least."

"My *chai*?" Justine's fingers reflexively touched the gold charm on her necklace, the Hebrew word for life. "Of course. I wouldn't go for a haircut without it, you think I'd leave it behind for a meeting like this?"

"That's my girl. Now I have some news for you."

"Okay. What?"

"I'm having an engagement party in two weeks and you have to be here because, you, girlfriend, are my maid of honor."

"No way! What about our pact, *single and free forever*? And who is this person stealing my Dani from me? Your gorgeous Italian movie producer? And why such short notice?"

"What pact? Yes, it's him. And I'm a little bit pregnant. Just a few weeks, but the test was a strong positive."

"Pregnant? Are you ready for a kid?"

"Yes, and yes. But Alessandro doesn't know yet. I plan to fit into the wedding dress that Lise promised me, so no wedding until after the baby."

"Well, hey, that's fine with me. E-mail me the invite and I'll be there. With Scott. I do get a plus one, right?"

"Of course!"

"I better get going. Let's talk later."

CHAPTER 13

Justine put the Porsche in gear and raced a bit too fast to the restaurant. She arrived a few minutes early. As she climbed the winding stairs up from the parking lot to the restaurant, the sun slipped to the horizon, casting different hues of red and purple onto the fluffy white clouds nestled over the Pacific.

Walking through the restaurant to the bar, she scanned the eyes of dozens of men of all ages and races, alone or with their wives or dates. All heads turned as she passed, and she realized that she was out of place in her stiletto heels, skinny designer jeans and white silk blouse. Her ostrich purse alone cost what many of these men and women earned in a month. What was she thinking? This wasn't LA, or Manhattan, or even Miami! This was earthy, organic, marijuana-ville, and she had dressed for a fashion show.

She headed straight for the bathroom and into a stall, where she pulled down her jeans and thong, and sat down, and started to cry. What had she gotten herself into?

At the sink she wiped the eyeliner from the rims of her eyes, then rifled through her bag for her lip gloss. The woman in the mirror looked just like her, she thought as she painted the gloss on her lips. *She's brave. You be brave too. Go find that man they call Don.*

Back by the bar she didn't see anyone who looked like the bad-ass Lily had described. Justine started to feel annoyed. Men waited for her, not the other way around. She found an empty seat at the long bar and ordered a sparkling water with lime.

Don had started hacking and tracking her cell phone the moment Justine arrived at the San Jose Airport to pick the Porsche. He'd heard her conversation with Danisha and was amused.

He'd been seated by the window next to the bar, with his back to the main entrance for the better part of an hour. Justine didn't see him because his bullet-proof vest made him look thick, out of shape, and his gray wig made him look old. As the sun went down, the lights of the bar became brighter and the window became his own wide-angle mirror. From his chosen perch he could watch the whole bar and restaurant. He wore glasses with small mirrors on the inside the outer lenses, so even without the window-mirror he could always see behind him. The polycarbonate glasses also protected his eyes; the Israelis taught him that secondary fragments lodged in soldiers' eyes account for twenty percent of all casualties in urban warfare. Most his clients lived and worked in urban environments. The glasses also made him appear studious, unthreatening. An excellent disguise.

When Justine first arrived, Don had set his nondescript brown corduroy jacket on his stool and ambled down to the parking lot to watch her make her entrance. As she strutted up the stairs, he walked past, down to her car, ran a transmission scan to make sure no one else was watching her, and then slipped a small Faraday Cage, a radar-absorbent cloth, over the Porsche's GPS antenna to block any tracking devices.

Lily had told him that Justine was attractive, but this woman had something more than just looks. She had style. She was dressed better than anyone else in the room. She knew how to take center stage—even in a parking lot. She had a great walk. Like a dancer. It seemed as if everyone—even the women—watched her, which was good for his plans.

Justine checked the time on her iPhone: seven-eighteen and still no man named Don. She endured the clichéd pick-up lines of assorted big-belly drunks, tourists, and stoner locals. Her standard response was always polite: *Thank you, but I'm waiting for my husband. He'll be here any minute.*

The ice in her second sparkling water was almost completely melted when a big, belligerently blasted and massively muscled man she'd already rebuffed walked up to her, slapped his huge paw on the shoulder of her silk blouse, and smirked, "Looks like *you* got stood up by your own goddamn husband, ya stuck-up bitch!"

Justine slipped her shoulder from under his hand and pivoted on her barstool to face him. In a measured but even tone, she said, "Get away from me!"

One of the guy's motorcycle gang buddies at their table roared with laughter. "Looks like you got yourself a fighter!"

"Fight, my ass, one cunt-slap and she'd be suckin' dirt before she sucks my cock." But then he suddenly tottered up on his tiptoes with a surprised wince of pain, his eyes wide. An older man, with gray hair and glasses, was behind him, pinning both of his massive arms behind his back. Then he gripped the middle fingers of both his hands and bent them backwards.

"Back off," the old man growled. Justine had noticed him earlier, sitting at a window with his back to her.

The drunk spun around and the gray-haired man nudged him toward his buddies. Shaking the pain from his hands, he bellowed, "You fuckin' asshole!" He charged back and threw a wide haymaker punch.

The older man dodged the punch, stepped under the drunk's arm, and slipped behind him. Suddenly the drunk's head hit the bar with a satisfying *clonk*. His huge body plopped to the floor. It happened so fast that even though Justine was watching, she wouldn't be able to describe what she'd just seen.

The room went silent.

The old man turned to face the unruly gang, raised his hands in a conciliatory manner, and bowed his head and apologized. "I'm sorry for your friend. He tripped. He'll wake soon, but for now, he feels no pain. This restaurant is named for an ancient drink that makes you forget your pain and sorrows. I am sure he's forgetting his."

The men could do nothing but stare down at their huge friend. He was actually *snoring*. They murmured amongst themselves, trying to figure out what to do next. The stranger took Justine by her elbow and led her away.

"Justine," he whispered in her ear, "Don." He placed a hundred-dollar bill on the bar with a nod to the bartender, then led Justine quickly toward the patio.

She hadn't noticed the narrow path under the patio that led to an exit. Either Don knew the place quite well or he had the eyes of a cat. He walked her through a grove of redwoods, down a narrow dirt path.

"What just happened back there?" she asked, taking off her stilettos.

"You passed your first test. But we need to hurry."

"I noticed you when I first walked into the bar! Saw the back of your head. Why did you make me sit there for an hour?"

"You waited for forty-seven minutes. You arrived at six thirty-one. It's good that you were early."

Justine exclaimed, "Oh my God, my purse!"

Don handed it to her, smiling.

She stared at her purse in disbelief and then at him. "How'd you get it?"

"You left it. I picked it up."

Don slipped Justine's iPhone into a radar-absorbent pouch to block her cell phone provider from tracking it. His own phone had a multiband scanner that could tell whether any other devices were tracking Justine or her car. He still didn't trust her.

Nor did she trust him. When they got to the parking lot Don guided Justine to the passenger door of the Porsche, and opened it for her. She was scared. Paralyzed. He pushed her in, slammed the door and then quickly walked around, got in the driver's seat, started the engine, and turned the lights off.

"Get down, they're coming," he told her, nodding his head toward the restaurant stairs.

Justine crouched under the sight line as Don accelerated smoothly, quietly driving without headlights in the darkening twilight. They headed north. Don disconnected the battery from his cell phone, then did a U-turn and drove south. He never touched the brakes. Using only the gears and engine to control it, he easily spun the Porsche spun around the curves of the highway. The tires barely squealed.

"Aren't you glad you have the right car for your first escapade?" Don laughed. They heard the sound of motorcycles and cars engines revving, then peeling out of the *Nepenthe* lot. Justine looked in the rearview mirror. Some headed north, others south.

"How'd you steal my keys?" she asked as she put on her shoes back on.

"They were on top of your purse. I know where we're going and you don't."

CHAPTER 14

She had no idea where she was. Don had turned onto a dirt road about a mile back, though it could have been two miles for all Justine knew. The Porsche rode so smoothly, purring like a cougar cub even in second gear, she thought it could've been going anywhere from fifteen to fifty miles per hour. Twilight had given way to the phenomenal radiance of the Northern California night, even the darkness shined.

"I don't think I've ever seen a sky this color," Justine heard herself saying.

"The Milky Way and the ocean make a spectacular couple," Don replied, slowing the car to a rolling stop. Justine noticed a gate swinging open about a hundred feet ahead. He shifted the gear into first, then gave the car just enough gas to move it forward without raising any dust. When the gate closed behind them and Don pulled the gearshift to neutral, Justine would've sworn he hadn't moved a muscle.

"Did you just shift without touching the clutch?" she asked as the Porsche rolled down a narrow dirt path.

Don nodded. "The engine tells me when it's ready to change gears."

"But it's not..." her incredulous reaction to the car whisperer in the seat beside her was interrupted by the sight of a small cabin perched on a hill overlooking the ocean. Don parked the Porsche near three vehicles with canvass covers.

"Is this your home?" Justine asked.

"I have no home, as you use the word, but this is where you'll sleep tonight."

"Alone?" She was so confused.

"Alone with your thoughts." As Don spoke he pulled the hair off his head, and Justine got even more confused. She saw his hands on his temples, on his cheeks, *was he pinching his cheeks?* And then he did that thing she'd seen in too many James Bond movies and thought, *I can't believe it! That was a mask? He just peeled off his face.*

Suddenly a completely different man was sitting next to her. Don had literally transformed himself. He was no longer an old white dude. Justine wasn't exactly sure how to describe him. He *was* James Bond, the Daniel Craig version, but Eurasian. Handsome, yes. With high cheekbones and chiseled jaw. Even in the starlight she could see the intelligence in his eyes, the shine of his jet black hair.

They turned off onto a winding graveled road and finally stopped. Walking on the rocky path to the cabin in her stilettos was a challenge, but Justine managed to navigate it without twisting an ankle. Don stopped on the porch, offered Justine a seat on a weathered bench, and took off his boots. Following his lead, she slipped off her shoes. Their paper-thin sole, sexy black leather straps and five-inch heels looked silly next to his battered, water buffalo hide, cowboy boots, especially when he pulled two small pistols and two palm-sized stainless steel folding knives from inside each boot.

"Great boots. Did you get them at Saks or are they Internet and gun show only?" she asked him, remembering Lily's story of the hide-a-pistol-purse. When Don didn't respond to her retail humor she tried another tack. "Nice hardware," she said, her thoughts racing between *he's so beautifully mysterious* to *oh my god he's a fucking assassin.*

"Back-ups," he said.

"Hard to run in those boots."

"Too battered to run. Have to stand and fight."

"You or the boots?"

"All of us."

Justine thought she saw him smile, but she forgot all about that when he took *another* gun from his *pants.* "And I thought you were just happy to see me," she quipped.

That one worked. He definitely smiled. "Thank you. But that is a ten-shot Glock twenty-six."

"I'd hate to be stranded on a deserted highway and have you show up," she said with a nod to his arsenal.

"If you were stranded anywhere, I'm the one you would want to show up."

"Clients ninety-nine, stalkers zero," said Justine, deadpan.

"Okay, Client one-hundred." Don winked and reached under his shirt. Then, with the grace of a master magician, he produced another pistol.

"I swear, you gun people have the most fascinating accessories."

"This is a Glock eighteen pistol. Shoulder holster under my shirt." He stashed the gun with the others in his boots. "And we don't like being referred to as *you people*."

How had she missed those bulges? He never looked heavy or bulky, and he moved with such grace, even laden with so much steel. "So all together that's four pistols. You expecting a war?"

He lifted his belt buckle to reveal a tiny revolver. "Five." This is a Freedom Arms mini-revolver. That biker gang at Nepenthe had even more."

The moon reflected an ethereal light on Don's face. Justine could swear she saw a ring of crystal clear blue around his light brown eyes. *Was this guy for real?* He was Jon Hamm and Ryan Gosling and Ken Watanabe all rolled into one Double O Seven. *You can look, but don't touch,* she reminded herself.

He unlocked the cabin door and, with a subtle nod, directed her to enter. She looked into the room, hesitating in the doorway as Don turned on some lights. *Of course his secluded cabin is gorgeous.* The room was small, but spacious. A futon with a white down comforter and four fluffy pillows sat on tatami mats in the middle of the floor, two shoji screens covered the walls adjacent to the floor-to-ceiling windows, which slid open to an expansive wood deck overlooking the ocean.

The sound of the surf crashing onto the rocks below the cabin reminded Justine of all the sparkling water she'd drank while waiting for Don at the bar. "Does this little Zen palace have one of those awesome Japanese toilets?" she asked her host.

Don slid one of the shoji screens to reveal a small bathroom. Justine went in, turned and bowed to Don as though she were leaving a dojo, and slid the shoji closed. Motion-activated, soft candle-like LEDs gently illuminated the cream-and-white-colored marble and bamboo décor, including the *Toto* toilet slash bidet. *Even his goddamn bathroom is high-tech perfection.*

Back in the main room she found a white terrycloth robe folded on the futon, but no Don. Then she heard his voice from outside the front door. "Leave *everything* of yours in this room. It'll be safe. If I find anything on you—jewelry, tampons, whatever—your interview will be over. You'll become a potential foe instead of an ally."

What the fuck? He goes straight from jewelry to tampons. And he thought she could be foe. Who uses that word? She heard a car engine start —not the Porsche. He was waiting for her. *Now where's he taking me?*

Her suitcase was still in the Porsche. Reflexively, she looked for her purse, she had to talk to Danisha. But her purse and cell phone were also in the rented car. She paced in a circle, *what to do, what to do. Think.* Her situation suddenly felt grim; no one knew where she was and only Lily knew who she was with. *Could Lily have set her up? Maybe Don was the voice on the other end of her attacker's phone call? Maybe they were kidnapping her?*

She slid open the doors to the deck looking for a way out. The strong ocean wind chilled her. She heard the distant sound of the surf crashing on the rocks below and realized there was no escape that way. Behind her was a strange man who could overpower her in seconds, yet he rescued her from the biker gang and, so far, had only shown kindness. She slid the doors closed.

CHAPTER 15

It's now or never. Justine stripped down to her thong and wrapped herself in the robe. It was warm, and so soft. Reluctantly she pulled down her thong, folded it and left it with the rest of her clothes on the futon.

She closed her eyes and did a slow, ten-second breathing meditation to steady her nerves. Then she left the cabin, barefoot.

In the pale moonlight she could see exhaust rising from the tail pipes of an old, battered Volvo station wagon. But the engine didn't sound like an ordinary Volvo; it had a rumble in its exhaust. The passenger side door opened. The rented Porsche was gone. She thought it must be under one of the dusty canvas covers.

She padded cautiously across the cold stone path and climbed into the welcoming warmth of the heated Volvo. "Not quite an Aston Martin, but I love the thermostat."

"I never said my name was Bond."

"Is that Esalen? The lights at the bottom of the cliff?" Don didn't answer. "Are we going to the legendary Esalen hot springs?" Justine asked, sounding like a precocious teenager.

"Lily said you were sharp."

"Just my luck, you're gonna waterboard me," Justine retorted.

"You'll be in hot water but I doubt you'll be bored."

"Quick question. How do you plan to do my tampon check? Will I get the full body cavity search?"

"Yes. Electronically. With scanners, not fingers,"

After a few silent minutes of driving over curving, bumpy roads, they finally stopped. Justine waited in the car until Don opened the door for her and took her hand. She smelled the sulfur of the hot springs before she saw them.

Don reassured her. "Our noses only have five million receptors, our skin has billions. Your skin will be so happy your brain will ignore your nose."

"I should get you together with my best friend Dani for a Trivial Pursuit tournament," muttered Justine.

They stepped into a secluded cave with a pool, carved over thousands of years into the ocean cliff.

"Leave your robe on and lift your arms up over your head." Justine shot him a look. "Please." She complied. "Now spread your legs like you're going through airport security," Don ordered.

Justine stood very still. His sudden military tone surprised her.

"Problem?" he asked.

"No…" Once again she felt like she had lost all her power, but she yielded to his command.

Don pulled out what looked like two cell phones from his robe pockets and pushed some buttons. The phones, or whatever they were, began to emit a subtle humming tone. "You getting a busy signal?" Justine asked in an effort to diminish her own discomfort. Don smiled, but had no witty comeback. He guided the instruments over her entire body, almost but never quite touching her, like a *reiki* master. They continued humming until they came near her left ankle, when they both beeped.

"I fell off of a horse in college. Broke my left leg. Titanium screws." she said.

"These detect metal. They also measure the electrical dipole constant, so they will find any unusual cavities or implants."

"You know, I've been felt up by a few guys, but never by remote control."

Don continued in his business-like tone, "Please, turn around. Close your eyes."

"Yes, sir," Justine saluted. "I knew you'd get me naked, eventually," she snapped as she waited for him to remove her robe. When she heard him set his gadgets on a ledge, she closed her eyes and held her breath.

Nothing happened. Suddenly she heard the swish of Don's robe slipping to the ground, followed by the sounds of his feet splashing into the pool. She turned for a quick peek. The half-moon shone on Don's muscular back, revealing a series of jagged scars. Her eyes locked on his bare ass as he descended into the swirling water. *Stop it, he's off limits.* She averted her eyes. The echoes of his voice whispered from the back wall of the cave. "Come on in."

When she turned around Justine saw that Don was facing away from her. Surprised at his modesty, she paused, inhaled deeply and exhaled, dropped her robe, and entered the swirling water. She waded in, sat on a submerged bench beside him, and slid down until the water covered her breasts. Don looked into her eyes for a split second, and then looked down into the water. His profile was striking. Justine felt her vagina contract involuntarily, and despite the heat coming off the water, her nipples tingled as they hardened.

She felt Don's presence like an electric jolt through the water. They were both quiet for a few minutes. *He sure was right about the nerve receptors in my skin.* She felt completely relaxed.

Don broke the silence. "This is a mutual interview. You get to ask me a question for every one of mine that you answer truthfully. I will never lie to you, but I can't answer everything."

Justine's mind raced with questions. "Okay. Is Don your real name?"

"I'm supposed to ask the questions first but, okay, yes. In the West, that is my name. I was born in Japan. My mother named me Akisume —Autumn Rain—but you can call me Ki or stick with my American name, Don. I answer to both."

"I knew you were a mix, but in the darkness you could be Mexican, Mongolian, Uzbek, even Native American. So you're half Japanese. What's the other half?"

"I don't know."

"Where's your mother now?"

"She gave me to an American family when I was a boy."

"Lily told me the story."

"After they took me to the States she knelt in front of an oncoming train."

He was silent for a moment. Justine wondered what he wasn't telling her.

"I've answered many of your questions. Now it's my turn. Why do you want to become your own bodyguard when you can afford to hire the best?"

Justine looked into his eyes, wanting to trust him. "I was almost raped on my own bed. I was terrified. Lily told me that the police couldn't protect me twenty-four-seven but I could learn to protect myself if I trained with you. So, after crying and moaning a lot, I turned my fear into anger and decided to take control. Lily probably told you about teaching me to shoot. I learn quickly. I know it sounds cliché but I felt *empowered*. I'm a successful business woman. Just like my mom. I also enjoy extreme sports, I'm competitive, don't feel comfortable if I'm too comfortable. This whole experience—the attacker, the shooting lessons, meeting you—makes me realize I need to be a fighter. Like you. I don't really know you, but I get a sense that I want to be a version of you."

Don put his hands together as if in prayer and bowed. "You've passed the second test."

Justine smiled and returned the bow. But she still was anxious. This feeling she had for him was foreign, not overtly sexual but *pleasant*.

"I'd like to be your student, but I have so many questions. Like what exactly were you doing with those cell phones thingies and my body?"

"I needed to make sure that you were not recording my words. The first pass was to detect any unusual passive chips, bombs, etcetera. Though from your profile—yeah, I did have Lily profile you—I had no serious suspicions. The second pass was to detect any transmitting devices."

"You're my own private MacGyver."

Don remained serious. "I'm training you to protect yourself. From anyone and anything. You'll need to think like an assassin in order to prevent your own assassination. When Lily first met you, before she sent you to me, she ran background checks on you."

"Lily ran background checks on me?"

"She doesn't give lessons to criminals."

"So I passed Lily's tests."

"If you had failed my interview or chose to walk away, you would sleep in a beautiful hotel in Monterey tonight. You just wouldn't remember how you got there."

"So this must be my stress interview? If I'd failed, you'd use some drug to make me forget everything about tonight, right?"

"Lily said you were sharp."

"But I passed?"

"Yes. You'll sleep alone in the cabin by the ocean. I'm closing my eyes now. There's a shower in the dressing room to your right. Go rinse off.

The path to the cabin is well lit. It's just above us, less than a two-minute walk. Your clothes, purse, and the key to the Porsche are still there."

"We're not in Esalen?"

"No. You're the one who said that I was taking you to Esalen. I only said that Lily said that you're sharp. We drove around in the dark in a circle. You didn't pay attention to the turns so you became lost in reality because you were lost in your mind."

"You tricked me!"

"I just taught you to count your turns wherever you go because you'll always want to know your way home," Don told her. "I'll see you on your deck at eight for breakfast."

CHAPTER 16

On Thursday morning Eniko and Iya landed at San Francisco International airport and picked up the Ford Fiesta Lise had booked for them at Avis. Forty-five minutes later, they checked in to the Westin Palo Alto Hotel. Lise had picked both the hotel and the car for their practicality. The Ford, a nondescript gray box with wheels, would draw no unwanted attention to her two beautiful dominatrices, and the Westin was perfectly located, about a mile from Justine's Edgewood Drive home and adjacent to the Stanford campus. The girls would blend in with the students; no one would suspect the real reason for their trip to Palo Alto.

They were checked into their room by noon, changed into their yoga clothes and put all their necessary equipment in crossbody messenger bags, the kind the Stanford kids used. Iya had done their homework and mapped out the route to Justine's house on Edgewood Drive and found the best place to rent bikes. Eniko had learned all about Bay Area Bike Share from Google. She used the Citibikes in New York City regularly, though Iya thought it was little more than a fleet of clunky rolling ads for a bank. At least the California bikes had no corporate logo. They walked a half-mile or so to the bike station at the Caltrain depot and chose the 24-hour rental option.

They hopped on their bikes and headed east, away from the sprawling university campus and congestion of University Avenue and El Camino Real. Soon they were riding down tree-lined suburban streets. So quiet. So *American*.

Iya was the first to notice the black Toyota Highlander parked across the street from Justine's house. The only other vehicles not parked in driveways were service vans and trucks with company names painted on their doors. She nodded to Eniko, who rode her bicycle slowly past the Toyota to try to get a look through its darkened windows. Empty.

Iya stopped, ostensibly to tie her shoe. Eniko caught up and stopped beside Iya. "Someone's in the house," Eniko said.

"You saw him?" Iya was sure someone was there too.

"No, I can feel it." Eniko always had an uncanny intuition about this sort of thing.

"I'll go back and sit watch. Did you see that hedge about a hundred meters back?"

Iya smiled and said, "*Kanyeshna*. The light green hydrangea? You know I did. I'll head there first, then I'll take care of the Toyota."

Eniko nodded her agreement and rode ahead to the next intersection, then did a wide U-turn. Iya rode to the hedge and stashed her bike beneath it. The light green of the bike's frame blended beautifully with the pastel green petals, unless someone was actively searching for a Bay Area Rideshare bicycle, they'd never notice it there. She strolled towards Justine's house with her iPhone to her ear, speaking in impassioned Russian to no one.

Eniko meanwhile walked her bike, limping, towards the mysterious black Toyota. Once she reached its back wheels she leaned over to massage an ankle, and surreptitiously placed a Sentinel Micro transponder, a tracking device in a magnetic box about the size of a pack of matches, in the wheel-well. She hobbled along for a few more meters, then laid the bike on its side, sat on the grass, took an ace bandage out of her messenger bag and wrapped her faux-sprained ankle. Then, continuing her act of the wounded co-ed, she carefully mounted her bike and slowly rode back to the hotel.

Meanwhile, Iya found another flowering bush, a Cape Honeysuckle, diagonally across the street from Justine's house. Keeping her phone pressed to her ear, she slowed her pace to inspect the vermillion-flowered hedge. It was actually a line of small trees, at least two meters high, with thin trunks. If she could squeeze herself through two of those trunks she would have a clear view of Justine's front door and upstairs windows, as well as the rear end of the Toyota.

Squeezing through was easier than she thought. She couldn't have asked for a better hiding place; no one who wasn't actively searching for a tall thin blonde would see her lurking in those bushes. The hard part was standing still.

The first thing she noticed was just a hint of movement through one of Justine's upstairs windows. A few minutes later she saw a man walking from the house towards the parked Toyota SUV. She couldn't see his face—he wore a black baseball cap and black-rimmed sunglasses, but she could see that he walked with a strange gait; his right foot turned out just slightly, like a dancer who'd only learned half the first lesson. She could also see a fairly large canvas bag slung over his left shoulder. The Toyota's break lights flickered and she heard the two short beeps of a remote lock. The man got behind the wheel, turned on the engine, and drove off.

CHAPTER 17

Justine awoke in the darkened room. "Oh shit, what time is it?" she said out loud to no one. She felt around for her phone, shook the bedding, lifted the duvet, turned over pillows, and then finally flopped on her belly to feel around the floor. She found it near the wall, plugged into the charger, right where she left it last night, before she crashed on the futon. Holding her thumb on the phone's home button, the screen lit up and she saw the digital clock. "Ten twenty-nine? Holy crap." She hadn't slept this late since, well, ever. And she was supposed to be up at eight. *Don's gonna' be pissed.*

She eased her naked body out from under the warm down comforter, shivering as she slipped into the cold terrycloth robe and found her way to the shoji screen that doubled as a bathroom door, slid it aside and turned on the light.

Sure, the bathroom had a state-of-the-art wash-your-ass-with-warm-water-heated-seat toilet, but no water glass, toothpaste, or mouthwash. She cupped her hands under the tap and scooped handfuls of water into her mouth. The sulfur and whatever other new-age minerals in the pool last night must've robbed her body of hydration, even as it healed and relaxed her after her exhausting two-day odyssey.

"You need food," she told her reflection. The only thing she'd ingested since breakfast yesterday was the Nepenthe sparkling water. And a wedge of lime. *At least you won't get scurvy, matey.* Yeah, she definitely needed to eat something—she was talking to her reflection about an obscure nineteenth century disease. She must be delirious.

Through the open doorway she could see the other shoji screen in the darkened futon room, and spied a hint of daylight behind it. *There were huge windows last night, leading to the deck.* The shoji screens she remembered. And the floor-to-ceiling windows behind them. And the view of the ocean.

She walked to the screen, slid it aside and was suddenly bathed in glorious morning light. The view in the daylight was breathtaking; cobalt blue ocean and azure sky. Justine grabbed her phone to take a take few pictures of the place, then remembered Don. This was his hideaway, not a bed and breakfast. Also he would know if she used her phone for anything, even pictures. Her visual memory would have to suffice.

Just next to the front doorway she found a pair of black cotton drawstring pants, a black cotton shirt, and black slippers—her size—neatly folded on a built-in wooden ledge. *Ooh comfy karate outfit, fashionable and practical.* She quickly put the clothes on. So warm, and they smelled like a sunny Saturday afternoon. The slippers felt like, well, like slippers. She had no idea what they were made of, some new high tech material, but it sure was soft. And tough.

Outside on the teak deck that ran the length of the cabin, Justine inhaled the clean midmorning air. She noticed a place setting for one on the redwood deck table.

"Don," she called out over the deck. "I'm up! Are you here?"

His reply came from below, "Be right up!"

Don, dressed in his black *Karate-gi* and carrying a small bowl, bounded up the stairs. "Glad you stayed. Sorry you missed breakfast. I brought you granola with berries and almond milk." He handed her the bowl.

"Thanks. I like the service in this place."

"You are now my student, not a guest. I'm your teacher, not your servant."

"I see. Well, sorry I overslept. That *never* happens. When do I start my training?"

"You're always training, if you pay attention.

Don led Justine back inside the cabin. He rolled up the futon, unplugged a single wire from a socket deep in the tatami mats. Justine was confused. "I slept on an electric bed? Were you going to fry me if I was bad?"

"You slept on an *Earthing* grounding sheet. It removes the static electricity from your body—which fries you from within. I bet you slept really well last night."

"Sure did. Slept so well I missed your breakfast. What's a grounding sheet?"

"We are bioelectrical beings. With the synthetic fibers of our clothes, insulation in our homes, rubber tires on our cars, we allow static electrical charges to build up in our bodies. In more primitive cultures people walk barefoot. They're connected to the earth. They don't have many of the diseases we have in our civilization, the diseases that came with industrialization. When you go to the beach and walk barefoot on the wet sand you feel better, right?"

"Depends on who I'm with," Justine replied with a big grin.

Don ignored her flirting. "We can't walk barefoot on the beach every day but we can ground ourselves when we sleep. This allows our bodies to heal faster and increases deep REM sleep. So we wake up more refreshed."

"So in essence you're using high tech to get back to nature?"

"Well…You could just sleep naked on a dirt floor."

"Thank you for the grounding sheet." Justine smiled. "I do appreciate it. Really. I'm learning about stuff I never knew existed. What's next?"

Now, I'm sure Lily already taught you enough to defend yourself against the more common threats the *average* woman might encounter. Now you need to learn *awareness*. You must prepare for a three-hundred-sixty-degree circle of possible threats. Cowards travel in packs. You need to go from zero to hero in the blink of an eye. Once you've learned lethal force, you have a responsibility to prevent violence. That's the paradox. But lethal force must be a *final* option. You must be prepared to shoot accurately and quickly under tremendous stress. Even after you've been shot."

"Won't this training take forever?" Justine asked, nervously twisting a strand of hair.

"If you already have law enforcement or military training, the Secret Service training would take a year. The top private executive protection academy would take half a year. I'll train you in three months. You will pay me back with three months of work."

This new contingency surprised Justine. "What kind of work?"

"Protection. For *my* clients."

"Can't I just pay you to train me? I can afford it."

"That's too easy. I only train heroes. Those rare human beings, like Lily Marshall, who have a sense of duty. Who use their power to protect others in need of help. "

"Okay. I...I...I never thought of myself as a hero..."

"Lily saw the power in you. So it must be there."

"I guess I should be flattered," she said demurely. "Actually, honored is the better word."

"It's both an honor and a responsibility."

"I appreciate your trust and I'm ready for the responsibility. I do need to go to Los Angeles next week. Danisha's engagement party."

"That's fine. My goal is to have you trained and ready for the Academy Awards."

Academy Awards? What the hell was he talking about? "Was I nominated? I gotta get a gown!" she joked, covering for her confusion.

"I suspect that many of my clients will be nominees. Having you there and well-trained will be an invaluable asset for them and for me. You'll blend in with the crowd. I bet that doesn't happen often."

"I'm going to the *Oscars*?" Don nodded. "I'm going to the Oscars!" Maybe this three-months of work payback contingency was a blessing in disguise.

"If I believe you are ready. We'll start your official three-month training when you get back from LA."

As Justine followed Don along a narrow dirt path towards the cliff, she felt an inexplicable loneliness welling up within her. She didn't want to leave this place, this man. *Wait a second girl. Check those gooey emotions at the door. You have a boyfriend, remember?* She wondered what Scott was doing. *She hadn't even thought about him for the past couple of days.*

They stopped at a promontory at the edge of the cliff. Don told her to step in front of him.

Justine found herself standing two feet from the edge of what had to be a thousand-foot drop to the jagged rocks below. "Roger that," she said, feigning courage before she instinctually reached for Don's hand. He eluded her grasp, which scared her even more.

"Now you'll learn to focus on the here and now. Not the past. Not the future. Don't let your imagination distort your perception. I want you to see, hear, and feel three hundred and sixty degrees around you," Don continued. He led Justine through the *realm of the senses*, a Zen exercise that heightened her awareness of all her sensory organs. Looking over the edge of the cliff, she started to feel faint.

Somehow Don sensed that. "Focus on your breathing," he said.

"Okay, just don't let me go over the cliff."

Don stood behind her, placed a blindfold over her eyes and a pair of noise-canceling ear-buds over her ears.

"Who are you Mary Poppins? Pulling all this equipment out of nowhere. What's next, a table lamp?"

"Use your calming breath," Don said softly though some kind of radio link in the headphones. "Please turn around without stepping backwards." Justine complied. "What do you feel?"

"I'm scared."

"Your fear is a gift that arouses the primitive portions of your brain to peak performance. Focus on your physical senses rather than your emotions. Now what do you feel?"

"I feel the wind on my face and both forearms, which means you're stepping away from me."

"I've made myself undetectable. You can't see, hear, or touch me. In ten seconds I want you to tell me whether I've moved to your right or to your left."

Justine felt her heart pounding. "I have no clue!"

"Take two steps forward. Rotate slowly to your left and then to your right. Use your breasts and genitals to find me."

"Wait. Use my *what*?"

"Please open your top."

"All the way?"

"Yes please. We were both comfortable seeing each other naked last night. Now, feel my presence through the sensations of your nipples."

Standing on the precipice of an abyss, blindfolded, Justine felt oddly safe. She opened her shirt and exposed her bare breasts to the elements. As she slowly rotated from left to right she became aware of a subtle tingling in her nipples. "What am I going for here?"

"Just breathe. Concentrate. Your body will send you messages. Pay close attention."

Justine forced her mind to concentrate on her body. Stepping carefully to her right, she suddenly sensed his presence. "Oh my God! I can feel you. You walked away from me. You're about…eight to ten feet to my right."

"Close your top. Lift your blindfold and open your eyes."

Justine saw only grass and trees. "Where are you?"

Don rose from behind a log ten feet to her right.

"How'd you do that?"

"I visualized caressing one of your breasts with one hand as I licked the nipple of the other. The energy of lust is remarkably similar to that of a kill. They affect adjacent portions of your primitive brain. How many times have you felt a man lusting after your ass at a party and you turned around to catch him staring?"

"That's happened," she said shyly.

"I understand. You're a beautiful woman so you arouse primitive desires in men. We have the five obvious senses, but we have other, more primitive senses. When we work to develop those, we paradoxically become more evolved. How do you feel now?"

"A bit confused, but fine. Relaxed."

"Good. You can go home now. Focus on your driving. Don't think about your lessons until you're safe in your own bed. You know your way home. Have a safe journey," Don said as he gently embraced her.

A new feeling swept through her body as she hugged him back. She couldn't define it, and for the first time she could remember, she wasn't sure how to respond. She didn't know why, but she wanted to hold him tighter.

As Justine hiked back to the cabin she thought about Scott. *She did miss him*, all the confusing reactions to Don were actually misdirected longing for Scott. *Shit, I haven't written to him since he left.* She wondered how he was dealing with the trauma of Friday night, or *if* he was dealing with it. All of a sudden she was eager to get to a spot with *WiFi* or cell service so she could check her email.

From the deck of the cabin she could see Don standing on the promontory, wearing nothing. He raised his arms, palms out as though hugging the setting sun, started spinning slowly to his left, moving in a complete circle, then to his right, back and forth, faster and faster, with his feet just inches from the edge of the abyss. Justine couldn't see his face, but she knew that his eyes were closed. Even at that distance she could make out the muscular contours of his perfect ass.

Don suddenly stopped, his back to her, and waved goodbye over his shoulder.

CHAPTER 18

Justine made it to the Avis lot at San Jose International in less than two hours. Starting the engine of her Tesla, Justine waited for the sound of the engine revving, then she remembered it was electric. She kind of missed the purr of the Porsche as she drove her silent high-performance vehicle up the 101 to Palo Alto.

Traffic came to a standstill outside Mountain View, so the ride home from San Jose took longer than the ninety-five mile drive from Big Sur to the airport. By the time Justine pulled into her driveway she was famished. Instead of parking in her garage she left the Tesla in the circular driveway and took her bag from the trunk, and hurried to open her front door. She entered the security code on the alarm panel. Green lights flashed and she heard the "all-clear" *beep-beep*. Once inside the house, she plopped her bags by the front door and made a bee-line for the kitchen.

The Sub-Zero was practically empty. *Granola, blueberries and almond milk, again.* She wondered how long she could survive on those ingredients alone, and prepared a large bowl. With honey. "I really need to get to the grocery store," she said to herself.

Finally sated and hydrated, she carried her bags upstairs. As soon as she opened the bedroom door she let out a scream.

Her dresser had gaping spaces where the drawers should've been. The entire bedroom floor was strewn with clothes, papers, photographs. Her safe room door was open. She walked towards it slowly and peered inside. The cabinets were open. More photographs littered the floor. She knelt down, picked up a handful of pictures. Hawaii, her last vacation with Scott. *Oh my God, the nudes!* She shuffled through the mess, looking for the private pictures Scott had taken of her. Gone. She searched an overturned drawer for her passport. Also gone.

She ran into the study, the room adjacent to her bedroom and found the same chaos. Her laptop, gone.

Her head began to pound. She felt like the *beep-beep* of her security system's all clear signal was still going, over and over in her ears, haunting her. Mocking her. *What the fuck happened with my security system?*

She called Lily's private number.

"You're back already?"

Justine cut her off. "I'm home. Can you get over here right now? You have to see this," she said in a voice she hoped was calm.

"Are you hurt?"

"No. But someone broke into my house."

"I'll send the B and E guys over there, but you have to leave your house."

"What? No!"

"Yes. You don't want to compromise the crime scene and you could still be in danger. Did you touch anything?"

"Of course I touched something. I came home, everything looked normal, I ate a bowl of cereal, I went upstairs and found Armageddon." *What did she touch?* Remembering Don's instructions of three-hundred-sixty-degree awareness, she mentally traced every step she'd taken since she walked in her front door. "I picked up some photographs on the safe room floor. That's it. Didn't touch anything else."

"Good. Listen, I'm already in my car on my way over there. I want you to leave the house. You don't have a gun yet and I'm worried about your safety."

"I have to pee first," Justine sulked. "And call my mother."

"Oh for fuck's sake woman! At least go outside. Out front."

Justine had no intention of going anywhere until Lily showed up. Sitting on the toilet, she called Lise. "I thought you were sending me two women who could find my scumbag."

"Hello Justine, how are you this fine autumn day?"

"Cut the polite pleasantries, Lise. Someone broke into my house."

"Yes, and?"

"And I wasn't here. I left late yesterday morning for Big Sur. Just came back a half hour ago. Downstairs everything was fine. Upstairs looked like a scene from CSI. My detective friend said I'm not safe. Did you send those women yet?"

"Yes Justine, I sent *those women.* Eniko and Iya are their names. They got there yesterday. They already told me that someone was in your house."

"Lise, what the fuck? And you didn't tell me?"

"Justine. Calm down please. Everything is under control. I promise you, you're safe."

"How? How do you know that I'm safe?"

"Eniko and Iya are on it. I trust them. I trust them with *your* life. You'll meet them soon. Very soon."

Before Justine could ask any more questions her doorbell rang. "Cops are here," she told her mother. "Gotta go. I'll call you as soon as I have anything to report."

"Justine, wait. Don't mention my girls to the cops."

"Fine, whatever. Love you," Justine said as she opened her front door for Lily.

"What's missing?" Lily asked. "And what happened with your alarm system? Did you call the security company?"

"The alarm never went off. At least I think it didn't, someone would've let me know. My laptop, my jewelry—or some of it, I haven't done an inventory. And a bunch of personal stuff, like photographs."

"Okay, I'll deal with the security company and the crime scene guys from B and E. You really should go now. But first I'm dying to hear. How'd it go with Don? Are you in?"

Ah, Don. Just the thought of him calmed her. "You were right. About everything. I'm in. *All in.*"

Lily smiled like a proud big sister. "After three months with him a little break-in like this will feel like a paper cut. When do you start?"

"Next week. I'm going to LA for my best friend's engagement party next Saturday. But last night? That was one fascinating lesson."

"Right. You've already started." Then Lily's expression got serious. "I've got everything covered here. Don't you have anything to do outside the house this afternoon? Maybe you need a new lipstick?"

"I could use some food."

"Perfect. Go. I'll call you as soon as I have any info for you."

CHAPTER 19

Justine parked in the rear lot of the Country Sun Organic Supermarket on California Avenue. She strolled into the store through the back entrance, grabbed a small rolling cart and went directly to the produce aisle. Everything looked new, different, even though she'd shopped in the same store hundreds if not thousands of times. Her senses were definitely evolving, growing sharper. Standing by the pyramid of avocados, she sensed someone following her. *Or maybe she was just being paranoid?*

"Is that really *you*?" It was a woman's voice, a woman that sounded like she'd just found a long-lost friend.

Not paranoid. Justine turned around and saw two young women. Undergraduate young. And tall. One had long blond hair pulled into a high ponytail, the other was a brunette with an Audrey Hepburn pixie cut. They were both strikingly attractive, like models dressed up as college students. "Do I know you?"

The brunette leaned in to kiss Justine's cheek. "Lise sent us," she said, *soto voce.*

Justine accepted the kisses, then stepped back to take a good look at the two girls. "You're the, um, dominatrices?"

The blonde smiled, puting an index finger to her lips in the international sign for *shut up*.

"How did you know I'd be here?"

"The same way we found the scumbag that broke into your house," Pixie Cut answered.

"Wait, what?" Justine was incredulous. "You know about that? Who *are* you?"

"Eniko *lapochka*" said Ponytail to her friend. "Where are our manners? Allow us to introduce ourselves. This is my dear friend Eniko. My name is Iya."

"You're Russian?

"Ukrainian." Ponytail/Iya responded. "We need to talk."

"Lemme pay for this stuff. Then we can sit outside at one of the tables and have a drink or something." Justine nodded towards the case of fresh-pressed juices. "Over there, get whatever you like."

The girls grabbed a few bottles of the brightly colored beverages and followed Justine through the checkout counter and out the front exit to the shaded tables. Justine had to admit that they were both exceptional-looking women, but she sensed in both of them an intensity that discomfited her. She momentarily thought of fleeing.

Only two of the outside tables were occupied. Justine and the girls sat as far from the other patrons as possible. They sipped from their bottles, not saying a word. Iya smiled at Justine, her expression silently reassuring. *They can feel my anxiety,* Justine thought. *Don would not be pleased with me right now.* She took a deep cleansing breath and finished her drink.

As soon as Justine put her empty bottle in the recycling can Iya took her elbow and whispered, "Follow us."

Justine felt a chill go up her spine. She didn't trust these two. They were far too wholesome-looking to be dominatrices. What the hell did Lise see in them?

Still, she followed them to a gray car in the back parking lot. On the way there she noticed that they purposely avoided the field of view of the store's security cameras, both of them seemed to be using the same three-hundred-sixty-degree visual awareness that Don had taught her. *Maybe I misjudged them, maybe they can be useful?*

"We saw the break-in," said Eniko from the front passenger seat, with no discernable accent.

"What do you mean you *saw* it? How'd you get past the alarm? And if you're so sharp, why didn't you stop them?" Justine demanded.

"We have our ways," explained Iya from the driver's seat. She turned onto El Camino and headed north. "And it wasn't *them*, it was just *him*. One guy."

"We watched him leave your house, then followed him to his sleazy motel room," Eniko explained.

"When?"

"Yesterday," said Iya in a happy, sing-song voice. "Your neighbor across the street has the most wonderful hedge for playing, how do you call it in English, hide and seek?"

"Stop teasing her, *lapochka*," Eniko interrupted. "She's Lise's daughter. We work for *her*, remember?" She turned to face Justine. "We put a device on his car, like we did with yours. Then later we found him and invited him to party with us."

"When did you put a device on my car? I've been out of town for the past day."

"About an hour ago. It was in your driveway," Eniko continued. "Anyway, he wasn't in the mood to party. So we just took him."

"Took him?"

"Yes. For you. Since Lise is paying us, we thought you should have the honor of loosening his lips—and then closing them."

Now Justine was frightened. Her mother hadn't always been the best judge of character. "Hold up a sec. I gotta call Lise. I promised to call her back and I wanna make sure you are who you say you are before we go anywhere."

They both laughed. "Call her," said Iya.

Justine opened the FaceTime app on her iPhone and called her mother.

"You finally got off the toilet?" Lise said when she answered.

"Hello *mother*." Justine said through her teeth before pointing the camera's lens at the front seats. "Are these your dominatrices?"

Lise cracked up when she saw the girls. "You two look adorable! Where'd you find those outfits? Did you line up any dates with the Stanford football team?"

Justine turned the phone back toward herself, exasperated. "Okay, Lise, thanks for identifying them for me. Talk to you later."

CHAPTER 20

Justine hated sitting in the back seat of any car, but this was worse than any car. The traffic on El Camino, as usual, was a horror show. Justine felt every bump in the road, heard every honk amplified through the cheap metal and creaky windows. "What is this vehicle you have me in? A rental? I can't stand it back here. Can't we just go back and take my car?"

"Not to where we're going," Iya smirked.

"Again, where *are* we going?"

"To solve your problems," answered Eniko. "But we need to hurry. Your police lady friend will start to worry if your fancy car stays in that lot too long."

"You know Lily?"

"We know everything."

No you don't. Justine thought about Don and felt an odd sense of comfort. Then she asked the dominatrices, "How can you solve my problems? Shouldn't we call the police if you already found the guy?"

"Do you want Scott's naked photos of you or do you want the police to scan them for their own personal photo collection before they log them in as evidence?" Iya asked facetiously.

Justine understood that was a rhetorical question, yet she had so many other questions she knew they wouldn't answer. Resigning herself to their plans, she sat back and stared at the scenery along Page Mill Road. The glass facades of office buildings and corporate research parks gave way to oak-studded foothills behind Stanford, then a winding ascent to the crest of the Santa Cruz Mountains. Justine focused on what

Don taught her about counting the turns so she could always find her way home.

Iya turned south on the Skyline Highway. Justine knew the area, but only vaguely. It was popular with the outdoorsy Stanford kids, hikers and cyclists. From what she could recall there was nothing up there but campsites and hiking trails. *What could they possibly do to the guy up there, hike him to death?* Then Iya turned right onto a dirt road leading into the redwood forest.

Justine figured they'd driven a quarter of a mile when Iya pulled up to the barbed-wire gate. Eniko jumped out to open it, and Justine tried to help, but her door was locked.

"Child safety lock," Iya said through the rearview mirror. "Another great American invention." She unlocked the doors. "We're not there yet, but you're free to go if you wish."

Justine remained silent as Iya drove through the gate and then waited for Eniko to close it and climb back into the passenger's seat. They drove in silence down a dirt road through a canopy of redwoods. After about a minute they arrived at a dilapidated cabin with peeling gray paint and broken windows.

"This doesn't look like a sleazy motel," Justine said, breaking the uncomfortable silence.

"That dump was a palace compared to this place," snickered Eniko. "This is an abandoned meth lab. No one's lived here since the cops shut it down years ago."

"How the hell did you find it?" asked Justine.

"Google. I just typed *police reports* and *meth lab raids* in the search bar," Iya explained. "This place stood out because the last hit was like five years ago. Then we used *Google Earth* to find it."

"Once we actually got here we knew we'd found our own private Gulag," said Eniko.

Now Justine was intrigued. "How'd you get access to police reports? Aren't they confidential?"

"With enough time—and will—we can hack through any security system," said Eniko.

"Now what are you doing?" Justine asked Iya, who was out of the car, crouched over a rusty metal contraption.

"The meth cookers left these as booby traps. I reset them when we left and now I have to deactivate them. We wouldn't want to scratch your delicate body."

Justine ignored the jab, got out of the car and followed the two women to a cellar door at the back of the cabin. The stench of urine and feces overpowered her. Iya covered her face with a handkerchief and then descended the ladder that led into the abyss.

From the top of the cellar steps Justine could hear a panoply of unpleasant sounds. Eniko was nonchalant. "No water or food for over twenty-four and he still pees and shits."

"Did you torture him?"

"He would have done worse to you." Eniko handed Justine a handkerchief and a pair of surgical gloves and motioned for her to follow Iya down the rickety stairs. Eniko was close behind her. Too close. Justine felt trapped.

She reached the bottom and stepped aside to let Eniko pass. The smell of terror was even stronger, more putrid in the underground darkness. She pulled the gloves over her hands and covered her mouth and nose with the handkerchief.

A thin shaft of light filtered through the open cellar windows, but that was all she could see. As her eyes gradually adjusted to the cellar's darkness, she could discern the shape of a body on the floor. "What am I looking at?" she asked.

"Lights!" Eniko said with a theatrical flourish. She turned on the flashlight app on her phone and pointed the light at the lump on the floor. Justine could see the hairy body of a muscular, olive-skinned man with a hood over his head. Stark naked and handcuffed spread-eagle to rusty iron bolts embedded in the cold, slimy concrete floor. A pile of soiled adult diapers surrounded his head.

"Camera!" Iya said. Then, as she ceremoniously held the top of her prisoner's hood, she yelled, "Action!" then pulled it off. "Do you know this man?" she asked Justine.

He was barely conscious. But his eyes opened wide when he noticed Justine.

She summoned every ounce of strength she had to stay calm, to not shriek out in terror. Her instincts told her to back away, to avoid his body as though it were a mound of slithering snakes.

Iya, waiting for an answer to what she must've thought was a reasonable question, continued to stare at her. "Well," she asked impatiently, "is this the man that attacked you on Friday night?"

Justine shivered when she remembered Gondo running his knife over her naked body.

"Yes," she finally managed to say. "I'll call the police."

Iya let out a laugh worthy of a Disney villain. "How can you possibly be the daughter of Lise Baron?" she screamed. "Lise would never raise such a stupid child. The police? Who do you think you're dealing with here? This monster does not care about the law. He doesn't *deserve* the dignity of your American justice. *We kill* him. That's justice."

"Payback's a bitch, right *monstra?*" Iya said to the quivering mass of feces at her feet. "And you are the perfect bitch." She turned to Justine and handed her a knife, similar to the one Scott kept under his pillow. "Here you go, *printsessa*. You still need for him to tell you how to get your photos back, so don't kill him too fast."

"Me? Can't you get my photos back?"

"Justine, you can do this." Eniko's voice sounded kind, encouraging. She pointed to the knife in Justine's quivering hands. "It's sharp as a scalpel. *Use* it."

"That would make me like him. Evil."

Iya shrugged. "Sure. We can be your *mercenaries*. But evil is also hiding behind morals and having someone else do your dirty work."

And I don't want you to *murder* him. I just want my pictures back. And I want to get out of this hell hole.

"Right now he's barely conscious, so we need to wake him up," Eniko said, opening a canvas bag she'd retrieved from the shadows. From it she took a syringe, a whip, and a flogger. She injected whatever liquid was in the syringe into the vein of the man Justine knew as Gondo. His muscles immediately started to shake uncontrollably, his limp penis became engorged, turning red and purple as his veins bulged. Eniko handed the black-leather flogger to Justine.

"Don't you want your photos back?"

Justine looked down. Eniko shrugged, and, with the grace of a ballerina started to flog Gondo on his knees, then thighs, each swat closer and closer to his erect penis and shrunken balls. She grinned wickedly.

Scared and repulsed, Justine bit her lower lip until it hurt.

"Not even one little lash?" chided Eniko.

Justine shook her head no. She felt as if she were in an alternate universe, a mountaintop hell, with two beautiful agents of the devil. Eniko flogged Gondo again. Justine turned her back on all of it.

But the noises alone were more than she could stomach. The *swoosh* of Eniko's flogger, the *slap* of its leather on his flesh, the thud of his body as it slammed onto the concrete floor, again and again. The screams.

"Stop!" she shrieked, covering her ears with her hands. She closed her eyes tightly.

Iya reprimanded her. "Can't you see? Open your eyes!"

"No!" Justine was adamant.

Iya continued in a steady, measured tone. "If we let him go, he'll hunt you down. Torture you. Rape you. Sodomize you. You will pray for the angel of death to end your agony. But this guy," she nodded at the filthy lump chained to the floor, "this guy will keep you just barely alive. To suffer."

"I am not a murderer."

"It's not murder, Justine. It's justice," Eniko reasoned.

"Please, let him go," Justine said. "I can't. I'm not. I..." She climbed up the ladder into the blinding afternoon sun. The fresh, sage-scented air calmed her, but she couldn't stop shaking.

She pulled away in a reflexive jerk when she felt a hand gently rest on her shoulder. She hadn't heard Eniko climbing the ladder after her, didn't know she was right there, standing behind her.

Justine sat on the dirt and tried to regain her composure. She hugged her knees and rocked herself back and forth.

Eniko sat beside her. "Listen, we are women of our word. We have to trust that you, too, are a woman of your word. Tell no one that you met us or what you saw today." She nodded toward the cabin. "You should have killed him, or at least let us kill him. You will meet him again and again in your nightmares and then your nightmares will someday become a reality when he hunts you down." She waited for Justine to react. Nothing. "Let us at least end this."

"Let him live. Warn him to never come near me again. Tell him that if he hurts me, or even tries to scare me, you will finish him off."

"You think that's a realistic plan? You have no idea." She stood up, and with her hands planted on her hips looked down at Justine and said in an even, measured tone; "Your so-called morality is your greatest weakness. But okay, have it your way *printsessa*. I'm gonna hose myself off and take you home. Iya will take care of him, but he will live."

Justine nodded her thanks, then stood up, brushed herself off, and crawled into the passenger seat of the gray car. She fastened her seat belt —muscle memory—then sat back and sobbed.

A minute later, Eniko got into the driver's seat and started the car. She reached into the center console and handed Justine a small sealed envelope. "Storage unit 1812" Justine stared the envelope, confused. She could feel a small key inside. "Public Storage in Redwood City," Eniko continued. "The street address is written on the inside flap. Everything's there, including the photos. All of them. But your friend back there took pictures of your pictures and sent them to his boss."

"His boss?"

"Yes. That idiot wasn't working alone. We have his cell phone. The same burner he used to send close-ups of your tear-streaked face and wet pussy. Remember that?" She looked back at Justine, who nodded silently. "Of course you do. We'll keep his cell phone. You might want to trash the photos since this pervert masturbated all over them. They're covered with his cum." She looked at Justine again. "Do you understand us a little better now?"

As the gray car descended the winding mountain road Justine held onto the storage unit keychain like a security blanket. *At least I'll have my dignity,* she said to herself.

CHAPTER 21

Justine wanted to get to Los Angeles on Friday, the day before Danisha's engagement party. Lise would meet her there, they could spend an entire evening together, just the two of them, then have all of Saturday morning to get ready for the big event at Danisha's house. But Justine also wanted to get away from the madness and recent memories of Palo Alto. No way was she going to spend seven more days there.

Lily's text came in just as Eniko pulled the gray car up to the Country Sun parking lot. *All clear. You can go back to your house now.* Justine walked the few yards to her Tesla in a daze. She didn't want to go back to her house so she invited Lily to meet her for a late lunch at Café Brioche, right on the other side of California Avenue. They ate and talked and drank and talked some more. Mostly they talked about Don. Lily understood Justine's reluctance to go home, and why she was so anxious to continue her training. When Justine excused herself to go to the ladies' room, Lily contacted Don. "I'll follow you back to your house," she said when Justine returned to the table. "Pack a bag for a week at the cabin and a weekend in Malibu. I'll drive you to Santa Cruz. Don will pick you up there, in the parking lot of Whole Foods, then take you to Monterey Airport on Friday. There's a flight to LA just about every hour."

The next six days were physically grueling and mentally challenging. Justine was already in superb shape. She'd been a fitness fanatic since high school, had years of intense Krav Maga training, practiced Ashtanga yoga for ninety-five minutes six mornings a week. On top of that her extreme sports training—jumping out of planes and off cliffs, swimming upstream and canoeing in whitewater rapids—put her in the most elite of elite amateur athletes. But none of that compared to the training regimen Don had designed for her. His methods combined jujitsu, karate, Krav Maga, yoga, tai chi, triathlon training and Ian Fleming.

Every morning at eight Don led Justine down the same steps she'd climbed the first night she was there, past the hot springs cave to another set of steps carved into the side of the cliff. At the bottom of those stairs he opened a heavy door that opened like a bank vault. The space beyond the door felt cool, like a wine cellar.

"Holy nautilus, Batman. This is the workout cave?" Justine said the first time Don triggered the lights. From the entrance she could see exercise equipment, weights, an endless pool, and what looked like an entrance to yet another cavernous room.

Using ancient yoga and martial arts systems and modern cutting edge technology she learned to breathe all over again. Don taught her to look for behavioral clues to avoid conflict and recognize danger and deception. He had her use *Bodyblades*—a sort of vibrating stringless archer's bow that made her muscles contract and relax five times per second. He trained her to use counterforce rotation, which quickly increased the power of her strikes. He taught her Bruce Lee's *forward strike* and *one-inch punch* in all directions. It wasn't long before he had her starting, stopping and changing directions with precision so she could ward off attackers from any direction.

On Sunday, Tuesday and Thursday, he attached her to a *Vasper* unit, a machine that looked like an elliptical glider and a stationary bicycle had a baby and attached what looked like a bunch of blood-pressure cuffs to it. The first time she saw it she cracked up. "You cannot be serious," she said as he attached pads and cuffs attached to tubes to her arms and legs.

Don was always serious during training hours. "Vasper was designed for astronauts. In essence it's a combination of compression, cold, grounding and interval training. The compression fools your brain into thinking your muscles are damaged. Cuts muscle recovery time in half," he explained, strapping a George Jetson-like helmet to her head. "The Air Force para-rescue teams use it too. So do Navy SEALs. And Special Ops."

"I get it," Justine cut him off. "Elite military forces love this contraption. But I don't even break a sweat."

"Cooling liquid in the vest, cuffs and helmet. When your blood temperature goes up, it can't absorb enough oxygen. Cooling the muscles as you work them makes your exercise far more efficient and speeds recovery. It also boosts human growth and anabolic hormone levels. It's the closest thing I've ever seen to a fountain of youth."

"Alrighty then, beam me up, Scotty!" Don didn't crack a smile. "Really? Nothing? You never watched Star Trek?"

"You do look kinda fetching in that hat," he said, but still no smile. Justine marveled at his self-control.

All week her feet never touched shoes. Don even made her run barefoot, teaching her his running style, first on an Alter G antigravity treadmill then on an Athletic Republic treadmill. The Alter G forced her use all of the muscles of her legs, and the treadmill forced her to sprint as fast as she could as multiple video cameras provided biofeedback. After her fourth session on those machines Justine could run like a gazelle.

After a light lunch on the cabin's deck he let her rest for thirty minutes before starting her upper body workout. She started on the Free Motion Dual Cable Cross, which she used at her office gym, but the way Don had her use it gave her a complete upper-body workout in twenty minutes.

Next up on the training schedule was video game swim time. The endless pool Justine had spied the first morning was actually a custom designed pool with powerful water pumps that created currents that she had to swim against, combined with above water and underwater cameras. Don handed her a one-piece bathing suit and a smart mask, like a bathing cap for her face that somehow connected to the cameras above and below the water and had a teeny-tiny video monitor built into the lenses of the goggles. She could actually watch herself swimming in real time on the monitor, and then later observe the details of her strokes on an iPad to learn visualization techniques that would eventually help her to improve her personal energy efficiency.

Her muscles lengthened and strengthened symmetrically without adding bulk. After five days swimming felt more natural, easier, but still not up to her own self-imposed level of perfection.

"Rome wasn't built in a day," Don said when she expressed her disappointment.

By Thursday night Justine's muscles looked incredible, but they weren't happy. At dinner Don noticed her rubbing the back of her neck. "You okay?"

"Just a little sore. Can't imagine why. First thing I'm gonna do when I get to LA is get a massage." Justine sighed, rolling her shoulders.

"You can get a massage here."

"I don't mean the kind with happy endings."

"Your endings depend on you. Wear your swimsuit. I won't cross those boundaries."

"I'm not sure I'd be uncomfortable with that."

"It's ironic that you feel comfortable with me teaching you to kill but you're uncomfortable with me giving you physical comfort."

"Okay, you know what? I want to trust you. And I want a massage. But my one piece swim suit covers too much of me."

"Your underwear will work as boundaries."

Justine thought about her lace bra and thong. Scott's favorite. Then again, her back, neck, butt...even muscles she didn't know she had ached. "What if I want you to stop?"

"I've given you my word," Don said. He stood and headed down the steps to the hot springs.

Don was relaxing with his eyes closed in the hot spring pool by the time Justine got there. She hung her robe on a warming rack, contemplated removing her underwear, but then she thought of Scott and kept them on. Don's eyes were still closed as she stepped into the steaming pool. Despite its warmth, she felt a shiver of apprehension—though it could have been primitive desire.

"I didn't expect boot camp to start this way," said Justine, as she nervously fussed with her hair.

"Your boot camp started the moment you made your decision to train with me. My job is to train you the best way I can, with kindness and positive reinforcement so that you can reach your own personal nirvana here on earth. After you reach your mental, physical, and emotional peak you'll find stress exciting, even thrilling. Eventually you'll be able to endure almost anything so that you can survive and return to what you care about in the here and now. I don't offer promises of Pearly Gates or seventy-two virgins, or even an afterlife. I can offer ocean-side hot springs and an occasional massage."

Justine nodded, then relaxed and let the heat of the mineral water penetrate her body.

"Shall I begin your massage?"

Justine, her eyes closed, nodded again.

Don effortlessly lifted her body onto a ledge where she could lie, still partially submerged, in the hot water on her back. Her head rested on a soft sponge above the waterline. Don started at Justine's feet, gently massaging her toes with strong, gentle fingers. Gradually he increased the intensity as his expert fingers detected minute lesions in her tiny toe muscles—old wounds from wars of high heels and pointy-toed boots. He stretched and rotated the joints of her toes—slowly, methodically— almost to the point of pain. But he never crossed that threshold. Waves of pleasure followed each stretch.

Don started working on her calves and the thin muscles on the sides of her shins. His expert fingers probed, discovering more scars from shin splints and calf cramps past. It took him a while to knead them out. Again he flirted with her threshold for pain-slash-pleasure. She had never felt so blissful, and from a foot and calf massage? When he began massaging the tendons around her knees, her thighs started to quiver in anticipation. *If he can make my feet feel so good, what could he do to the rest of me?*

Don pulled his hands away. "I think it's time to stop."

"You're a tease," Justine said, looking into his eyes.

"I haven't even begun to tease you," Don said with a slight smile, tilting his head. "I'll leave you on your own. There are no cameras on. You have total privacy."

"Okay, you can skip my thighs, but my back still hurts. Can you at least relax my back?"

"If you insist."

"I'm requesting, not insisting."

"Then please roll over."

Justine settled onto her stomach, her back still submerged in the hot spring water.

She felt Don rise out of the water and placed his knees on the shelf, straddling her thighs, and sat carefully on her calves. She was startled when she felt his testicles, bare gluteus muscles, and the tip of his penis; it was as if a jolt of electricity had flashed up her spine. His hands probed the muscles at the base of her spine with the same magic he had worked on her toes. Again he pushed her thresholds.

He worked up her back to just below her shoulders, and then returned to the base of her spine and probed outward, then downward, stimulating her gluteus muscles. As he probed deeper, he began to move his fingers in a fluttering, vibrating motion; gently at first, but then the intensity increased. She felt a sensation in her clitoris. *But he's nowhere near there, what the fuck?* Suddenly, she lost control. Intense, electrifying spasms wracked her entire body; waves and waves of pleasure sent her over the edge into a powerful, overwhelming orgasm.

Justine had experienced countless genital orgasms in her life, but she'd never felt anything like this; erotic, electrical currents pulsing through her body. From what she had thought would be a simple massage! After a minute of silence, Justine asked in bewilderment, "What did you just do to me?"

"Do to you? I don't know what you mean."

"I've never had a massage like that before."

"Does your back feel better?"

"You're avoiding my question. What did you just do to me?"

"Do you want me to tell you or show you?"

"You can do it again?"

"No, but you can let me. Women can orgasm multiple times from a variety of triggers. Men, need twenty minutes to recover from their first, then twice that time from their second."

"Okay, just tell me! *What* did you just do to me?"

"I gave you your best back rub ever. You did the rest. What would you like me to do now?"

Don got up and Justine rolled over onto her back. He returned to his knees, astride her shins. Justine could see that he was well made, but not totally excited—*still, he was, a little,* she thought. Her nipples, on the other hand, were straining against the sheer lace of her wet bra.

"You're not wearing a swimsuit, so by your boundary definitions, I could touch you anywhere," Justine said, feeling breathless.

"I don't have clothing or touching boundaries. But I do think I should leave you to your thoughts."

"And what are you going to do?"

"Be alone with my thoughts."

"I think we'll both be rather confused."

"That's an understatement." Don stood up and stepped out of the pool.

"Sweet dreams."

CHAPTER 22

Justine was aroused, scared, and all but panicked. Her thoughts went from delirium to clarity. Why had she gotten herself into this sexual situation? Too many times before she'd let herself become sexually vulnerable; it always led to her getting hurt. She wanted to call Danisha, but Don would probably hear her conversation with his ubiquitous high-tech spy gadgets. She ran her hands over her body, searching for any tiny foreign object—something he might have implanted while she was delirious with pleasure. She reached between her legs but then pulled her hand back. Don hadn't touched her there. Part of her was relieved; but another part—the part she had touched—longed for him?

She stepped out of the hot springs, removed her wet underwear and put on the robe. Then, still flushed from her *massage,* she climbed the steps back to the cabin, fished her cell phone from her luggage, and slipped under the down comforter. The phone showed five bars of reception. She hit the phone icon, then favorites, then Danisha.

"Hey, girlfriend, I think I'm in trouble."

"What's new?" Danisha asked, laughing.

"Don just gave me a massage. It's been a long week, I've been training with him."

"You've been what? With the mystery man from Nepenthe?"

"Yeah, we were in the hot springs and I had this long orgasm-type thing filled with electric shocks followed by more, gentle ones—and he was only rubbing my back! I wasn't even naked! I was wearing a bra and panties. Dani, help me. I'm in panic mode." She lowered her voice. "If he can do this to my back, imagine what he could do with his tongue on my clit!"

"Wow, lucky you! You *are* a superwoman! Was it that good? Without penetration or clitoral stimulation? You're not in trouble, girl—you're in paradise," Danisha laughed.

"Stop it. I'm being serious."

"There are all sorts of ways to orgasm. What you just experienced sounds like it was tantric sex. You reached a level of physical ecstasy. This guy, Don—he's a master. I bet he can take you to emotional ecstasy and then to spiritual ecstasy. Really, think about how fortunate you are. Very few women reach orgasms from just a back rub. What are you complaining about? Go to sleep."

"Right! Like I can sleep after what just happened to me?"

Danisha was still laughing. "We should all have your problems."

"I guess I just feel guilty. Because of, you know, Scott."

"Don't worry, baby girl. I'll always love you. Just try to keep your panties on for now. When do you get here?"

"Tomorrow morning. Catching a flight out of Monterey. Meeting Lise for dinner."

"See you at the party then. Saturday!"

"Saturday. Yes…with Scott."

CHAPTER 23

Don drove Justine to Monterey Regional airport just after dawn on Friday morning. The fifty-minute ride was another lesson for her, an oral recap of the past six days' instruction. He briefly explained the next phase of her training, which entailed something he referred to as the "avoidance of negative stimulus learning principle." It sounded ominous —Justine heard the words *mistakes* and *pain* a few times too many, but Don looked so serene as he spoke she didn't pay much attention to the negative—which was kind of his point after all. Besides, in her entire life she'd never felt more alive or energized.

While waiting to board the Alaska Airways turbo prop plane, Justine reflected that one week ago she was an innocent, rushing home to primp for her big night with Scott. Now she began to doubt her own perceptions of reality, too many shocks to her system had left her feeling distorted. If Superman suddenly showed up at the window she'd proba-bly invite him in for a cup of coffee. She desperately needed a dose of Danisha. She wanted the grounding wisdom of a best friend/college roommate/sister-she-never-had/most trusted confidante.

Of course Justine also needed her mother. Lise—one of many A-lis-ters that happily and hastily rearranged her schedule to fly across the continent for Danisha's engagement party; she was after all Dani's (un-official) god-mother. Lise needed Justine, too. Needed to see her safe, delivered from the nightmare of the attack. Mother and daughter met in the lobby of Shutters, the swank five-star-hotel on the beach just south of the Santa Monica Pier, at seven o'clock on Friday evening. Lise, having just arrived from the airport, asked Justine to come to her suite while she freshened up. Once they started chatting they lost track of time, and rather than go to the trouble of choosing a restaurant and going out they decided to order in from room service from One Pico, one of the restaurants in the hotel, and eat dinner on Lise's ocean-front balcony. It was tough to beat that view.

Only one person could drag Justine away from Lise that night. Well, maybe two. Justine's mind craved Don but her body yearned for Scott. She'd read and re-read his emails, searching between the lines and punctuation for hidden messages, any sign that he would make it back in time for the party. Swiping through the few he'd managed to send since arriving in Uganda five days earlier, she noticed a new one. "Made it to Kinshasa in time for the last flight out to Paris. Made it to Paris in time for the connecting flight to LAX. About to board. I. Cannot. Wait. To. See. You."

"Good news?" Lise asked.

"Am I that transparent?" Justine responded, setting her phone on the table beside her plate.

"I'm your mother. I can read your every micro-expression. But anyone with eyes could read what just happened on your face. Scott?"

Justine nodded, still smiling. "He's on his way." She picked up her phone again and opened a flight tracker app. "He didn't say what airline or what time he's arriving. I shall research the possibilities on my handy..." She was interrupted by three loud knocks on the door. "You expecting anyone?" Justine asked Lise.

"Everyone I know thinks I'm at my apartment in Century City. What's the matter Jussy? You look nervous." Once again, Lise didn't have to use her mother's intuition to read her daughter's expression. Justine was suddenly very, very nervous.

"Could they have followed me here?"

"Who? Jussy calm down. Eniko and Iya took care of your problem. It's probably just room service, or housekeeping."

"Yeah," Justine responded tentatively. "But still, I wish I had a gun right about now."

"Oh dear lord. She's off with the guns again. You realize we're not in Texas, right?"

Justine walked to the door ready to disarm whoever was out there with the self-defense techniques Don had just begun to teach her. "Yes, who's there?" she said in her best *I'm not at all concerned that my stalker could be knocking at the door at this hour* voice.

"It's me. Scott."

Justine couldn't open the door fast enough.

CHAPTER 24

Not everyone in Hollywood knew the producer Alessandro Stellini, but he was working on that. A few people had heard of his brother, Roberto, the director of one moderately successful Italian import, a sappy romantic comedy. But Roberto rarely left *Cinecittà*, much less Rome, and had never been to the States, much less Hollywood. Alessandro was on a mission to become the more successful brother; he wanted to play in the big game—or as he called it, *il gran gioco*. He arrived in Los Angeles with nothing but a stunning wardrobe, a hefty bank account, and a whole lot of charm. A natural charmer with movie-star good looks, he could turn on the charisma to make anyone feel special, mesmerize the right actors, directors and agents, and easily get into the hottest restaurants without a reservation. And Alessandro always picked up the check. But only one person in the entire entertainment industry knew the real power of Alessandro Stellini's personality; his brand new fiancé, the award-winning costume designer Danisha Howard.

Danisha wanted a simple gathering to celebrate her engagement, but Alessandro couldn't quite grasp the concept of simple. He wanted to throw the party right away, as soon as she said yes. He hired the top event planner in Los Angeles, gave her an unlimited budget to produce the affair in ten days. Booking a venue wasn't a problem. Dani's house, built into an expansive hilltop lot landscaped with water-conserving succulents, had magnificent views of Santa Monica, Malibu and the Pacific. She insisted on having the party there. Then, as she was pinning a costume on the pop diva Leila Del Rio, who was just wrapping up her world tour with three sold-out shows at the Hollywood Bowl, Danisha mentioned her party-planning nightmares. Leila immediately corralled an impromptu party band, all big names in the music business and invited guests. The entertainment would be impromptu, like open mic night at the Viper Room, except everyone that would approach the mic at Danisha's was already a star. Just like half the guests that rearranged their schedule to attend. To make sure he had "covered all his bases," Alessandro hired a gospel choir and a Dean Martin impersonator.

The party started at three, so Justine let Scott sleep in and, carrying her party dress and shoes in a garment bag, got to Dani's at noon. "Holy shit," Justine said when she first saw Dani. "You look gorgeous. Beyond gorgeous. I hope you didn't invite Kerry Washington. People will get confused."

"I'm a half a head taller. And yes, she's coming."

"You're also more beautiful."

"Shut up. All I want to do is puke."

"You are actually glowing. Puke away Dani-girl, 'cause it don't matter how you *feel*. You *look* great. Pregnancy agrees with you. Let's see the dress."

"Where's your boy-toy?" Danisha asked as she led Justine to her dressing room.

"You mean Scott or Don?"

"Scott. He's your plus-one, no?"

"Yes. Don's not exactly the plus-one type. Besides, that's all business."

"Ah-huh," Dani replied in her *I-know-you-better-than-you-know-you* tone.

"Scott's sleeping. He got in late last night. Flew twenty-three hours."

"You didn't have an, um, *active* night together?"

"Active enough. I have no complaints." Justine's smile spoke volumes. "He got some great news so he was feeling especially, well, I dunno, *accomplished*."

"Great news? I love great news. Do tell."

"His agent called from New York this morning at six to tell him he's on the short list for the Pulitzer."

"Oh my god oh my god that's huge! For that cat thing?"

"Yeah, the black leopard photo essay in National Geographic. No so huge, he hasn't won yet."

"This is Hollywood, baby. Until the winners are announced nominees are all winners. Alessandro is gonna milk this with every introduction. *Theese is Signore Scott Reddington, my Pulitzer Prize winning photo-journalist friend.*"

"He'll jinx it!" Justine laughed.

Dani shrugged. "Just warning you. Alessandro's a world-class schmoozer. It's part of his allure…his sexiness. "

A couple of hours later, all dolled up in a Tom Ford midnight blue silk backless dress, Justine finally got to meet her best friend's fiancé. She was standing with Scott, who'd just arrived and looked like he belonged on the cover of GQ, beside the pool. Danisha walked over to them on the arm of a man in an exquisitely-cut navy-blue suit. *That has to be Alessandro*, she thought. He wasn't as tall as she'd imagined, about the same height as Dani in her three-inch heels, but maybe he seemed taller because his legs were long compared to the rest of his body.

"Juss," Danisha called out from a few yards away, "come meet Alessandro!"

He wore his black hair combed straight back even though he was starting to lose some. Face-to-face Justine could see that the hairstyle framed a powerful-looking face. He had an air of gravitas and wealth, a combination that women found irresistible. "*Ciao Bellissima,*" Alessandro said as he kissed Justine on each cheek. "You're even more beautiful than your pictures."

"Now I'm wondering which pictures you've seen," Justine replied. Alessandro was holding onto her shoulders, looking at her as though he *needed* to study her face.

"So many pictures. In college, at the beach, even a few in front of the coliseum, in my hometown." He pulled her to him again for a full body hug.

"You showed him our European vacation pictures?" Justine directed her words at Dani with a look that said *you know he's grabbing my ass, right?*

"I've told him a lot about our adventures. Not everything, but a lot." Dani's expression said, *Don't worry about his hands, he's Italian.*

"*Ma che, bellissima Giustina,* you don't wearing the under clothes?" Even his mistaken grammar was charming, though Justine thought maybe he laid it on a bit too thick. She could've sworn she felt his semi-erect dick pressing against her hip as his hands rested on her butt. *Is anyone else seeing this?*

"*Giustina,* you could give the Pope a hard-on," Alessandro said to her.

Scott's photographer's visual awareness easily detected what was happening. He calmly looked into Alessandro's eyes as he used his fingers to scoop under Alessandro's thumb and twisted it into a wrist lock. Alessandro involuntarily stiffened in pain but didn't let go.

Scott twisted harder until Alessandro's hand fell away from Justine's body. Only then did Scott release Alessandro's thumb. The two men glared at each other with forced smiles.

Justine turned and introduced Scott.

"Ah yes, the famous Pulitzer Prize winning journalist! It's an honor to meet you Signore Reddington," Alessandro said, attempting to shake Scott's hand but instead put his arm around Justine's shoulder.

"Please, call me Scott. Nominee, not winner. And I'm a *photo-journalist.*"

"Meaningless details!" Alessandro responded as he withdrew his hand. "You will win, I have no doubt."

Scott laughed, "I've already won the most important prize of all," as he slipped his hand to Justine's waist. She knew that he didn't trust Alessandro as he gently pulled her away.

"I adore you," Justine whispered as she playfully bit Scott's ear.

Between talking to Lise and Danisha's mother, and all Dani and Justine's college friends that made it to the party—and all the dancing!—Justine and Scott didn't have a moment alone until well past sundown. Justine could see that Scott was struggling with jetlag, though he'd never admit it, world traveler that he was. During their final slow dance she whispered to him in her most seductive tone, "What do you say we blow this Popsicle stand and go to my place?" She didn't have to ask twice.

The driver Justine had hired for the weekend was waiting out front. She had long since abandoned her heels, and had to search under the poolside furniture to recover them. "You poor babies," she said to her feet as she sat to put the strappy sandals back on.

"Leave 'em," Scott said as he scooped her up in his arms, romance-novel style.

"I paid eight-hundred-dollars for those shoes!" Justine protested.

"I kinda wish you hadn't told me that," Scott said, laughing. He picked up the shoes and carried them and Justine out to the car.

The moon floated high above the Pacific Coast Highway, its light magically bright. In the back seat of the Town car Scott pulled Justine close to him, unaware that the driver could watch them in his rearview mirror. They shared a deep, long kiss. "Maybe someday you and I can have a party like that. What do you think?"

"A party? Sure." She looked at him. *What's he trying to say?* "Scott, are you proposing to me?"

His smile lit up the back seat. "Well. I suppose. Um. Sure. I mean. Yes. I am. Justine Baron, will you marry me? And we can honeymoon in Burundi. I'll be there on assignment in about six months."

"Burundi? In Africa?"

"East Africa, to be exact. I'll be covering the misery, the human cost of the political corruption and resulting genocide."

"That sounds like the *ideal* honeymoon spot."

"I figure that since you're into guns now, you can be my body guard," Scott joked, "It's Africa's second-most densely populated country and the world's poorest. Lake Tanganyika is beautiful in April, makes you forget about all the highly lethal infectious diseases," he said in his most romantic voice.

"Do you want to marry me or kill me?" she said, slapping him playfully on his chest.

"Okay, we can go wherever you want. Cape Town. Bali. Paris. Ahhh, Rio de Janeiro?"

"Rio, one of the most dangerous cities in the world. But since I'll be your bodyguard, we can samba all night."

Justine would have gone anywhere with Scott, would've been thrilled to spend a few more days with him, would have stayed in Santa Monica for months given half a chance. But she always knew that their fairy tale reunion would be fleeting; he had a crew waiting for him in Kinshasa, ready to finish the job he'd started. He didn't have much choice, he'd told her, had to get back there by Tuesday. Her cajoling whispers, begging him to stay just one more day, fell on deaf ears. Neither did he respond to her more vocal statement that he'd long ago surpassed the stigma of Daddy's Money so what the fuck was he still trying to prove, he was the fucking boss, he could stay with her one more day goddamnit. She had to admit that his Episcopalian aloofness annoyed the shit out of her.

Before the sun rose on Monday morning her driver took them both to LAX. Scott's flight left earlier than hers, so she waited with him at the international departures terminal until the last possible minute, then watched as he made his way through security and disappear into the crowd. As she made her way to the Alaska Airlines terminal for her 9 AM flight to Monterey, Justine didn't even bother trying to fight back the tears.

CHAPTER 25

Near the baggage claim carousel at Monterey Regional Airport she noticed a heavy-set man in a mis-shapened suit holding a dry-erase board with her name on it. Don hadn't said anything about sending a driver to pick her up, she was sure he'd be there himself waiting outside in one of his cars. *But which car?* She'd actually only seen the one Volvo, so she'd just assumed…*Shit. He's testing me. I've been gone less than three days and he thinks I've lost my edge.*

But how was she supposed to respond to this new driver curveball? *He hasn't seen me yet,* she thought, *I could just walk past him.* But that was pointless. Don must've sent the man for a reason. She decided to walk right up to him and introduce herself.

"Good morning sir, I'm Justine Baron. Did my client send you?"

He nodded, took her carry-on bag, and, with a swing of his head beckoned her to follow him.

His car, a perfectly acceptable black BMW 750Li—probably three or four years old—was on the first floor of the parking structure, close to the entrance. *Strange car for a livery service,* Justine wanted to say out loud, but didn't. Her nerves were acting up again. Something was not right. She stood behind the driver and watched as he carefully laid her carry-on bag inside the trunk, then opened the back right door and waited for her.

She didn't budge.

"Getting in?" he said with a gesture of impatience. It wasn't really a question. But there was something about his voice…suddenly she got it.

"Don?"

"I charge in fifteen minute intervals ma'am. You wanna stand there and stare, it's on your dime."

She got in the car.

Don picked up a black baseball cap with an orange visor from the front seat and handed it back to Justine. "How'd you guess I was a Giant's fan?" she asked as she inspected the gift. Inside the cap was a hard eyeglass case with a pair of Ray Ban Aviators. "You want me to wear these now?" He nodded. She pulled the cap on her head, took it off, adjusted the rim, put it back on. As soon as the glasses were on her face he started the engine and drove out of the parking lot.

"We have to talk about the call you made from the cabin on Thursday night," Don warned, after he paid the parking lot attendant and drove through the gate.

"And good morning to you, Don. My weekend was delightful, thanks for asking."

Ignoring both her words and her tone, Don continued his lecture. "You thought it was innocent."

"You told me I'd have total privacy!" Justine protested, furious.

"I told you the cameras were off. This is not a reprimand. It's a lesson. If your enemies were tracking your cell, that one innocent call would have led them here and all of my years of careful physical and electromagnetic secrecy would have been for naught. Because of one phone call."

"Oh my God. I actually believed you when you said I had total privacy, I'm such an idiot."

"Don't worry, there's also good news. *This time.* Your room is also a Faraday cage that blocks all incoming and outgoing electromagnetic energy."

"Wait, what? If I was in a Faraday cage how'd my call even go through?"

"Your signals stayed within the room. An internal antenna led to a hard-line router, which bounced your signals around the world to different routers, eventually routing into the millions of bytes of message chatter of a mainstream Internet provider. I expect you to make mistakes, but I can't let your mistakes compromise our security."

"You eavesdropped on my conversation with Danisha?"

"Well, the NSA recorded it. We can't know if they listened to it."

"Oh for the love of...what the fucking fuck? The National Security Agency is listening to *me?*"

"You are a person of interest to them, though I'm not sure why yet."

"So wait, I'm a slow learner. Were you listening or not?"

"I respect your privacy. My associate warned me that you breached my security."

"Your *associate*? Who's your associate? Is he the gremlin that cleans my tatami mats just before I arrive? Does he slip into my room at night and put a clean *karate gi* by the door?"

"My associates choose to remain in the shadows. *I* clean the tatami mats. *I* put your clothes in your room."

"Why are your ninjas lurking in the shadows? I'd like to meet them, thank them for taking care of me, and ask for forgiveness for my mistakes," she said with a heavy dose of sarcasm.

"It's their choice whether or not to meet you, not yours. I will relay your appreciation to M," he responded without a trace of sarcasm.

"M?"

"That's the name my associate uses. You two may or may not meet eventually, but all your needs—security, information, tech support—will be taken care of and you will be grateful."

"M. I get it, kinda like Bond's Q. Okay. Good to know. Do I get to meet this person any time soon? How will I know him? Or is he a her?'"

"Don't worry. You're already known."

"And you're sure I can trust, um, him?" Justine ventured, hoping for at least an acknowledgment of the gender of this mysterious person.

"We served together in Afghanistan. After what we went through there, yes I trust her with my life and yours."

"Because there's not greater bond than the one forged between two soldiers in combat?"

"Don't turn this into a platitude, Justine. You're part of my team now. You will meet M eventually, if and when she finds it necessary."

Justine sat back and reflected on this new bit of information. Her romantic weekend was now officially and irrevocably over; not a trace of the warm fuzzy feeling that had been so strong just a few hours back remained. She wasn't in La-La Land any more. No more room service, no getting lost in Scott's blue eyes, no more parties with movie stars. She was back to boot camp on steroids. Back to Don. Back to the cabin, which, come to think of it, wasn't so awful.

"I also appreciate you letting me sleep in your room. Where are you sleeping?"

"You're welcome…and again—"

"Right, I've got it: your choice. Did you watch me sleep?"

"I'm your teacher, not your lover."

"You know, if I really think about what's going on here I can get the feeling that this is kinda like a cult? Total isolation. Total dependency. Your way or the highway?"

"Your life started with the cult, or as some would call it, the culture of your family—their home, their food, their belief systems, and their choice of schools. The military has its boot camps. The police have academies. Every religion has its seminaries, synagogues, churches, monasteries, or madrasas. By that logic, every training situation is kinda like a cult. Isolation, dependency, and authority figures."

Justine didn't want to argue with him. She knew he was right. They rode the rest of the way back to Big Sur in silence.

Returning to the cabin felt natural, like she was home. Justine carried her own bag inside– Don told her he'd meet her on the deck in precisely fifteen minutes for lunch. She unpacked her bag, and stretched out on the bed to clear her brain of clutter. *You're ready for this. You want this. You don't have a choice.*

Two minutes later she stepped out on the deck. The sun hung high in the cloudless azure sky, the sea was calm. Don ascended the stairs with a tray of grilled red snapper, salad of fennel and endive and sliced macadamia nuts, sprouted brown rice, and a pitcher of green water.

"You just made all that? In ten minutes?"

"Fifteen. I prepared everything before leaving for the airport. The fish is room temperature. You'll need the protein."

"Green Kool-Aid?" Justine asked, pointing to the pitcher.

At least that got a smile out of him. "Chlorophyll water. Powerful antioxidant, which I'm guessing you'll need after a weekend in Malibu."

"I was actually pretty good. No weed, not much wine."

"Excellent." Don filled the water glasses, handed one to Justine, and raised his, smiling broadly as he said, "Now drink the Kool-Aid."

When they finished eating Don stood up and began to clear the table. "I'll clean the plates. You go inside and get ready. Make sure to thoroughly clear your bowels. Training starts in thirty minutes."

"You're even controlling my *toilet* time?"

"Real-world practicality. When you protect a client you must focus on your mission, not the state of your bladder or bowels."

Justine placed her hands together in prayer position. "Thank you Obi Wan Kenobi. Learn I shall try," she said, bowing respectfully to her teacher.

Don returned her bow. "Do. Or do not. There is no try," he said with mock seriousness. Then he winked and said in his best Yoda-voice, "Truly wonderful, the mind of a child is."

She easily adjusted to the quotidian routine; though to be fair Justine's days were anything but quotidian. Don expected her at the breakfast table every morning, seven days a week, at sunrise. That first Tuesday morning he handed her a manila folder filled with photos, drawings, and diagrams of various firearms and pages of charts—weekly timetables for sunrise, sunset, moon phases and tides.

"Memorize it," he told her as she leafed through the pages.

"All of it?"

"Every word. Except for the solar table. You can keep that. Check it every night before you go to sleep. We will meet for breakfast right here every morning at sunrise."

"So seven-twelve tomorrow morning," Justine said, studying the timetable.

"Precisely. We will work from sunup to sundown."

"I get an extra minute each morning!" she said, laughing.

"For the next few weeks, yes. First Sunday next month you lose an hour."

"More time with you then," Justine winked.

"Daylight Saving Time is an artifice. Daylight only changes with the tilt of the earth."

She didn't notice the days getting shorter, completely forgot about the holidays that had marked the season every autumn of her previous life. No pumpkins or witches or ghosts; no signs of the traditional harvest holidays like Suk, Diwali or Ramadan. No roast Turkey or stuffing. Not in Big Sur. She did manage to get back to Palo Alto to spend Thanksgiving Day with Scott and Lise. But no four-day college-student weekend for her; the most Don would grant her was a forty-eight hour pass.

Falling into the routine was easy; the actual work, not so much. Every morning Justine ate breakfast, cleared her bowels, then met Don in his Bat Cave training facility. Every morning he started her with the same state-of-the-art, peak-performance physiology exercise programs and machines she'd started on the week before Dani's party in Malibu.

Using his own system, a combination of more than thirty martial arts techniques and ancient yoga *asanas*, Don taught her to use her breath to control her physiology as well as her psychology. She learned to control her reactions to stress and danger.

Using mock assaults with Model Mugging—Don playing the role of Mugger, his costume, a sort of padded Darth Vader-with-ginormous-helmet meets industrial-strength oven mitt—for full-speed, full-contact combat simulations under increasing levels of adrenaline stress in daylight and in the dark, since most combat takes place under low-light conditions.

The afternoons passed in a whirlwind of pistols, machine guns, assault and sniper rifles. Don's system integrated the martial arts with modern weapons; his pedagogical method was scientific, precise, and efficient.

"Just having firearm doesn't make you safer," Don told her that fist afternoon. "Just like owning a piano doesn't make you a piano player. We start by educating your mind. You will train and practice until your firearm becomes an extension of your will and you become one with your weapon."

"Oh, I must've missed the neon sign outside," Justine said, mentally trying to translate his new age vocabulary.

"Okay, I'll play the straight man for you. What sign?"

"The one that says *Don's Zen and the Art of the Pistol Training Camp*."

"Great idea. I should copyright that. Now pay attention. If you do it right, you'll feel that you and your weapon are one entity. Whatever you see you will be able to hit with tremendous speed and accuracy. The next phase is what I will from now on call my *Zen and the Art of the Sniper Rifle*. We're gonna increase your effective combat range. You'll have the ability to shoot at a target from a distance of more than ten football fields."

"As in one kilometer? Like, more than half a mile?"

"Yes, just like that."

"So we're leaving Luke Skywalker to return to James Bond and you actually think *I* will be able to shoot *that far*?"

"Of course. A Jedi's strength flows from the force."

"And we're back to Star Wars!"

"Yeah, sorry about that lapse. I couldn't think of any Bond quotes other than *shaken not stirred*."

"Cultural reference lapse forgiven, Master." Justine bowed again, laughing this time. "I still think half a mile is a fuck of a long way to hit a target."

Three afternoons a week were spent behind the wheels of Don's assortment of battered cars. Don taught Justine how to use her vehicle not only for escape but also as a weapon. While she enjoyed the shooting sessions she absolutely *loved* the driving lessons. What could be better than ramming cars with impunity and doing three-sixty spins on a deserted raceway? Nothing. Except maybe drive-by shootings using live ammo to shoot at human-shaped metal targets. Within a month Justine's driving skills reached peak performance levels.

On the rare occasions that she made mistakes, Don's responses could be more than a little painful. That was how he reinforced his *avoidance of a negative stimulus* learning principle. As a result Justine learned to avoid making mistakes while simultaneously developing a higher tolerance for pain. Day after day she felt more alive and energized. As her bone density increased, she could smash Don's human-shaped punching bags harder and harder. Her muscles grew supple and strong. She'd always been a graceful runner, but now there was no slowing her down, no panting, no gasping for breath, even after five-miles.

Her only heavy breathing happened during Don's occasional tantric massages. He could be ruthless in his training sessions, but the orgasms he gave her more than made up for any discomfort.

CHAPTER 26

As an undergraduate Justine toyed with the idea of majoring in psychology. The study of human behavior promised vast and unpredictable rewards, not the least of which was an understanding—if only academic —of whatever the fuck it is that motivates people to do the crazy shit they do. Now, more than a decade after graduating from college, Justine stood on the deck in Big Sur staring out at the turbulent ocean and thinking about one of her old psyche courses. *The Neurophysiology of Pleasure*, or something like that. The title of her final paper—*Olds and Milner's Rats and The Deadly Power of Orgasm*—and the basic details of the experiment she remembered well; the pleasure center of rats' brains were wired to receive electrical stimulation every time the rat pulled a lever. Once the critter discovered the mechanism to achieve pleasure— academic-code for orgasm—he or she would abandon all other activities, ignore all diversions and survival instincts. They'd literally do anything to keep getting that sweet shot of euphoria; ignore their children and friends, ditch their fiancés. They'd just pull that lever until they died of dehydration.

Justine totally understood the rats' predicament. Once she'd experienced the stimulating current of Don's hands she was hooked; she'd do whatever it took to get access to that lever. And Don knew exactly how and when to give Justine access to the pleasure center. He knew exactly how hard he could push her during the day because he knew how much she could take *and* how much she desired the reward. Of course she also understood that the reward encompassed so more much more than the pleasure of orgasms. Don's intense daily physical training sessions were also subtly disguised lessons in learning to see, hear, smell, taste, feel and think all over again, but through the lens of Don's enigmatic camera.

Yet a thin shadow of suspicion, a protective cloak of doubt, still floated through the rational portions of her brain. Justine felt like she was part lab rat learning her way through Don's mazes and part Alice in Wonderland, endlessly awed and astonished in this magical and frightening land beyond the looking glass. Don wasn't just her teacher. He was her stealthy guide. Her Cheshire Cat.

Maybe she was overthinking it. Maybe the day's training had made her particularly exhausted. Most nights when she got back to the cabin all she wanted was sleep, and this day hadn't been much different from any other. But tonight she felt energized. Perhaps it was the afternoon meditation session that had revitalized her. Then again, Don had offered to give her one of his occasional evening massages, which always led to the intense pleasure of release, the perfect antidote for the accumulated almost super-human physical and mental exertion he commanded. Her orgasms were becoming even more intense as she allowed Don's fingers access to parts of her body that contained senses she hadn't known existed. She'd *earned* that release.

Still, her rational senses could resist Don's magic fingers, especially when Justine consciously conjured memories of Scott. But more often than not those memories led her to wonder if Scott could learn Don's techniques, but that was a scenario that was too convoluted for even her way-above-average intelligence. Besides, Justine had lived enough to know the difference between explosive orgasms and *love*. With Scott she had both. From Don she craved only the *release*. Or that's what she told herself.

Sometimes, when Justine was completely lost in orgasmic pleasure with Don, she believed that his tantric massages were even better than actual sex. Without the complications of emotion and commitment and planning for a future, without the minutiae of details involved in a *relationship*, her orgasms transported her to a separate plain, an ethereal place of what she could only describe as cosmic perfection in colors.

And now she was ready to go even further. Don was waiting for her in the hot spring cave. Walking into the cabin she remembered a stash of candles and hurricane lanterns in one of the cabinets—leave it to Don to be prepared for anything. Once the candles were set up and lit she looked through her lingerie drawer for her sexiest bra and panties before deciding that all she really needed was her robe. No bra. No thong.

By the time she got down to the cave Don was already unwinding in the hot spring. In her most matter-of-fact tone she asked him if they could change up the massage venue tonight, do it in the cabin instead of the cave.

"Why?" he asked. "You wanna test a new boundary?"

"Why not let me worry about my boundaries."

It wasn't a question. Don's eyebrows rose slightly. *He's surprised?* Justine thought. Whatever he was feeling, his facial expression was a new one for her.

Don nodded, rose from the pool, and wrapped himself in his terrycloth robe. "Lead the way," he said.

The cabin looked different in candlelight, warmer maybe. Justine stole a glance at Don as they entered, trying to get a read on his reaction. If he was surprised, angry, or pleased, he wasn't letting on. Justine walked straight to the futon, turned to face Don, and dropped her robe. His eyes locked on hers for what seemed like an eternity before he let them take her in fully.

"I am your teacher," he said with great effort.

"Yes," Justine said, noticing the erection that was tenting his robe. "And I'm grateful for all you've taught me." She knelt on the futon, holding his eyes, then turned and lay on her belly. She heard Don's robe drop to the floor.

He began massaging her toes, probing and kneading the tiny muscles, gently tugging at the joints before working his hands up her calves. He reached her thighs. Justine felt herself quiver. Her heart raced.

"Wait," she whispered. He stopped, but didn't say a word.

Justine rolled onto her side. With her back facing Don, she wrapped her forearms loosely around her knees and stared out at the flickering flame of a candle, unable—or unwilling—to budge a muscle. Emotions and memories churned though her mind and she tried to tame their chaos with a dollop of logical reasoning. Who was in charge here? She initiated it. *Right? You wanted this! The candles. Shit, the fucking candles!* Or had she followed his lead? Or was it his kind of mind fuck, did he somehow coerce her to seduce him? What was this *experience* she was having with this extraordinary man that she should trust him in such an intimate way?

Danisha warned her about the link between emotional ecstasy and spiritual ecstasy. Except it wasn't a warning, it was a fact. Danisha was just explaining one of the many facts of life that she knew Justine still needed to learn.

Breathe. Long, slow breaths. Justine focused on her breath, as Don had taught her, to slow her pulse. Her muscles relaxed. Her mind signed out. All thoughts ceased. She felt her body floating almost imperceptibly above the futon. The only thing she could feel was the throbbing of her clitoris. She rolled onto her back, crossed her hands behind her neck, and closed her eyes. "Okay," she said. "I'm ready."

Don placed both his hands on the outside of her right knee and gently pressed the joints of his knuckles into her muscle as his fingers started searching and manipulating the fibers and tendons. His hands moved slowly up the outside of her leg, sending waves of warmth through the skin of her outer thighs, her ass, her hips. He kneaded her flesh with a firm, even rhythm, playing her like the keyboard of a Steinway Grand. *He's a fucking maestro,* Justine thought. She could feel every minute contraction, flutter, twitch of his palms, knuckles, every joint of his fingers, pushing, pulling, playing. He rolled her onto her right side, ran his hands softly up the curve of her waist, to her ribs, shoulders, upper arms. Her body moved to the lead of his hands, like they were performing a ballet of his creation that they'd already done a thousand times. He turned her onto her belly and started massaging the back of her knees, thighs, her ass.

Don definitely had a method, slow and precise. He took Justine through a field of pleasure, a field teeming with wildflowers and roses cultivated and feral, and stinging thistle, thorns, and poppies. With only his touch he showed her those places that hide between pleasure and pain. She felt herself get wetter. Her clit was swollen, throbbing. With great tenderness he ran his fingertips across it and she exploded in an electrifying spasm.

Justine opened her eyes as she tried to catch her breath. Don took hold of her hips and turned her onto her back, then gently explored the muscles along the insides of her thighs. She gasped as he gently spread her legs, then massaged up to without quite touching her outer labia. He continued with the lightest of touch, upward on the crease between the insides of her thighs and edges of the lips of her vagina, then up between the cheeks of her ass, around her anus, hips, waist. She rolled onto her belly. He laid his palms on the small of her back and began to flutter his fingers, gradually increasing the intensity of speed and pressure. Justine moaned. Her hips rocked, swayed. And then she couldn't hold it back. *Did she scream?* Her entire body shuddered. Again and again. Behind her tightly shut eyelids she saw bolts of lightning, as if she were being flung into space on the current of an electrical storm. "Oh. *God…*" She might've screamed.

Just when she thought she was finished, Don reached down, grasped her waist, and turned her onto her back. Justine opened her eyes and looked up at his face then down at his erection, seeing it for the first time. She wanted it. In her mouth. In her pussy. She felt such a scalding flood of desire she thought she might pass out.

Don spread her legs wide and his fingers explored the muscles and tendons of her thighs, working up to her outer labia, but stopping there. Again, he ruthlessly pushed the boundaries of pleasure and pain until all feeling merged into a single sensation. Justine was on the verge of another orgasm. His fingers played the insides of her thighs, increasing in speed and power, until she exploded again.

Suddenly Don lifted her legs high, spread them wide and knelt between them. His cock was so close, so ready to penetrate her. Justine wanted him inside her. She desired him with every fiber of her being. All of a sudden in her mind's eye she saw Scott. He was smiling, but then a shadow crossed his features. Justine's lust suddenly morphed into sadness. Both emotions were too intense to bear for too long. She felt overwhelmed. Her body went limp.

"Boundaries," Don said, or maybe he asked. Justine nodded. He shifted his body away from hers, but he was breathing hard. He stood to put on his robe. "I understand," he said, and turned to go.

"No, wait," said Justine. "Don't go. Not like this. I want you to understand me. I'm…You…You've given me a sense of myself—of my power. But what we were about to do…it was wrong. I had to stop.I didn't want to. But I had to. Not my most eloquent speech, but, do you understand what I'm trying to say?"

"Yes…I think I do. And your training is almost complete."

He knelt on the futon, picked up Justine's robe, and draped it over her shoulders.

"You're almost ready to be…I was going to say, your own body-guard. But more important, you're ready to be your own woman. Your own person."

To Justine's astonishment, he cupped her face and gently kissed her lips—a chaste kiss, but with the heat of a banked fire beneath it. She could feel it, just as she could feel the tremble in his hands. "That is the significance of our time together tonight. Tomorrow, we meet again at the same time."

He got up, and, with a friendly wave, walked out of the cabin.

Now, naked except for her down comforter, Justine was alone. Don had taken her to a place she'd never been, and she was grateful—grateful that he'd returned her to *her*. Safe and sound. She thought of Scott, her fiancé. She loved him. She held on to that thought as she sank into the sweet oblivion of sleep.

CHAPTER 27

Getting out of bed felt like a serious challenge. Justine had slept a deep, dreamless sleep, and the futon felt so warm and cozy, and she really didn't want to face Don. She didn't want to even think about—much less discuss—what happened between them a few hours earlier. The fluttery feeling in her gut felt nauseatingly familiar, like Awkward Monday. Anyone who ever attended a New York City private school knew the feeling, the one they invariably woke up with on the morning of the first school day after Homecoming Weekend, as well as the term.

Justine had learned the hard way sophomore year when she hooked up with Streeter Williams, a senior who was President of the student body, quarterback and captain of the football team, and had the dreamiest amber eyes. When he started flirting with Justine at the non-school-sanctioned, alcohol-fueled Homecoming party, her girlfriends acted like she'd landed a date with Jonathan Taylor Thomas himself. All eyes in the room followed them as Streeter held her hand and led her to a dark corner. The pride she felt at that moment was palpable. Hooking up with Streeter Williams was the Holy Grail, every girl wanted some of that.

When he got her alone his hands went straight to her breasts, which she didn't mind, then under her skirt, which she did. He was sensitive enough to her discomfort, kissed her gently on the lips and said thanks, then went hunting for his next conquest. Justine had failed Homecoming Hookup 101. Her dread at the prospect of facing Streeter in school was formative; she swore she'd never let that happen again.

And yet here she was, more than fourteen years later, curled up in fetal position under a quilt dreading the prospect of facing the man she did not have sexual relations with despite wanting to more than anything.

Enough stupidity. Get up, she told herself.

Justine got up, wrapped herself in the terrycloth robe and walked to the ledge by the front door to pick up the clean *karate gi,* just like she did every other morning. But there was no *gi* on the ledge, only an unsealed manila envelope on the floor beside the door. She picked it up and opened it. Inside were one car key, a small portable GPS device, a burner phone, and a sheet of printer paper folded symmetrically in thirds. The key was for the Volvo. She unfolded the paper and read:

> *You're ready for your first assignment. Meet me tomorrow at precisely 09:00 hours.*
>
> *The address is programmed into the GPS. If you need to talk anyone use the burner but tell no one where you're going. I'll see you tomorrow.*

She must've reread the note thirty times. *He's gone? He just left me here? Alone?* If he was using military-speak this must be serious. Then again, when wasn't Don serious? She turned on the GPS to see where she'd have to be at precisely one o' clock tomorrow.

Malibu? Yep. Malibu Colony to be precise. *A beachfront address. Fancy.* Okay, she could handle that. *Some Beverly Hills Housewife at her beach house.* The drive would take around five hours, maybe four if she left before dawn. Or she could leave right away, take her time driving down the coast, then spend the night at Danisha's. A far more appealing option than spending an entire day and night in the cabin, without Don.

She figured she'd need a week's worth of clothes, which she packed in her personal bag. Don had already prepared three Go Bags containing her weapons, body armor, and electronics. Within a half hour she had all her gear assembled and packed it into Don's funky old gray Volvo wagon.

Driving a car like that would make quite the impression for the good folks of Malibu. Don had taught her the importance of blending in, but she never imagined herself having to blend in with the help. At least she'd get to learn how the other half lived.

The low, throaty rumble of the Volvo's engine reminded her that this wasn't a typical soccer mom's car. She sped around the twisting curves of Highway One, handling the souped-up Volvo like a pro. *Danica Patrick got nothin' on me*, she said to herself, thinking of the only professional racecar driver she knew. Whatever Don did to the suspension system was genius; the clunky-looking station wagon rode like a Formula One racecar on a roller coaster.

She decided to take her time. There was no reason to rush. Might as well take one day off, enjoy the ride and the view, and call Danisha.

She answered on the fourth ring.

"It's me, calling from a different phone."

"Why hello there! Long time no hear."

"Yeah, it's been intense. But I'll be in your neighborhood in a few hours."

"I'm in Beverly Hills, about to walk in to the hair salon. Not sure when I'll be home. I have a date with my fiancé, might not come home at all."

"You're such a slut."

"You're just jealous because your fiancé is shooting elephants in India."

"Leopards in Uganda."

"Whatevs. You have a key to my house, right?"

"Yep."

"Remember the code?"

"Yep. I'm just a little nervous parking this, um, car I'm using on the street. It's not mine."

"Put it in the garage. I'll park in the driveway if I have to. *If* I come home, that is."

"I'm not gonna wait up for you. I can *hear* the shit-eating grin on your face right now."

"You know me so well."

"Yeah I do. See you later?"

"Later. Yes. Love you mean it."

CHAPTER 28

Beverly Hills. Two words, one iconic place. Except it's not just *one* place, it's a city within a city, with its own mayor, city hall, courthouse, public library, police department, even an art deco jailhouse. For most people, Beverly Hills conjures images of mansions, Mercedes and Ferraris, and housewives with collagen-enhanced lips and surgically-enhanced everything else. Those images were created and reinforced by the media, so many TV shows and magazine spreads fed the American appetite for scandalous and salacious stories of the rich and famous. Danisha didn't care about any of that. When it came to Beverly Hills, she could take it or leave it. She could've lived without the restaurants and boutiques, but she couldn't live without her hair stylist, Dino Diamante.

Danisha had probably spent more time with Dino than any other man in her life. She'd found him on a movie set when she first started working in Los Angeles, right after graduating from Stanford. They were both assistants back then, now she was one of the most sought-after costume designers in the business and he was the owner of Salon Dino on North Canon Drive, in the heart of the Beverly Hills business district. He knew many of her secrets, and she knew all of his. Walking into his salon was like walking into the home of an old friend. Or rather *friends*. Everyone greeted her as if she were the most beautiful and important woman in the world. She never felt attractive when she walked in, but she always said she looked so much better when she walked out.

She entered the salon to a chorus of *ciao bellas* and air kisses, apologized for being late and strode back to the shampoo sinks, grabbing a black satin smock on her way.

"Today I do the shampoo," Dino announced, making his grand entrance from the break room. He spoke with a trace of an Italian accent. Danisha was one of the few people who knew that he was actually from Bayonne, New Jersey, not Milan.

"Lucky me!" she responded. Dino had fantastic hands, but he rarely got them wet, that's what assistants were for. "What's the occasion?"

"No occasion, I just love you. Big night tonight?"

"Dinner with Alessandro. No big deal. He made reservations at *Matsuhisa*. You been there?"

"*Certo!* Spectacular sushi." Dino's rave reviews of the meals he'd enjoyed at the trendy West Hollywood eatery was interrupted by the buzzing of Danisha's phone.

"Hold that thought," she told him. "It's Alessandro, one sec." Then, into her phone she said, "Hi hon. What's up?"

"I'm so sorry, *mi amore*, but I must cancel our plans for tonight. Something important came up."

"No problem, you're easily replaceable," Danisha said with an exaggerated nonchalance.

"Ah, you beautiful fickle woman. I bought you a little something."

"A guilt present? My favorite! What is it? Does it shine? Can I eat it?"

"It's a surprise. I'll see you tomorrow, yes? You'll find out then."

"Alrighty then. I'll go and have dinner with Lyndsey, my nutty actress friend and spend some time with her. Good luck with whatever it is that's so important you have to cancel your date with me."

"You look sad! What happened?" Dino asked. Danisha thought she could hide her disappointment, but he knew her too well.

"*Something* came up. No trendy sushi for me tonight, but tomorrow I get a..."

"Surprise?" Dino finished Danisha's sentence. "Alessandro gives the best surprises. I say this will be jewelry. No. Shoes. Yes, that's it. Shoes. *Manolos*."

"He does like to spoil me," Danisha said. She had the means to spoil herself, but she liked having a man that bought her presents, took her to beautiful places, escorted her to industry parties and events. After years of dating actors, A-list agents and managers, a studio head, screenwriters, men who called themselves producers, and two bona fide directors, as well as some civilians—men who worked outside the industry—

Danisha finally met Alessandro Stellini– the cosmopolitan, charming, tall, dark and handsome man of her dreams.

Alessandro liked being in Danisha's orbit. She was an Oscar-nominated costume designer with access to tons of Hollywood insiders. He was a relative newcomer to Hollywood, a film producer from Rome. Danisha was a great asset to him. And to be fair he did spend all of his free time with her. He'd never canceled on her before, and spent most nights with her at her place. He still kept his penthouse at The Century, which he used as his production office. Danisha stayed in his Century City penthouse when she couldn't make it back to Malibu or had an early-morning meeting in LA. She loved it up there. It was like a gilded nest in the sky, with the most extraordinary views. The building was five miles inland, but on a clear day she could actually see the Pacific Ocean from his terrace on the thirty-ninth floor.

Primped and coiffed, Danisha left the salon with time to spare before her next meeting. She stopped at one of her favorite Beverly Hills haunts, the American Tea Room, which just happened to be right across the street from Dino's salon. Danisha called Lyndsey.

"Hey girl, you wanna meet for dinner tonight in Koreatown?

"Sure!"

"I've been dying to go to the OpenAire at the Line Hotel. Can we get a table?"

"Yeah, it's not that busy if we're there by six."

'I'm in B.H. Let's see, I have a meeting with my agent around the corner from here at four. I should be able to make it down there by six," Danisha said, mentally mapping out her route downtown at rush hour. "Alright, I'm down. See you in a few hours."

Her phone dinged. It was Alessandro.

"*Sorry about tonight. Don't be made with me. I'm stuck in the Valley*".

"*I am mad with you. Deal with it*".

Within seconds of pressing send, her phone rang. Alessandro. Her text worked.

"*Cara mia*, I'm driving now, you're on speaker. I don't like that you be unhappy for me.

"*With you*. I'm unhappy *with* you, not *for* you, Alessandro. Prepositions. Learn them"

"Dani, Dani, *principessa*. Stop the angry. I cancel my meeting so we can have dinner together just as I promised. And you still get the surprise."

"I can't. I already made a date with Lyndsey."

"Bring her!"

"No."

Dani, *carissima bambina*. Please forgive me. At least come to me after your dinner. Please?"

"Okay, I'll have an early dinner and meet you at the condo after. What time will you be home? "I will be siting on the couch all of the evening waiting for you to walk in the door." Her anger had started to dissipate when Danisha heard Alessandro's Italian voice.

She was in her car and on her way to Koreatown by five. Her Waze app took her down Wilshire, with a few side trips over to Olympic then back north to Charleville for a mile or so, then back over to Wilshire. She pulled up to the Line Hotel, a stark, concrete and glass rectangle, or rather collection of rectangles, a few minutes before six, handed her keys to the valet, then walked through the hotel's ultra modern lobby and up the stairs to the restaurant.

At first she thought she'd stumbled onto the wrong set. The Openaire was a functioning greenhouse. Just the idea of dining in the verdant comfort of the place was enough to make her happy. Plants hung from the rafters, trees and bushes grew in terra cotta pots scattered throughout the room like a curated urban jungle, and the glow of dusk bathed all of it in a magical golden light. Danisha sat down at one of the two-tops in a glassed-in corner of the huge space and ordered a bottle of Prosecco.

"Can you feel the oxygen coursing through your lungs?" Danisha was deep into her Instagram feed when she heard Lyndsey's question.

"You're early?"

"Nice to see you too, Ms. Howard. And no, I'm not early. It's exactly six."

"Shit. I was gonna get so much work done."

"Don't kid yourself, girl. Instagram *is* work," Lyndsey said as she leaned in to give Danisha a hug.

"I love this place. Koreatown, who knew?"

"Right? Well, for the record, I knew."

"My own personal trend-setter. And makeup artist. Now settle in and start drinking. I'm ready for some gossip," Danisha said, rubbing her hands together like a cartoon villain.

"Ah, yes," Lyndsey said, rolling her made-up eyes. "This is a good one. You know Julianne McQueen, the star of that show *Hidden Rooms*? The real pretty one with a pixie cut? Bitch makes two hundred thousand an episode. Well, the night before last, her maid found her half-dead on her bathroom floor. Her house is up in Mandeville Canyon, way at the top. And get this. Rather than call an ambulance? She called the agent!"

"Holy shit. Classic Hollywood story. Poor Julianne. What'd she take?"

"Pharmaceuticals and heroin. Just like Philip Seymour Hoffman."

"May he rest in peace," Danisha interjected.

"Indeed, poor baby," Lyndsey agreed. "The word is that the agent knew she had a *problem* and he had this easy-to-use FDA-approved device that automatically injects an overdose antidote."

"Naloxone?"

"Fuck you Danisha. I shoulda known you'd have that fact filed in that computer you call a brain. Anyway, he gave her the Naloxa-whatever, *then* called an ambulance. They got her to Saint John's hospital just in time."

Danisha didn't say anything to Lyndsey, but Alessandro had told her that he was trying to get Julianne to star in one of his new movie projects. She wondered if he knew about the overdose story.

"Apparently, the producers of *Hidden Rooms* are talking about changing the storyline a bit. But you *know* Julianne's agent is fighting them on *that*. But now all these other agents are pushing their ingénues for whatever new starring role the producers create to replace Julianne," Lyndsey said. "And then, last night at Nobu, this agent, Jack Foster from ICM, accidentally—and I use the term loosely—pushed his wine glass off the table just as another agent, Jon Lindner from CAA, was walking by. And it just so happened that Lindner was wearing a great-looking white shirt that got most of the wine. Did I mention it was a claret? Very red. Dark red. Well, Lindner punched Foster in the face and his nose started bleeding—and the blood went flying all over his wife's pink dress. The two guys were swearing like Mafiosi and Foster's wife was screaming profanities like I've never heard!" Lyndsey laughed.

"You were there?"

"Yes! I saw the whole thing! I swear, it was all I could do not to grab my phone and record the entire show to post to YouTube. Can you imagine how many hits that video would get?"

"Yep, but you'd never work again," Danisha reminded her.

"Exactly. That's why the phone stayed in my purse. Anyway, I gotta pee. Can you order me a kale salad and anything salmon?"

"Of course. While you're gone I'll scour the trade blogs to see if the story has any legs."

Again Danisha was lost in the magical information provided by her iPhone when Lyndsey returned to the table. This time she was out of breath, agitated. She pulled her chair as close to Danisha's as possible and said in a hushed tone, "Dani, this is a little weird and I don't want you to get upset."

"Yes, and?" Dani responded, her curiosity piqued.

"Alessandro is here. He must be on Virbila's, you know the Time's food columnist's private E-mail list of chic hangouts, which I admit is how I found out about this place."

"Wait, what?"

"I just saw him! With two other guys, in the back corner. He didn't see me. And I gotta say, those guys? The men he's with? They don't look like our type of people, if you know what I mean."

"No. I don't know what you mean." Danisha sat up very straight and looked toward the back of the restaurant.

"Don't look, for God's sake," Lyndsey hissed. "And put your head down!"

"What's making you so crazy?"

"Well, one of them had this long, scraggily beard…He looked…I dunno…Middle Eastern."

"You're profiling! Maybe he's an Orthodox rabbi."

"I know what rabbis look like. All the flavors. And that was no rabbi. Besides, what kind of Orthodox rabbi goes to a non-kosher restaurant with Alessandro Stellini?"

"Alright, you make a valid point. So, what should I do?"

They looked at each other, silent. For the first time, Danisha realized how blue Lyndsey's eyes were. Dark blue. It surprised her, because she had known Lyndsey for so many years.

"Just wait. You just got engaged. No need to give up such a beautiful specimen of a man. Not yet anyway. This could all be innocent."

"Give him up? I'm in love with him. And he's in love with me! I can tell. I see it in his eyes when he looks at me. And the way he holds me in bed?" Danisha sighed, suddenly overwhelmed with affection. "No, I'm not giving him up."

Lyndsey took Danisha's hands and held them between hers. "Dani, you're a brilliant woman, especially when it comes to design and business. But your track record with men? Not so great. Disastrous, if I'm gonna be honest. I'm your friend. We help each other, look out for each other. And I gotta say, I don't have a good feeling about this. And neither would you if you saw these guys."

"Oh come on!"

"Dani, I'm serious. Are you seeing him later?"

"Yeah?"

"Okay. Okay. We can work with this. Okay, when you see him later, don't say you were here. Lie to him."

"I can't lie."

"You have to. Please. For me? Say we went to…um…Nobu!" Lyndsey said. "We should leave right now. Alessandro *cannot* see you here. You go first. Now."

Danisha had never heard Lyndsey sound so adamant. Pulling her hands away from Lyndsey, Danisha bit her lower lip and then nervously rubbed it with her fingers.

"I'll pay the bill, I have cash," Lyndsey said, taking her wallet from her bag. "Go. Right now," she ordered.

Danisha took the black cotton napkin from her lap, folded it into a square and placed it on the table. "Okay, Meet me outside?"

"Yeah. Two minutes. Don't look at anyone on your way out."

A few minutes later Lyndsey met Danisha in front of the hotel. "Dani, how did you meet Alessandro?"

"At a wrap party…a TV series."

Lyndsey quickly turned away, but not before Danisha noticed the look of alarm on her friend's face. "Hold up a sec here girl, why'd you ask me that? I swear I just saw something flash across those blue eyes. Was that shock?"

Lyndsey turned back to face Danisha. "I love you, Dani," she sighed. "You know that. I just want you to be careful. You've always been too trusting."

"You shitting me? I grew up on the South Side of Chicago; I know all the games," Dani protested.

"Hollywood games and South Side games? Not the same thing. Not even close. But enough negative bullshit. I'm still hungry. Let's go get some Korean barbeque."

CHAPTER 29

Alessandro was waiting for her on his couch, just as he promised.

"Oh, you're here," she said as she walked through the front door of his apartment.

"Where else would I be?" He asked, perplexed.

"I dunno. At dinner somewhere with some starlet?"

"Dani, are you jealous? Is that what this is about? You know how it hurts me to disappoint you. *Carissima* Dani, *amore mia, bella donna, ti amo moltissimo.* I cannot get enough of you." He was standing beside her now, taking her into his arms. "So many women I have fucked. Hundreds of womens!"

"Not helping!" Danisha interjected, not sure whether to laugh or cry.

"*Ma, va bene.* I will try to be more, how do you say, politically correct?"

"Um, no, that's something completely different. Just try to avoid painting me too detailed a picture of your sexual history."

"Ah. Okay. I talk only about you. I want only you. No actress. No movie star. You. My Dani." He took her in his arms again, held her chin in his hand and gently guided his lips to hers. "I love these lips." He unbuttoned her blouse and kissed the tops of her breasts. "This. I cannot ever have enough of this." He freed a breast from the cup of her bra, kissed her nipple, then lifted her into his arms and carried her into the bedroom.

She was naked before her ass hit the mattress. Alessandro started kissing her belly and worked his way down, kissing every centimeter of skin. He stopped just short of her labia, then licked the inside of her thighs. Dani groaned. She could feel the moisture building up between her legs. Alessandro dipped his tongue into her vagina, then slowly let it glide up to her clit. Her first orgasm started then, but it didn't stop. He kept licking and sucking, drinking the juices that flowed from inside her. She moaned louder, then screamed and she shuddered in orgasmic convulsions.

Danisha counted three more orgasms before Alessandro finally allowed himself to come. They lay tangled in each other's limbs, Danisha struggling to catch her breath. Within a few minutes she was ready for sleep, but Alessandro had something else in mind.

"Time for your surprise," he told her as he opened his nightstand drawer and took out two small rope-handled Neiman Marcus shopping bags. "*Eccolo*, this one first."

Inside the bag was a four-ounce bottle of Danisha's favorite perfume, *Santal* by Le Labo. Before she could take it out he handed her the second bag, "That's just the appetizer. This is the entree. I don't have the patience to wait. Open it now, *mi amore*."

Dani looked up at him. This was too much. It wasn't her birthday, or Christmas or even Valentine's Day. "But, why?" she asked him.

"Because I adore you...too much," he answered with Roman pride.

Inside the bag she found a small, square, black velvet box. Jewelry. Her heart raced. She lifted the lid to find an emerald bracelet. "Holy shit, Alessandro, this is fucking gorgeous. Wait, this matches the earrings you gave me for Christmas?"

"But of course! Tell me you love it."

"I love it!" He could always make her feel happy, at least for a few days. The smile on his face as he put the bracelet on Dani's wrist could've lit up the room. It was genuine, she was sure of that. They made love again, and she was happy.

But just as she was about to fall asleep, Alessandro whispered something in her ear that she didn't understand.

"Hmmm?" Danisha snuggled closer to him, then turned and nestled her back and ass into his belly. "I'm the inside spoon tonight," she said groggily.

"You are *adorabile*. How will I sleep without you tomorrow night?"

"What you talkin' 'bout Willis?" Dani asked, thinking he was joking. "Who is Willis?"

"It's from a seventies sitcom. But that doesn't matter. Are you going somewhere tomorrow or are you playing with me?"

"Playing? Sit com?"

"Stop with the innocent foreigner routine 'Sandro. Answer my question."

"Yes, I just told you. I have to go to Rome tomorrow."

"Wait. What?" Dani sat up and turned on the lamp on the nightstand beside her. Now she was really pissed. "Rome? Tomorrow?"

"Yes. I told you. My brother. He is very ill. I promised I would go to him for a few days to take care of his business affairs."

"Hah. The perfume and the bracelet were props? Bagatelles to butter me up?" *He thinks I'm that easy? Fuck this shit.*

"No, Dani. How could you say this? It's a family emergency. I would never leave you if I did not absolutely have to. I go for Rome tomorrow afternoon at four. I'll be back in a week. I promise."

Danisha didn't cry or argue, didn't say a word. She turned off the light and tried to clear her mind. Staring out into the darkness, she could still see the worry in Lyndsey's deep-blue eyes.

CHAPTER 30

Justine woke up as usual, thirty minutes before dawn, but this time at Danisha's house the following morning feeling well rested and ready —though she did have more than a trace of trepidation—to face the day. Her first assignment. After eating a bowl of yogurt with blueberries in the kitchen, she made herself a cup of cappuccino. The floor-to-ceiling windows of the great room overlooked the ocean and the Malibu Colony to the west. From her vantage point it all seemed so peaceful down there. Why would anyone surrounded by such placid beauty possibly need protection when she has her own personal arsenal? But, that's where she was going to:

Guard a celebrity who lived in Malibu.

She'd heard about the Colony but had never actually been there. It looked deceptively simple. If she didn't have to clear the guard and gate she'd never have guessed this was some of the most valuable real estate in the world.

The guard was expecting her and waved her through. The houses got bigger as she drove, following the directions on the GPS. She arrived at her destination at precisely eight-fifty-eight AM. Don, sweating in his workout clothes, was waiting outside the front door of a white stone mansion. He greeted her in his most professional tone and took her four bags from the trunk.

"Whose house is this?" she asked before walking inside.

"Alyssa Stewart," Don replied.

"*The* Alyssa Stewart?" Justine's eyes widened in awe.

He nodded. "She has an appointment in Beverly Hills this morning. A fitting for her Oscar gown. You'll be escorting her. First you'll need to unpack. Your room is back here." Don led her through a side door of the enormous house. "You're going solo; I need to leave on another assignment."

He dropped the bags in a room then led her up a staircase. "Time to meet the client, it'll be a good test of your patience and resilience."

"Why?"

"You'll see. Come on, she's at the pool." They walked out a door at the back of the house, onto the pool deck overlooking the ocean. Alyssa was sunning herself, topless, with just the smallest possible triangle of diaphanous cloth covering her crotch.

"I didn't know you were back." Alyssa cooed, her eyes closed behind her sunglasses. "Would you be a love and put more sunscreen on me?"

Don picked up a bottle from the glass table beside Alyssa's chaise. Justine noticed the label, *Guerlain Orchidée Impériale*. *That shit costs over four hundred dollars*, she thought to herself. Don poured some lotion into his palm, set the bottle down, rubbed his hands together and gently applied it to Alyssa's shoulders. Justine couldn't take her eyes off of Alyssa's breasts, shaped to perfection by one of Beverly Hills's top cosmetic surgeons. As Don smoothed his hands over the famous breasts Alyssa purred with pleasure, her ample nipples hardened. Justine noticed that the way Don touched the great movie star was casual. He gave her none of the sensual, penetrating attention he'd given Justine in his hot springs in Big Sur. *You think you're all it, hey girl? You don't know what you're missing*, Justine thought to herself. Clearly Don had never given Alyssa a tantric massage.

"I'd like to introduce you to my replacement close-protection specialist—Diana," Don told Alyssa once he'd finished coating her in overpriced French sunscreen.

This name change caught Justine off-guard. *Diana? Like the Princess or like the goddess of the hunt?*

"I don't want Diana," Alyssa said with her eyes still closed. "I want you."

"I'm sorry, but I have a national security assignment. Diana is perfectly capable of protecting you."

That got Alyssa's eyes open. She looked at Justine as if she were a dress she was considering trying on. "Just 'cause she's your fuck bunny, doesn't mean she can protect me."

"Our relationship is professional."

Alyssa shrugged, her eyes still glued on Justine. "Fine. She's older and flatter. If you can resist *me*, you're *definitely* not interested in *her*."

Don smiled. Justine put on her best poker-face and focused on keeping her mind blank.

"God, I hope I don't look as bad as you in twenty years," Alyssa continued with a snarl.

Justine remained expressionless. After all of Don's verbal drills to inure her to insults, Alyssa's attack was pathetic. Amateur insult drivel.

"Doesn't she speak English?" Alyssa asked Don.

"I speak English. And French, and Spanish, and Italian. I can also carry on a conversation in Hebrew."

"You brought me a fuckin' Jew? You know how much I hate being surrounded by Jews in Hollywood and now you bring one into my home? Get her the fuck out of here!"

Justine had no patience for bigots, but then Don did say this client would test her patience.

She focused on her calming breath and thought, *if anyone wants to shoot her, I'll loan them a gun.*

"Alyssa," Don responded politely, "If you want to hire another security company, that's your choice."

Justine wondered why he would put up with this bitch. His financial situation must've been extremely precarious.

"I hired you even though you're an old, half-breed Jap," Alyssa snapped, "*Not her!*"

"I think you owe Diana an apology. We're a team. If you don't want her, this 'old, half-breed Jap' will leave with her.

"Okay, whatever. I apologize to both of you," Alyssa said irritably, waving her arms in the air and the she turned her attention Justine. "But tell me this. What do you see in her that you don't see in me?"

Now Don was getting pissed. "Our relationship is professional, as I just said. She's a highly trained professional with a perfect protection record. No client has ever been lost under her watch."

Justine struggled not to crack a smile at Don's retort. Though technically he was telling the truth; she'd certainly never lost a client.

"So Diana, or whatever your real name is, is this true?"

"We are both professionals," said Justine in a monotone but stern voice.

"But, the prerequisite to rule number one is the golden rule," Don responded.

Justine was sure she saw a smile creep around his eyes.

"Golden rule? 'Those with the gold, make the rules,' " retorted Alyssa.

"No. Do unto others *before* they do unto you."

Justine nodded as she turned away and walked away, she thought, "I got it all right here, boss," she said, tapping her temple.

Her first solo gig. Don said it would be an easy job, but he didn't have to listen to the inane conversation going on in the back seat of the Alyssa Stewart's Mercedes. If he ever did have to hear it he'd already mastered the art of blocking all superfluous noise. Justine hadn't yet reached that phase of security professional evolution. She heard every word of the ethnic slurs and clichéd phrases that gushed from Alyssa Stewart's perfect mouth like crude oil from *Deepwater Horizon.*

Alyssa's chauffeur wove through the mid-day West Side traffic like a pro; Justine figured he must've been a stunt driver in a past life. She wondered which job was more dangerous, driving off cliffs for a J.J. Abrams movie or carting around America's most beautiful bigot.

He turned south on Beverly Drive, then left onto one of the smaller side streets, and pulled up to the front entrance of an unmarked, two-story red brick building. And a pack of paparazzi waiting for them on the sidewalk, their cameras ready to attack.

"Who tipped off the wolf pack?" she asked Raphael, Aylassa's assistant,

"Beats me," the young man responded, jutting his head in the general direction of his boss.

"All publicity is good publicity, right?" Alyssa cooed sweetly. "Bring 'em on."

"Perfect," Justine hissed as she put on her photochromic sunglasses to ready herself for the barrage of camera flashes, then took the Glock 17 from her purse. Her backup pistol, a Glock 26, only holding eleven rounds, was hidden in her thigh-holster. In her left hand she held a folded, GoLite silver umbrella that she could open to reflect camera flashes back onto the photographers, ruining any shots they took. As an added bonus, the folded umbrella made a terrific improvised weapon.

Still, Justine felt nervous. She opened her door, stood up and started her three-sixty degree surveillance scan.

A dozen strobe lights fired at once, all aimed at her. Motorized camera shutters fired thousands of rounds. Television cameras with more blinding LEDs competed for space on the sidewalk. Momentarily confused, Justine hesitated.

"What the fuck, bodyguard lady?" Raphael called out a small crack in his window. "You look like the proverbial deer caught in the headlights."

So much for all my realistic simulation training, Justine grumbled inwardly.

"Are they seriously taking pictures of *her*?" Alyssa asked Raphael.

"I'd say, yes. Definitely."

"These idiots think she's *someone*? Wait. They think she's *me*?"

Raphael shrugged. "She does have a great butt."

When the driver opened Alyssa's door she struck a few well-rehearsed poses before slipping her long, shapely legs out the car and onto the sidewalk. It was sheer old Hollywood. Then, Alyssa then did a graceful pirouette, giving it enough swirl to hike her *Dolce & Gabbana* silk chiffon skirt in a high circle, revealing the outline of her Commando thong. *Great,* Justine thought, *she's prepared a little song and dance number for the boys here.* The strobes lights would make Alyssa's top and thong appear almost sheer in any photo. The girl was giving the wolf pack a feast of pink meat.

But then Justine noticed something strange. Not one of the cameras was aimed at the press-hungry movie star. *Shit, they're taking pictures of me?*

"Wrong blonde," she said to the two hundred millimeter lens of a Nikon D5 XQD. The man behind that camera must've been paying attention. In a split second he'd spun around and located the real target. His camera's isolated flashes alerted the rest of the pack and they all followed his lead. Alyssa rewarded them all with the honey-moncy shots they craved, flaunting the best breasts money could buy and jiggling her surgically enhanced ass, while maintaining her thin veneer of disdain. The wolf pack howled in appreciation. She was America's Reigning Queen of Sex.

As if she had done it before, Justine stepped in front of Alyssa, using her GoLite to leverage her way through the crowd. Alyssa didn't follow her, but continued her series of poses, pretending to be surprised, then contemptuous, then charming.

Fucking actors, Justine thought, masking her aversion with the blank expression of a professional. She turned back, placed herself in front of her client and got ready for round two. With her right hand on the Glock in her purse, she used her elbows and her improvised baton to navigate her way through the crowd. They pushed back. They shoved. Justine smiled politely but spoke with authority. "Excuse me…Pardon me…Thank you," she said with as much decency as she could muster. But that didn't work. So, jutting her knees into the sides of any unfortunate set of knees that got in her way, she toppled her human obstacles into each other until the ones on the edges of the pack fell back on their asses. They never knew what hit them and turned on each other instead, cursing and shoving.

Alyssa and Raphael followed the path Justine cleared for them. Once they were all safely in the designer's *atelier,* Justine noticed one photographer handing a fist-full of hundred-dollar bills to an attractive young man standing by the front door. *One of the designer's assistants. Bastards! This whole ambush was a set up.*

Another man appeared on the scene. Tall, skinny, bald, he wore wide-leg black cropped pants—though they could just as easily have been long shorts, and a matching asymmetrical panel jacket with a funnel neck and enough zippers and studs to fill the hardware aisle at a Michael's arts and crafts shop. Justine was momentarily mesmerized by the outfit—*he pulls off that overgrown school-boy meets the Matrix look so well*—until the whiz-click din of motorized camera shutters reminded her what she was doing there in the first place. She had just begun to consider her best angle of attack when Alyssa shrieked with joy. Justine watched as her client sauntered into the strange man's arms.

"Hi there Kenneth," Raphael said with a wink.

Kenneth Garletti, the designer. *Well that explains the outfit.* Kenneth listened to Alyssa's long-winded apology, nodding sympathetically, until he spotted Justine. *Shit, am I still staring? Nope, he's the one who's staring. At me. What the fuck?*

Kenneth took a few steps away from Alyssa to get a good look at Justine. Then he stood for a moment, his left hand holding his chin and his other hand planted on his right hip, and sized her up like she was a racehorse at an auction. "Manolo Blahnik on the feet and Christian

Dior on the ears. The dress is, Alaia? Yes of course it is. I forgive you for not wearing one piece of mine. This time." He then took Justine by the waist and waltzed her around in a circle. "Alyssa, why did you never tell me you had such an elegant sister?"

"She's my bodyguard, you moron. If you wanna fuck her, do it on your own time. I'm here for my fitting."

Kenneth glanced dramatically at the Howard Miller mantel clock. "Yes…and only two hours late."

"Raphael told you the traffic was a nightmare."

"I know. I know. *I* was driving from my partner's beach house in Malibu, too. It only took me thirty minutes. You're not my only fitting today."

"But I'm your number one."

"You know you are," Kenneth cooed back, as he twirled his graceful, manicured fingers through Alyssa's perfect hair.

Number one pain in the ass, Justine thought.

Kenneth led Alyssa and her entourage into an ornate fitting room. While Kenneth's assistant—Justine never did get his name—sat Alyssa on the in rose-gold velvet tufted sofa. The room was lit by an enormous Venetian glass chandelier of varying jewel-tone colors, as well as a series of matching sconces along the *trompe l'oiel* gold marble walls. A bottle of Veuve Cliquot was chilling in a silver ice bucket on top of what could've been a genuine Louis XIV *Bouillotte* gilt-painted wood table set in front of a row of potted dwarf palm and giant Bonsai trees. Justine appreciated the eclecticism, overdone as it might've been. Kenneth poured everyone a glass of champagne, which Justine politely declined, before beginning the delicate process of getting Alyssa into a luminous, yellow-silk chiffon, Garletti gown.

"The gown is almost perfect," Kenneth announced once it was securely attached to Alyssa. "It only needs a slight nip and tuck to reveal more your gorgeous breasts. After all the work you did to get them, you might as well show them off as well as possible, no?"

The nipping and tucking took two hours. Alyssa stood motionless on the platform the entire time, as Kenneth, armed with pins and a tape measure, perfected his masterpiece.

No one noticed the noisy commotion going on a few yards away in Kenneth's showroom. Not at first anyway. It was the sound of a fist banging on the fitting room door that finally caught everyone's attention. Someone was pissed. Justine reflexively turned to shield Alyssa before the door burst open and Justine found herself face to face with America's *former* favorite movie star, Kandace Jordan. An exceptionally angry Kandace Jordan.

Screaming, Kandace pushed her way into the fitting room. Her perfectly manicured hands extended like claws, went straight for Justine's face, one hand grasping for her hair and the other desperately trying to scratch out her eyes. Using Don's *drunken client, roving hands* evasion technique, Justine easily blocked Kandace's hands. Then, with the patience and skill of a kindergarten teacher, she pushed the infuriated celebrity away like a child covered in tempera paint.

Kandace stood stock still, momentarily dumbfounded. But soon enough she started screaming again, at Justine. "You fucking cunt. First you fuck my husband and now you steal my designer!"

Wait, what? What is with these Hollywood people and blondes, how can they possibly think we all look alike?

Justine's hesitation gave Alyssa an opportunity to slam into Kandace. "You're so fucking stupid. You got the wrong bitch, yo!" She was screaming at Kandace but the brunt of her invective went straight into Justine's ear. Clasping the gown to her torso, Alyssa continued her rant. "And for the record? Your man's a lousy lay. You two deserve each other!"

Finding herself smack in the middle of a celebrity catfight, Justine wanted to strangle them both. Drawing from her training in Don's unique version of Aikido, she stepped between the two beautiful adversaries and pressed her left hip into Alyssa, who pushed back even harder to get to Kandace. After a quick calculation Justine decided that she should place Alyssa on the ground rather than allow Kandace to push her down in the melee. With an almost maternal caution, Justine lifted Alyssa onto her right hip, and with one swift twist, carefully guided the screaming actress to soft landing on her back.

"On my god the pins!" shrieked Raphael.

"Fuck the pins," shrieked Kenneth. "That dress cost twelve grand, wholesale!"

"She's not paying for it," Raphael reminded the designer. "I don't give a shit about the dress. Torn skin takes time to heal. You can have one of your *rice queens* sew up the dress."

Justine began to check her client for signs of pin-injury, but stopped when she saw Kandace at the edge of her field of vision. The other crazed actress was coming at her with a vengeance. Justine's instincts were sharp—*thank you Don!*—and, with the grace of a prima ballerina, she easily blocked both of Kandace's outstretched claws, then foot-swept her to the ground, rolled her over, and took a large zip tie from inside her belt.

She had both of Kandace's wrists cinched tight behind her back when she was suddenly blindsided by an enormous object. She looked up to see the small mountain that was one of Kandace's three-hundred-pound bodyguards, then yielded her entire body to his weight, causing him to overshoot her. He flew over the Persian rug and skidded face down on the polished marble floor, colliding head first into the wall, out cold.

But as luck would have it, Kandace had two bodyguards, and the second looked like a clone of the first. Justine watched in awe as he came at her. His outstretched monster arms wrapped around her chest and slammed her to the ground, knocking the wind out of her. Again, her instincts kicked in instantaneously; she tucked her chin so her head wouldn't hit the floor, and then, in spite of the throbbing pain in her chest, she grabbed his pinkie, *hey, look at that, he has a pinkie ring, what a surprise,* and twisted it backwards. The ape howled in agony, his arm relaxed to give Justine enough space to twist her body out of his grip, which gave both of her knees more leverage. She rose to her knees, bent over him, and pinned him face down on the floor, using his pinkie as a joystick.

Bending over her prey, Justine beamed with pride. She'd just broken almost every rule of mixed martial arts full contact matches. Her opponents were a combined six hundred pounds to her one hundred and fifteen, so she had no choice but to even the playing field with illegal moves. Twisting the big boy's pinkie finger back a little more, she whispered in his ear, "We're all professionals doing our jobs, so no need to get hurt, right?"

The lug was eager to surrender. "Alright, alright! Jeez woman, where'd you learn to fight?"

"*Arrest and Control,* Bob Koga style." Justine knew any security guy worth his paycheck would recognize the name of the world's foremost law enforcement martial arts instructor.

Still pinned under her knees, the enormous man relaxed. "That explains a lot. I give up," he sighed.

Justine felt a delicious rush of adrenaline. Ah, success!

Except now Alyssa was up. Her almost-fitted gown was falling off her torso. She looked down at Kandace, who was curled into a fetal position on the carpet. "You stupid bitch!" Alyssa screamed, repeatedly kicking Kandace's body with her bare right foot. Justine had just begun to pull her client off of her defenseless victim when the paparazzi burst in, their cameras blazing.

Their flashes were blinding. Justine closed her eyes, and, using Don's method of fighting in total darkness, used her other senses to locate Alyssa, whose angry curses continued unabated. Justine followed the shrieking sounds to Alyssa's arm, then, gently grabbing her neck, wrapped her furious client in a rear carotid choke. Next she swiftly wrapped her legs around Alyssa's chest in a double leg hook, squeezing the air out of her lungs.

Within seconds Alyssa was unconscious. Justine released her gently onto the rug.

The intruding paparazzi cameras continued to flash, aimed both at the unconscious Alyssa and Kandace's bloodied and shrieking face.

Don is not gonna to be pleased with my work today. So much for my first low-key, low-risk assignment.

CHAPTER 31

Alyssa was uncharacteristically silent on the drive back to Malibu. Raphael fielded all the calls from her agent, manager, publicist, life coach, and everyone else that had set Google alerts for Alyssa Stewart.

"Actually, your publicist is thrilled," Raphael said, summarizing his many conversations with Team Alyssa. "She said, you *literally* just got yourself a million dollars worth of free publicity. And the agent's not even pissed. You really should talk to him."

Alyssa shook her head and continued to pout.

"You really did kick that ugly bitch's ass. Aly? *Hello?* I'm proud of you?"

Alyssa perked up. Something Raphael said had caught her attention. "Stop the car!" she said to the driver. They were heading north on the Pacific Coast Highway. "Just pull over to the side of the road."

"We'll be home in like ten minutes," Raphael protested.

"Now. Put this fucking car over right now!" she commanded. The driver pulled onto a wide shoulder. Alyssa was out of the back seat before the car had come to a complete stop.

What the fuck is she doing now, Justine thought as she clasped the handle to open her door, which flew open before she had the chance to pull it.

"Diana!" As soon as Justine stepped out of the car Alyssa was hugging and kissing her like a long lost child. "Thank you, thank you, my goddess Diana! I never saw anyone fight like you. I totally underestimated you."

"Um," Justine wasn't sure how to react to this new public display of affection.

"I'm really sorry about how I treated you before," Alyssa continued. "Do you forgive me?"

"I...I...yes. Of course."

"Yay! I'm so happy you'll be walking the red carpet with me! You, my goddess, are my new BFF."

Lucky me, Justine wanted to say. Instead she just nodded.

Later that evening, Justine, her arms and back aching and covered with purple bruises, escorted Alyssa on a stroll down the beach. Flood-lights illuminated Alyssa's pool deck and the ocean surf. In spite of her not insignificant aches and pains, Justine felt remarkably calm.

"Something wrong Diana?" Alyssa asked.

"Nope. Why?"

"You're just, like, I dunno, quiet or something?"

Justine let out a chuckle. "Kandace's six hundred pounds of body-guard beef got to my hundred fifteen pounds of girl power," Justine said, barely smiling. "I'll need to heal if I'm gonna protect you at the Oscars. Which means I have to go back to Don. He's the only person I know who can fix me in time. His treatments work twice as fast as any other miracle cure you LA health freaks can come up with."

"Then you should probably leave right away," Alyssa said with gen-uine concern. "I can hire a team of off-duty Malibu cops but I need you at a hundred percent for the Oscars."

"Don't worry, that's a whole month away. I'll be back," said Justine, realizing that Alyssa was so needy because she was really not much more than a child. She wanted to say 'call me Justine,' to tell this vulnerable little girl a piece of the truth, but she knew that would go against all of Don's rules. Instead, she put an arm around Alyssa's shoulder, and Alyssa turned to give Justine a full body hug.

"Such a pretty necklace," Alyssa said, fingering the *chai* charm on Justine's gold chain. "Is that Sanskrit for something?"

"Hebrew. Which is kinda like Sanskrit, I guess. Except people actu-ally speak it. Anyway, it's my good luck charm. It's actually two letters that spell *chai,* which means *life.*"

"I love it. You think I could find one just like it?"

"I thought you hated Jews," Justine laughed.

"My bad. I was in a mood. I promise I won't do that again. Forgive me?"

Justine hugged Alyssa, kissed her cheek, then took her hand and walked her back to the house.

Driving back to Big Sur, random fragments of scenes from the afternoon's violent altercation flooded Justine's mind. Trying to find some sense in the chaos, she forced herself to go over every detail of her first day of work.

The next day's tabloids, entertainment and gossip television shows and Internet sites all ran stories, complete with full-color photos, on the mysterious hot body that guarded America's favorite movie star. Justine Baron, the former Silicon Valley CEO, had suddenly become first-class clickbait.

CHAPTER 32

Danisha was starting to doubt her perception of reality. Was Justine right about her disastrous track record with men? Alessandro had been so loving, so gentle the night before he left for Rome, why should she doubt him? And why didn't she just ask him what he'd ended up doing that night? It was a natural question for a fiancé to ask, especially since he'd tried to make a date with her. Right? She told him she wasn't available so he found alternate dinner companions. She definitely should've asked.

But she hadn't asked, and now a sense of paranoia had co-opted her entire being. So maybe her suspicions about Alessandro were valid. Then again, maybe she was just being overly sensitive, again. Growing up in South Chicago—one of the worst urban neighborhoods in the country had taught her to be vigilant; she refused to play the victim. And being a successful black woman in the entertainment industry meant she had to deal with racism and sexism every single day. So yeah, maybe her sensitivity had morphed into full-blown paranoia.

But she knew that Alessandro was in the same Korean restaurant she was in and it wasn't in The Valley.

Lyndsey saw him with the Imam, or whatever he was, the *not-rabbi* at Openaire. Lyndsey wouldn't make that shit up, would she? Danisha didn't care who Alessandro met for dinner or where he went, she cared that he *lied* to her. But then again, did he lie to her? He hadn't actually said anything about having dinner with anyone. So technically he hadn't *lied*, it was more like a lie of omission. Which was just as bad. Wasn't it? The perfume and bracelet shouldn't have been a problem, except he gave them to her right before he told her about his sudden need to go to Rome. It was all a bit too perfect. *Wasn't it?*

Justine would know what to do. Danisha reflexively picked up her phone then realized she had no clue how to contact her best friend. All this new super-secret nonsense was so annoying. Then she remembered that Justine had called yesterday. From a different number. *Did that number show up when her phone rang?* Danisha scrolled through the list of received calls. Nothing. Of course.

And then it rang. No caller ID. *Please be Justine, please be Justine,* Danisha thought as she pressed *accept.* "Hello?"

"None of it is true. Well, some of it is, I guess."

Danisha sighed with relief. "Thank God you can still read my mind."

"Oh come on, Dani. Don't tell me you believed any of that crap clogging up your Facebook and Twitter feeds."

"I'm not sure what you're talking about since I haven't looked at social media all day…"

Justine cut her off. "So you haven't even seen the tabloids?"

"I have an actual job, so no. I also have a major conundrum. And I mean *major.*"

"Where are you?

"At work."

"On a set?"

"No. My office. Sony. Culver City."

"So you're safe?"

"What? Yes! I mean. Yeah, I'm safe. I'm just really confused. I think I might have a problem with Alessandro," Danisha said quietly.

"What? So soon? He's not hot anymore?" What?

Danisha gave Justine the Reader's Digest version of her conundrum in the calmest tone she could summon. "You still at my place? I can fill you in on all the sordid details over dinner."

"No I left LA last night. Taking my last solo stroll along the water before I head back to training."

"Damn it girl, I need you!"

"Yeah, I can hear that. What you really need is to get a look at his computer."

"How can I do that?"

"You still have that whiz-kid IT guy?"

"Yeah."

"And Alessandro's in Rome for how long?"

"He said no more than a week."

"Perfect. You can get into his condo, right?"

"Yes, of course."

"Then it should be simple enough. You've been there before when he's not there, right?"

"Well…Yeah. Yes."

"Perfect. This'll be easy-peasy. I'm gonna tell you exactly what to look for. Grab a pen, write this down." Justine recited a basic *Sleuthing For Dummies* list of items that Danisha would need to find useful information in Alessandro's apartment. "Got it?"

"Yeah."

"Great. Now, memorize everything on that list."

"Okay."

"Then burn it."

"You're kidding, right?"

"Honey, my new, um, boss has put my sense of humor into what I like to call the bodyguard equivalent of a medically-induced coma. So no. I'm not kidding."

Danisha hesitated, unsure how to respond. "Okay, I'll do it and get back to you with any news," she said finally.

"Yeah, about that getting back to me part?"

"No. Jussy please. Make it not be true," Danisha said, doing her best Maria from *West Side Story* impression.

"A boy like that…" Justine started to sing.

"And she's back!" Dani laughed, relieved.

"Yeah, start with the show tunes and you can always get me back, metaphorically at least."

"At least some things never change. When you hear me singing Officer Krupke you'll know I've totally lost it."

"It's just your neurosis that oughta be curbed…," Justine sang in her best Bronx accent. "But seriously, call your IT guy. Now. Once you find out the truth, which is probably innocent, you'll feel better."

"Right. Call me soon?"

"As soon as I possibly can. I promise. Meanwhile, if you need me desperately, text SOS to this number. If I'm not actively working, I'll respond right away."

Danisha sat at her desk contemplating her choices when she felt her phone vibrate beneath her fingertips. Turning it over, she saw Alessandro's name flashing across the screen and a warm wave of relief washed away all her all doubts and suspicions.

"Alessandro?"

"Yes. *mi amore.* How are you?"

"Fine. I was just thinking about you. Why aren't you on the plane yet, doesn't it take off in a few minutes?"

"Dani, I gave you the flight tracker information, no?"

"Yeah, but I haven't checked it yet."

"Of course, busy woman you are. The flight is delayed, but only for one hour. I miss you already. I wanted to hear your voice. You sound good. Are you good?"

"Yes, 'Sandro, I'm good. You left me less than three hours ago!"

"What is it you Americans say, absence makes the heart grow lonelier?"

"Fonder." Danisha laughed. How could she possibly doubt this man?

"*Ma,* I have *una problema.* I thought I grabbed all of my cell phones except I left one of my European cell phones in my office. It's the one with all the important contact information, so I need it. Usually Arturo can get into the condo but he's already in Rome, waiting for me. Miguel will Fedex it to me but he doesn't have a key to the apartment. Can you go to my condo now, find the phone and bring it to the concierge?"

"Uh, sure. Right now?"

"Whenever you can get there is fine my love. The phone is in the top right drawer of my desk. Put it in an envelope and bring it to the lobby on your way out? I left my office door unlocked for the housekeeper, but you'll need the code to unlock my desk. Do you mind?"

"No, of course I don't mind," Danisha replied, both anxious and excited by this serendipitous opportunity to snoop.

"You have paper and pen?"

"Yup."

"I will give you the code now. Write it down on a small piece of paper. How do you call the little square yellow paper that sticks to things?"

"Post-its?"

"Yes! That's it. You have the *posts it,* yes?"

"Yes, Alessandro, I have the post-its."

"Write down the combination. Ready?"

"Uh huh," Dani answered patiently.

"*Allora*, write this now. Sixty-nine. Sixty-nine."

"Got it."

"*Va bene*. Now, memorize this combination, then burn the paper."

"You're kidding, right?" Danisha said, laughing playfully.

"This is amusing you?"

"Well, yeah, kinda. It's just that..." she had to think fast, "That same line, those exact words, are in the script for my next project." She wasn't lying.

"Listen, *amore*, I'll call you when I get to Rome. I should to go. Thank you for doing this for me. I love you."

"I'll do my best. I love you more, by the way. *Ciao, mi amore.*"

Danish paused for a moment before clicking off. She hated what she had said—

"I love you more, by the way—"

CHAPTER 33

Traffic on Motor Avenue was lighter than usual. The first red light she hit was at Pico Boulevard, where she turned right, then took the next left onto Avenue of the Stars and practically coasted the final two blocks to the expansive driveway of Alessandro's Century City condominium building.

So far, so good, she thought as she pulled up to the main entrance. Raul, the valet, greeted her by name as he opened her door, as did Miguel the concierge when she walked past him to the elevator bank. By the time Danisha reached the penthouse floor she felt remarkably calm. Arturo, who ran security for that floor, was not there. At Alessandro's apartment door she punched in his security code: six-nine-six-nine —*not obvious at all,* she thought to herself, *I really should talk to him about that.*

Danisha opened the door to find complete darkness. Every light was off, every blackout shutter closed. The space felt like a black hole, a dark corner of the universe. "He's forty-two flights up," Danisha said out loud to herself. "What's he afraid of, ninjas scaling the building under the cover of night and breaking in to his office?" She flipped a light switch, then punched in the six-digit code, which was merely a repeated extension of the front door security code, and watched as all the shutters opened simultaneously, and the lights of the city sparkled like a jeweled blanket spread out just for her.

Justine's list. Danisha had memorized it, as per Justine's explicit instructions, then put in through the shredder. There wasn't much to memorize.

1) Gloves
2) Ziplock bags for evidence
3) Fingerprints
4) DNA
5) Credit card statements
6) Copy the entire contents of his hard drive onto a flash drive

Numbers one and two were easy. Danisha had as many boxes of super-fine cotton gloves at her studio, in her office and at home as she had ziplock bags. Finding fingerprints might not be so easy. DNA she could get from a toothbrush or comb. Now that she had the code to get into his desk, finding credit card statements wouldn't be a problem. Copying his computer's hard drive would not be possible since Alessandro most definitely would have taken his laptop and his iPad with him to Rome.

She took a pair of brand new white cotton gloves from her bag and slipped them on, then went straight to the kitchen. Alessandro had to have left something in there with his fingerprints. *Oh yes he did,* she thought when she saw the small juice glass on the counter. She picked it up and smelled it. Orange juice. Definitely his, he drank four ounces of fresh squeezed OJ every morning with his vitamins *Fingerprints, check.* She took a zip-lock baggie from a drawer and slipped it over the glass, then sealed the bag and dropped it in her purse before heading back to Alessandro's office.

Walking through the main hallway, Danisha noticed that every door was closed. She tried opening one. Locked. Then another. Same. She tried them all, and they were locked.

Alessandro's office door at the end of the hallway was wide open. The room was impeccably clean, not even a piece of paper or tissue in the leather wastebasket. Danisha pulled the chair from his desk, sat down, and said, "It's show time folks!"

She punched in the code she'd memorized and unlocked the desk. The European cell phone was right there where he said it would be, top right drawer. Danisha then took a deep breath, and, mentally reviewing Justine's detective to-do list, carefully opened the next drawer. Nothing interesting there, just your typical business papers. No credit card receipts. She repeated her inspection of the desk's six drawers, finding nothing of interest. Then, in bottom left drawer, she noticed a laptop.

An Origin PC-19. *What the hell is he doing with a PC?* She'd never seen her fiancé with anything but a Mac.

Danisha carefully lifted Alessandro's laptop onto the desk. "You, my pretty little friend, are the key to my entire future," she said out loud to the machine. "Okay, maybe that's some bullshit hyperbole on my part, but maybe you know something I don't?"

It took a minute or so to figure out how to open the stupid thing. Once she had the lid unhitched from the keyboard, the first thing she saw on the screen was a photo of her own face. She remembered when he'd taken the picture. They'd been walking together, watching the fisherman on the Santa Monica Pier. It was the morning they'd made love for the first time. It lasted two hours. They couldn't stop kissing and touching each other. She had never experienced anything that before. Alessandro said the same was true for him.

Seeing that photo made Danisha feel guilty. She had to stop looking. She started to close the screen, but hesitated. She knew she had to find out more about him. About what was really going on.

But the computer was password protected. Danisha closed her eyes and visualized the movements of Alessandro's hands when he unlocked one of his other laptops. That technique proved useless. She closed her eyes again and tried the next technique in her mental bag of tricks. Manifestation. Focusing on her memories of time spent with Alessandro, Danisha remembered the time that he ignored her because he was too preoccupied with opening up his laptop. "The video!" she said, recalling the episode. She'd recorded it with her phone. *Please tell me I didn't delete it,* she thought as she searched her phone for the video. "Yes!" she practically screamed when she found it. Then she enlarged the moving image on her phone's screen and could see that his fingers went to the letters W, H, and O.

Alessandro once told Danisha about his admiration for the British Special Air Services. He especially admired their motto, *Who dares Wins.* Danisha's fingers typed *whodareswins* on the keys. The computer screen lit up.

She found an app called *My Pictures,* and clicked on it. Hundreds of files opened. She could actually hear her heart pounding as she started scrolling through photos of women's faces. Blondes, brunettes, redheads, white women, brown women, black women, Asian women, Indian women. Some beautiful, others not so much.

Danisha clicked on a random face. The caption said, "Colleen, Dublin Beauty." Dozens of images appeared on the screen. High-resolution photos of Colleen the Dublin beauty naked, beckoning, masturbating, giving head, handcuffed to two bedposts. And so many more Danisha didn't have the stomach to look at. *Who is this man I'm in love with?*

Now she was sweating. Couldn't breathe. Then she thought, *fuck this. Since when have you allowed fear to get in your way?* And then she was furious.

She hadn't brought a flash drive. *Okay, don't panic. What would Justine do? She'd improvise. I don't have a flash drive but I do have my laptop. All I need is a USB cable…*and she'd just seen one in Alessandro's desk drawers. Problem solved. She took her own MacBook Air from her bag, connected the two computers, and started to copy all of his photos to her laptop.

The entire process took twelve agonizing minutes. When it was finally complete, Danisha closed both computers, returned Alessandro's to its drawer, then put her computer back in her bag.

Sitting back, she tried to control her rage. "Long slow breaths," she told herself. Except what she wanted more than anything at that moment was to vomit. *So many contradictions. So many lies.* All this time he'd told her that he loved her, so why all these pictures? Was he a sex addict? Had he actually fucked any of these women or were they merely his fluffers? Would she ever know the truth?

Calm yourself down woman! She focused on her breath, visualized a flowering meadow and crisp blue sky. Her pulse slowed. Her mind cleared.

She looked at the clock. Twenty minutes had passed since she walked in the building. Miguel-at-the-desk would know how much time she'd spent up there, might wonder what she was doing. No one needed twenty minutes to pick up one thing.

She hiked up her skirt, spread her legs, put her fingers on the part of her thong that covered her pussy, and, with her middle finger, pushed the fabric into her vagina. She stood up, pulled off her thong, and dropped it onto Alessandro's desk. *That ought to distract him when he gets back.* And it explained what she did with her extra time. Men stop thinking with their brains when they start thinking with their dicks.

As she pulled into her driveway, still reeling with anger and shock, she realized that in her excitement-slash-confusion at finding Alessandro's secret computer, she'd completely forgotten to look for a sample of his DNA.

CHAPTER 34

Justine wanted to enjoy her last solo stroll along the water before heading back to training. She wanted to *revel* in it, to be perfectly present in the moment. But her pain had a mind of its own. Her spine and chest and every perceptible muscle of her body silently begged her to get back to Big Sur, to the healing hot springs. To Don.

She hoped he'd be there. How long can a top secret national security mission last for a guy like Don anyway? Then again, if he did make it back sooner rather than later the sting of her failures would still be fresh. *Let a few days pass,* she thought, *and he won't care so much that I fucked up so badly with Alyssa.* Just in case he did get back early Justine prepared a mental list of every little thing she'd gotten right.

I kept my client from getting attacked. I subdued two huge meathead rivals. The client wasn't really hurt when I choked her out. The press loves the story. My client can now triple her fee for her next movie. Her agents and managers love me. She loves me, for chrissake. She considers me her new best friend.

No matter how she tried to spin it, though, Justine knew she'd fucked up. Bad. Still, her return to the cabin in Big Sur brought an enormous sense of relief. As soon as she walked through the door and unloaded her gear, she tore off her clothes, grabbed the terrycloth robe and hobbled down the steps to the hot springs.

Just the smell of the water was enough to lift her spirits and take the edge off her aches and bruises. She hung the robe on a hook and stepped under the waterfall they called the shower. As the warm water and soap washed away her sweat and anguish, Justine began to feel at home again. She told herself that if she was ever going to be able to relax and start healing, she'd have to stop worrying about any eventual Don debriefing.

She turned on the Jacuzzi pumps that Don had installed into nature's hot springs and stepped into the swirling water. Powerful jets of hot mineral water pummeled her back. Within minutes Justine felt her muscles de-tense, her breath became deeper. Finally, she allowed herself to close her eyes and think of absolutely nothing. But then she *felt* it.

Her eyes still closed, Justine's rapidly developing sixth sense told her she was not alone. *A coyote maybe?* She scoured her memory for facts about the wild animals of California as she slowly opened her eyes and lifted her arms and hands to defend herself against whatever was sharing the cave with her. When she saw that there was a man sitting in the pool beside her, and that man was Don. She screamed, or laughed, depending on who was the interpreter.

"You scared me!" she scolded him, as she wrapped a towel around her body.

"I didn't scare you. You allowed yourself to be scared. I'm no threat to you."

"What kind of answer is that? What are you doing here? I thought you were working on a national security threat?"

"Alyssa called me. She's extremely worried about your injuries."

"Is she okay?"

"Alyssa? She's fine. The Malibu cops, on the other hand, couldn't handle the mob of reporters so I moved her to a safe house."

"Safe house? Oh my god, I'm so sorry."

"No apologies necessary. It's standard procedure. As I said, Alyssa is fine. Trust me, the safe house is up to the lady's standards. I'm more concerned about you, which is why I'm here. Let's get out of this water so I can check your injuries."

With gentle probing fingers, Don examined Justine's back and sternum. "No broken bones, just some bruises. Rest here, use the Vasper, and you'll heal in no time."

She took a deep breath to gather her nerve. "It didn't go as I expected."

Justine had never heard Don laugh so loud. "I got the Google alerts."

"I'm sorry. I screwed up."

"I didn't know you had such mastery of understatement," Don said, still laughing. Then he put a hand on her shoulder and said, "All's well that ends well."

"Wait, what?" Justine exhaled in relief. "I thought you were going to tear me a new one."

"Everyone makes mistakes. If we're lucky, our mistakes will teach us to push ourselves beyond our limits. In our line of work, events never go as planned, which is why we plan for all kinds of contingencies. And even then we sometimes have to improvise in the moment. You improvised quite well, and you accomplished your objectives."

Justine was both surprised and gracious. "Wow. Thanks for noticing. And thank you for being so nice to me."

"Perhaps I sent you off to battle a little too soon, before you were fully trained. But I've learned not to second-guess myself. There's no profit in that. You were my best option for protecting Alyssa for what should have been an easy dress fitting. Now we need to get on with your after-action debriefing. Did you read my briefing on your way to the fitting?"

"What briefing?"

"On your cellphone."

"Too busy dealing with Alyssa. I didn't have time."

"What do you mean you didn't have time? Prioritize your attention. Always. While the driver was doing *his* job, you should have been doing *yours*. Your job is to protect Alyssa so you have to be aware of every potential threat. Does she have allergies? What is her blood type? Who are her rivals? What was the external layout of the boutique? Where were the closest emergency rooms, police and fire stations? All the answers were in the briefing. I gave it to you for a reason."

Justine looked straight into Don's eyes. "I apologize, I should have read it on the way to the fitting. I will next time…if you give me a next time…please…"

"You've just learned another excellent lesson. I'm sorry you had to learn it the hard way, and I'm sure it'll happen again. Human nature. Now, as soon as you saw the paparazzi at the main entrance, what should you have done?"

"I thought Alyssa wanted them there. Isn't any publicity good publicity?"

"That's not an answer. You're not her publicist. You're her security. If you had read the advance work, you'd have known all the entrances and exits to the boutique, so you could've told the driver to circle, you could've picked the most secure entrance with the fewest paparazzi. Better yet, you could have had him drop you off a block away and then sneak in the lowest-risk entry. Had you read the briefing you would have known the layout of the fitting rooms and the entrances and exits. You could have secured them all."

Justine looked down, embarrassed. "I fucked up."

"Well, yes and no. You were a beginner but now you have some experience and hindsight."

Justine stepped back into the water and immersed herself, hoping maybe she'd dissolve, or at least her shame would. Being CEO of a multimillion-dollar company was a far easier job than this one.

But both her shame and Don were still there when she re-emerged. "Justine," he said in a tone that was at once firmer, but kind, "you exhibited a grace under pressure that was nothing short of remarkable. Your used your physical and mental skills to protect Alyssa without seriously harming her assailants. Like I said before—we learn from our mistakes."

"That's very kind of you to say, and I thank you."

"I wasn't trying to be kind. That was honesty. Now, let's move on. You will recover. We will protect Alyssa," he said with an encouraging smile. "In the meantime," he said, "you still have to wait while your bruises are healing."

"Can't I go on a vacation to heal?"

"Evil doesn't stop, so neither can we."

"I just got slammed by six-hundred pounds of Candace's bodyguards. I hurt all over."

"Your trigger fingers still work. Practice with them."

CHAPTER 35

Ajit Pandeek was one of those guys that could change your life, for better or for worse, with a few strokes on a computer keyboard. He knew his way around the hardware as well as the software of any device with a chip. Every major company in Silicon Valley had tried to recruit him while he was still a student at the India Institute of Technology in Mumbai. But Ajit wasn't interested in living and working in a community of geeks; he liked girls too much, so he'd only considered offers from companies in New York City and anywhere in Southern California. When he got the offer from the head of IT at Sony Pictures he was intrigued. When he met Danisha during his interview process there, he was sold.

Danisha needed him more than she'd realized. In the eighteen months or so since he'd started working at Sony Pictures, she'd kept him busy writing—or tweaking—code for design programs, 3D printing, and anything else she could think of. He didn't mind; he would do anything for her and she knew it. Before she met Alessandro, Danisha even had a crush on Ajit. She'd slept with him twice, the first time in a moment of weakness and the second in genuine gratitude, which made Ajit both loyal to her and jealous of Alessandro. She debated whether or not to show him the files she'd found on Alessandro's computer, but in the end the decision was easy.

As soon as everyone else had left the building at the end of the work day, Danisha walked across the hallway to Ajit's office and knocked on the door. He immediately opened the door. She quickly explained what she needed to do.

"What project do you have for me? You have my undivided attention."

"I bet I will, especially when you see my, um, subject matter. By the way, this is personal, not business. For me I mean. We both know you're a porn addict, so I want you to examine some porn for me."

Ajit sat down in front of the computer. Danisha pressed a few of the keyboard buttons.

"Tell me about *these* files," she said as she opened the file with Alessandro's photos.

"Whoa! That's Allie McCain! She got out of the business a year or so ago. God, could she suck—oops, I'm sorry. There's Tiffany Jewels! She vanished three months ago. Where'd you find all these? They were never on my computer."

Danisha nudged Ajit aside and took control of his keyboard, typing *Allie McCain* into the search bar. In less than a second a list of at least two-dozen movie files appeared on the screen. She clicked on the first one and watched for about thirty seconds. "This Allie chick sure is a deep-throating sword swallower. That's the correct term, right?"

"It'll do, yeah," Ajit answered.

"Now who are the rest of these bitches?"

Ajit knew about half of the women in the photos by their screen names. "Porn is a huge business. Did you know that porn sites get more traffic than any other sector?

"Fascinating."

"Did you know that most teen-age boys whack off twice a day or more watching porn that's illegal for them to view?"

"Still fascinating. Can you answer my question or not? Who are the rest of these naked-ass bitches?" Danisha was losing patience.

"Move over. Lemme see something. The girls I recognize haven't been seen in a new film for a while. Some of them more than a year. I wanna check the national registry for missing persons."

As Ajit's fingers flew over the keyboard, the screen filled with pictures of faces that matched the ones in Alessandro's file. But these missing-persons photos were nothing like the glamorous shots of the porn starlets. "You see, you've got to wake up pretty early to fool my facial recognition software."

"What's going on?" Danisha asked, feeling both intrigued and appalled.

Ajit shrugged as if to suggest that the answer was simple. "You know —you've been around the entertainment business for a while. A lot of young, innocent girls come to Hollywood to become stars, even though there're already fifty thousand unemployed actors in LA. Some arrive with no savings. Others get ripped off by greedy managers and agents. Most just return home broke and disillusioned. They're the lucky ones. Others turn to stripping, hooking, or porn. Some get strung out on drugs and need their fixes. The easiest way to do that is by opening their mouths or spreading their legs."

"Yeah, I always *see something* in the news now. I know all this shit."

"That's New York. Hollywood is just as bad, maybe worse. Girls want to make it here, they gotta put out. It's an ugly business. Girls just vanish with no trace. Some of them as young as twelve. Where'd you get these files?"

"Tell me about the other files. The pictures in, say, Tiffany's file. You said she just disappeared? Recently?"

"About a year ago, yeah." Ajit opened the file. It started out with ordinary headshots, then became more and more sexually explicit, evolving into bondage photos of Tiffany in apparent agony. "I'm afraid she's really in a lotta pain here," Ajit said, "because she was a terrible actress."

"Then why'd you watch her?"

"Why do you think? Look at the size of her tits! I mean breasts."

"Just speak the truth. No filters."

Ajit looked at the bondage photos again.

"Here's the thing. Tiffany could take three men on simultaneously, and she play-acted like she enjoyed it, but you could tell she really didn't. Here she's really getting hurt and not even pretending to like it."

"What does all of this mean?"

"Either these files came from a cop, an investigative reporter, or an ST."

"What's an ST?"

"Sex trafficker. Let's say an independent producer holds an audition for new talent. He asks some agents he knows—and probably pays off —to send some desperate actresses, then he takes photos and short video clips to see how much they'll show and how far they'll go. He'll ask them if they want to party. If they do, he'll drug 'em, fuck 'em, and then never give them any role. Or, if they're hot enough, he'll put them in some porn clips. Dozens of girls come to these auditions, and they all get naked."

"How do you know all of this?"

"I was asked to do a little editing on a few films." Danisha gave him a hard look and he shrugged again. "Hey, it was *free, fresh* porn."

"So you moonlight in porn and still have porn on my company's computer?"

"Dani, I'm a sex addict. At least I'm not a junkie or a pedophile, right?" Danisha showed no response. "And I'd never hurt anyone. Ever. The only person I'm hurting, I suppose, is me." Still nothing from Danisha. "So where'd you get these files? Isn't your boyfriend a producer? Whoa, wait! These are *his* files!"

Danisha blanched and turned away.

"Damn, I'm good! I figured it out, right? Dani?"

"That's enough," Danisha said. Trying desperately not to cry, she focused on the motion of Ajit's fingers on his keyboard.

"Looks like he runs a website on the Dark Web," he announced a minute or so later.

"A website? Does it have a name?"

"*Aqua Blu Shadows*. Pretty, don't you think? Hey, you wanna really do some digging?"

Danisha nodded, reluctantly.

"I'm keying into the metadata on Tiffany's file. Some other encrypted files are embedded in the photos as well," Ajit explained. "Now, I will launch a few of my handy-dandy National Security Agency decryption algorithms." Within seconds a long series of numbers flashed on the screen. "Oh, shit..."

Danisha asked, "What 'oh shit'? What do those numbers mean?"

"There was an online auction for Tiffany. It closed the day before Christmas, last year. Client number two-four-three won the bid. One hundred twenty grand, U.S. He—that's an educated guess, I've never seen a woman involved with this stuff, not on the business side anyway —he deposited sixty grand as soon as he won her, then another sixty when she was delivered on New Year's Eve. Looks like client number one-seven-one was the second closest bidder at one-hundred-fifteen thousand. You wanna hear about the other bids?"

"Are you shitting me?"

"So. We know that client one-seven-one likes this type of girl. He was willing to pay up to one-hundred-fifteen thousand dollars for her, so your ST is gonna search for a similar girl to sell to him, at probably a slightly higher price since he'll be pissed that he did a snooze-and-lose on this girl. Clever marketing strategy, actually." Dani shot him some serious shade. "If you disregard the product, that is."

"This is the bookkeeping of a sex slaver? What happens to the girls afterward?"

"Who knows? And really, who even cares? I mean, I care, of course, but the public in general? The CIA released a report, not too long ago, that said something like fifty thousand women are smuggled into the U.S. every year. Most of them vanish. What happens in Eastern Europe and Asia? Even worse. At best, your boyfriend—if he's involved, I mean —is just helping worn-out porn stars get some overseas work."

"He's my fucking fiancé, and he *can't* be involved. Something's wrong with this picture. With all these pictures."

"Right. Fiancé. Wait, what? You got engaged?" Sorry, back to business. Let's see...I don't really know what happened to Tiffany but," Ajit's fingers worked the keyboard, "if I enter the reverse encryption algorithms, I should be able to get the information..."

Another photo appeared on his screen, this one of a cute redhead. "She's only twelve," Ajit sighed. "Or rather, she *was*. This auction was three days after Tiffany's." He turned away from the screen to stare at the wall.

"What?"

"Look, I admit to being a porn addict. But I'm not a pedophile. I guess client two-four-three got tired of his bleach-blonde, fucked-every-way-imaginable Tiffany, disposed of her and wanted a red-headed virgin. Little Orphan Annie here sold for three hundred thousand dollars. Red hair is the rarest hair color in the world, highly prized in the Middle East and Southeast Asia. Of course, in Japan red hair is considered the sign of the devil. But real blondes are the gold standard for sex slavers. And these guys check the pubic hair roots to make sure."

"I think I'm gonna puke." Danisha said. She started crying, first for these young women, and then for herself, for falling in love with Alessandro.

"I wonder what he's done with all of this money? He's probably made tens of millions! I'm gonna do some research, follow the money trail."

"Please. Stop. Make it all just fucking *stop*." She sat back and started to sob.

"Dani?" Ajit said, concerned now at her sudden outburst at emotion. He put his hand on her shoulder in an effort to comfort her. "I'm sorry, I was…"

"Don't you understand? I fell in love with Alessandro. I…I'm carrying his baby."

"Oh. No. I had no idea. Dani, this is totally effed up."

"That motherfucker! I'm gonna kill him." Lightning bolts of rage coursed through every cell of Danisha's body, and then she went stone cold.

"Dani?" Ajit said quietly, "Are you okay?"

"Of course I'm not fucking *okay*, Ajit. What kind of idiotic question is that?" She stood up and kicked her chair over. "I'm furious," she shouted as she kicked the overturned chair. "Humiliated." She kicked it again. "Enraged!"

"Dani? You're scaring me."

"Am I? Are you seriously scared of me right now, Ajit?" She picked up a small screwdriver-like tool from the cup of pens on his desk. "Because right now I seriously feel like taking this," she looked at the tool, confused, "whatever the fuck it is…"

"Philips head screwdriver. For the motherboard…"

"…and shoving it in that motherfucker's eyeball! Then I'd find another *tool*, and flay the motherfucker."

"Dani, we might be getting ahead of ourselves here."

"How do you figure that, Ajit? We don't have enough evidence with the disappearing porn stars?"

"Well, *maybe*? Just maybe there's another explanation?"

"Yeah? Like what?"

"I dunno. I mean, we need to find out who he really is, right? If you could maybe get his fingerprints somehow? I could run a legit background check."

"I can do that," Danisha said, her rage giving way to excitement. She grabbed her bag. "My girlfriend works for some super secret private security company. She told me to find something with his fingerprints and DNA. I totally flaked on the DNA but I did find this," she said, fishing the zip-locked orange juice glass from her purse. "I followed standard CSI procedure, wore gloves and everything. The glass has to have his fingerprints, right?"

Ajit grinned. "Nice work Veronica Mars!"

"Not sure I love the white-girl sleuth reference, but thanks?"

"What you talking about? I loved that show. Besides, she had a black side-kick, remember? Anyhow, now *I* get to play real life CSI. This is totally hot. First, I'm gonna need some water."

"As it happens," Danisha said, handing him a sealed bottle of Evian from her bag.

"Damn, Dani! What else you got in that Mary Poppins bag of yours?" Ajit said, as excited as a kid at his own birthday party. "Do you have face powder so I can lift the print?

"It costs $150 a jar. So, just use a little."

"Okay. I got a buddy downtown, works forensics for the LAPD. He owes me. Might take a while, but he'll run this sample for me. The fingerprint check I can do myself. Watch and learn, my beautiful Danisha. Watch and learn!"

Danisha sat back down to watch Ajit play crime scene investigator.

Ajit winked, and soon asked Dani to turn off the lights. Once the room was dark, he used the flashlight on his iPhone to side-illuminate the prints. "Sweet! Lookie here, Dani. An almost perfect thumbprint. Lights please, he said, as he continued to make a transfer.

"And there it is! A perfect beige-on-black thumb print." Ajit then repeated the fingerprint dusting process with the other print on the glass.

"Now what?" Danisha asked.

"Now we feed these babies to the scanner," he answered, sounding a lot like Mr. Rogers. "Then we use Photoshop. And by we, I mean me."

"Obvi."

Ajit was back at his computer, happily plugging away at his keyboard and muttering words like database, Interpol and Homeland Security.

"These are easier hacks than most people think," he muttered proudly. "Okay! We're in the California DMV fingerprint database and…"

"And?"

Ajit's fingers stopped. He leaned in to get a closer look at his screen. "One sec."

"No one sec. What did you find? Tell me. *Now*!"

"Alessandro's California driver's license and Italian passport."

"What about them?"

"Well, according to Homeland Security—they're authentic."

Danisha breathed a very audible sigh of relief. "So he's not a sex trafficker?"

"We don't know that. All we know for sure right now is that these two documents, his driver's license and passport, are legit."

"So that's good, no?"

"It's not bad. I still wanna have my buddy run the DNA. I'll bring all this *evidence* to his lab on my way home later. He'll be able to get more info for us in a few days."

"I'm not sure I want any more information."

"Dani, you most definitely want more info. But go home now. You look awful."

"Thanks a lot. But seriously, Ajit, I can't tell you how grateful I am right now.

CHAPTER 36

Danisha hadn't lied to Ajit—she was grateful for his help as well as his friendship. But the information he'd discovered, the stories—it seemed like every picture Danisha had ripped from her fiancé's secret hard drive told a more horrendous one. If she didn't stop thinking about them, at least until she could more pieces of the puzzle, if she didn't whup her thoughts into submission, she knew that her emotions would send her straight to crazyville. To accomplish that goal, Danisha needed to do a serious personal inventory. After leaving Ajit's office she fled the Sony lot and drove home on autopilot, her mind cluttered with memories of relationships past.

What was it that Lyndsey said about her track record with men? *Not so great. Disastrous, if I'm gonna be honest.*

It was time for that Come to Jesus Talk. With herself. Time to face the harsh fact of her own naivety, especially when it came to men. Ever since her Stanford days, every relationship that tasted so sweet at first soon enough went sour. Darnell and Freddie, both starters on the football team, and both two-timing egomaniacs. Jean Paul…ahh, yes, Jean Paul the gorgeous son of the Belgian ambassador. Must've learned his lying skills from his daddy, 'cause that son ofa bitch would lie about the color of his goddamn shirt. John the blue-blood WASP med student, slumming it with the undergrads, and in Danisha's case he was actually slummin' it, in his own mind anyway. Bastard had the balls to tell her that his parents wouldn't approve of him dating 'a woman of color. Even Ron, the last guy she dated in Hollywood, a successful music video director, turned out to be a punk-ass tail chaser. Danisha felt the familiar rush of bile to her chest when she thought about all the *video hoes* Ron was screwing while he professed his undying love to her, and all those wanna-be dancers with their constant offers for blow-jobs. Lindsey, who'd been on so many of those video shoots, told Danisha that Ron was a man-whore, but Danisha refused to listen. Until she caught him with his pants down, and a buxom bottle blonde on her knees with his cock in her mouth.

And now Alessandro. Danisha loved him, she was sure of that. And he loved her. Right? Just thinking about him made her want to cry again. *Oh hell no!* She told herself she was being weak, that she'd allowed herself to get soft. If ever there was a time to toughen up, this was it. She needed some inspiration, the familiar voice of a friend, someone who understood, who could feel her pain. She needed music. Loud music.

She pressed the voice command button on her steering wheel. "Play Lemonade by Beyoncé."

The solemn tone of the first song, the gospel prayer of Beyoncé's breathy, layered vocal tracks, transported Danisha to a more peaceful place. Her anguish evaporated—if only temporarily—into the familiar, hypnotic beat of the song. All thoughts of Alessandro and his vanishing porn stars ceased. As the album progressed, its range of emotions—as well as its beat—intensified. Danisha was buckled in for the ride, and her sense of peace seamlessly morphed into full-on rage. "Who the fuck do you think I am?" she screamed. *Fuck it. Beyoncé isn't sorry, why the hell should I be?*

By the time she reached her house, Danisha was ready to unload a shit-ton of pain onto her fiancé. The song *Sorry* was still playing in her head, blaring like an orphan anthem waiting to be adopted: "*Looking at my watch he shoulda been home. Today I regret the night I put that ring on. He always got them fucking excuses. I pray to the Lord you reveal what his truth is.*"

Truth. What the fuck was Alessandro's *truth*? The only way to find out was to ask him. She sat on her couch with her laptop to write him an email.

"My trusty radar is bugging out. Something about your story doesn't make sense. We need to talk as soon as you get home."

Her message wasn't as vitriolic or explicit as she'd planned, but it did get Alessandro's attention. Less than fifteen minutes after she'd pressed send, Alessandro called.

"*Cara-mia*, what is this trust radar you write about? *Non capisco*, I don't understand."

"Where are you Alessandro? You sound close."

"In Rome. Just as I told you. We have an excellent connection."

"Uh-huh. An excellent phone connection, you mean?"

"So many confusing phrases, Dani. Tell me in simple English, what's the matter?"

She looked at the clock. Eight-forty-seven. Rome was nine hours ahead of Los Angeles, so it was five-forty-seven tomorrow morning for Alessandro. If he was in Rome. "Why you up so early?" she asked him without a trace of affection.

"I have early meetings. I'm trying to finish up all my work here so I can get back to you."

Danisha softened. He sounded so genuine. So concerned about her. So sweet. "When do you think you'll be back?"

"Soon, my love. Very soon."

"No, Alessandro. That's not good enough. I'm not gonna be placated with empty promises."

"What is placate?"

Danisha sighed as she thought of a succinct definition. But then she started laughing, at herself mainly. She couldn't help it. He was so adorable. So helpless when he tried to keep up with her in English. "Can you just tell me straight when you plan to come back? I really do want to talk to you face to face. Give me a day and time. Soon is not an answer."

"Ah. I think I understand. Okay. I promise I will be on a plane by Tuesday."

"Thank you, that's all I wanted to know."

"Dani?"

"Yes Alessandro?"

"Are you sure that's all you wanted to know? You sound so upset, it can't be just about me going away."

"No. You're right. It's not just that. I…I've been…um, hearing things. Rumors mostly." She had to think quickly, couldn't let him know she'd been snooping through his desk. "Except some of it comes from people I trust. People who say they've, um, seen you…"

"Yes?"

"Out with other women."

"Ah, the actresses."

"Actresses?" *Could he have a legit reason? Was it possible?*

"I will explain when I see you, how you say, face to face?"

"Yes, Alessandro. That's how we say. Face to face."

"*Va bene.* Tuesday night then. I will explain everything. I promise you have nothing to worry about, *mi amore.*"

Danisha wasn't ready to buy his bullshit.

CHAPTER 37

Justine sat in the hot springs wishing Don were there to give her one of his Tantric massage. But he was with Alyssa. She wondered if she was jealous, had to remind herself that she had a fiancé. Of course she wanted Don, but she also wanted Scott. Scott was far better husband material than Don. Besides, for the time being, Don was her boss. Any businesswoman worth her stock options knew better than to mix business with pleasure.

So what about all those orgasmic massages? What's your rationalization for that stroll on the wild side?

Justine shook off those thoughts as she walked from the hot springs to the cabin. The air felt different up here. Cooler maybe, or lighter. It smelled different too, conjured sense memories of physical extremes; working her muscles and brain to the point of exhaustion, aching muscles, jostled bones, and the calm tranquility of the hot springs, the welcome relief of the showers.

That's exactly what she needed to facilitate her transition from alert protection detail to recovering killer-with-a-conscience; a quick dip in the mineral springs followed by an afternoon nap.

She was deep into a REM cycle of her nap when the voice invaded her dream. "You have a critical e-mail," it told her. Her dreaming self didn't care about a critical e-mail, didn't care about anything except the hands of the dream-man on her aching shoulders. But the voice was persistent. And kind of obnoxious.

"But I don't wanna wake up," she whined, hiding her head under a pillow.

"You have a critical email." It was a man's voice. Justine moved the pillow so she could hear it better. "You have a critical email." A computer-generated male voice.

She looked around to find the source, a speaker tucked into the ceiling. "What? How did I not know about you, speaker?" *Great. I've been here alone for less than two hours and already I'm talking to myself.*

"All your communications devices are activated."

Justine hollered at the speaker, "Who are you?" then wrapped herself in the comforter and rolled over to grab her iPad from her purse. She opened her mailbox to find dozens of e-mails. One of them was blinking. It was from Lily Marshall , marked URGENT, in all caps.

"Who are you?" Justine asked again. "And why are you reading my e-mails?"

"Your lack of cyber security must not compromise the integrity of our networks," the voice answered impatiently.

"And your lack of answers to my one single question is pissing me off!"

Still no response.

"Hello?"

Again, silence.

"Fine. Be that way. I have an urgent email to read," Justine said, turning her attention back to her iPad. She opened Lily's e-mail to find the photo of a young girl. *Huh, she kinda looks like me when I was thirteen. That's so cute. But why would Lily send me a picture of a girl that looks like me and mark it urgent?* She scrolled down below the photo and read Lily's message:

> *Justine, see amber alert below. Witness ID'd your sketch artist's drawing of the man who attacked you as a prime suspect in Gemma's abduction. Be alert, Lily.*

> **AMBER ALERT 13 yr old Gemma Rutlidge abducted 3:18 p.m. Palo Alto Middlefield & Forest; 5 ft 4 in 100 lbs blonde hair blue eyes blue jean shorts white tank top blue zippered sweatshirt; suspect vehicle white van CA 7W???3 Suspect black hair 6 ft 200 lbs bandage/cast left arm.**

Justine flopped back onto the futon, closed her eyes, and buried her head in her hands. In a flash, she relived the night of the attack—Scott naked and unconscious, cuffed to the banister, the glistening edge of her assailant's knife, his foul breath and disgusting threats. Her eyes filled with tears as she imagined the horrors that same fiend might inflict on an innocent, defenseless young girl. If she'd allowed Iya and Eniko to kill that monster, if she hadn't been such a fucking *humanitarian,* Gemma would be safe at home—that is *if* her monster was the same one that abducted poor Gemma.

She looked at the email again. Gemma had been kidnapped four hours ago. Don had briefed her on the rudimentary facts of child kidnappings during one of their many client protection study sessions. One fact flashed in her head; seventy-five percent of child victims are murdered within three hours.

Justine brushed the tears from her eyes, grabbed her cell phone, and called her mother. "Damn it, Lise! Answer your damn phone, for fuck sake," she screamed when she heard the familiar voice mail recording. The second she hung up her phone rang again. She answered without looking at the caller ID.

"Lise?"

"No, it's Lily."

"Oh my god, Lily. That poor girl. Please tell me you're calling with good news."

"Well, I do have news. There's been a break in Gemma's case—a big one. We had state and local law enforcement checking out every white van within a fifty-mile radius of Gemma's abduction. They had a report of one with a seven in its tag spotted on your street. The driver sped off when he spotted the patrol car, and they lost him in traffic. They did find the van about ten minutes later, parked near the Stanford Shopping Center, empty. He'd taken off on foot, so he's still at large. My first thought was to check your house. I'm afraid we found Gemma's body in your bed."

"Oh, no."

"Justine? I need you to listen to me now, this is important. I'm absolutely sure that the perp is the same guy that attacked you."

"That poor girl. Her poor mother. How's her mother ever going to live after this?"

"Justine? You need to go into witness protection."

"I'm not going into witness protection, Lily."

"Where are you now?"

Justine hesitated to answer, thinking about the voice in the ceiling. "I'm safe."

"With the man of Nepenthe?"

"Something like that," Justine said, her voice breaking with the effort to hold back a river of tears. "All I can see is that poor girl, dead. In my bed." She started to sob.

"There's nothing you could have done," Lily said, trying to reassure her.

But Justine knew better. There was something she could have done. She had the chance to stop the fiend that killed this poor girl. She had him at her mercy. She could have—no, she *should* have slaughtered the fucking monster.

CHAPTER 38

Alessandro made it back to Los Angeles two days earlier than promised. He called Danisha very late on Saturday night—or rather, very early Sunday morning.

"Cara mia! Im just about to board my flight at *Fiumicino*. How 'bout I take you to brunch tomorrow?" he said when she finally answered her phone.

"Alessandro? What time is it?"

"For me is nine on Sunday morning. For you, is still Saturday night. Did I wake you, *amore?*"

Danisha looked at the clock on the screen of her phone. "Yeah. It's midnight here. I've been working nonstop, fell asleep a few hours ago, I guess. You're coming home?" Her heart started to pound, she didn't know if that was out of fear or excited anticipation. Probably both.

Falling back to sleep was difficult, but somehow she managed to doze off before dawn. Her heart was still pounding when her doorbell rang at two the next afternoon. Seeing Alessandro standing there with his suitcase, looking happy and handsome, Danisha forgot about the laptop she'd found in his desk. She threw her arms around his neck and kissed every inch of his exquisite face. She couldn't help herself.

They never made it to brunch. The first thing he said was he wanted to talk, tell her the truth about his businesses. All his businesses. She didn't even have to ask.

They sat on her patio. It was one of those perfect mid-winter Southern California afternoons. The sun hovered over the Pacific and a few white clouds floated lazily in the bright blue sky. Danisha was both starving and nauseated from her pregnancy, news she still hadn't shared with Alessandro.

"Dani," he said with a heartfelt sincerity. "I adore you. You must know this. You are the *only* woman I want. The only woman I need. If any of your spies…"

"Hey!"

Alessandro shot her one of his wicked-charm smiles to let her know he was kidding. His blue eyes sparkled. Dani was done. "Any woman seen with me was, how do they say here…ah, yes, *talent*."

A niggling voice in the back of her head told Danisha that he was lying. He didn't even look jetlagged. *Keep it together, girl. Ask a question, he's in answer mode now.* "Why do you have lunch meetings at Hollywood hotspots with *talent?*"

"I find them jobs overseas."

"What jobs overseas?"

"Dani, you know how it is here with the actresses. They come because in their home town, how you say, Peoria?" Dani smiled and nodded. He'd already learned the old Peoria cliché. "So. She's the prettiest girl in Peoria. Everyone says she should be in the movies. So she comes to Hollywood. Hurray for Hollywood. But once they get here, they are alone. So much competition, so many other beautiful girls from the other small towns. I don't know any of the names. Kansas maybe?"

Dani laughed out loud. "That doesn't matter, keep talking Sandro."

"Yes. So very soon, she's broke. Can't find a job. Has to pay for singing lessons, acting lessons. You know, you see them all the time. Tens of thousands of them are here, but less than a thousand of them make money acting. *Ma*, some, if they get very lucky, maybe make a commercial or find some work as a face in the crowd, how you call that job?"

"An extra?"

"*Va bene, si.* extra. That work might pay for the singing lesson, but it doesn't pay the rent."

"You're not telling me anything I don't already know, Sandro."

"Yes, I'm getting to that. You see, there are lots of overseas jobs for American actresses, even if they've just performed minor roles on American or even Canadian TV. So. I find for them work. They get paid for acting. Doing what they want to do. For this I get a fee."

"A fee? Like an agent?"

"*Esatto*! Ten percent. Just like an agent. My connections overseas, the producers, they treat my clients like goddesses. They don't even have the expenses for the living. No rent. No groceries. They can save money, go back to their hometowns and say they worked in movies if they want to, marry a hometown boy, have kids, and do all of those normal things."

Danisha considered the details of the story her fiancé was telling her. They did jibe with what Ajit's information, but what about all those S&M and bondage pictures? No way could she let him know that she'd seen those, but the fact they existed at all still disturbed her.

"What is it Dani? You look, *come si dice*, worrying?"

"Um, it's a lot to take in, I guess.

Alessandro leaned over and kissed her gently. "*Capisco.* Tomorrow I introduce you to Samantha."

"Samantha?"

"My talent."

"You mean client?"

"If you wish. She recently returned from a big job in Dubai and wants to take me to lunch at Spago's to thank me. Of course I told her no."

"Why?"

"Because Spago is passé! Nobody goes there anymore, only tourists. So we will go to Capo instead. In Santa Monica. I call her now, see if she can go with us tomorrow."

"You're taking me on your lunch date?"

"Not date. *Client.* And yes of course I'm taking you. Samantha has wanted to meet you ever since the first time I mentioned you, after our first date. Besides, she can afford to feed us both many, many lunches. And dinners. She married a billionaire prince and is a *very* rich woman now. A true rags to riches American fairy-tale."

"Prince of what?"

"I don't know," his hands moved at a breakneck pace, as though they fueled the engine of his memory. "His name is Nawaf Bin something or other…I don't remember exactly right now, jetlag…"

"Ah, you should probably rest. What time is it for you now?"

"Doesn't matter. All you really need to know about Nawaf is that he's the heir to one of the largest oil exporting families in the Middle East."

Danisha's thoughts bounced from trust to suspicion. Her nature was trusting, naïve some would say, as she tended to look for the safest resolution to any conflict. She tried to shrug off the ominous thoughts that had been haunting her, wanting more than anything to believe Alessandro.

"Now, I confess, I used to play around...until I met you," Alessandro said, taking her hands in his. He kissed each of her fingers. "You are the most wonderful, beautiful, brilliant, accomplished woman I've ever met. You're also the sexiest. Even now that you have the extra kilo or two."

"I beg your pardon?" Danisha was aghast. The same niggling voice that a few minutes earlier told her he was lying had more influence when it told her not to tell him about her pregnancy. She didn't think she was showing yet. But was she?

"*Ma*, Dani, I do not criticizing. You were maybe too skinny before, no? Happiness can make us comfortable, no? You look more *comfortable* to me. That is what I want to say."

"Comfortable?"

"Dani, come to me, *mi amore*." He stood up, walked around the table and scooped her into his arms. "You have total control of me. You've given me the most intense pleasure of my life, and the most happiness. Now, we go to the bedroom, yes?"

Danisha let go of any lingering doubts, buried her face in his neck and inhaled his scent. "To the bedroom," she whispered in his ear. "*Certamente che si.*"

Alessandro grabbed Danisha's hair then threw her onto the bed. Shocked at his sudden aggressive passion, she submitted as he pulled off her yoga pants and top. When he used her bra and panties to tie her arms to her headboard posts, she felt both frightened, and excited. She didn't fight back.

Without removing his own clothes, Alessandro kissed Danisha with unprecedented passion. Her heart pounded in apprehension, her tongue and lips intertwined with his. She needed to touch him, tear his clothes off and wrap her arms around his torso, to pull his face to hers and hold onto his cock. The dual sensation of pain and pleasure gave way to frustration.

"Untie me," she purred. He didn't respond. "'Sandro, please. I can't make love like this." Still no response. Finally she yelled, "Stop!"

This time Alessandro listened. Rising to his knees, he freed her from her bondage, then pinned her arms as he gently kissed her face and neck. "I love you," he whispered. "I love you. You are mine. Forever."

"I love you, Sandro."

CHAPTER 39

Danisha walked into Capo on Alessandro's arm. The place was packed, and every head in the room turned to watch as they walked by. Both had the dreamy, slightly unfocused eyes of spent lovers. Danisha thought she recognized a gorgeous redhead sitting alone at a corner table. "Isn't that what's-her-name?" she whispered to Alessandro. "The actress that starred in the TV series about the mixed-race family in Iowa?"

"Another reason why I love you so, you have such a good eye." Alessandro led Danisha directly to the actress, then pulled out one of the chairs at the table and motioned for her to sit. "Danisha, allow me to introduce you to my dear friend, Samantha Addams. Samantha, this is the woman I've told you about, my beautiful fiancé, Danisha."

"Of course I recognize you," Danisha said graciously, "from your show. What's it called?"

"Doesn't matter," Samantha answered with a huge smile. "It was canceled over a year ago. It's such a pleasure to meet you. Miss Howard. An honor actually."

"Danisha, please. I'm sorry to hear that the show was canceled. I thought it would go on forever."

"So did I," Samantha said, laughing. Then she stood up and gave Alessandro a warm, full-body hug, before turning to Danisha. "I absolutely adore that dress. And the rest of you! No wonder you stole Alessandro's heart. He's told me so much about you."

A waiter opened the bottle of champagne that was chilling in an ice bucket beside the table. He filled three chilled flutes, bowed silently and departed.

"I see you ordered the Krug Brut, my favorite."

"Only the best for you, Alessandro."

"But so expensive! I would have been happy with Perrier."

"You know I don't care about money. Not any more." She raised her glass to her two guests. "To the dreamer who made my fairy tale come true! Because of you I'm living my dream. I married a handsome, glamorous prince. I feel like a twenty-first century, red-headed Grace Kelly!"

"And you look like one, too," Alessandro said. He clinked his glass to hers. Danisha thought she saw him wink. "*Tanti auguri!*"

"*Tanti auguri!*" the women repeated.

They ordered the seafood platter lunch, which they ate while Samantha entertained them with stories of culture shock and the many wonders of Dubai.

Once the seafood carcasses were cleared Samantha took out her cell phone. "Dani, can I call you that?" Danisha nodded. "You have to see these pictures. I started a foundation for the illegitimate children of sex workers in the Emirates. We provide education and a hot meal to the older ones, but the babies. Just look. They're so adorable. And so grateful." She scrolled though photos of children of various nationalities opening presents, eating French fries, hamburgers and ice cream. She stopped at one image of Alessandro surrounded by laughing kids. "Look how they adore him."

"Alessandro!" Danisha said with genuine admiration. "Why did you never tell me about these children? All the work you do for them, I never knew."

As they were leaving the restaurant Samantha turned to Danisha. The look on her face was serious. Danisha braced herself for the worst.

"If Alessandro hadn't taken me under his wing, I would have never met my prince. But you don't have to worry about meeting princes. You already captured the heart of the most wonderful man in the world—besides my husband of course," Samantha said with a light laugh. "Alessandro is the very definition of Prince Charming."

Danisha smiled as she fought back her tears. She'd actually considered leaving him. "Excuse me," she said, turning to dab the corners of her eyes.

She didn't see Alessandro slip Samantha a wad of hundred-dollar bills, or take Samantha's phone—the same phone with the pictures of the adoring children—and slip it into his own pocket as he opened the door of the limo he'd rented for her. So when Alessandro kissed Samantha good-bye, Danisha thought nothing of it.

CHAPTER 40

As a kid, Ajit taught himself the basics of computer programming. Before he started high school he'd progressed far beyond the basics, all the way to world-class coder, which, as any tech-geek knows, is code for hacker. He was always intrigued by the idea of hacking, but it wasn't until he was in university that he understood that hacking wasn't something people just do for the heck of it; they have to have a reason, a goal.

He'd learned a lot from American television shows, preferring the complex dramas like *Criminal Minds*, *CSI*, and *Numbers*. He loved the IT nerds, the guy or gal—on American shows it could go either way—the technical analyst or forensic specialist or software engineer who saved the day while sitting at a computer screen analyzing data. He wanted to *be* one of those guys. While still a student in Mumbai he applied for IT positions with every intelligence agency in the US. The NSA and FBI wanted him, and, since they only hired American citizens, offered to expedite his immigration and naturalization papers. But then the offers from the private sector started rolling in, and they were simply too lucrative to ignore. Besides, no government agency in any country would let him get away with watching porn, at work or at home.

Danisha's dilemma worried Ajit, but it also rekindled his old dream of playing real a life CSI data analyst. He took the juice glass Danisha had so carefully lifted from her sleazy boyfriend's apartment to his friend at the LAPD forensics lab, who was able to get a pretty decent DNA sample. Using his home computers, Ajit ran that info through international demographic databases. The process was slow and tedious, and while he waited for a hit, which could take up to a week, he used the supercomputing power of the Sony Pictures mainframe to dig into the life of Alessandro Stellini.

The picture Ajit uncovered wasn't pretty. He dreaded telling Danisha; for some inconceivable reason she was in love with the sleaze bucket. When she came to his office late Monday afternoon, he almost didn't want to tell her the truth, but he cared too much about her to keep her in the dark.

"You'd better sit down," he told her as she walked through his door.

"Why, am I showing so much already?'

"What? No, you...I mean, you're..." This was going to be tougher than he'd anticipated. She looked so happy. She was literally *glowing*.

"Chill out AJ, I'm just kidding. Kinda. What did you find out about Alessandro?"

"You really do look beautiful, Dani. I'm sorry to be the party pooper here, but your boyfriend..."

"Fiancé," Danisha corrected him.

"Dani, please. Just sit down and listen to me."

She sat in the chair facing him. "Okay, shoot. Tell me what you got."

"Your fiancé is a money launderer. He uses an unregulated private bank in the US to transfer funds to the Bahamas. That money then goes to Switzerland where it disappears into the Dark Web. I was able to trace most of it to Dubai. On top of that, his name and many organizations linked to him showed up on the Panama Papers."

"Wait, what?"

"The Panama Papers. You know, the dude that hacked that Panamanian law firm's financial and legal records of all their shady clients with secret offshore companies and then leaked more than eleven million documents to the international press?"

"I know what the Panama Papers are, Ajit. What do they have to do with Alessandro?"

"He's dirty, Danisha. Financially, he's a major player in a vast system of crime and corruption. The Panama Papers are just the tip of that proverbial iceberg."

"You run IT for the creative department of a major film studio. What the fuck do you know about money laundering?"

Ajit did his best to ignore her nasty tone. "I was also able to track all of his, um merchandise. You really should come over here and look at the screen. I found more pictures."

Mesmerized and horrified, Danisha watched Ajit as he scanned through what seemed like hundreds of photos, mostly of very young girls.

"This is disgusting," she told him. "I knew about these already. He explained it to me, the whole business. Most of them are street kids, runaways. Or former porn stars looking for work overseas."

Ajit came to a folder marked *DH*. When he clicked on it, Danisha saw thumbnails of hundreds of photos of herself naked. She leaned in to get a closer look. "What the hell? That looks like me."

"That *is* you. See the links?"

Beside maybe every third or fourth picture was a link to web page. "Yes. Do I want to see the sites they link to?"

"I've looked at all of them. You've already seen them. Or at least you've already experienced them."

"Don't speak in fucking *koans*, Ajit. Just tell me what's there."

"Okay, first of all I'm Hindu not Buddhist, so I don't speak in *koans*. And second, they link to videos of you having sex with your, um, fiancé."

"Bullshit." Danisha pushed Ajit off his chair and clicked on a link.

"You really don't want to do that," Ajit said, springing back in an effort to protect her from herself.

But he was too late. Watching a video clip of an engorged cock pumping in and out of her own mouth. She gagged, too shocked to speak. Ajit handed her a bottle of sparkling water. She took a swig.

"There's more. A lot more. You strong enough to see this?" She shook her head no. "I gotta say, I know this isn't the most sensitive thing to say to you right now, but I've watched a lot of porn, and you're pretty fucking hot."

"Fuck you, Ajit. Turn that shit off." She pushed herself away from his desk, walked over to the window, and covering her eyes, started to cry. *You are my angel,* Alessandro told her, over and over again. *You're everything I've ever wanted in a woman, a partner, a wife.*

Danisha turned and stared at Ajit. "No. He wouldn't hurt me. I don't believe it. I won't believe it. He loves me."

Ajit glanced at his screen. "There's more. It's worse. Much worse."

"What are you saying?"

Ajit's fingers took to the keyboard again.

"Here's it is."

"Here what is?"

"Your auction site."

All the blood rushed from Danisha's face. She gagged again, then staggered towards the desk and collapsed. Ajit jumped up and helped her into her chair.

"I think I'm gonna throw up," she managed to say. He looked around for an acceptable receptacle, handed her a waste bin, then went back to work on his computer.

"Dani?" he said, handing her a wad of tissues and the bottle of sparkling water.

"Yeah?"

"He set up an auction for you. It doesn't start for another six months though. I bet he's waiting until after your baby's born."

"He doesn't know about the baby yet."

"Why not?

"I dunno. Waiting for the right moment, maybe? I've only told you and Justine." Danisha buried her head in her hands for a moment to steady herself. Then she looked at Ajit and asked in her low-talking Chicago Southside talk, "Okay, how do we take this mother fucker down?"

"Danisha, he's not just dirty. He's dangerous."

"You think I don't get that? He's already destroyed me."

"I'm talking serious danger. Remember when I said he could be a sex trafficker?" Danisha nodded, but refused to show any signs of fear. "Well, he is. But it's worse than just sex traffic. He *sells* human beings. I already told you that the money ends up in Dubai," Ajit explained in his best CSI tech-guy voice. "They use a charity, ostensibly for widows and orphans in Afghanistan, Iraq and Syrian refugee camps. But this foundation? It's high up on the State Department's watch list."

"What the fuck? The State Department? Why?"

"Because it's linked to a lot of the jihadist groups, they're pretty fucking sophisticated when it comes to raising funds. They funnel funds through charities, which are basically just financial facades. To raise the amounts they need to run an illegal state, do things like bribe officials, buy weapons, build bombs, recruit suicide bombers, they sell women and girls into slavery."

"You saying my Alessandro is connected to ISIS?"

"At first I didn't see how that was possible, though it was the only thing that made sense. Then my friend came through with the DNA report."

"And?"

"And you couldn't possibly have known who he really is."

"But you do?"

"I do now, yeah. Look at this picture."

"Oh god no, no more pictures, please."

"It's not what you think. It's actually worse."

"I see why you didn't go into sales," Danisha said, scooting her chair closer to *Ajit's*. "Who's this dude? He kinda looks like a younger version of…" Danisha stared, dumbfounded, at the grainy photo on the screen.

"It is. I found it on the Interpol database. An old Syrian passport. Your fiancé isn't Italian at all. His real name, or rather his original name is Tarik Nader."

"He's an Arab?"

"Syrian father, Dutch mother. He's also on the State Department watch list. Terrorist watch list."

"Holy mother of Christ."

"Danisha? We really need to call the FBI."

"Ajit, this time you're wrong. This time I actually know something you don't. We need to call someone, that's for damn sure. But not the FBI. There's only one person I trust. The only person we're gonna call is Justine."

CHAPTER 41

Justine thought about driving up to Palo Alto. She wanted to check on her house and to pay her respects to the family of the murdered girl. She also wanted to see Scott, and talk to Don and flee to the emotional shelter of her mother. Lise was probably her best bet at the moment; Don was with Alyssa and so unreachable, and Scott was somewhere in the wilds of the Northern Territories of Canada photographing musk oxen and tundra wolves.

Just as she picked up her phone to call Lise, it buzzed. Text notification. From Danisha. "SOS."

Justine looked up at the cabin's ceiling and spoke in the direction of the hidden speaker, "It's from Danisha. You know, my best friend? I'm gonna call her now, just so's you know. I won't be long and I will be discreet. It's ringing, but you already know that. Oh hey Dani, I just got your text..."

"Oh my fucking god Justine! I'm *totally* fucked. Alessandro's not..."

"Whoa girl, take it down a notch please. I'm a bit slow this morning, just got some awful news. What about him?"

"He's not who I thought he was. He's not a film producer. He's not even Italian."

"Wait, what? Did you copy his hard drive?"

"I did everything you told me. Even got fingerprints and DNA. I found a secret laptop in his desk. I've only seen him use his MacBook, this was an Origin 19, hidden in the back of a drawer. Justine, he's bad. Really bad. I found hard-core porn, tons of pictures of women tied up.

S and M shit, totally nasty. And nude photos of me! He runs a website called *Aqua Blu Shadows*."

"Wait, what? You mean like, www dot aqua blu shadows dot com?"

"No. No. Not like that at all. My IT guy, Ajit, found it on the Dark Web."

"Holy shit, Dani. Talk about international intrigue," Justine said dramatically.

"Jus, I haven't told you the worst part. These women? He *sells* them. He's a sex trafficker. I'm in some deep shit here. Can you help me?"

Justine could've sworn she felt her heart skip a beat. "Hold up, this is too much information for a phone conversation. Your phone isn't secure. We need to meet face to face."

"Where are you? I can meet you whenever you're ready."

"I'm in…" Justine looked up at the ceiling again. "I'll meet you at Lise's LA condo in four hours. You still have the key and the security code?"

"Possible interference detected." The voice was back. "Use only burner phones and tablets. Out."

"What's going on?" Danisha asked.

"Listen, I'll explain later," Justine responded calmly. "Alessandro doesn't know about Lise's apartment. Go there *now*. If he calls you, answer him. Don't let him hear or see your fear. Just be yourself."

"I don't know if I can do that."

"Well, I *do* know that you can. Be strong girlfriend. I will see you in a few hours, and I promise I will guard you with my life."

"Okay, that makes me feel a little better. I guess."

"It's all gonna work out. I promise," Justine swore as she hung up.

"You're booked on flight 5020." It was the voice again. "Departing Monterey Regional at two-forty-seven, arriving LAX at four."

"Who *are* you?" Justine asked as she tossed some clean clothes into her case.

"Traffic is light but you should leave here now. Your burner is compromised, take a fresh one. Middle drawer to the left of the stove."

"Thank you Mr. Disembodied Voice," Justine answered facetiously. "I'll forgive your eavesdropping this time. Okay, new burner, check. Now where did I put my go-bag?"

"Foot of the bed," said the voice.

Chapter 42

As soon as Justine was in the car and off the property she used a fresh burner to call her mother.

"Lise, Danisha is in big trouble with Alessandro. I can't go into details, but she's on her way to your place so can you call security so she has no problem getting in?"

"Not necessary. They know her there. She has a key."

"That's what I thought, just wanted to double check. I'm on my way now, should get there by five. We're gonna need Iya and Eniko too. Right away. Any chance they can get to LA by tomorrow? I also need you."

"They're already there, getting intel for some federal agency. The *doms* are pretty quick, so they should be finished with their work by now."

Good. Get them to the apartment, asap."

"Justine, what's going on? You sound stressed."

"Ya think?"

"Well, if you're asking for Iya and Eniko you must be desperate. I'm on a set in Aspen, shooting a commercial, but I can leave tonight. As for the girls, only the devil knows where they are. I'll have to track them down, but I'll get them there. Can you tell me more?"

"Not on the phone. I'll tell you everything when I see you."

"Now I'm worried."

"That makes three of us. I'll see you tomorrow?"

"Maybe even tonight, if I can get out of here."

Justine allowed herself to breathe a sigh of relief. "Thanks Lise. Just knowing that makes me feel better. Now go find your psychotic dominatrices. We need to start spreading some pain."

The travel gods must've decided to bless Justine that day. Her flight from Monterey to LAX landed fifteen minutes early, just as her flight from LAX to Monterey early that morning had. She wasn't too stressed to appreciate the irony of her present professional situation. As CEO of TruYouth she refused to travel more than five days in any financial quarter. Outside of that, anyone who wanted to meet with her had to fly to Palo Alto. Now that she was a few hundred million dollars richer, had a new job for a nebulous security company based in a secret cabin perched on a cliff on the mid-California coastline, Justine was flying up and down California like an old timey-salesman and not even earning an hourly wage.

CHAPTER 43

Stepping off the elevator on the sixteenth floor, Justine scanned the hallway and saw no one. She expected to find Danisha safely barricaded behind Lise's apartment door, anxiously pacing the living room or hiding in a bathroom. But the front door was locked from the outside only, no deadbolt or chain blocked her entrance. No lights had been turned on either, and the drapes were still drawn closed. The place was empty. Justine's initial reaction was panic, but she checked that right away. After all, she told herself, it was barely five o'clock on a weekday and Danisha still had a corporate job.

She grabbed a bottle of Evian from the well-stocked fridge and plopped down into one of the leather barrel-chairs in the living room and swiveled around to gaze out the windows. Magic hour. Golden light bathed the hills, ribbons of boulevards, the West LA and Santa Monica sky-scrapers, and, just a few hundred yards ahead of her, the copper-hued Fox Plaza sky-scraper.

Her brief reverie was interrupted by the sound of a key turning in the lock of the front door, followed by the frustrated and voluble tenor of a weary traveler.

"Lise!" Justine bayed when she heard her mother's voice.

"Hello Justine. I'm thrilled to see you and so happy that you're comfortable over there on the swivel throne, but can you please help me? I'm not built to schlepp my own luggage."

"Not to worry Queen Mother, I've been training for just this type of emergency," Justine responded in mock seriousness. Then she picked up every one of Lise's cases and started carrying them to the master bedroom.

"You know, I thought you were kidding with that quip but now I'm not so sure. If all else fails, you could always get a job as a Pullman Porter or a Red Cap," Lise joked.

"You should never doubt me." Justine said, returning back into the living room, and abruptly but easily hoisted her couture-clad mother over her shoulder in a fireman's carry.

Lise shrieked in amused surprise, "Careful, I'm wearing Dior Après Ski. Vintage, if you don't mind."

"Of course you are." Justine tossed her mother onto the couch as though she was nothing more than an overstuffed Balenciaga tote bag.

"Skill Demonstration One," Justine recited. "Watch and learn. That's how you handle a drunken client."

"I'm not drunk, thank you very much. But after that greeting I definitely need a drink. And a hug." Justine eagerly complied with the latter demand first, then, as they both laughed playfully, went to the kitchen and poured them each a glass of Sancerre.

"What's happening with Scott? You still engaged now that you're an international woman of mystery?"

"That's a bit of an exaggeration Lise. And yes, I'm still engaged."

"I don't see a ring," Lise said, inspecting Justine's left hand.

"Lise, don't be ridiculous. First of all, we're Millennials, the hyper-educated, socially aware generation. We disdain diamonds and everything connected to the DeBeers blood cartel. And second, you know I would never let him buy a diamond at retail. When he gets back from the furthest reaches of Canada he's gonna call you. I told him you'd take him to your guy on Forty-Seventh Street."

"I can think of no better way to spend a Thursday afternoon than looking at five-carat stones with Samuel and Scott in the diamond district," Lise said, laughing.

Justine cracked up. "Oh my god, I just got that visual. It's hysterical!"

"Your security sucks." The woman's voice came from the living room.

Lise let out a barely audible screech. Justine rushed to see who it was.

"You left the door wide open. You're lucky we are your friends."

"Top of the evening to you Ms. Eniko," Justine said with a snicker when she saw her old friends, the Ukrainian dominatrices.

"She's right, you know. We could've been bad guys," said Iya.

"And Ms. Iya! So nice to see you again," Justine said through almost gritted teeth. Then she smiled, relinquishing any negative feelings she might've been harboring for these two enigmatic beauties.

They looked stunning. Dressed in couture outfits and Manolo heels, they hardly looked like killers, let alone former KGB Swallows. Justine had to remind herself that these were the same co-eds she'd met in Palo Alto a few weeks back. She didn't even want to think about the last time she'd seen them, naked and spattered with the blood of her freshly tortured attacker.

"Actually, it's good to see you guys," Justine said. "And I gotta say, you two clean up good."

"What does this mean, clean up good?" Iya asked, suspicious.

"To put it in terms you can understand," Justine explained playfully, "you look super hot."

Lise greeted Eniko and Iyo with kisses planted right on their lips. "Yes, the two of you are always hot. Thanks for coming so quickly."

"Wasn't problem, we were here already in Los Angeles doing some consulting work," Eniko explained with a wink. "Timing was perfect since we make our clients come quickly too."

"Lise tells us you are badass now," Iya said to Justine. "That you are bodyguard for rich famous people. We are impressed."

"We prefer the term *security detail*," Justine said, smiling.

At the sudden sound of the doorbell, Iya and Eniko quickly slipped off their heels, drew twin Makarov pistols from their bra holsters, and moved stealthily towards the front door.

"Chill ladies," said Justine. "It's probably Danisha. You know, the woman we're all here to protect? Geez Louise, you do take this shit seriously, don't you?"

"Of course," said Eniko, aiming a quick glance of disdain at Justine. "You should take seriously too."

"Ooh," Justine responded, "that's some serious shade you're throwing at me, Bond girl."

"What means this shade?" Iya asked, her eyes and her Makarovs still trained on the front door.

"Put down the weapon and I'll tell ya," Justine said jovially.

"Oh for the love of Pete, girls," said Lise as she tried to look through the peephole.

"No!" Iya hissed, pushing Lise away from the door. "Whoever's there could shoot your eye right through your head." Eniko nodded in agreement.

Justine looked at her mother and rolled her eyes.

Lise shrugged and stepped away from the door. "Who is it?" she asked with an exaggerated nonchalance.

"It's me, Danisha," said the voice on the other side of the door.

Eniko opened the door a crack, her pistol ready.

"Oh for fuck's sake. I know my girlfriend's voice, why not just ask me if that's her?" Justine said, taking control of the situation by opening the door. "Dani! Do come in." Danisha walked through the doorway, dragging her luggage behind her.

"Just leave your bag right there for now," said Lise while Justine embraced her friend. Eniko peeped her head through the door, checking the hallway for anyone that might be following Danisha.

Then, Eniko closed and locked the door, making sure the deadbolt was secure. They effortlessly re-holstered their pistols into their push up bras.

It was Lise's turn to give Danisha a welcoming embrace. "You're safe now, my beautiful girl," she cooed. The relief on both women's faces was palpable. "Allow me to introduce my friends, Eniko and Iya." The girls nodded as Lise said their names. "They're also my partners in a few, um, business ventures. They can teach you everything you need to know to become a sexual master over men," Lise added with a sly smile.

"Um, yeah, thanks. I'll keep that in mind," Danisha said, staring at Eniko and Iya with unabashed suspicion. "What is it that you two do exactly?"

"We do all sorts of things. You know, women's work," Eniko said, and Iya laughed.

"Nonsense," said Lise. "You're being uncharacteristically modest.' She turned her attention to Danisha "These two waifs are here to help protect *you*. They worked for the FSB, which is part of what used to be called the KGB."

"You're Russian?" Danisha asked Eniko.

"Ukrainian." Big difference," Iya answered for her friend.

"Yes, well in any case," Lise continued, "they were *Sparrows*, part of an elite group of female spies."

"Meaning we fucked a lot of men we didn't want to fuck," said Eniko, deadpan.

Now Danisha was really confused. "Why?"

"To get information," Eniko responded. "You hear her say the part about spies? I had over eighty successful fucks. Iya had even more."

"Is true," Iya piped in. "We are professional information extractors. Because we did that work so well, we decided to use what we learned about the sexual desires of men, powerful men, and some women, to make money. Only now, here in America, we provide dominatrix service."

"Wait, you do what?" Danisha asked. Then to Justine she said, "They're kidding, right?"

"Nope." The answer came from both Justine and Lise, like a Greek chorus.

"As you can see," Eniko continued, taking control of the explanation, "we don't wear black leather bustiers and thigh-high boots. We learned our trade from the best, a group of very intelligent, highly skilled women in Paris."

"Oh. Paris. Of course," said Danisha, not sure she wanted to know what skills these two pretty young women were talking about.

"You see, some men, and also a few women, enjoy pain. They get sexual pleasure from being submissive." Eniko shrugged, then looked appreciatively at her partner. "Me and Iya, we enjoy our work. We get sexual satisfaction dominating men, filling their desire. We get paid well."

"Iya and I," Justine interjected. Danisha chuckled. "And it's fulfilling, not filling."

Lise shot them both a nasty look. "Enough now, *girls*," she said.

"What? I'm helping them learn English!" Justine whined, winking at Danisha.

"We need to get to business, not grammar lessons." Lise was not amused. She turned to face Eniko and Iya. "I didn't want to say anything about this over the phone. Danisha has a serious problem with her fiancé."

"There's an understatement," Justine mumbled.

Lise ignored her daughter and continued her explanation. "You see, he's a sex trafficker."

"You told Lise?" Danisha said to Justine, furious. "I told you that in confidence."

"Of course I told her. You need my help, yes. But I can't do it alone. We, you and I, *we* need them. I swear Dani, even I'm surprised that I can admit that," said Justine.

Eniko and Iya stared at Danisha. "Sex trafficker? You are sure?" Eniko asked, surprised by what she had heard.

Dani nodded, then dropped her head in shame.

"If this is truth, if you have involvement with sex traffickers, you *need* us. You need our *expertise*. We understand the twisted minds of men like this. We lived as sex slaves, but we got lucky. We escaped our captors. Most women don't."

Danisha remained silent. She gazed at her left hand, focusing on the glimmering diamond on her ring finger. Finally she spoke. "Okay, yes. Yes, I'm in a ridiculous and dangerous situation. Being involved with Alessandro could cost me my life. If I lived, no one would hire me if they knew the truth. I'd have to start all over designing prom dresses for debutantes in Tallahassee."

"That's where you go, Tallahassee?" Justine asked, incredulous.

"Best I could do off the cuff," Danisha said, her voice cracking under the strain of oncoming tears. She tried to pull off her ring, but gave up when she couldn't get it past her knuckle.

"Danisha?" Eniko said with a surprising kindness. But Danisha wouldn't look at her.

Eniko continued in her sympathetic tone. "Justine will make sure you're safe. Iya and *I* will teach her how to retrieve more information from him."

Danisha did not like the sound of that. "How?"

Iya laughed as she explained, "We'll teach her the Way Of The Dominatrix."

"Ew," said Justine.

"No!" Danisha protested. "No sex. No violence."

"It is obvious that you understand nothing about the realities of the world." Eniko had clearly run out of patience. "The real world, behind the illusions you project here in your make believe world. This man Alessandro is your enemy. And now he is our enemy too. Our *target*. Justine may have to do to him what we have done to other men. Evil men like him."

"It's for the best, believe me." Iya added.

Justine took Danisha's hand and told her, "Just remember that what-ever we have to do we will do. For you. That starts with getting our hands on Alessandro's other computer, and any other data we can find."

Danisha shook her head.

"No?" Eniko asked her sweetly. Danisha shook her head again. Eniko stepped closer to her. "Listen to me, Danisha. He will hurt you. You and hundreds of other women."

Justine stepped between Eniko and Danisha and took her best friend's hand. "The hard sell ain't gonna work here, *muchachas.* Let me talk to her. Alone." Then to Danisha she said, "We're sharing my room. Let's go rest for a spell."

Sitting on Justine's bed, surrounded by framed pictures of happier, simpler days, Danisha let herself collapse in tears. "This is not my life. I do not want any of this," she whimpered.

"Good. But you have to get away from Alessandro."

"You think I don't know that?"

"I know you know, Dani. It's just, well, not as easy as you think to just walk away from a man like that." Again Danisha shook her head no. "Dani, please. Listen to me. We, those beautiful dominatrices and I, we're willing to risk our lives to protect you. And it's not just you. There are thousands of women out there, potential future victims. You already found one laptop with a list of victims. I'm certain he has other lists. Lists of buyers. Think about it Dani. What and who enables these crimes? Money. *Men* with money. Loads and loads of it. They don't give a shit about human dignity, or individual rights. We're talking about pure *evil* here. And you and me? We have an opportunity here. We can put a big fat dent in the front fender of this evil machine."

"You and me," Danisha whimpered.

"Touché," Justine said, laughing. She pulled a tissue from the box on the nightstand beside the bed and handed it to Danisha, who was also laughing, but through a torrent of tears.

"Dani, I'm serious now. Think about it. Do you realize how many women and even kids, you and I and those two Ukrainians out there can save from abduction, slavery, rape, torture, even murder?"

Danisha sat up straight, trying to gather her composure. "Okay, you're right. But I can't go back to his place. If he catches me...I don't have your nerve, Jussy. Never did."

"You don't have to do anything but act as if nothing has changed. You can do that, right?"

Danisha nodded, then started crying again. "I don't know."

"I do. You're stronger than you think. *I'll* go in. You just give me any information I'll need, like names of security guys and the dudes at the front desk and any codes I might need."

"Okay. You're right, as usual. I'll do whatever you say. I'm scared. And so tired."

"I know. Can't be easy carrying around all this angst as well as a baby." At the mention of her unborn child, Danisha started whimpering again. "Shit, I'm sorry Dani. And I was doing so well," Justine said, taking Danisha into her arms. "Go ahead and cry. You deserve it."

"I'm all cried out. Got no more tears, just like the shampoo," Dani mumbled, her head on Justine's shoulder.

"You hungry?" Justine asked.

Danisha shook her head. "Sleepy maybe. Feels like I haven't slept in days."

"That makes perfect sense to me. Lie back. Take a nap. Maybe even sleep through the night. I'll be right out there in the living room. Just holler if you need anything." Justine waited for a response, and, hearing none, noticed that her friend was fast asleep.

She left the bedroom on tiptoe and quietly closed the door behind her. Eniko, Iya, and Lise were sitting in the living room, waiting.

"So? Do we work? Eniko asked Justine.

"Yeah. Give her a break, will you? She's naïve, you said it yourself. And I don't want to fight with you guys. We need to work together. You two helped each other escape from a nightmare. Now the three of us need to help Danisha escape from hers."

Iya glared at Justine. "Tell me one thing first. Why should I trust you? Perhaps you are CIA agent trying to get us."

Justine blanched, unsure whether to laugh or scream. "Me? I'm a former executive of a cosmetic company now training like an idiot to protect myself. The only thing I've ever done for the government is pay them a fortune in taxes."

Iya ignored the joke. "Perhaps it is your handler that works for CIA. Perhaps he's the cat and you're his mouse."

"Okay, I'm not sure what your analogy is supposed to mean there but okay. I'll tell you whatever I know about my, what do you call him, my handler? To me he's a teacher. And yes he might've worked with the CIA once upon a time, but he went rogue. Just like I imagine you went rogue from the FSB."

Again Iya ignored her jab. "Does he fuck you?"

"Why do you insist on being so disgusting? Don has never fucked me."

"He must be too old, then, fat and ugly. With a shriveled-up dick," laughed Iya.

"Why does any of that matter? He's my teacher, not my lover. But I will tell you that the only thing soft about him is that one spot in his heart, and that's only for women that need protection."

Eniko asked, "What does he look like?"

Justine was taken aback. "Why does that matter?"

"I'm curious. This teacher of yours, you make him sound like super-hero."

"He's actually very handsome, in a unique, almost exotic sort of way."

Eniko blanched. "Is he part Asian?"

"How'd you know to ask that?"

A knowing smile crept across Eniko's face. "So that means yes, he is, how you say, Eurasian?"

"As a matter of fact, yes," said Justine.

Eniko's smile lit up her entire face, but only briefly. A moment later she was crying.

"What happened? Did I say something wrong?"

Eniko mumbled something in Ukrainian to Iya. She sounded ex-cited. Happy.

"Seriously, what's happening here?" Justine asked again.

"I'm telling Iya that we found him. I mean *you* found him," she said kindly, throwing her arms around Justine. "And together, *we* must pro-tect *him*."

Shocked, Justine tried to wriggle out of Eniko's embrace but couldn't. "From whom?" she asked.

"Can't be true," Iya said with an utter lack of emotion.

Eniko let go of Justine and turned to Iya. "He's *not* just a legend. He's real."

Then, facing Justine, she explained, "He rescued Irina, one of the *Sparrows*. She was supposed to be my FSB mentor, but to me, she was like a sister. Until I met you," she added, glancing over her shoulder at Iya. "You are my partner, my sister, my lover," she said tenderly.

Iya looked down, but said nothing.

Eniko's eyes were shining. "Your American knew my Irina," she continued telling Justine. She was KGB, he CIA. They began as enemies. But then they fell in love. They ran away, betrayed their countries by leaving, so they could be together. There was a rumor that they had a daughter, the prettiest girl in the world. Their story was like a fairy tale."

Iya broke in. "But their fairy tale was not happily ever after. So many evil men, capos of drug cartels in Russia and Asia, they all wanted him dead. For years they searched for him, but never found him. Then they captured Irina and the child. Tortured them for weeks. When the girl finally died they fed her body to tigers while Irina was forced to watch.

"Her lover, the great American spy, he couldn't protect them. But he got his revenge a thousand times over. On six continents."

Justine shuddered. "This sounds like some nasty Joseph Conrad shit."

"But is true," Iya assured her. "Now everyone wants him dead. There is very real bounty on his head."

Eniko nodded in agreement. "Five-million dollars for proof of death, twenty million for bringing him in alive."

Justine's eyes narrowed. "And you two want me to believe you're not one of the many bounty hunters you talk about?"

Eniko looked into Justine's eyes. "I understand that you want to protect him. We want to protect him, too," she explained patiently.

Lise, who had been sitting quietly by, asked, "So, what are we gonna do now ladies?"

"Eniko still believes in fairy tales," Iya sneered. "And Justine is fucking her fairy-tale *prince*, and lying to us about it."

Lise threw up her hands. "I've had enough of the high school locker gossip. Iya, chill the fuck out. Justine, give Iya a hug."

Eniko was the first to offer her hand in a truce, which Justine happily accepted. "Come Justine," Eniko said. "Iya and I will teach you all you need to know about, how you call it? Breaking and entering."

CHAPTER 44

When she accepted the offer of instruction in the fine art of burglary, Justine assumed Eniko would want to begin the lessons when they returned in the morning, after they'd all had a good night's sleep. Justine had no clue what the Ukrainians had been up to before they arrived at Lise's place; Eniko had said something about consulting work in LA. Whatever that was, it couldn't have been too physically taxing. They both looked stunningly well rested when they arrived. When Iya busted out her super-secret-spy tool kit, Justine was intrigued. All those tiny gadgets meant for picking locks, cracking safes and probing other people's hard drives looked like so much fun, even through her weary eyes. But when the girls started talking, explaining and demonstrating, Justine realized that the lesson had already begun.

She acquiesced to every physical and mental exercise no matter how strenuous, picked every lock—after many failed attempts—in Lise's apartment, and disabled both Lise's security system and the alarm for the building's gym. It was well past midnight when she successfully, and illegally, gained access to the condominium's roof. By the time she completed her first intense breaking and entering training session—or as Don would call it, covert entry and data extraction—Justine was literally seeing double.

"You sleep now," Eniko told Justine when they returned to Lise's apartment. "We start again tomorrow morning at ten."

"You're leaving now?"

"We need sleep too," said Eniko.

"Not just sleep," said Iya, tossing a lustful look at Eniko. "All work and no play makes Jack dull boy."

"You're quoting Stephen King now. I'd prefer to avoid the horror genre all together and stick with John Le Carre or Ian Fleming," Justine said as the girls stepped onto the elevator and waved goodbye.

They were back and ready to kick her butt into fighting shape at precisely nine-fifty-five the next morning. The lesson began with a recap of the previous night's lock-picking and security alarm disarming lesson, followed by a two-hour mixed-martial arts workout in the condo's gym space. Justine was thrilled to have new sparring partners; so far the only opponent she'd had outside of her years of Krav Maga training was Don who always let her barely win and then made winning even harder the next time.

"You have fascinating style," Iya to Justine.

"Fascinating meaning *interesting?*" Justine responded suspiciously.

"Is Iya's way of saying she respects your skills," Eniko interjected. "You learned this method from the teacher you told us about? The Eurasian?"

"Some," Justine answered, still unsure how much information to share with these two. "But I had training before I met him. Did Krav Maga for years when I was a kid, and in college."

"Israelis are great fighters. But you have something else. Is good. Very good."

"Um, thanks," Justine said, shocked by Eniko's unguarded compliment. "You're not too bad yourselves. The KGB taught you well."

"FSB," Eniko and Iya countered simultaneously.

"Whatever. I'm hungry. I saw a coffee shop up the block. Let's take a walk and grab some lunch."

"We don't have time," Eniko said, dismissing Justine's suggestion.

So much for girl talk, Justine thought. "Well I have to eat something and I don't want to go upstairs and disturb Lise and Danisha."

"We have to go there eventually," Eniko said.

"What for?" Justine asked.

"For private dominatrix lesson, of course," Eniko answered.

Justine did not like the hyena grin on Iya's face.

Justine got her way, but Eniko made sure they were back at Lise's apartment within a half hour.

Lise was on her way out to a meeting in Brentwood. She told them that Danisha was working in Justine's room, but they could use her room if they needed privacy. Justine could've sworn she saw her mother wink at Eniko when she said the word *privacy*.

The afternoon session began and ended in Lise's bedroom. The second Iya started unpacking her tool kit, a sturdy and stylish black leather satchel, an all too familiar feeling of dread washed over Justine.

"So what is all this stuff?" she asked Eniko.

"Tools of trade." Eniko picked up an enormous black dildo attached to a leather harness sort of thing. "Lesson One, how to use strap-on."

"Oh dear god," Justine mumbled.

"No kvetching," Eniko barked.

"Did Lise teach you that word?" Justine asked her. "I know it's not Russian or Ukrainian. Though it might be considered English by now."

Eniko, ignoring Justine's banter, continued rattling off words such as bondage and humiliation, cock and ball torture, spikey wheel, blindfolding, paddles, corporal punishment, cat o' nine tails and candle waxing. Trying to memorize the odious vocabulary and various methods of using the equipment, Justine did what she told Danisha to do to get through the difficult parts of her ordeal; she acted *as if*. For Justine, studying the many elements of sexual domination, what Eniko so proudly called *The Way of the Dominatrix,* became the equivalent of taking a prerequisite course for her undergraduate degree, like physics or statistical analysis.

The afternoon session went on well into the night. Justine noticed the colors of sunset at one point, around the time the flogging lesson began. When Iya lit a candle and started explaining the nuance of wax dripping Justine said she thought she'd learned enough for one day.

"I mean seriously, do I need to know all of this just to break into Alessandro's apartment tomorrow night?"

"You never know what you will need," Iya snapped.

"She's right," Eniko added. "Best to be prepared for anything."

"Unless I want to set up shop grooming bikini lines at Kappa Kappa Gamma, I don't see how learning to drip wax prepares me for anything." Justine protested. "It's disgusting."

"You make face like that and no one will ever want you as dominatrix," Iya scolded.

Justine smiled proudly. "Mission accomplished, then."

CHAPTER 45

The next morning Justine woke up feeling agitated. The thought of breaking into Alessandro's apartment terrified her. She knew from her studies with Don that breaking into a target's space was among the most dangerous of operations, one that under normal circumstances she would not have to undertake. Now she wondered what *normal* meant to him; so far every aspect of her experience with Don fell far from any accepted interpretation of the word. Eniko had come up with a brilliant, if close to impossible plan, the details of which were still settling in Justine's memory banks. But they didn't make her feel any less terrified. She would have to replay, review, and repeat those details, every single one of them, as the day progressed. But first she needed to contact Don.

He'd given her three phone numbers, all burner cells, and told her to memorize them. No problem there, Justine Baron was a champion memorizer. Actually contacting Don was another matter altogether. Come to think of it, nothing about Don was easy, so why should she expect to be able to call him any time she needed him?

What she really needed was caffeine. She grabbed her burner phone and pressed the first number as she headed to the kitchen but got a recorded message apologizing for the number being out of service. She dialed the second one while grinding coffee beans in her mother's Miele espresso machine so she didn't hear the ring tone or the voice asking for ID verification. Not at first.

"Please tell me you have soy milk," Justine called out to Lise, who was sitting at the kitchen table.

"Don't hold your phone to your ear with your shoulder, Jussy. You'll get a hunchback," Lise answered.

"Yeah, right. That's what I need to worry about now."

"ID VERIFICATION." The voice on the other end of the call was not a happy one.

"Hello?" Justine said, as if she had just answered the call instead of placed it.

"Verification of your identity. Now please."

"You know who I am," Justine whisper-hissed. "I need to talk to Don. Put me through, please."

"ID verified. But I cannot put you through."

"Oh. You can't? Why not?" Justine recognized the voice. It was the same disembodied interloper from the cabin.

"These phones are for emergencies only," the voice answered impatiently.

"This is an emergency. I need to do a covert entry to retrieve encrypted files, so I need tech support."

"I am tech support. And you're not yet trained in covert entry."

"That's funny, all of a sudden you sound human."

"I am human."

"Okay, good to know, and nice to meet you. I did learn about covert entry, just not from Don. I had a pretty intense lesson last night with two former FSB agents. They had me totally immersed in a comprehensive course."

"Russians?"

"Ukrainians, as it happens."

"Names?"

"I know them only as Eniko and Iya. But they know Don. Or at least they seemed to know a lot about his past. They told me about Irina and a daughter." Justine waited for a response. When none came, she continued her story about the Don story. "They told me there's a bounty on Don, five-million if he's dead or twenty million if he's alive."

"What do they know of your relationship with him?"

"I apologize if this sounds rude, but I don't know you. You *tell* me you're human, but I don't know if you're a real person or a conglomeration of people typing commands into a keyboard to animate this voice that pretends every now and then to be a machine and then a man and then a woman. So why should I answer any of your questions? I called this number to talk to Don. So. Would you please put me through to him?"

"How much did you reveal to them?" She sounded sincere, concerned. A woman now, not a machine.

"Who are you?" Justine was so confused.

"I'm either your best friend or your worst nightmare. It's your choice."

CHAPTER 46

She called herself Marisol. At least that's the name she finally gave Justine at the end of their conversation. Justine never did get through to Don before she embarked on her non-Don-related mission, but Marisol was only too happy to help once Justine had enlightened her with the details of Danisha's nightmare. She enthusiastically agreed to provide tech support and offered to be on-call during the operation, an offer Justine enthusiastically accepted. Marisol told Justine to get Alessandro's license plate and cell phone numbers, anything she could use to track his movements. Then, using the devices Don packed in her go-bag, which included an invisible earpiece and microphone and the tiny camera embedded in a choker necklace, Justine told herself she wouldn't be alone in Alessandro's apartment. She'd have Marisol with her, an extra set of eyes as well as a reassuring and omniscient voice in her ear. Just knowing Marisol was backing her up gave Justine much-needed confidence.

The Ukrainians would also be with her, waiting in the getaway car. Justine didn't think they needed to know about Marisol. Not yet. Don hadn't told her about Marisol's existence, much less her purpose, so she figured it was best to keep her separate sources separate, and his secret, secret.

Danisha emerged from Justine's bedroom wearing yoga pants and a loose-fitting tank, her eyes still swollen with sleep and sorrow. Justine had purposely blocked all thoughts of Danisha's pregnancy, but seeing her now, fresh out of bed after thirteen hours of sleep, she couldn't help but note the changes in her friend's body. The fertility goddess breasts and blossoming baby bump; a ripeness that seemed to emerge overnight.

Justine's heart melted. She wanted to say something, anything, to brighten Danisha's gloom. But what, what could she possibly say that wouldn't spark another torrent of tears?

Eniko and Iya arrived with two rolling suitcases and a serious attitude. No greetings, no small talk. They might've looked like vapid super models who'd just left a photo shoot, but these two beauties were pure business. They planted themselves at the kitchen table and started talking strategy.

"What's in the suitcases?" Justine asked Iya.

"Wigs. Clothing. Lipstick."

"Why?"

"We play dress-up."

"We have a plan already?" Justine asked anxiously.

"We always play dress-up," Eniko said, winking.

"That's a big suitcase for wigs and lipstick," Justine noted.

"Tools of the trade," Lise chimed in. She knew what they were dealing with. She also knew that her daughter still had a lot to learn.

Eniko grilled Danisha about every detail of Alessandro's life; the layout of his apartment, his schedule and habits, the names of any close friends or known associates. At first Danisha said she didn't know much, but Eniko was a skilled interrogator. By the time Lise put the eggs on the table, Iya had drawn a detailed floor plan of Alessandro's apartment, and had started writing a list of items for Justine to either find or avoid.

When everyone had finished eating, Eniko told Justine it was time for one more lesson. This session had nothing to do with the picking of locks or disarming of security systems. Eniko told Justine to be prepared for the worst, and in her experience, the only way to deal with life's most serious challenges was by taking advantage of the opponent's weaknesses. When it came to men in general, and—from the information Danisha had given them—Alessandro in particular, their weakness usually had something to do with sex. Eniko wanted to teach Justine how to exploit those 'sexual flaws.' She even had a name for her tutorial: "*The Secret Way Of The Dominatrix*."

CHAPTER 47

Alessandro had told Danisha that he had meetings all afternoon in the Valley and plans to meet a business associate for dinner in Encino. He didn't say when or with whom he was meeting. Danisha, trying her best to stick to Justine's *act as if everything is okay* edict, thought it best not to ask. After much discussion, Eniko and Justine decided to take the risk and break into Alessandro's apartment before seven that same evening.

But first they had to play dress-up. Eniko didn't give Justine a chance to choose her own outfit. She handed her a red leather mini-dress and red patent leather Yves Saint Laurent strappy platform sandals with five-inch heels.

"I'm doing this thing dressed up as a sexy fire hydrant?"

"Very funny. I'm laughing on inside," Eniko responded, stone faced.

"You're serious about these shoes? What if I have to make a quick getaway? I'll break an ankle."

"Americans always say break a leg. So for you tonight it's ankle."

"That's actually kinda amusing, Eniko. Nice comeback."

"Now wig," Eniko said, trying to repress a smile. "Then makeup. Those shoes you can slip off easily. Trust me. They are, how you say, tried and true."

"Got it."

Justine took the outfit to her room, where Danisha helped her squeeze into the dress. "Fits like a glove," she said once she'd zipped Justine in.

"A very short glove," Justine grunted. "How'm I supposed to breathe in this torture device?"

Danisha cracked up. "You gotta appreciate the irony. You're playing the dominatrix and the masochist at the same time."

"True that," Justine said. "The minute I signed up for this training madness I unwittingly became a disciple of the Marquis de Sade. Do me a favor," she said, removing her gold chain with the *chai* charm. "Keep this safe for me."

"But it's your good luck charm. Are you sure you don't need it with you tonight?"

"Someone might remember seeing it. Hebrew letters make a statement. Tonight that could be dangerous."

Danisha staggered to the bed and sat on the edge of the mattress, looking like she was about to be sick.

Justine sat down beside her. "What's wrong?" she asked, taking Danisha's hand. "You look like you just saw a ghost."

"There's more about Alessandro."

"More what?"

"Information. I couldn't tell you on the phone before you cut me off. Ajit ran his fingerprints and had a friend at the LAPD run his DNA. Apparently Alessandro was born in Syria and his name isn't Alessandro. It's something Arabic."

"He's an Arab?"

"According to the DNA report, yeah."

"Where'd you get the sample?"

"From an orange juice glass I found on his kitchen counter when he went to Rome."

"Did you see him drink from that glass?"

"No. He was already gone. You told me to find anything with fingerprints, I grabbed the OJ glass before I left."

"Okay. So we know that someone who was in his apartment drinking orange juice is this Arab guy, but we don't know for a fact that that someone was Alessandro."

Danisha's eyes lit up. "Holy crap Justine. I never thought of that. So he might be exactly who he says he is?"

"I don't know about that. Maybe, maybe not. Right now we need more evidence." More than anything Justine wanted to make Danisha happy, to let her have this glimmer of hope. But she knew that for

Danisha the line between hope and naivety had always been thin, and in this case it was also sharp and dangerous. "I'll have to get another DNA sample from his place to confirm the orange juice glass DNA. From his hairbrush or something, I'll figure that out when I get there. Right now I need help putting on my hooker jewelry."

CHAPTER 48

Eniko's plan was simple. Speaking heavily accented English, Justine plays high-class French escort to get past the doorman and front desk of Alessandro's condominium building. Then, using the security codes provided by Danisha, she breaks into his apartment, copies the encrypted contents of the laptop Danisha found hidden in his desk drawer as well as any other computer, cell phone or tablet she finds, and collects any physical evidence that could have samples of his DNA and/or fingerprints. Iya plays the role of chauffeur and Eniko provides tactical coordination and tech support. While Justine infiltrates the inner sanctum of Alessandro's evil empire, Eniko and Iya wait in the getaway car, which in this case is a getaway stretch limo with windows tinted to the legal limit of opacity, communicating with Justine through the dedicated radio frequency link in the earpiece and mic from Don's go-bag. Eniko figured Justine would need twelve minutes max to accomplish the mission. *Easy peasy.*

Except Justine didn't think any of it sounded easy. Teetering through her mother's garage in Eniko's come-fuck-me-pumps and dressed in full sexy-fire hydrant-meets-fifteen-hundred dollar-an-hour-escort regalia topped off with a Jessica Rabbit red wig and kabuki doll makeup, Justine thought the entire plan sounded like madness. Justine was petrified.

Seeing her reflection in the tinted window of the Ukrainians' rented Cadillac limousine, all dressed up and ready to go, Justine didn't recognize herself. She wriggled her tush into the back seat, and pretended to be brave. *Act as if* was the mantra she chanted silently in her head. But the second Iya, disguised in a bob-cut brunette wig and the black uniform of a professional livery driver, drove through the gated entrance of Alessandro's apartment building, and Justine's doubts threatened to overpower her.

She froze when Iya pulled up to the front entrance, couldn't get out of the car. Every negative emotion she'd experienced over the past four months converged in her gut. The mantra she'd so carefully cultivated was silenced by another more powerful voice in her head. *What the fuck are you thinking, woman? You can't do this. Get the fuck out of here.*

"Well, you plan to sit there all night?" hissed Eniko, crouched near Justine's feet.

"What?" Justine had forgotten about crouching Eniko.

"We're here. Now get out of this car and do your job."

A uniformed doorman approached the limo. Iya lowered the back window enough for him to talk to her passenger.

Justine tried desperately to control her breath.

"Good evening, Ma'am. May I help you?" he asked, offering his hand.

Justine didn't answer; she couldn't, every one of her muscles was paralyzed. Eniko pinched her thigh and hissed, "Go."

The pinch was painful enough to startle Justine back to her present reality. Silently cursing Eniko's ridiculously strong fingers and praying they didn't leave a bruise, Justine smiled at the doorman.

"Ah, oui, Monsieur Stellini," she heard herself say as he opened her door. She took his hand and shimmied out onto the pavement.

"He's expecting you?" The doorman couldn't take his eyes off Justine's cleavage. She silently thanked whoever invented the push-up bra.

"I am, how you say, *surprise*," she said with a coquettish wink.

"I see. But you must be early. He just left. You can wait in the lobby."

Justine flashed him her most dazzling smile, then leaned in and whispered conspiratorially, "I was told is important to be discreet., yes? Zey give to me ze key for his *appartement*. And *code de sécurité*." She slid her hand down the front of her teeny dress and pulled Danisha's key from between her breasts, giving him the best possible view.

That did it. The doorman's jaw literally dropped. He was like a cartoon character; Justine could almost see his eyes popping out of their sockets. He held open the heavy glass door for her, his eyes glued to her ass as it shimmied into the lobby. Every man in the lobby watched appreciatively as she strode confidently past on Eniko's strappy red patent leather five-inch stilts. The doorman walked proudly as he accompanied her past the reception desk, tossing an *it's okay, she's cool* look to the receptionist, all the way to the elevator. Justine slipped him a twenty-dollar bill as she stepped in.

To steady her nerves on the ride up, Justine thought about the many gadgets concealed in her red Proenza Schouler shoulder bag; a small elegant Seecamp .32, semiautomatic pistol loaded with pre-fragmented bullets—*ninety percent stop rate in five seconds!*—and a second camera, a miniscule Sony QX10 video transmitter. She also had the tiny camera at her throat, the one hidden in her choker, as well as the invisible earpiece and microphone. Those gadgets were connected only to Marisol. The Ukrainians knew nothing about the cameras or Marisol.

The elevator door opened on the penthouse floor. Justine crossed the hall to Alessandro's door, punched in the alarm code she'd memorized, used Danisha's key to enter the apartment. It took a moment for her eyes to adjust to the dimmed lights.

The first thing she did was kick off the fucking shoes. Then she quickly scanned the large foyer and walked through the living room to the study.

"Nice crib," Justine heard someone say into her right ear. She turned reflexively to the voice before remembering the earpiece.

"Marisol?"

"Who else?"

"Good point. I'm kinda nervous, if you couldn't tell."

"Whatever. Do me a favor, do a slow three-sixty so I can get the lay of the land." Justine did a slow pirouette. "How's that?"

"Perfect. Now put on the gloves and take me to the study."

Justine smacked herself on the forehead, then reached into her bag for a pair of surgical gloves. "Can't believe I almost forgot about these. I'm such a fucking amateur."

"Maybe. But you're a smart amateur. And you have me. Now, you all set to pick a lock or two?"

"Yeah," Justine said, dropping to her knees and fishing her tiny tool kit from her shoulder bag. "One sec..." she said as her turning wrench and steel pick penetrated the key slot. She felt the click, turned the knob. "And we're in."

She punched the code Danisha used to unlock Alessandro's desk. "You seeing all this?" she asked Marisol. "The code still works, so that either means he doesn't suspect Danisha or he's set a trap."

"You're getting ahead of yourself," Marisol said. "Just find the laptop."

"Here it is." Justine placed Alessandro's laptop on the desk, turned it on, and entered the password that Danisha had given her. The computer screen came to life. "Now what?"

"Just touch the lower left screen with the stylus from your go bag," Marisol instructed.

"That sounds easy enough," Justine said, following Marisol's instructions. A file icon appeared on the screen, requesting a password. She connected her flash drive to the USB port. Within seconds the file opened. "I'm in. That was easy. But was it maybe too easy?"

"This was never the part I worried about," said Marisol.

"Do I wanna ask what was?"

"Getting caught. Listen, we're tracking Alessandro's movements through his cell phone and his license plate."

"Oh, that's brilliant. Where is the gentleman now?"

"Well he's not in Encino. He just got off the 405 at Santa Monica Boulevard. There's a chance he's headed home."

"Home? Here? Now?"

"Maybe. You need to be prepared."

"Can't you just, I dunno, disable his car?" Justine asked.

"Not tonight I can't."

"Okay. How 'bout this? Call Highway Patrol and report him. Say he's driving recklessly, going over a hundred miles an hour and weaving in and out of lanes. Make it sound bad."

"Not a bad idea. Back in a sec." Marisol's flash drive blinked away, copying every bit of data on the laptop. Within thirty seconds she was back on the line. "Okay, that bought you another ten minutes. The CHP is in hot pursuit."

As the flash drive churned though the laptop's files, the images it was ripping from the hard drive flashed on the screen. Justine nervously nibbled on a fingernail as she watched photos of one naked woman after another, each more sexually explicit and disturbing. It was disgusting, far worse than anything she'd seen in any erotic magazine or porn flick. What angered her most was the series of photos of one particular girl. A young redhead. Very young. Her left eye was swollen shut, both cheeks bruised. She appeared to be crying or screaming, and there was blood seeping from whip marks on her tiny breasts and skinny thighs. Her arms were tied to ceiling restraints and her legs were spread, her ankles tied to iron rings drilled to the floor. In some shots she could see the muscular right arm of a man holding a whip. Justine took a closer look at one of those shots and saw a jagged scar on the man's large bicep.

"How's the file transfer going?" Marisol chirped in Justine's ear.

"Disgustingly well, thanks. Two more minutes."

"Great, that'll give you exactly sixty seconds to get out of there."

"What you talkin' 'bout?"

"I'm monitoring the CHP radio. He turned onto one of the side streets off Santa Monica and they lost him. I got him on Beverly Glen, looks like he's winding his way back to his apartment. You've got maybe three minutes."

Justine's terror returned with a vengeance. "He catches me here and I become the next woman in his kinky pictures."

"Justine, you need to calm down. I swear I can hear your heartbeat," Marisol warned her.

"I'm scared," Justine whispered. "The files haven't finished downloading yet, I didn't get finger prints or DNA or paper files. And you're tell me I'm going to have to face the devil in three minutes?"

"Two minutes."

"Shit. Shit. Shit."

"Justine…"

"You'd be scared too. Unless you really are a machine."

"Yeah, we're not playing that game again. This is not the time to be scared. Breathe. Use your training."

My training. Yes. Plan B. The Ukrainian Plan.

"Okay Marisol. You're right. I got this." She grabbed her purse and made a bee-line for the master bedroom.

Justine, what are you doing?" Marisol asked calmly.

"Executing Plan B. I'm putting my bag on the night stand so you can monitor my next moves."

"But we don't have a Plan B."

"*We* don't, but I do," Justine said. "Remember the Ukrainians I told you about, the former FSB agents? They trained me for precisely this kind of situation. As long as I don't vomit I just might be able to pull this off."

She set her bag on the nightstand and made sure the camera inside had a clear shot of the bed. Then she tugged off her dress as she hurried to the entrance hallway, where she dropped it by the front door next to her shoes, leaving a trail of honey to lure the hungry Alessandro bear into her trap. The final piece of bait she would leave closer to the trap. She hurried back to the bedroom, pulled off her thong and dropped it just outside the door.

"He's back," Justine heard Marisol say. "His car pulled up to the front door and is now on its way to the building garage. He must've dropped it with the valet, which means he's walking through the lobby right now."

"You can see me, right?"

"Yes. Nice outfit."

"Very funny. My heart is pounding so fast I swear its gonna explode. Do I look nervous?"

"You look naked. Except for the jewelry. Did you get the flash drive and put the computer back?"

"Shit. Shit. Right. On my way." She dashed from the bedroom to the study, where the images of victims continued to scroll while Marisol's flash drive continued to blink. Sweat poured from Justine's underarms, even though the air conditioning was on full blast. No way would all the files be copied to the flash drive before Alessandro arrived.

She closed the study door, hurried back to the bedroom, and took the pistol from her purse. If Alessandro was armed she might have to stop him instantaneously with one shot to the head. Armed and Female —and naked—she stood behind the open doorframe, out of sight and in the shadows.

CHAPTER 49

Lise was working in her bedroom when the music started blaring. The girls had left to deal with the Alessandro conundrum—she didn't ask, didn't want to know what they had planned—so it had to be Danisha listening to…Lise closed her laptop and listened for a moment. Neil Young?

I was thinking about what a friend had said. I was hoping it was a lie.

Danisha had every right to feel miserable, confused, dejected. Lise knew that the healing process would take time, but she loved Danisha too much to feel sorry for her. It was time for a dose of pragmatic mother love. She found Danisha sitting alone in the fading light of the living room. The sun had set, but the sky was bright with dusky colors of sunset. Golden light shone through the enormous windows onto Danisha's melancholy silhouette and glowed like a halo.

Neil Young gave way to Tom Petty.

I'm a bad boy, 'cause I don't even miss her. I'm a bad boy for breakin' her heart. And I'm free, free fallin'…

"Free Falling? What is this, the Spotify *depressed-hippie* playlist? That's what you want to listen to on a night like this?" Lise asked. Danisha didn't respond, she just sang along with Tom and stared at her engagement ring.

Lise sat, looked straight into Danisha's eyes and tried again. "Danisha?"

Nothing.

"Dani?" She snapped her fingers, clapped her hands. "Danisha Howard. You are a disgrace to your generation."

"What?" Dani shook her head like she was shaking off a pesky insect. "Why?"

"You should be listening to Beyoncé or Justin Timberlake. You're also supposed to be socially aware. Apparently you didn't read the memo about blood diamonds."

Danisha's eyes welled up. "I missed more than a memo. I missed every fucking clue. Oh Lise, what am I gonna do?" She couldn't hold back the tears. Sobs wracked her entire body.

Lise had never claimed to be the most maternal of mothers, but she was empathetic. "Dani," she said firmly, "you're going to be sad, there's no way around that. What's happening to you is horrendous. You don't deserve it. If I could make it all go away you know I would. But sweetheart?" Lise sat up straight, held Danisha's face in her hands and looked directly into her swollen red eyes. "Shit happens. There may be such a thing as karma, I don't know. That's all way beyond my pay grade. What I do know is that bad things happen to good people all the time. That's life, as cliché as it sounds. And you *know* that I'm serious when *three* worn-out clichés come out of my mouth in one short monologue, right?"

Danisha laughed feebly. "Yeah, I was gonna say something about that but couldn't because I was crying too hard."

"I noticed. And it's okay to cry. But it's not okay to mope."

Danisha sighed. "I don't know how to stop."

"Go to work," Lise said.

"But it's after six. No one will be there."

"Danisha Howard, who do you think you're talking to? I know a thing or two about Hollywood movie studios. The entire lot doesn't close down at seven. Aren't you working on some new Spielberg epic?"

"You obviously don't know that much about Hollywood. Spielberg doesn't work with Sony."

"There she is! You just need to get out of your head. Stop sulking. Start thinking about other people. People with bigger problems than yours."

Images from her childhood flashed through Danisha's memory. Poverty, violence, the mothers crying over their slain sons, the babies clinging to their strung out mothers. "You're right," she told Lise. She pulled a couple of tissues from the box and blew her nose hard. "But I'm gonna need an ice pack before I go anywhere."

"Did you sprain something?" Lise asked, suddenly concerned.

"Nah," Danisha said, waving a hand like she was wiping away that possibility. "I can't go out in public with my eyes all puffy like this. You're the one that taught me that ice is the world's cheapest beauty secret."

CHAPTER 50

Lise was right. Danisha could feel the weight of her ennui lift as soon as she made the decision to get dressed and go to work. She felt even lighter when she got to the costume department on the Sony Pictures lot, which wasn't exactly buzzing with the activity it would've had a few hours earlier, but it was definitely humming at an acceptable pace of distraction.

Ajit was still there. "How are you doing?" he asked with genuine concern.

"Y'know…We don't actually know anything about Alessandro yet. Not for sure."

"We know enough. I can't believe you can be so naïve. The man sells women. He's a sex trafficker. Why can't you accept that? He's selling you after you give him a kid! And after he's finished with her, he'll sell her too!"

"It's not that simple, Ajit. He explained everything to me, and even introduced me to one of the women. Samantha Addams, you know, the actress."

Ajit dropped his head and shook it slowly, like he was listening to an improvised jazz fugue. "No. No. Listen to me, Danisha. Or better yet, look. I found more pictures in Alessandro's files."

"No thanks, I've seen enough."

"These are of someone you know. Your hot best friend, the Silicon Valley cosmetics woman."

"Justine?"

"Come see for yourself."

Ajit pushed against his desk and rolled his chair back to give Danisha room to stand by his enormous computer screen, which was plastered with nude photos of Justine. Ajit clicked his track pad and all the pictures snapped into one neat pile. He clicked on the first pic in the pile.

"Are you ready for the *Justine Baron As You've Never Seen Her Before* slide show?"

Danisha shook her head no. "I'll never be ready for this. But yeah, go ahead."

The first two dozen shots were tastefully erotic, beautifully composed and well-lit. But all of a sudden the photos became sordid as well as slipshod. Justine, her white silk robe pulled wide open, gagged and tied spread-eagled to a bed. She wasn't exactly naked, but she might as well have been.

Danisha wasn't sure what she was seeing. "What is this?" she asked Ajit. "Some kind of fetish thing?"

"Something like that, maybe. But maybe not. They were all in the same file, buried deep in the laptop's operating system. Someone worked hard to hide these, so they must be pretty fucking valuable."

Danisha buried her face in her hands. "She betrayed me," she said.

"I don't know about that. They weren't taken by the same person. Look," Ajit said, typing a command into his keyboard.

Danisha looked but all she could see was a series of what looked like random letters and symbols. "I can't read code, Ajit. What is that?"

"Oh right, sorry. This is the metadata for every item in this particular file. It proves that the first set of photos, the tasteful more arty shots, were taken with a camera, not a cell phone. Probably by a professional photographer, then stored on the hard drive of a computer. But the second set was taken with a cell phone camera. A burner phone."

"I don't know what that means. And right now I don't care. Oh god, Ajit. Can we just go somewhere and get shit-face drunk?"

"No Danisha. I think I should just take you home. But we could stop at my dispensary on the way."

CHAPTER 51

The front door opened slowly. Justine heard a murmur of men's voices moving through the living room. *Shit, there's two of them,* she thought. That was not part of the plan. She focused on listening, tried to make out what they were saying. But all she heard was silence. Alessandro must've spotted her trail of breadcrumbs.

The men started speaking again. Justine put her ear to the door and heard bits of their conversation. Italian. Macho stuff she'd heard a thousand times when she lived in Florence during her two quarters abroad her junior year. But then she heard Alessandro say something about Danisha and a surprise, followed by the sound of the front door closing. Whoever was with him had left.

Okay, now she only had to deal with one man. She quietly set her pistol on the floor, close to the doorjamb. Then she took off her gloves and tucked them into her purse.

"Dani! Is that you? Come out, come out, you dirty little vixen! Show me my surprise!"

This is it. You can do it, just go, Justine whispered to herself. She stepped through the bedroom door into the hallway where she found herself face to face with a totally surprised Alessandro.

"*Bon soir, cheri.* I am Jacqueline," Justine whispered in a faux-hoarse voice. "You speak French, *n'est-ce pas?*" She was so close she could smell the alcohol on his breath.

"Jacqueline you say? Who sent you?" Alessandro seemed suspicious, but Justine could see the tent pitching in his pants.

"I am a gift, *un cadeau,* from your dear friend Samantha."

"Samantha?"

"*Oui.* Zee *actrice?* She instructs me to tell you zat Samantha says *merci beaucoup.*" Justine took slow steps backwards into the bedroom, making sure she landed in the sightline of her purse on the nightstand, and beckoned Alessandro to follow. "Why you don't come here and show me what you can do weez zat *enorme* bump in your pants?"

Alessandro smiled, an ugly lustful smirk, and started unbuttoning his shirt before he got through the bedroom doorway. Once inside, he closed the door. He slipped off his loafers, then his shirt, and finally his pants, without taking his eyes off Justine's breasts as she slowly sauntered around him, enticing him with her eyes, her hips, lips.

Standing at the foot of the bed stark naked, Alessandro started stroking his semi-hard erection. Justine figured he wasn't planning on a lot of foreplay. But she was.

She rested a hand on his shoulder, then raised her eyes and looked into his face. It revolted her; Justine had to summon every drop of stamina she could muster to continue touching him. She told herself that it would all be over soon enough, and started sensually massaging his shoulder as she leaned in to kiss his neck. Still clasping his engorged cock, Alessandro sighed.

Justine shimmied around him, rubbing her breasts against his shoulders, side, and back. Once she was standing steadily behind him, she jumped on his back wrapping her thighs around his waist and squeezing hard. She wrapped her right arm around his neck and swiftly squeeze his throat with her bicep and forearm. By squeezing the carotid sinuses tight and firm, just as Don taught her, she cut off the blood supply to his brain. Within seconds Alessandro fell backwards onto the bed, unconscious, pinning poor Justine beneath him.

The dead weight of his body on her chest knocked the wind out of her. Struggling to catch her breath, she squirmed out from under him. Every muscle in Alessandro's body had gone limp, so Justine was shocked that he still had a hard-on.

She got off the bed, grabbed Alessandro's wrists and pulled his arms to the bedposts. When she finally had him spread-eagle face up on the bed, Justine reached under the corners of the bed and pulled out the restraining straps she'd seen in the photos on his laptop. She cinched him up tightly, then hopped off the bed and grabbed her thong from the floor near the doorway, which she used to gag him. One of his black pillowcases made a perfect blindfold. Once she had him securely bound and gagged, she took her pistol from her purse.

Justine took a step back to inspect her work—and the body of the man that snagged her best friend. She detested him and everything about him, yet she was captivated by the perfection of his body and the beauty of his face. *So male beauty is a thing after all,* she thought as she admired his wavy dark brown hair, square jaw, muscular shoulders, washboard abs, and his dick. It was *ginormous.* She had to admit it; this Alessandro dude was a knockout. No wonder Danisha fell in love with him.

"*Ay dios mio,*" Justine heard someone say. She'd completely forgotten about Marisol and the cameras, mic and ear piece.

"I take it the light in here is good enough for you to see everything you need to see?" Justine said softly.

"He's absolutely gorgeous," Marisol whispered.

That's when Justine saw it, the jagged scar on his right arm. Was Alessandro the monster in the photos? She took a closer look. No doubt about it, it was him.

"Look at the scar," she whispered to Marisol. "I don't know if you could see any of the pictures when they were scrolling on his computer screen. There was one nasty series of a red haired girl, barely pubescent. I could see the arm of the man that was beating her. It's him."

"I'm not surprised," Marisol said. "He might be gorgeous on the outside, but inside he's pure rot."

Justine decided to take a look around the room while she had the chance, before she had to run back to the study to grab the flash drive. She opened the top drawer of the nightstand. Nothing interesting there. Same with the next three drawers. In the fourth drawer she struck pervert gold.

"That looks like a pharmacy," said Marisol.

Justine picked up one of the prescription bottles and read the label. "Flunitrazepam," she said, stumbling over the syllables.

"Generic Rohypnol. Date rape drug."

"Charming. He just gets better and better," Justine said, inspecting the next few bottles. "This one's gamma hydroxybutyric acid, and this is ketamine. And lookie here, he's even got Viagra."

"GMBH, Kit-Kat and Viagra. You would be so popular in the West Hollywood gay clubs with that shit."

"Hey, some of my best friends…holy crap, what's this?" Justine had opened the next drawer, and was staring at a collection of sexual torture instruments that would've put the Grand Inquisitor of Spain to shame.

Now Justine was pissed. She picked up a whip that looked like an extra long leather tassel. It was the same device she'd seen Alessandro use on the girl in the pictures. She turned to Alessandro and started hitting him on the chest. She shouted, "Mother." *Swoosh*. "Fucker!" *Swoosh*. *Swoosh*. *Swoosh*.

"You're a natural with that flogger," Marisol said, slightly amused at the scene she was watching. Justine didn't respond. She was in a groove, taking all her frustration out on Alessandro. Marisol spoke again. "Justine, you need to stop. Do you hear me? Stop! We have more important work to do and not much time."

But Justine was only more enraged. She moved from his chest to his now flaccid penis.

"Justine! Listen to me. You're acting just like he would. Is that what you want? To become the same kind of beast as him? Now stop. That's an order!" Marisol was clearly no longer amused.

But Justine couldn't stop. She continued her furious thrashing, until she heard a different voice say, "You're damaging the evidence we need."

"Justine, who is that?" yelled Marisol.

"I'm sorry Marisol, this isn't how I would've introduced you to Eniko. She's the one I told you about, from the FSB?"

Iya interjected next. "I'm here too. Nice to meet you, Marisol.

"Who the fuck are *you*, and how did you hack in to our conversation?" Marisol asked.

Eniko calmly answered, "Ex-FSB, rogues just like you. Independent contractors, working against the same enemies. I checked Justine's equipment before we left, and was able to isolate her broadcast frequency. My comrade Iya and I still have a mission to finish. Justine, you need to get Alessandro's semen."

"What?" Justine and Marisol asked simultaneously. Then Justine added with a whine, "Why?"

"We need his DNA, remember?"

"You can get his DNA with an inner cheek swab with a q-tip," said Marisol.

Iya interrupted. "We need large quantities of un-contaminated DNA to run batteries of tests for crimes committed all over the world. We need his sperm."

"That's a helluva a lot of DNA," retorted Marisol.

"He's committed a lot of crime all over the world. Each agency would want to do their own tests," said Eniko.

Justine didn't know whether to believe the Sparrows or Marisol.

"Get the sperm," commanded Eniko.

"Sperm, oh yuck. How am I gonna do that? And where am I gonna put it?" Justine was incredulous and disgusted.

"Jerk him off or suck him off," Iya answered dryly. "It's your choice."

"I love all these *choices* people keep offering me lately. Fine. I'll jerk him off, but where do I put it once I get it, um, out?"

"Zip-lock bags," laughed Eniko. "In your purse, remember?"

Justine dug into her purse and pulled out a couple of zip-lock bags.

"Start jerking him off," said Iya.

For the first time since she was a teenager, Justine was anxious about jerking off a guy. And Alessandro was barely conscious.

"He's soft as a strand of overcooked spaghetti. How do I get sperm from *that*?" she said, pointing to the sad hunk of flesh curled up on Alessandro's crotch.

"You found Viagra in his rape drawer, no? Crush half a pill, dip a dildo into the powder and shove it up his ass," Iya ordered. She sounded like a drill sergeant from a bad Cold War spy movie.

"*Ay dios mio*, said Marisol with a chuckle. "Now I want to meet both of you. In person."

"For heaven's sake, woman," Iya continued. "You've never milked a prostate?"

"Until two seconds ago I didn't know that was possible. I wish I still didn't." Justine found a dildo in Alessandro's sex toy drawer, and used it to crush a small handful of Viagra tablets. Once she had the dildo coated with Viagra powder she said to Eniko and Iya, "Alright, here goes. My first venture up the ass of a supine pervert."

Iya responded with gusto. "Atta' girl! Jam it in."

Justine looked away as she used her left hand to spread Alessandro's butt cheeks and her right hand to shove his dildo up his rectum. "Nothing's happening," she complained.

"Turn it on!" The answer came from all three women at the same time, like a choral concert.

Justine pushed the vibrator's on button and let it work its prostate stimulating magic. Within two minutes Alessandro's penis had stiffened into a giant erection. She placed the plastic bag over it and waited.

Marisol laughed in her ear.

"This is funny?" Justine asked, pissed.

"If you could see the look on your face," Marisol said in between guffaws. "Eniko, I wish you could see this. Oh, I'll take a screen shot so you can see later."

"Marisol! Don't you dare!" Justine screamed.

"But you look like you're changing the most disgusting diaper. It's priceless."

Just then Alessandro's breathing intensified, getting deeper, faster. His body tensed. He sighed. He moaned. And finally, he came. Justine watched wide-eyed as white viscous fluid shot out of his cock and flowed into the baggie. She sighed with relief as she pulled it off and zipped it shut. She could hear her three spy-buddies clapping and laughing inside her ear.

"Brava. Good work," said Iya.

"Get dressed," said Marisol. "And don't forget the flash drive."

"And clean up after yourself," added Eniko.

Justine placed the jizz-filled bag into a zippered compartment of her purse, then untied her thong from Alessandro's face and crumpled it into her bag. Her next struggle was getting herself back into the leather dress. She was shocked that she managed to get the zipper half way up without any help. Then, wearing a fresh pair of surgical gloves, she collected her gear from the bedroom and went to the den to retrieve the flash drive from Alessandro's computer.

In the hallway mirror she noticed her reflection. "Holy Mother of Dragons, Marisol! Why didn't you tell me that I look like a reject from a Romanian Knife Throwers convention. You were actually gonna let me walk out of here with my hair looking like this?"

"Trust me honey," Marisol laughed, "in that outfit, no one's looking at your hair."

Justine shrugged and fluffed up her hair with her fingers. "All that fancy gear and not even a damned comb."

She grabbed her shoes in the entrance foyer, stepped into the hallway and closed the door. She didn't arm the security system because once Alessandro gained consciousness, his slightest movement would set it off.

As soon as Justine was in the elevator she heard Marisol chuckling again. "Seriously?" she asked. "You're still amused?"

"Nice improv! Academy Award-worthy, actually," Marisol said.

Justine smiled at the two men working in the lobby. Night shift. They didn't know her, and didn't seem concerned as she hurried out into the waiting black Cadillac limo.

"Ugh, Iya. Thank god it's you," Justine said to her driver. "I never thought I'd hear myself say those words."

"What am I, chopped liver?" It was Eniko, crouching on the floor of the other side of the back seat.

Justine handed her the flash drive and sperm bag. "Nope. You're the keeper of the jizz. I'm so damned tired I don't even know what time it is. Now I need a drink," she sighed.

"Shaken, not stirred," said Iya in her best imitation of a British accent.

Eniko emerged from her spot on the floor and took the seat beside Justine and chimed in with a heartfelt chuckle. "Yes Ms. Bond—Jamie Bond."

CHAPTER 52

Iya dropped Justine off at Lise's condo and sped away. As soon as Justine opened the door, Danisha asked how Alessandro was.

"I had to choke him out in order to collect his sperm."

"You did *what?* You're always stealing my men!" she yelled as she stormed out.

There had to be a way to get rid of the lingering yuck factor. Justine knew that no amount of soap and water would cleanse her body, mind and spirit of her breaking-and-entering slash fledgling-dominatrix ordeal. The residual pollutants were tenacious; images of women, bound, gagged and frightened floated through her dreams like goblins on Halloween. Flashes of sense memories haunted her waking hours too; a certain peculiar odor—a mixture of department store cologne, sweat, semen, and fear—sporadically invaded her nostrils. And just in case Justine wasn't feeling miserable enough, Danisha wasn't returning her calls.

They'd had a few tussles over the almost fifteen year history of their friendship, and a few of those had been doozies. The first one was towards the end of their junior year at Stanford after Justine slept with Danisha's ex-boyfriend Rand Kimball during spring break in Cabo San Lucas. Danisha hadn't gone on that trip, said she had no interest in participating in a "pseudo-sorority beach orgy," and preferred to stay in Palo Alto during the break and work on her portfolio while the campus was quiet. Justine suspected that the real reason Danisha didn't go had to do with money. Her casual offer to cover Danisha's expenses, she realized later, was ill conceived; Dani didn't say no, she didn't say anything. She just glared at Justine, expressionless.

Dani's description turned out to be pretty accurate. Justine missed her a lot that week, and, though she'd never admit it to anyone, she also resented Danisha for not coming and for her silent reaction—a look so cold, so angry, one would've thought Justine had just wrapped herself in a Confederate flag. She partied a lot that week with other kids from Stanford and USC, and emailed Dani every other day with status reports and gossip. It never occurred to her that her drunken hook-up with Rand would upset Danisha, so she included that bit of news in her last email, and when she got back to the dorm Danisha was even angrier than she'd been before the break.

"You seriously fucked Rand Kimball?" she asked, furious.

"Well I don't know that it qualifies as actual fucking." Justine responded, laughing.

"What's that supposed to mean?"

"Oh come on Dani! You aren't serious, right? I mean, it was a quick grope and pant on the beach. During Spring Break. Everyone knows spring break doesn't count."

"*Everyone* knows? I don't know, am I no one?"

"You don't get it, do you? It's not him Jussy, it's you. You get everything you want."

"And you don't?"

"No I don't. You don't realize what it's like to have to prove yourself at every step. I have to work a thousand times harder at everything I do just to get people to take me seriously."

Justine had understood then how thoughtless her offer to pay Dani's way had been, and how tone deaf she'd been to all of Danisha's complaints about their privileged and entitled peers.

Justine calmly told Dani that she was wrong, that she wasn't thinking straight. That she wasn't making this shit up, that Danisha had seen the evidence with her own eyes.

But Danisha wasn't interested in facts or evidence. She was falling apart, irrational, and lashing out as she stormed out of Lise's apartment.

That was almost five days ago.

Lise, who stayed with Justine, sensed her daughter's anxiety. "Give her time," Lise advised.

"I've called her a hundred times. Sent texts, emails, Facebook messages. Hell, I'd send smoke signals if I knew how. But she's not responding."

"She's suffering, Jussy. PTSD."

Justine sighed. "Yeah. Even though *she* wasn't the one that had to go into battle."

"Stop that right now," Lise ordered. "You want glory? Go back to Palo Alto and start another company. You did what you had to do and I'm proud of you. Believe me, I've seen Eniko and Iya in action and I'm still traumatized."

"Do me a favor and *never* tell me *that* story," Justine responded, trying desperately to block the image of Lise holding a flogger from her mind. "But Danisha? I get it. She's also got the pregnancy hormone surge. I hear that can make girls get all cray-cray."

"I wouldn't know. And don't reduce your best friend to a concoction of chemicals. Just get on with your own life, deal with your own issues. How long do you think you'll stay in LA?"

"Good question. I should look into that," Justine said, reaching for her cell phone. The alert banner showed two new text messages, and an email from Scott.

Greetings from the top of the world. It's outrageously beautiful up here. You'd hate it, nothing but snow and mountains and sky, plus the occasional bear trying to eat me, but don't worry, not in the sexual way. I did kind of fall in love with another woman. A harp seal. She fell in love with me, actually. Kept bringing me dead fish as presents. Anyway that relationship would never have worked and we both knew it. Besides, I miss you.

I am so fucking cold, can't wait to warm up in your bed. Between your legs. Leaving for Winnipeg tomorrow. It's only a fucking 12-hour snowmobile drive from here. Will let you know when my flight gets in to SFO."

"Good news?" Lise asked Justine, whose sudden happiness was unmistakable.

"Yep. Scott's coming home. But I should tell him to come to LA, not San Francisco. I'm not going back there any time soon. The Oscars are next week end, I might have to stick around these parts."

"You're going to the Academy Awards?"

Justine realized that she shouldn't have mentioned the Oscars. She hated having to lie to her mother, but she had no choice. Lise knew that Justine was in training, learning to protect herself, but she did not know about the terms of Justine's arrangement with Don. The fact that she was paying for her training with three months of what Justine knew

Lise would consider *manual labor*, working for Don's organization protecting the rich and famous, had to remain a secret.

"Wouldn't that be something? But no, I'm not going to the awards," Justine said. It wasn't exactly a lie; Don told Justine she'd only be on the red carpet with Alyssa Stewart. "My teacher is here and he doesn't want to interrupt my training."

"I was invited to one of the after parties," said Lise, oblivious to Justine's inner struggle. "Since I'm here anyway I think I'll just stay. You know you're welcome here, but why don't you go check into one of the spa resorts in the desert? You and Scott will have more privacy."

"You always know just what to say, Lise. I will most definitely look into that possibility."

"No you won't," said Lise. "I know just the place in Desert Hot Springs. If you leave here after rush hour you can get there by midnight. I'll make the reservation for you in my name, just in case the psycho that attacked you is tracking your card. Take my car."

The texts were from Marisol. Justine clicked on the first one: *El jefe says you can take the next 5 days off.*

Thank you Don. The idea of spending five days in the desert, one or two of those days with Scott, suddenly seemed extremely appealing.

She clicked on the second text: *Scratch that. Call me on the primary number.*

Now what? Justine grabbed her burner cell and told Lise she was going for a walk.

CHAPTER 53

Marisol answered on the first ring. "You sure it's safe to talk?"

"I just walked out of Lise's building, walking east on Olympic Boulevard. No one walks here so there's not much chance of me bumping into another pedestrian or being overheard. What's up?"

"You know you'll be escorting Alyssa on Sunday, right?"

"Right."

"Alyssa has officially chosen publicity over security. She doesn't want Don beside her on the red carpet or in the venue."

Justine smiled. "Don must be relieved."

"Security will be tight," Marisol continued, ignoring Justine's small talk. "The usual radical groups have promised to protest every cause imaginable, and of course there's always the professional hooligans. Any minor incident, someone throws a rock that lands near a celebrity—suddenly becomes a major publicity coup. Even the threat of a suicide bomber would end the whole ceremony."

"So much for *the show must go on*," Justine interjected with a little friendly banter. "But won't there be a small army of federal, state, county, city and private security protecting the stars from the public?"

Marisol snickered. "Yeah. Bodyguards will be piled up like sandbags for a hurricane. Only they'll be walking sandbags, each jockeying to look more important than the next one. Meanwhile, Don, who is arguably the best professional protection money can buy and the best tactical profiler on the planet, will have to wait in Alyssa's limo with her personal assistant, watching the TV news feeds on six small monitors."

"Don already told me I'd be on the red carpet with her," Justine said, wondering which designer dress she'd get to wear.

"Right. And I'm telling you what happens after they roll up that carpet. The after parties start around nine. Security at these things varies, we never know if they'll let Don inspect the venues in advance. Your first stop is the Stars for Peace Foundation event."

"Never heard of them."

"It's a Jewish American charity that supports cultural interchange between Israel and other countries in the Middle East. They're honoring the Swedish director Lars Karlsson. He was nominated for Best Documentary. According to *Variety* it's a, quote, *Insightful Israeli-Palestinian retelling of Romeo and Juliet, with—spoiler-alert—a give-peace-a-chance ending*. End quote. The group hasn't received much coverage, so it shouldn't be on the radar of the media-savvy protestors. They'll go to the more publicized star-studded extravaganzas instead."

Justine stopped walking. "Lars Karlsson? My fiancé photographed him in Rwanda. It was his first assignment for *National Geographic*. Karlsson was working to save the mountain gorillas."

"That's a fascinating coincidence, Justine, but right now I need you to focus on *your* next assignment."

"Right. Go ahead, I'm all ears."

"The Israelis will take care of security for that first party so you don't have to worry about pre-checks, just stay close to the client."

"What Israelis? Like, official IDF soldiers connected to the consulate?"

"Not quite. They're mostly ex-Mossad, with a few active duty agents. We are not privy to that information, and to tell you the truth, I don't care. They're good. That's all that matters," Marisol explained.

"Cool. But what are ex-Mossad agents doing in Hollywood?"

"Working. Following the money, just like Don. Celebrities love having ex-Mossad on their security team. It's a huge status boost."

Justine thought about her first trip to Israel, the summer before her senior year in high school. She lived on the *Neve Eitan* kibbutz for two months. Her official job was tending livestock, but her actual job was rubbing antibiotic ointment on the rear ends of chickens. She shook off the image of her Israeli commune friends playing bad ass. "So why are we going to this party? Alyssa's a rabid anti-Semite."

"That's just an act. Besides, she loves you now. The producers of her next film are sponsoring the party. She'll make an appearance, then rush off to the next event on the list."

"Which is?" Justine asked with mock curiosity.

"You will have all of that information as soon as her team finalizes her schedule. Speaking of running, Don wanted me to discuss your outfit for Sunday night."

"That's up to Alyssa. She said she wants me to look like her hot best friend, or whatever. Just *not* like a bodyguard. I'll wear something of hers, a dress she's already been seen in."

"What about shoes?"

"I told her I'd bring my own."

"Don wants you to blend in. He said to tell you to dress like a personal assistant. To look sweet, not hot. You need to be invisible. Maybe look a little overweight."

"Yeah, that's *not* gonna happen. You know what they say in Hollywood, 'Those with the gold make the rules.' On Sunday Alyssa makes the rules."

"Don will allow some of Alyssa's suggestions, like the wig."

"What wig?" Just hearing the word *wig* reminded Justine of her dominatrix costume.

"Alyssa wants to be the only hot blonde in her entourage. You'll be wearing a brunette wig. Short, with bangs."

"Charming. As long as I don't have to wear a skin-tight leather mini dress."

"That was a *muy memorable facha*. But fat chicks can't pull that off. And Don wants you to be a fat chick so..."

"Well how'm I gonna pull *that* off?"

"It's not so difficult. Looking thinner is much more tricky, which is why no one in Los Angeles eats anything but celery sticks for the entire month of February."

"Exactly. And Don wants me to blend in. I'll stick out like a pervert in a playground if I have to look like a," Justine made the universally recognized hand signal for air quotes, as if Marisol could actually see her, " *fat chick*."

"What you wear and how you look is up to Don. Next topic. You may take the next five days for yourself. Go to a spa in Carmel, or a

Buddhist monastery in the desert. Whatever makes you happy. Don will pick up the tab. Just be rested and ready to kick butt by Saturday."

"Um, okay," Justine said through a fresh smile. Maybe she should get laid after all. *For days.* She was glad Marisol couldn't actually see her face. "I can do that."

"There is one more small detail. You won't recognize Don, not at first. He has made some changes since the last time you saw him."

"You using *made* as a transitive or reflexive verb?"

"Justine, this is important!" Marisol scolded.

"I know! That's why I want you to clarify your intended meaning of the word *made*. Did Don change something or did something change Don?"

"Huh?"

"He made some changes *to what?*"

"To *himself*. Physical, surgically-aided changes."

"Why?"

"Because there's a five million dollar bounty on his head and every assassin in the world is gunning for him. So, don't be surprised if he looks like a Nordic carpenter. The FAA has facial recognition software with age progression in every airport. It's cutting edge technology, impossible to hack. But this state of the art technology *cannot* identify Don now, post-op. I doubt that even his old friends, the ones trying to silence him, could recognize him. They know nothing of age-*regression* and race-shifting, in their software or in real life."

"You are making this up, right?"

"It's amazing what plastic surgeons can do these days."

CHAPTER 54

Justine didn't want to waste any time deciding where to go. Marisol's suggestions of a spa in Carmel or Buddhist monastery in the desert didn't sound too appealing; Carmel was too far and the idea of anything monastic was antithetical to Justine's goal of having as much sex as possible. Her best move would be to go wherever Lise sent her. Justine could always count on Lise and her superb sense of everything.

"It's official," Justine said to her mother when she got back to the apartment. "My teacher is busy for the rest of the week and won't have time for me. I have five glorious days to myself. Where am I going?"

"I was thinking of a little place in Desert Hot Springs. The general manager is one of my best friends. I'll call him."

"Exactly how many *best friends* do you have, Lise?"

"Justine, it's a category, not a person. I've told you that, and you're not allowed to make fun of me. Anyway, the place is perfect. We'll get you a Soulstice room. That's s-o-u-l-s-t-i-c-e—FYI."

"Of course it is. This is some new age chakra balancing resort I take it?"

"It can be if that's what you want. They do have a resident shamanic healer, but you can also just hang around your own suite. They all have private patios with fire pits and a hammock."

"I love that word, *private*. A lot more than those other words you used, *shamanic* and *healer*."

While Lise called her best friend at Two Bunch Palms, Justine researched flights from Winnipeg to anywhere close to Palm Springs. She was pleasantly surprised to find that United had a flight with only one stop that would land Scott at Palm Springs before nine the next night. She tapped out a quick email to him with the name of the hotel and the flight information she'd found, then prayed that he could make the twelve-hour journey.

"You're all set," Lise announced when she got off the phone. "Use my name when you check in, they'll be waiting for you. I forgot to tell you the best part. It's an adults only resort, and everybody whispers in the common areas."

"Can I leave right now?" Justine responded, laughing.

"Baby girl, if I could teleport you there I would. Unfortunately, I can't do that yet, so you'll have to take my car."

Lise's car wasn't too shabby of an option. If one had to drive across the Mohave Desert it might as well be in a brand new BMW Z4 convertible. Justine started the journey with the top down, something she'd never do during the day. She cursed that decision as she drove east on the Ten, as Angelinos called that numbered Interstate freeway. Traffic was heavy, nothing unusual there, but convoys of semi-trucks and SUVs belched nasty exhaust fumes that engulfed her sporty little vehicle. She stopped at the a gas station somewhere near West Covina, closed the convertible roof, topped off the gas tank, then continued east into the darkness.

The young woman at the reception desk was expecting her. "Good evening, Ms Baron. I trust you had a pleasant drive this evening?"

"Yes, thank you. I'd forgotten how chilly it gets out here at night."

"We'll warm you right up. Your husband arrived about a half hour ago. I can call him and tell him to meet you at the grotto, the smaller pool is a constant one hundred and four degrees. It's one of the few mineral springs in the world with no sulfurous odor. It actually has a lovely, almost woodsy scent."

"Excuse me?" Justine interjected.

"I said the scent is kind of woodsy…"

"Not that part. You said my *husband* was here?"

"Yes! I'm sorry, of course you must be eager to see him. He sure was excited to be here."

Did she just wink? A familiar feeling of impatience mixed with dread swept over Justine. Furtively, she slipped her hand into her shoulder bag and wrapped her fingers around her back up gun, a Glock 26. "No problem, I wasn't expecting him until tomorrow," she said through a forced smile. "I'll just meet him in the room, if you can point me in the right direction."

"I'll accompany you there…"

"That's okay. I want to start my urban disconnect right now, enjoy the absolute silence between here and there."

"Very well. You're in the Soulstice King. That's solstice with a *U*."

"I saw that, very clever word play."

"Right? I can have someone bring your luggage to the room."

"It's still in the car, I'll get it later. Right now I'm kind of excited to see my husband."

"Okay, you can always call the front desk if you change your mind. Here's your key, and our brochure of spa services. I highly recommend the oxygen facial. It stimulates your skin with oxygen, more of an anti-aging treatment than a classic facial, not that you need it…"

"Good to know," Justine said, grabbing the key and brochure with her free hand. If she survived whoever was waiting for her in the Soulstice room, she would definitely get a facial.

Lise must've told her best friend the hotel manager that Justine would be expecting a gentleman caller. That would explain the receptionist's merry demeanor, and the hotel's willingness to give whoever had told them he was her husband a key. But how did that man know she would be here? Not even Don had that information. Justine wasn't taking any chances. She took the pistol from her bag and held it at a low ready position, both hands wrapped firmly around the grip and her right index finger on the trigger.

The door to the room was ajar. Justine pushed it open slowly, silently. Raising the gun to chin-level, she scanned the room. Only one light was turned on, a hanging lamp near the sliding doors that led to the patio.

He was out there. On the patio.

Standing in the dark at the doorway, she knew he hadn't seen her, and unless he had night vision goggles he wouldn't be able to detect her. *He might have night vision goggles.* She had to take every precaution. She pointed her gun at the man, who was bending over what looked like a low table, and kept her eye trained on him as she walked slowly towards the sliding doors.

"Put your hands up where I can see them," she barked when she got to the doorway. "I have a gun pointed at your head and I know how to use it."

He froze.

"Now stand up. Slowly."

"Justine," the man said. "Can you please put the gun down?"

She lowered her pistol. "Scott?"

CHAPTER 55

Justine set the safety and set gun on the nightstand. "Your wish is my command, scaredy cat. And it's Wonder Woman, not Super Girl. Try not to call out the wrong name when you're fucking me."

"And there it is, the super hero stand-up routine."

"You've forgotten how amusing I can be?"

"I've forgotten nothing. Every night I think about this. You, lying on a bed, any bed, underneath me. On top of me. Next to me. Sit up for one moment, please. This dress looks cumbersome. Let's get it off you, set that gorgeous body free."

Still smiling, Justine obeyed. Scott lifted her thin cotton dress over her head and gently laid her back against the pillows. With his left hand he caressed the contours of her belly, hips, shoulders, while his right hand undid the buttons of his white cotton shirt.

"Oh dear god you smell divine," Justine muttered. "Now take your pants off."

"Already done. Just lie back and relax now. I'm in charge here."

"I like that, for the next few hours anyway. Don't go getting any macho ideas for the future though," Justine said, her inner feminist overshadowing her romance novel heroine.

"Shhh, no talking. Just be."

When his lips finally touched hers Justine felt a delicious tingling in her upper thighs. Scott must have sensed it. He ran his fingers softly over the delicate skin of her inner thighs, just above her knee. His lips grazed the side of her neck, clavicle, shoulder. He bypassed her breast and belly and waist, went straight to the outside of her right hip. His left hand slid under her, onto her ass. He pulled her body closer to his lips.

Justine groaned.

Scott rolled her onto her back, and started to kiss the inside of her thighs.

Scott buried his tongue, or rather the tip of his tongue, on the tip of her clit. Justine felt the heat radiating from deep within her. Her groans grew louder.

"Fuck me please," she whispered.

"So was that one continuous orgasm or a series of serious earthquakes and aftershocks?" Scott asked a while later as Justine struggled to catch her breath.

"I lost count as soon as my pants hit the floor. Oh lord, can I tell you how often I've dreamed of this?"

Scott laughed. "You don't have to. I was right there with you."

"We have the next eighty hours and I want to last all night. Did you know we have a private hot tub and fire pit?"

"Yes, we've already discussed the fire pit, remember?"

"I remember everything, my love. Come, let's go outside. You won't believe how gorgeous the desert sky is at night."

Scott stepped off the bed and lifted Justine into his arms like she was a weightless nymph. She giggled again. A vision of the other hot spring, the one in the cave near Big Sur, flashed through her mind.

She opened her eyes wide and looked at her lover. He slid the glass door open and stepped outside to the small hot tub. His blue eyes sparkled in the reflection of the fire still burning in the pit.

"I really do love you, you know," she told him.

Scott's smile lit up his face. "She said the magic words! I'm going to set you down right..." he stepped into the tub and placed her on the tiled seat, "here."

The water was warm, the perfect contrast to the cool night air. Justine reclined against the tub's curved edge and watched as Scott stepped out, his cock still hard. "Hey, where do you think you're going?"

"I have something for you inside. Once sec. Soak up some of those magic desert minerals, get ready for round two."

As Scott disappeared into the room, Justine immersed herself under the water. She was floating on her back when he returned seconds later.

"Please tell me it's edible," she said. "All that activity, I'm famished."

"It's edible."

"Good." Justine sat up.

"Except it's not really." He stepped into the water and sat beside her. In his hand was a small black velvet box. "Food for your soul," he said, handing it to her.

Justine's eyes opened wide. Her heart beat so quickly in her chest she was afraid Scott could hear it pounding. She inspected the box with her fingers.

"Open it. Please?"

She lifted the lid. Nestled in a bed of alabaster silk she saw the ring. Its yellow stone glimmered in the reflected firelight. "Oh…" She couldn't find any other words.

"It was my mother's."

"It's exquisite. Is it actually yellow or are my sex addled eyes playing tricks on me?"

Scott laughed. "It's yellow. They call them canary diamonds now, but when my dad bought this for my mom it was just an ordinary old yellow diamond cut in the late nineteenth century."

"Ordinary? I love how you understate the extraordinary. Yellow diamonds, real ones, are some of the rarest stones on the planet."

"Well, I didn't want to brag."

"It's enormous. I'll need a security guard just for the ring."

"It's only six carats."

"Is that all?" Justine laughed. "Did you forget that you're dealing with a Park Avenue American Princess?"

"I know exactly who I'm dealing with. And I know the ring is a bit ostentatious, but it *is* a family heirloom. And since it was mine-cut a century or so ago, it's bloodless."

"Conflict free, eh? That fits my millennial perception perfectly, even though it was mined back then with slave labor."

Scott took the ring from out of the box and slid it onto Justine's finger. "I give you this from my heart, my mind, and my soul. Being away from you for so many months…" he stuttered, "I…I…I know now that I don't want that. I want to be with you. Always. Justine Baron, will you marry me?"

"I'm pretty sure I've said it before, but I'll say it again. And again and again." She was laughing now. A profound, uncontrollable smile took over her features. "Yes. Yes. Yes." She crawled onto his lap, wrapped her legs around his waist, and kissed every inch of his face.

Resting her head on Scott's shoulders, Justine gazed at the fiery yellow stone on her left ring finger. The smell of mesquite filled her nostrils, and for the first time since that horrible night in Palo Alto, she felt safe, and truly happy

They drove back to Los Angeles. She dropped Scott off at the Standard Hotel on Sunset. Reality was a buzz-kill, even in Hollywood—or maybe *especially* in Hollywood. It was the morning of the biggest night of the year, Oscar night.

Both Scott and Justine had to work. He had told her about his assignment to photograph the super-famous at the super-famous Vanity Fair magazine Academy Awards after-party. Of her assignment he knew nothing. In fact, he wasn't aware that she even had to work. Scott knew only enough about Justine's training to know not to ask her anything about it.

After three day of sex, Justine's heart grew heavy as she watched Scott disappear into the revolving doors of the hotel, and seeing the chaos of cars and humanity on the Sunset Strip only augmented its weight. The sound of a honking horn jarred Justine from her melancholy reverie. *Yeah, yeah, I'm going,* she said to the horn-honker as though he could hear her. Gripping the steering wheel with both hands, she caught a glimpse of her left ring finger. For one glorious moment she could believe that the stone, Scott's mother's diamond, emitted the energy– she didn't know what else to call it—of a tiny golden star. Her mood changed instantly. *Diamonds are forever.* Justine had never liked that slogan; she'd seen too many marriages crumble under the weight of fairytale expectations, but now at least she *understood* the sentiment that allowed—no, encouraged people to buy into the game. This one little lump of compressed carbon, worthless but for the faith men and women invest in its value, was a genuine symbol of *love.* Sure it was also a symbol of esteem and prestige, but Justine had no problem with that. The sparkling yellow gem reminded her that Scott was still with her, that he'd pledged his love to her, just as his father did with his wife, Scott's mother. *Forever.* Whatever that meant.

CHAPTER 56

When Justine arrived at the newly completed Beverly Stanton Hotel she thought that whoever said there was but one step from the sublime to the ridiculous must've experienced an awards ceremony in Hollywood. She'd been reading about the hotel in architectural, decor and gossip magazines; it was designed by a famous Spanish architect and had a six-month waiting list for an ordinary room. The lobby, with its towering white marble columns and billowing white silk chiffon curtains, felt like a corner of heaven. Justine thought that if they were even one tenth as beautiful as the lobby, the Viva's *ordinary* rooms had to be spectacular.

Marisol had sent the information Justine would need to access Alyssa Stewart's penthouse suite. The first text read, *Private elevator. Penthouse floor. Suite 3510.* Justine scanned the lobby and found the private elevator hiding in a quiet corner. Wearing faded jeans, a white cotton shirt and ivory Birkenstocks, she blended in perfectly with the pretentiously unpretentious crowd as she wheeled her carry-on around the perimeter and onto the private elevator. When the doors opened on the thirty-fifth floor, she checked her burner phone for the entrance code and punched it into the panel beside the suite's door. It opened with a satisfying swoosh, like a message being sent on an iPhone.

She inspected the suite. More white marble and silk, three bedrooms with their own bathrooms, and a living room with floor to ceiling windows. Justine gave herself a moment to take in the view; the skyscrapers of Century City, another cluster of high rise buildings downtown, and the hills in the distance. The skyline wasn't as fabulous as Manhattan, but some of the buildings were indeed spectacular. Her eye settled on one of them, a graceful oblong shaped behemoth with golden accents that glittered in the midday sun, kind of like her engagement ring. She knew the place, maybe because it was close to Lise's building. Her feeling of familiarity suddenly morphed into a memory.

Alessandro's building. Yuck, yuck, yuck.

Enough of that, she thought to herself. *Be here now.*

In the room that would be hers that night Justine saw a vision of feathers and organza in navy blue, spread out on the cream-colored velvet couch. A dress. *Karl Lagerfeld for Chanel.* She picked it up, held it to her torso and walked to the full-length mirror. Perfection.

Her burner phone buzzed. No caller ID, had to be Marisol. "Hey," she said, pushing the button on her earpiece.

"You're not wearing that dress."

"Party pooper. You're just jealous that I'm gonna look fantastic in navy blue. No one looks fantastic in navy blue, except me and Penelope Cruz. And Air Force, of course."

"You look good. But you won't be able to do your job with all those feathers."

She had a point. Justine inspected the dress. "They're detachable."

"Put the dress down. You should start getting ready. I take it you can do your own makeup?"

"Is the rabbi kosher? I'm just gonna try this baby on for a sec. See if it needs any alteration." Justine stepped out of her jeans and into the dress, which fit like it was made for her.

"Not bad, *chica,*" Marisol chimed in Justine's ear. "Too bad Don won't let you wear it. How you gonna carry a weapon in that?"

Justine opened her carry-on, pulled out her two Glock 26 pistols and her inner-thigh concealment holsters. "I won't need both of these, right?" she asked Marisol.

"Probably not. Don has faith in the ex-Mossad agents in charge of security."

"I'll only use one of them. They're heavy, especially under an evening gown. Eleven shots should handle anything the ex-Mossad couldn't."

"Head's up," Marisol said. "Don and client," ETA, sixty seconds."

Justine strapped on one holster, adjusted her breasts, and straightened her gown. Once she was sure that her inner-thigh-holstered pistol didn't show, she walked into the living room, faced the door, and waited.

It opened slowly. A man's voice said, "Don here."

"Duh. Justine here. But you already knew that." She chuckled, ready for a witty greeting. But when she actually saw Don's face, she was shocked. "Holy GQ, Don. You look like Thor."

He had somehow become a blue-eyed blond. He smiled as he re-holstered his pistol. His smile was the only part of him that Justine recognized. He looked like a sophisticated over-muscled movie star in his Tom Ford suit.

"Please tell me you look like Arnold Schwarzenegger in his prime because you're wearing your Spectra Shield body armor," Justine said to Don. She noticed that whatever brand of body armor he was wearing, it extended to his groin. Alyssa probably loved that.

And there she was, the movie star, Best Actress nominee, sweeping in right behind her favorite bodyguard.

Alyssa looked at Justine for a moment, her eyes taking in the sight of the beautiful woman wearing her cast-off couture dress, then ran over to her, squealing. "You look so fucking *hot* in that dress!" She threw her arms around Justine's naked shoulders and kissed her gently on the lips.

Justine suddenly noticed Raphael, Alyssa's assistant. "Hair and makeup are on their way up," he said.

"Where'd you come from?" Justine asked him playfully.

"He's always right behind me, like a shadow," Alyssa answered for Raphael. "Now, where's my room?"

"End of the hall," Justine said, pointing Alyssa in the right direction.

"Ugh, thank you. Raphael, wait here for the beauty committee." Alyssa kicked off her shoes and headed toward her room. "See you hotties later."

"Beauty committee at front door," Marisol told Justine.

"Got it, thanks Marisol," she responded as Don nodded and walked over to open the door.

Once Alyssa and her crew were safely settled in her room, Justine took a moment to study Don's face. She noticed the makeup he wore to hide the remnants of bruising. "When was the procedure?" she asked him.

"Two weeks ago. I've been recuperating at Big Sur, using the Vasper unit every day."

"Remarkable," Justine said. "That machine really does work. But the surgery, why'd you do it?" she asked.

"Because looks can kill. I have to hide in plain sight."

"Sorry for staring. This is gonna take some getting used to. You look, well, different, but still somehow gorgeous."

"Thanks. There were too many hired guns using my old photo for target practice. Probably including your two dominatrix *Swallows*."

"Marisol told you?"

"Of course I told him," Marisol snapped inside Justine's ear.

"How do I shut you up?" Justine asked the air around her.

"Did you make a new friend we can't see?" Don laughed as he pretended to look around the room.

"Everybody's a comedian today, eh? Listen, Iya and Eniko said that you were married to a Russian woman named Irina, that she was their mentor, and that they want to protect you."

"And you believe them?" Don and Marisol quipped in unison.

"They've actually been a huge help," Justine explained. "I could never have gotten the rest of the data off Alessandro without their help. And the Russians called them *Sparrows*. There's no need to insult them by calling them *Swallows*. We worked as a team. Marisol knows that."

"I like to err on the side of caution. Speaking of which, take that dress off."

"Yeah, I was just gonna do that. Don't want to mess it up before the big night."

"No Justine. You're not wearing it. Not tonight. I know Alyssa likes to dress you up like a movie star, but designer clothes won't stop bullets." Justine followed Don as he pulled his suitcase into her bedroom, where took out a pile of gray clothing. "Here. Try these on."

Justine did as she was told, and tried on Don's proffered outfit; a tarmac-gray boxy pantsuit, white cotton blouse, and a pair of sensible black flats. But she didn't even try to hide her disappointment. "I look like I gained twenty pounds and two bra sizes," she moaned. "And what's the deal with these granny shoes?"

"And this," Don said, tossing her a handful of hair.

"Yay. I get to be a brunette." Justine plopped the brown wig on her head. "Pixie cut. How original." She studied her reflection in the full-length mirror. "I look like an dowdy librarian."

"You wouldn't need that jacket in a library. It's lined with bullet and impact resistant plates."

"Even better. I'm going to the Oscars wearing some fucking dishes."

"It's not *your* fashion show. You're the help. Remember that."

"Yeah, yeah. I know. But this is too much," Justine said as she began to unbutton the jacket. "It's like I had a fashion lobotomy. I won't do it."

Don raised his finger. "Button it up," he ordered. "It's level IIA Spectra Shield, will stop most pistol bullets, and it has level IV ceramic trauma plates on the sternum and spine."

"Spectra shield?"

"It's the brand name of a super light-weight bullet-resistant fabric. You also have level III protection under your wig. A side or rear headshot might leave you with a concussion, but you'd survive. I've been shot eight different times and blown up once in my body armor. I was able to return fire eight times and my men took care of me when I got blown up. I'm alive. My enemies are not."

Justine pouted. "I can't do it. I admit I'm vain. And I look hideous in your outfit."

Don shrugged. "That's the point. Alyssa's the one on display. Not you. Not me. If you take off your makeup and stick in some cheek fillers, the paparazzi will ignore you. Remember your first job with Alyssa when you were on the front page of every tabloid?"

Justine surrendered. "Fine. Play that card. You win. Now, can I help you find a book? Something by Sinclair Lewis perhaps?"

"Very funny, Marian Madame Librarian."

"Ooh, a musical theater reference. I didn't know you had that in you," Justine laughed.

"Now these," Don said. He was serious now. No more laughing. He handed her a pair of clear wraparound glasses. "Polycarbonate. But, only level two. Twenty percent of urban warfare casualties are from secondary fragments in soldiers' eyes. These will at least give you some protection for your face. You can use your Spectra Shield–lined purse to stop most pistol bullets. These glasses have a mini-camera for Marisol's benefit. She'll be able to see everything you can see. You also have a mini-cam on the back of your suit collar so she can watch your rear. Hopefully you brought your contact lens so you can see Marisol as well. Your armor set me back five grand and that com-gear was more than twenty. But you're worth it," he added with a smile.

"Thanks a lot. And I'm already wearing my Google lens."

Don nodded approvingly. Justine gazed at herself in the mirror. She couldn't even laugh at how ridiculous she looked. With her Google lens she could actually see her armored butt in the mirror behind her. "Do me a favor and turn off my rear-view camera." Don glared at her. "Just for now. Please. Marisol?"

Her contact lens cleared and she could see normally again, but she heard Alyssa before she could see her.

"Oh my God! What is this? What happened to the Chanel I gave you?"

"Don said it wouldn't stop bullets, and as your walking sandbag I need to stop bullets."

Alyssa was clearly angry. "No. This will *not* do." Her tone was imperious.

"Alyssa, you need to listen…"

"No Don. *You* need to listen. You two are supposed to be my mysterious new lovers. You are *not* allowed to embarrass me in front of the press."

"We're here to protect you, not fuck you," Don stated bluntly.

"You're already fucked, 'cause you both work for me," Alyssa barked at him. "Your suit looks fine, I don't mind the extra bulk on a man. And, I like your new look. Better than before. But that old lady outfit? Alyssa Stewart doesn't do ugly."

"If we're going to risk taking bullets for you, we need to survive so we can return fire." Don countered.

"It's just a boring charity party," argued Alyssa.

Don lowered his voice. "It's a political as well as social event, so anything is possible."

"Don, you are a fucking buzz kill."

"I'm serious Alyssa. It's not just any charity party, it's a *Jewish* charity, which makes it a target. That's why they put ex-Mossad agents in charge of security."

"Then we have nothing to worry about," Alyssa snickered, reluctantly conceding the risk. "They're the best in the world, right?"

"True, but they're not on their home turf," Don countered. "They're not allowed to search, profile and detain here like they can in Israel."

"Yeah, yeah, yeah. Fine. Whatevs. But we're in Hollywood, USA, not the Middle East!" Alyssa stamped her foot like a child throwing a tantrum as she walked back to her bedroom. "Justine, change back into that Chanel gown. Now!"

Justine's glee overpowered her sense of safety. She practically tore off the gray armor on her way back to the dress.

"You wanna help me zip this baby up?" she asked Don, reclaiming her feminine allure.

"I can see your delight, Justine, and you do look nice in that dress."

"Nice? That's the best you can do?"

"I'm speaking from experience here. You two are making one dangerous decision," Don pronounced with sincere gravity.

"I have makeup to do. See you in ten," Justine said, grabbing her cosmetics bag as she headed to her bathroom. "Ooh, they even have makeup lights in here!"

Ten minutes later, Justine made her grand entrance into the suite's living room. Don grudgingly admitted that she looked stunning, but he reiterated his concern. "No body armor. It's a bad idea."

CHAPTER 57

They made it through the televised Academy Awards ceremony without incident—unless Alyssa's petulance counted as an incident; she didn't receive the Best Actress award, which put her in an especially foul mood, though she still managed to blow empty kisses to the winner. After the ceremony they'd breezed through the Governor's Ball; Alyssa had no statuette to engrave and she wasn't about to hang around her statuette-clutching competitors.

The first post-Oscar party on Alyssa's schedule was the Stars For Peace Foundation Ball. She wanted to breeze through that one as well, until Don reminded her that the event was in honor of the Swedish director, Lars Karlsson, whose documentary had just won an Oscar. Alyssa knew that being seen with Karlsson would improve her brand, increase her status with the intellectual crowd.

Justine was actually looking forward to this event. She'd read in the trades that Danisha, who still wouldn't return any of her calls, text messages, and emails, had recently signed on as costume designer for Karlsson's next feature and so would most likely be there to congratulate Lars on his Oscar. Justine didn't know what to expect from Danisha, and though she didn't delude herself with hopes of a warm embrace or a timid apology or even a slight shrug and forgiving smile, Justine hoped that maybe, just maybe, if she could just get a few seconds face to face with her dearest friend, the two of them could start mending the terrible rift in their friendship.

News vans topped with portable satellite dishes lined Canon Drive. The sidewalk and driveway outside the Beverly Stanton Hotel was jam-packed; reporters held microphones like lollipops, a swarm of paparazzi toting cameras with lenses that resembled bazookas mingled with the throng of crazed, impatient fans. Uniformed police stood at the perimeter of the property like soldiers.

The crowd parted at the sight of the limo and cheered as it pulled up to the velvet ropes at the hotel's elegant main entrance. Alyssa stepped out first, into an orgy of lights, cameras, and action. Justine hid behind her.

"Alyssa" Alyssa! Over here!"

"Who's your date Alyssa?"

"Who are you wearing, Alyssa?"

"Who's the hot brunette, Alyssa?"

"Alyssa, is this your new flame? Are you two an item now?"

The incessant camera flashes blinded Justine as she guided Alyssa through the glamorous obstacle course that was the hotel's red carpet. Navigating through random stands of klieg lights, herds of camera lenses, microphones, and disembodied broadcast-quality voices, Justine was actually living her dream of walking the fabled red carpet arm in arm with a famous movie star. It didn't even matter to her that her date had a vagina; the glamor of the event intoxicated her. Other celebrities approached Alyssa with their cell phones set to selfie-mode, and Alyssa did the self-mocking selfie-pose that had been studied and perfected by so many teen-age girls.

Inside the hotel, they approached the security line. Justine noted that the ex-Mossad security detail was comprised of an equal number of male and female agents. She'd never seen a woman agent in California. The Israeli security personnel were polite and thorough with the civilian, non-celebrity guests, and Justine noticed that even the few studio execs she recognized were treated like the proletariat. But no one dared bother any bona fide celebrity with a search. Justine wondered how many guests were actually covert security agents.

When they reached the front of the security line, a male agent guided Justine through the metal-detector scanning machine and left Don to guard Alyssa, his new blue eye scanning the room. The scanner beeped, of course; Justine's small Glock was still in her thigh holster, and a male agent told her to please wait while he found a female agent to pat her down. So she stood there and watched Don watch Alyssa breeze through the celebrity security station. Then Alyssa stood beside Justine as Don walked through the scanner. Justine could tell that Don wasn't happy.

"What's up?" she whispered to him.

"Separating us like that," he said, shaking his head. "Any observant enemy can see that we're security in tandem and not guests."

"Madame, this way please," said a heavily accented voice.

"That's *you*," Don said to Justine.

She stepped over to the security agent, an attractive woman with dark hair and steely blue eyes. She was probably in her early forties, but her outfit, an atrocious steel-gray pantsuit that looked a lot like the one Don brought for Justine, made her look older.

"They make you wear that?" Justine asked the woman in a conspiratorial tone.

"Excuse me?"

"The pantsuit. I almost had to wear one just like it."

"Ah yes, the uniform. I see that fashion beat security in your case. Raise your arms please." The woman smiled as she frisked Justine. "Oh-oh, what's this?" she said when she discovered Justine's thigh holster and Glock 26. "I'm afraid you'll have to leave that with us."

"I have my California concealed carry and my close protection guard permits."

"That doesn't count here. I'm sorry."

"But my..."

"We're running the security tonight and I promise you we know exactly what we're doing. So, you can either leave your weapon or wait outside. Those are the rules."

Justine forced a smile. "Here you go then," she said, relinquishing her pistol, which the Israeli woman tagged with a coat check label. "I really appreciate how well you guys do the security thing," Justine continued when the agent handed her the ticket stub. "But I have to say that I am a little concerned."

"About what?"

"Well, your covert team members know who I am, but I don't know who they are."

"Yes, I understand that could be a problem in a gunfight. However, since we are the only ones armed you don't have to worry. There will be no gunfights here. Not tonight."

"From your mouth to God's ears."

"Ah, so you're a member of the tribe?" the agent asked, recognizing the English translation of the old Yiddish adage.

"In more ways than one," Justine acknowledged. "Let me guess, you're old school, so you're carrying a Jericho 941 in .45 ACP with a ten-round magazine with two extra mags."

The agent smiled. "Yes. You've been well trained, I see. But tonight you can relax. We've taken care of all the details. Go. Eat. Enjoy the party. The food is delicious *and* kosher."

Justine felt a twinge of alarm. "Did you eat the same food before the party? Does it all come from the same source? Who screened it?"

"*Oy*, you *are* well trained. And so are we. Our chief oversaw all the preparations. Believe me, it's kosher."

"*Toda,*" Justine replied, using the Hebrew word for thanks.

The agent nodded. "*Tzeteh' Leshalom VeShuveh' Leshalom.*"

Justine bowed her head respectfully.

Alyssa floated through the security barricade like a Shakespearean sprite.

Don went into the Israeli Security screening room and emerged a minute later.

"That was quick," Justine said.

"Too quick," Don said. "Their attitude borders on complacent."

"Paranoid much?" Justine asked him. "They took your pistols too. That's not thorough enough?"

"They didn't find any on me," Don calmly assured her.

"What do you mean?"

Don surprised her by answering her with a hug. When she felt his hand slide through the side slit of her gown she was at first startled, until she realized he'd slipped her compact Glock 26 into her thigh holster.

"How the…" she started to say, but Don cut her off with a glance. "You always were good with your hands, but stealing my Glock back from Israeli security?" she whispered. Don barely nodded his head with a hint of a smile.

"She the only one that gets a hug?" Alyssa asked flirtatiously.

"I thought I already gave you one," he said, smiling.

"And now I want another one," Alyssa demanded with mock petulance.

"Well in that case," Don responded, still smiling. Then he winked at Justine, who watched carefully as he embraced his famous client, confident that her teacher had an ulterior motive.

Sure enough, she noticed that his hand found its way through the thigh slit of Alyssa's gown. When it reappeared Justine noticed that he had something in his palm. It had to be his pistol, which he surreptitiously slipped into his waist holster.

Alyssa, having spied the producer of her upcoming movie, rushed over to deliver her best Hollywood movie star meets Hollywood mogul public greeting. Don and Justine trotted along with her for a few steps like dutiful guard dogs. As Alyssa demonstratively embraced first the producer and then his wife, Don turned to Justine and kissed her seductively on her lips, which was the first time he had ever kissed her anywhere.

"What was that for?" Justine asked Don.

"You're a terrible actress."

"So I deserve a little public display of affection?"

"Okay so maybe I should question your memory and not your acting skills."

"I beg your pardon?"

"You've forgotten that she wants everyone to think we're a threesome."

"You're taking that seriously?"

Don shrugged. "Hey, it's the price you pay for wearing the dress."

Justine wasn't sure about any of Alyssa's bizarre commands, but she did take Don's hand and held onto it as though they were a couple. While Alyssa chatted with her producer, Justine scanned the room for Danisha, and prayed she wasn't with Alessandro.

She didn't find Danisha, but she did spot Lise. Justine knew her mother was a major contributor to the Stars For Peace foundation, and Lise did say that she was invited to one of the after parties, so Justine wasn't exactly surprised to see her there. She tried to avoid her gaze, but realized pretty quickly that her mother was too busy flirting with the honoree, Lars Karlsson, to notice that the brunette standing next to Alyssa Stewart was her own daughter.

Her daughter, meanwhile, was trying to act the part of the movie star's companion slash paramour slash protection detail, a delicate balance in this fantastical setting. Seeing so many A-list stars, directors and producers was so thrilling that her natural inclination was to rush over to Lise and say *Oh my god did you see who I was just talking to?* Justine kept her emotions in check by doing what she'd always done, working. She had no problem schmoozing in a room full of wealthy, idealistic people; the trick was to covertly survey the room at the same time.

But this *was* Hollywood, and in Hollywood everyone ogles. Why else spend weeks and weeks and tens of thousands of dollars preparing and getting all dressed up if not to be ogled? So Justine looked around to see how everyone else was looking around, and followed their lead. Many famous faces she recognized, the actors and actresses looked like they'd just walked off the pages of Vogue. Justine could've sworn they'd brought their own cinematographers to light their every step. Each gown was more glorious than the next. The majority of the other guests were middle aged and older men and women of obvious and substantial wealth. They too wore couture tuxes and gowns, only they looked thicker, more of this earth than the ultra-thin yet muscled luminaries in the room.

And then there were the others, the heavyset women in pantsuits and the stern-looking men who scanned the room instead of staring at the perfect bodies of the movie stars. Justine counted six of these women, all with lean, hard faces. *They're not heavy, they just have extra layers under their jackets. Armored vests.* These were undercover ex-Mossad agents, no doubt about it. The flaw in their disguise was their professionalism. They paid no attention to the glitter on the surface, didn't seem to care who was with whom or what anyone was wearing, so for Justine, they stood out. She glanced over at Don to study him for a moment. He laughed, casually placed an arm around Alyssa's bare shoulder or a hand on her ass. Justine clasped onto Alyssa's arm and joined the conversation, but continued her vigilant three-sixty scan of the room.

When Justine noticed Iya and Eniko on the arms of a smug-looking, older gentleman, her heart sank. The man had to be a producer, and perhaps he'd paid for their services for the evening, but Justine suspected that they might be after the bounty on Don's head. She feigned a slight cough, excused herself and covered her mouth with her hand and whispered, "Two *Sparrows*, twelve o'clock, platinum blonde wigs, black dresses," into her bone-conduction microphone.

Don cleared his throat, his signal for transmission received, and glanced at Iya and Eniko in passing. Justine watched them from two perspectives; Don's camera point of view through the Google contact lens in her left eye and the point of view of her own naked right eye. She wished she had Don's bullet-resistant glasses with the built-in mini-camera and she regretted her decision to turn down Don's offer of her own rear-vision camera. Now she felt stupid, vulnerable.

In the din of the room Marisol's voice came through Justine's ear canal radio with perfect clarity. "What the hell are they doing here?"

"Don't know," Justine mumbled, pretending to sip the champagne in her glass.

"We need to find out," said Don. Justine had been watching him. His lips didn't move.

Justine kept a close eye on the girls. They were definitely working some angle, scanning the attendees just as Justine and Don were doing. When their gaze paused too long at one corner of the room, Justine focused on that corner.

CHAPTER 58

That's when she saw them, Danisha and Alessandro. Justine felt a surge of disgust as Danisha buried her face in Alessandro's neck. He couldn't—or wouldn't—keep his hand off Danisha's ass and swollen belly. For a few seconds Justine forgot that she was a professional paid to protect her client. She felt the sweat break out on her forehead, was sure her face was turning red with indignation.

"Oh for the love of…" she muttered.

"What's the matter Jussy?" Alyssa asked, with a gentle caress.

Justine realized how much of a threat her emotions were to her composure. "Oh no, did I say that out loud?" Justine laughed as she took Alyssa's arm and whispered into her ear, "I just saw my um, friend. Guess she gave me a bit of a start."

"Aren't you full of surprises? Show me, where is she?"

"Over there, near the corner," Justine told Alyssa in a conspiratorial and girlish tone. She glanced at Don, who gave her the slightest of nods to let her know he got the message.

"The beauty in the green dress?" Alyssa asked.

"Yeah. And her asshole jerk-face *fiancé*. Just look at those two, chatting like a normal *straight* couple with that silver-haired man and his sweet young thing."

"Wow, not bad. Not bad at all. Her man isn't bad either. Oh look Justine, there's Mark Goffin and his new surfer boy. Let's go talk to them, get closer to your girl. Make her super jealous."

"Do it," Marisol barked into Justine's ear. "Get close to Alessandro and activate your directional cell phone hacker to grab their frequencies. There are too many other phones in the room, too much interference."

Don nodded in approval.

The last thing Justine wanted to do was start fiddling with her bra in front of this crowd, but since Marisol had hidden the cell-phone-hacking antennas in the under-wire of Justine's bra, following her order meant finding an acceptable way to do just that. As she held Alyssa's hand and followed her through the crowded room, her heart pounded like the bass-line of a Rihana hit.

"Alyssa, this is close enough," she said when they were within ten feet of Alessandro and Danisha. I don't want to take the chance of her recognizing me. Come stand close, pretend we're talking about something important. I wanna eavesdrop."

Alyssa was only too happy to take part in Justine's ruse. Justine gave her a warm hug as a cover to turn on the bra-encased antenna.

A moment later Justine heard Marisol: "Four active burner phones. If he's planning anything, we don't know what it is. I still haven't been able to break the encryption code you stole from him. Get back to Don with Alyssa now."

As Justine and Alyssa reached Don's side, Justine recognized Eniko's silky voice behind her. "Code Yellow, situation not good. We must leave."

Justine turned to Eniko and gave her the full Hollywood greeting, a warm phony smile, "Darling, you look stunning! I'm loving the understated makeup," she said loud enough for anyone to hear. And it was true, sheathed in a long black lace gown with a swathe of Van Cleef diamonds, Eniko looked marvelous. As she leaned in for a perfunctory hug and air kiss, Justine cooed into her ear, "What's up?"

Eniko whispered back, "Some code or combination of codes is being used—we can't break it. But whatever it is, *Elaimi-jihad* uses it."

"I don't know what that is."

"*Elaimi-jihad* is a terrorist group, the name means "global holy war" in English. It's the only one that has both Farsi and Arabic speakers working together. Usually they're at each other's throats. I'm detecting a high volume of transmissions."

"So that means..." Justine knew exactly what it meant.

"Right. Something's going down. Most likely tonight. Your friend's handsome sleaze bag is definitely involved. We just don't know how."

"The encryption, is it the same for the *Aqua Blu Shadows* website and *Elaimijihad*? Justine asked.

"Affirmative," said Marisol. "His sex trafficking business funds his terrorist cell."

"He must be directing the operation that's going to happen tonight, right here. Threat level orange," Don whispered to Justine.

"You gonna introduce me to your new friend?" Eniko asked. "Your blond stud over there. Whoever he is, he sure is fine. Don couldn't make it?"

Justine laughed. "Don never tells us where he's going. All I know is he's off somewhere doing his ghost protocol. He left us to do the grunt work." Eniko looked into Justine's eyes and whispered with a sardonic smile, "I must teach you to lie better. Your micro-expressions tell me a different story. Let's see…Don visited the surgeon a few months ago and now he looks like a Norwegian. A wise choice. Now certain people will find it much more difficult to get him."

Justine turned pale. "What are you talking about?"

"Great to work with you again!" This time it was Iya's voice joining the group chat in her earpiece. "Want to share Alessandro's cell phone numbers?"

"Okay, *Sparrows*," Marisol replied to all, "I can't wait to meet you in person, but right now we have a problem. Burner phone number one is active. I'll patch you in."

Don, nodded at the girls. "Good evening to you, too, Iya, Eniko. If Irina were here she would be so proud of you."

Just at the mention of the name, Irina, Eniko displayed a wave of emotion that surprised Justine. Biting her lower lip, she sauntered back towards Iya. Justine could swear she noticed tears welling up in Eniko's eyes. But there was no time for processing emotions, not if she was going to stay focused. She made the split second decision to approach Danisha. If Marisol was right about the elevated threat level, Justine had to protect her friend and the child she carried. She left Alyssa with Don and quickly worked her way through the crowd. But when Justine reached out to embrace her dearest friend, Danisha turned away.

"Hey, girlfriend," Justine said, trying to mask her astonishment. "Why the cold shoulder?"

Danisha scowled at her then hissed quietly in her ear, "I know you planted all that bullshit in my head just so you could fuck my fiancé."

Her vitriolic tone sliced through Justine's heart like a rusty scalpel. Justine was too shaken to respond before Alessandro, oblivious to the rift between the two women, turned around to greet her.

"Giustina!" he exclaimed, taking her in. Then, throwing his arms around her waist, he pulled her close and kissed her warmly on the cheek. "You look stunning. What brings *you* here with the dark hair?"

"I've heard that blondes have more fun but brunettes are smarter. I'm experimenting tonight. Scott's off taking photos somewhere and left me all alone." She ignored the crux of his question and he didn't follow up, most likely because he was distracted by the grand entrance of the honoree Lars Karlsson.

"*Ma, Giustina*—what are you talking about?" Alessandro said. "I see Scott right there. With Lars."

Justine saw him too, discreetly following the Swedish director, taking photos without a flash. She was not happy to see him. Scott could blow her cover. Justine was about to say something to Alessandro, but he had turned away to answer his cell phone.

She knew that Don wouldn't like it, but she walked across the ballroom to get closer to her Scott. *Why didn't he tell me he was going to be working one of these parties,* she thought as she observed him working. Of course he was too engrossed in whatever he saw through his camera's viewfinder to recognize her in as a brunette. She luxuriated in her temporary anonymity, and soaked in his presence. Until the sound of Marisol's voice broke her reverie.

"Alessandro's second burner phone is active," she said with an edge of alarm. "My Farsi might be a bit sketchy—I only really learned the Pashto dialect—but I can tell you that he received orders in Iranian Farsi, from a male. I could make out a few words. Ladies and gentleman, Jihad terrorism has come to Hollywood."

"Good work, Marisol," exclaimed Don. "Going to Plan X"

"Yeah, get the hell out of there. The pool exit extraction route is clear."

Don put his arm around Alyssa and whispered, "We have to leave now."

Alyssa scowled at him. "I have money men to greet. We're not going anywhere."

"This isn't a choice. It's no longer safe here," said Don.

"Isn't that why I hired you?" Alyssa demanded as she twisted away from him.

Justine could hear Alessandro in her earpiece speaking rapidly in what she assumed was Farsi. The voice that responded was also male, and spoke the same language.

"I speak Farsi," said Eniko.

"Of course you do," said Marisol.

"I'll ignore that and just tell you that they're saying the ETA is two minutes. He also said God is great."

"Terror alert upgraded to red," Don announced to the members of his team. "Possible suicide bomber or mass shooter. Or both. Primary threat profile: bomber, fat body, thin face, forehead sweat, dressed as law enforcement or religious leader. Secondary threat profile: Mass shooter; forehead sweat, nervous right hand checking his waist, also dressed like police or clergy. Either one will be targeting Lars."

Justine shadowed Alessandro from behind. Her earpiece picked up his third burner phone as it vibrated. A female voice spoke to him in Arabic. Justine recognized the phrase, *Allahu Akbar.*

"He said the security line is long so their ETA is now three minutes" said Eniko. "And the usual stuff about God being great."

"Make that two probable threats," Don said. "Look for forehead sweat on potential male and female suicide bombers. Female threat profile: large breasts or pregnant appearance with belly bomb implants."

"GPS tracking male bomber, one hundred yards, going through the outside kitchen entrance," said Marisol. "The kitchen workers are most likely Hispanic. They tend to be deferential to cops and priests. Female bomber GPS tracking, just outside of security."

Alessandro was talking again, first in Farsi and then in Arabic. Eniko translated, "Security still up, but they'll be neutralized soon. Get into position and wait."

"Justine. Over there. The priest," said Don. Justine followed Don's gaze and spotted a fat man in priest's vestments exiting the kitchen door. "Get Alyssa out *now!*"

Justine found Scott first. Grabbing his arm, she whispered urgently into his ear, "There's a bomb threat. Get out now."

Scott spun around. "What? Who are you?" But all he saw was a brunette hurrying towards Alyssa Stewart. He took photos of the back of her head and then a few of her shapely taut butt."

Justine grabbed Alyssa's arm. "Let's go. Now!"

But Alyssa was having none of it. "Don't touch me," she snapped. "And don't tell me what to do. You both work for me, try to remember that."

Alyssa Stewart, petulant Academy Award nominee, stormed off into the center of the room.

"She's acting like the jilted popular girl at the middle school dance," Justine said to Don.

"What's new? You going after her, or what?"

"Copy that, boss."

Justine grabbed Alyssa's hand and abruptly pulled her in for a dramatic embrace. "Don't run off like that, you know I only want what's best for you," she whispered in Alyssa's ear, before kissing the movie star passionately on the lips.

That did the trick. "Okay, Jussy. Forgive me?" Alyssa cooed, surrendering to her new favorite bodyguard.

"We actually care about you. You know that, right?"

"Yes."

"Good. Let's go back to Don. We really do need to leave. It's not safe here," Justine said, leading Alyssa back towards the kitchen exit.

"We have a situation," Justine heard Don say through her earpiece. "I've got two Mossad down. Looks like food poisoning."

"Copy that," responded Marisol.

"Okay, I see you. Be right there," said Justine. "Except I have the client."

"Sheri Paskell-Clemente is standing about three meters from me," said Don. "Alyssa loves seducing powerful studio heads, especially the female ones. Leave her there and we can keep eyes on her."

"On it," said Justine.

"Head's up guys," said Marisol. "I just heard Alessandro say it's happening soon. He's definitely command and control, so keep eyes on him. When he leaves the party you'll have sixty seconds to zero hour."

"So he leaves and lives to fight another day while his soldiers blow themselves to smithereens," Don acknowledged.

"They do get the martyr bonus," Marisol reminded everyone. "Seventy-Two virgins for eternity."

Justine managed to steer both Alyssa and the studio exec to a spot close to Don and the fallen Mossad agents. "Food poisoning?" she asked as she approached her teacher. "Are you sure?"

"That's my guess. Look at them," said Don.

He was right. The two Israelis, both small-framed men, looked pale and sick. Justine recognized the symptoms. "The entire security team as well as the support staff ate the same kosher meal before the party," she said.

"Looks like cholera toxin to me," said Eniko after checking one of the men's symptoms. "It always presents as a delayed reaction. Late Soviet-era biological weapon, until Gorbachev shut down the program in the mid-eighties. Their scientists defected to whoever paid. Iraq and Iran were always the top bidders."

"Thanks for the history lesson, Eniko." Justine actually enjoyed history trivia, especially Cold War trivia, but she wasn't interested in becoming a statistic herself. "What's next?"

Don stepped over to one of the stricken agents. "Code black. Zero hour imminent. We believe *Ealamijihad* poisoned your team. Cholera toxin. One hundred percent incapacity in five minutes, so you'll need IV electrolytes as soon as possible. The closest antidotes are with the SEALs in Coronado."

The man was sweating profusely. Mumbling in Hebrew into his sleeve, he managed to convey the danger to his superiors.

Justine saw Don's hand slip into the man's jacket as he helped him to his feet. He put up no resistance as Don lifted the pistol from its holster and slipped it into his own waistband. A female Mossad agent and her partner, both pale and soaked with sweat, appeared just in time to catch the agent as he collapsed. The partner picked up the other agent and stumbled toward an exit.

A new uproar was beginning. Justine heard calls for security and something about a drunk woman.

She and Don followed the sound of the voice, until she recognized it. "It's Alessandro," she whispered. Don nodded, beckoning her to follow him.

They saw the woman leaning against the wall beside the kitchen door. She definitely was not drunk. Alessandro stood close to her, still screaming for security.

"That one's poisoned, too," Don told Justine.

They both watched as Alessandro surreptitiously pressed his fist against the sick woman's diaphragm then stepped aside as she heaved. Anyone watching could see her vomit. Justine hoped that only she and

Don had noticed Alessandro reach under her jacket, steal her pistol and slip it into his waistband.

"Shit, did you see that?" Justine already knew the answer to that question. Don saw everything.

Two stern-looking agents, both perspiring heavily, pushed past Alessandro and escorted their team member out of the room.

"You've got eyes on Alyssa?" Don asked Justine.

"She's right there. Totally oblivious."

Don grabbed Alyssa's arm and guided her toward the glass doors that led outside to the pool. "We're under attack. Go with Justine. Now. This is not negotiable."

Justine, following close on Don's heels, took Alyssa's other arm.

"Let go of me! You're both fired!" Alyssa yelled as she jerked free.

Don glared, then smiled. "Thanks for releasing us. You still should leave. Now if you'll excuse me, I see a priest and I need to extract a confession from him."

"Justine. Get to the bar in the back, the one closest to the kitchen," he said with a sort of calm urgency. "I just saw Alessandro heading there with Danisha. She looks terrified."

Justine felt conflicted. She wanted to rescue Danisha, who clearly seemed to hate her, but she was also worried about Lise. Luckily she had the Ukrainians. "Eniko, Iya," she whispered, "have you guys seen Lise?"

"Yep," said Iya. "She's with the Swede, about two meters away from us."

"Can you…"

"We're on it," said Eniko. Justine looked back and watched the girls. Iya flirted with Lars as Eniko whispered into Lise's ear.

Either Lise was too tipsy to comprehend the danger or she simply wasn't listening. Iya continued her flirtatious conversation with the Swedish director while Eniko steered the four of them towards Justine and Don.

"What are you two beauties doing here?" Justine heard her mother say.

"We're here to help," hissed Eniko. "The entire Mossad security team has been poisoned and we know that at least two suicide bombers are either on their way or already here."

"You poisoned the Mossad?"

Iya grabbed Lise's arm and hissed, "Not us. *Ealamijihad.* Come on, follow us. Now. "

Lars looked both confused and intrigued. "Hello," he said to Eniko and Justine. "I don't think we've met. I'm Lars Karlsson. Did I hear you say something about poison?"

"It's an honor to meet you, Mr. Karlsson. I'm Justine, Lise's daughter. And these are my friends...Eniko and Iya, who, I'm sorry, are dying to meet Alyssa Stewart."

Iya nodded and Eniko led the way over to Alyssa's side. "Miss Stewart. We're with Mossad, here to protect you. Come with us."

Alyssa, instantly attracted to the women, would've followed them even if they'd never said the word *Mossad.* They led her outside, past the pool, towards her limo for her next party, where a crowd of eager paparazzi and semi-to-fully-crazed fans buzzed like a giant hive of hornets. When the first stargazer spotted Alyssa on the arms of the two unknown stunners, all hell broke loose. Justine could hear the commotion from the kitchen.

"Alyssa, over here!"

"Alyssa Stewart, oh my god it's Alyssa Stewart!"

"Alyssa, wanna introduce your new girl toys?"

"Did you get sick too, Alyssa?"

"Alyssa's sick everyone! Call an ambulance!"

Eniko downshifted into damage control/publicist mode. "Alyssa's fine, no need to worry. We have another party to get to. Excuse us."

"But they're carrying people *out.* People that look *sick,*" shouted a woman reporter. "Can you tell us anything about that?"

A chorus of chaos followed the woman's question.

"Yeah what's going on?"

"Is it true they were poisoned?"

"Who poisoned them?"

"Can you tell us what kind of poison?"

Justine listened through her earphones as Iya and Eniko steered Alyssa through the crazed crowd and thought that their ease and competence was admirable. Her brief reverie was interrupted by Marisol's voice.

"Male bomber, GPS tracking him outside the kitchen, heading toward the pool exit. Female bomber, GPS tracking her at the security booth entrance."

"I have a Catholic priest," added Don. "Fat body, thin face, sweaty forehead. Heading to the pool exit. Looks like he's coming for Karlsson."

Justine rushed back into the ballroom to see Don walking toward the man in the priest outfit. She followed, quickly closing the gap between herself and the two men.

Finally she got a good look at his face. There was something off about it. He looked nervous, no question about that, and not about being surrounded by celebrities.

He also looked familiar.

CHAPTER 59

Oh sweet mother of God. That's no priest. It's him.

That awful day at the cabin. Iya had warned her. Iya had handed her a knife—or was it a gun—and with the nonchalance of a woman dictating a grocery list, told her to kill him. But Justine had refused. Justine didn't want to play God, so she allowed the monster to live despite Iya's warnings. And now here he was trying to kill them all.

The photo of thirteen-year-old Gemma flashed through Justine's brain. Then the memory—a memory of her own creation—of poor Gemma being bound, raped, stabbed, her lifeless body left in a stranger's bedroom, Justine's bedroom. How naive she was. *Fuck you and your mercy.*

She should've known. She should've listened. She could kill him now. Her hand instinctively reached down to her thigh holster as she walked towards the man in the priest costume. All thoughts of the here and now faded like the stars at sunrise. Justine wanted nothing more than to use this opportunity to right her one lethal wrong.

The sound of Don's voice in her ear snapped her back to the present. "I'm on the priest. Justine. Find the female bomber before she blows us all to bits."

"Copy that." She ran toward the front security entrance, stepping over at least five fallen Israeli agents along the way. "All these agents here are down. Anyone know who the hell is in charge now?"

"We are," said Marisol.

One lone pregnant woman in a long shapeless black dress and head-scarf strolled casually toward the main entrance. Justine thought that something about her looked *off*. Her eyes were carefully lined with kohl but her pretty face was way too thin for pregnancy. A bump, too round and spherical for a baby, protruded unnaturally through the fabric of her shapeless black dress. *What the hell is she wearing, is that a kaftan?* The whole picture felt wrong, too easy. As the woman pushed her way through the metal detectors Justine could see sweat pouring off her forehead. Lights flashed and an alarm rang, but the security teams were too sick to respond.

Justine kicked off her heels and ran the last few steps to the metal detector. She got close enough to the pregnant woman to determine that whatever she carried under her dress was definitely not a human life.

Don had told her that *al-Qaeda* members in Yemen had experimented with implanting plastique explosives into women's breasts in order to get past airport security screeners. But those experiments had failed miserably; every one of their poor human guinea pigs had died of infections before they got anywhere near an airport. *Ealamijihad* had taken the surgical techniques to a whole new level of barbarity by removing the female organs that offended them—breasts, uterus, fallopian tubes, ovaries and probably even vagina—and replacing them with bombs.

Justine's instinct was to flee. She had no doubt that this poor woman was walking death. No one in that ballroom knew what Justine knew. No one else could see the fear-laced determination chiseled into the bomber's every feature. No one else could save the hundreds of innocent people at the event.

Determined to stop her, maybe even to save her, Justine lunged at the woman only to find herself suddenly blinded a split second later.

"Fuck!" she screamed. Her eyelids felt like they'd been set ablaze. She had seen the small plastic object in the woman's hand, and her first thought then was a detonator. But then she realized that it was actually a canister of pepper spray. Her reflexes had kicked in then. She squeezed her eyelids shut and held her breath. She felt, almost in slow motion, the tiny droplets of liquid tickle then tortured her eyelids and brow.

Immediately her thoughts flashed back to Don's lessons. *Sense memory.* She remembered that there was a waiter to her right with a bottle of champagne on a tray. With her eyes still shut tight, she moved swiftly, her hands in front of her, reaching, feeling for the waiter and his tray.

She found him in three steps, grabbed the bottle, placed her thumb over the top and shook it one, two, three times, then held the bottle close to her eyelids and released her thumb. Only when the champagne spray had washed and neutralized the offending chemicals from her eyelids, did Justine let herself breathe again.

Less than ten seconds had passed since the woman sprayed her, she was sure of that. Her hair was drenched with champagne foam and she knew her makeup was a mess. Her eyes still stung, but she could make out the shape of the suicide bomber, a black blob determinedly pushing her way through the brightly colored crowd.

"I found her, but she pepper sprayed me and she's getting away," Justine told her teammates. "Looks like she's heading to the pool."

"I'm on the priest, near the pool," said Don. "Remember the plate glass windows."

Of course, the enormous glass windows overlooking the pool. Justine had noticed them when she arrived because she knew that exploded glass shards become secondary missiles. If she or Don failed to stop either of these potential bombers, millions of razor-sharp projectiles would rip through the flesh and bone of every man and woman within ten yards of the window.

"I'm on it," she told Don, then ran as fast as she could to the pool.

From outside through the huge picture window, Justine could see the crowd milling about inside like sheep grazing in a bucolic pasture, completely oblivious to the possibility of a slaughterhouse.

"Look out, Justine," Marisol warned. "He's on his way."

"Who's on..." Justine started to say before she heard the tumult.

Then she saw Don about ten feet to her right, his hands holding tightly to the fake priest's neck as the two men burst outside through the patio doors toward the pool. The bomber, obviously well trained, fought back. He and Don toppled onto the Spanish tiled pool deck. Justine could hear the sickening sound of bones snapping. Glancing quickly over at Don, she saw him wrap his forearm over the man's white collar then lower him quickly to the ground, where he stayed, his eyes wide open, his head dangling from the neck.

"Is he...?"

"Yes. He was dead before he hit the ground," Don grunted. "But his bomb could very well still be alive." He stood up, and, holding the dead man's clenched fist, dragged the corpse toward the pool and shoved it into the water. Then, with his bare hands, he violently smashed his wrist against the marble edge of the pool. The hand muscles contracted and tightened around the switch. Justine watched in horrified fascination as Don shoved the clenched fist into the pool before he quickly rolled out of the way.

The explosion lifted tons of water up and out of the pool. A wall of it rose straight up, at least two stories high, mushroomed, then crashed down, shattering walls and walls of plate glass windows. The water fell back earthward. Some poured back into the pool, the rest onto the deck.

Justine's ear canal radios protected her ear drums from the explosion and allowed her to hear Don moaning. She looked around, trying to locate him, and spotted him lying still by the side of the pool. The wave of water had slammed him. She wanted to run to him, to make sure he was okay, help him get up and back to work, but her limbs refused to move.

CHAPTER 60

Everything froze for what seemed like hours, but was in reality less than three seconds. Then suddenly all was mayhem. Men and women, guests and staff scattered like ants at a picnic. Some cried out; others were too stunned to utter a sound. Inside the reception room, the crowd panicked as people ran for every obvious exit. The screams were deafening. Dozens of guests were lying unconscious, flattened and soaked. Some had landed in the pool; Justine wondered how many were still alive. Unless someone came to pull them out, they would surely drown.

Soaked to the bone, Justine slowly stood up and plucked the few small shards of glass that protruded from her arms and shoulders like they were excess feathers on a farmer's market chicken.

Oh shit, what the fuck happened to my suicide bomber? Justine thought, realizing she'd lost track of her.

Within seconds she spotted her standing dangerously close to a wall of still intact windows.

Justine summoned all her reserves of stamina and ran towards her target. But it wasn't enough; the woman was at the window by the time Justine reached her.

"Allahu akbar!" she screamed in ecstasy, her fist raised in defiance.

Oh no no no no no, Justine thought as the woman pulled the safety pin from the detonator in her right hand. The bomber's path to glorious martyrdom was so close; all she had to do was open those fingers.

Leaping on her prey like a lioness, Justine closed the gap between herself and the bomber. "Not on my fucking watch you stupid, ignorant cunt," she screamed as she grabbed the woman's right fist. Holding her left thumb firmly over the detonator switch, she wrapped her thighs around the bomber's waist, and, locked in this surreal death-grip, the two women tumbled onto the ground. Justine could feel the two breast bombs implanted in the woman's chest crushing into her own stomach.

Her opponent fought with admirable—and terrifying—determination. Her left handed punch landed squarely on Justine's cheekbone, unleashing a dizzying deluge of white-hot pain. Justine held fast to the woman's right fist—and the detonator switch. The thought of the destructive power that literally lay at her fingertips fueled and focused her rage.

For one brief moment she glanced inside at the first bomb's fallout; bodies draped in tattered couture gowns and tuxedoes, severed feet in thousand dollar shoes, the sparkle of brilliant white diamonds on detached hands and wrists, and so much blood. If she didn't know better, she would've sworn this was a film set. But the incessant cries of agony, the screams of confusion, the stink of vomit, emptied bowels and all that blood were too real. No wizard of special effects could replicate such horrific layers of carnage and destruction.

But plenty of people were still alive. *She could still save them. She had to save Lise and Scott. And Danisha.*

The bomber was determined to complete her jihadist mission. Still clasping the detonator switch in her left hand, Justine easily blocked the woman's second blow and smashed her attacker's face with her left elbow, knocking her down. With one knee she pinned the woman to the ground, then pulled off her headscarf and grabbed a handful of sweat-drenched black hair. Bones crackled like the drum section of a marching band as Justine pounded the woman's face onto the tiles.

The bomber screamed, her arms lashing out and legs thrashing. She managed to grab Justine's hair, but when she pulled it all she got was a handful of wig.

"Oh no, you ruined my do," Justine said in mock humiliation. A small smile crept across her face. "Now I'm angry. You. Wanna. Fuck. With. Me?" she screamed, punctuating each word with a smash of the bomber's head against the tiles. Even when she ran out of words, Justine kept pounding. Again and again and again.

"Enough," Marisol scolded. "Bitch can't get any more dead."

Justine stopped. The body convulsed in death throes, its skull crushed like a watermelon tossed from a roof. "I'm gonna be sick," she told Marisol.

"Not before you take care of that detonator."

Marisol was right. Vomiting over killing a woman with her bare hands made perfect sense to Justine, but being blown to pieces for that privilege, not so much. She focused her attention on the woman's right fist, the thumb still tight on the bombs' detonator button. Justine peeled the blood-soaked scarf from the dead woman's body and wrapped it tightly around her fist and thumb to secure the detonator's dead man's switch.

"Done," Justine announced. "Now I need to find Lise and Danisha."

"Not quite done," said Marisol. "Alessandro probably has a second remote trigger."

"Shit. So what should I..."

"Into the drink with our lady of perpetual suffering please."

"Copy that. Good riddance you stupid, misguided jihadist," Justine grunted as she rolled the body into the half-empty swimming pool. She braced herself for another explosion, but all she got was the splash of dead weight hitting the water.

"Now we done here?" she panted.

"She's still holding three live bombs. Right now the only thing preventing them from exploding is a scarf and your idea of a secure knot. If that scarf slips..."

"You know, we never covered underwater bomb disarming in my training," Justine said impatiently. The euphoria she'd felt just seconds ago had morphed into impatience laced with misery and pain. "The cops must be on their way by now. Can't they take care of it?"

"*Holy shit.*"

"What holy shit?" Marisol asked.

"Don."

"Where? Show me."

He was less than three yards away, lying on his back on the edge of the pool deck. Justine ran to him, around fallen bodies, some still twitching with life and struggling to breathe.

"Any pulse?" Marisol asked quietly. Her voice was surprisingly shaky.

Justine placed a forefinger on Don's wrist. "I, um," her voice cracked, "I don't feel one."

"You covered CPR in your training, no?"

Justine nodded and gently placed a hand under Don's neck, tilted his head back to clear his airway, pinched his nose and covered his mouth with hers. Her fingers trembled and, as she exhaled air into his lungs, she fought back an ocean of tears.

"Breathe," she whispered after several attempts to resuscitate him.

"Anything?" Marisol asked.

"Breathe, damn it," Justine begged. She breathed into his mouth again. "Don't leave me. Please. I can't do this on my own." She straddled his chest, felt for his sternum, and started counting ribs as he had taught her to prepare for CPR.

"Wait," said Marisol. "I thought I saw his chest rise. He's breathing?"

Justine put her head to Don's chest. "I can't tell," she said. The tears were flowing now, but she managed to stifle the sobs that were fighting their way out of her soul.

As she kissed Don's forehead, her tears soaked his brow.

The sound of gunshots put a quick end to Justine's attempts to revive Don. A blood-curdling shriek came next, a woman's voice, followed by more screams. Justine sprang to her feet and looked in the direction of the commotion. It was coming from just inside the floor-to-ceiling glass doors that led from the pool patio to the main room. She could see the silhouette of a man near the front, on the east end of the room, near the entrance to the kitchen.

"Can you see this?" Justine asked Marisol.

"Not really, too much visual interference. You have eyes on the shooter?"

"Almost. Right now I can't see much more than a shadow." She took the Glock from her thigh holster and, crouching slightly, ran towards the trouble.

"*Cuidado*," Marisol cautioned.

"I am being careful. Also the lights are out except for the Exit signs. The explosion must've cut the power. I don't think they can see me out here from in there."

"*Don't think* isn't good enough, *mi amor.*"

"'Fraid we don't have much of a choice at the moment," Justine said. The noise all around her was deafening—a cacophony of cries for help, agonized moans and screams. In the distance she could hear the wail of sirens. Too distant, she thought.

She stopped in the shadow of a potted ficus tree and surveyed the scene inside. "Hold up," she told Marisol. "I think I can see him now."

"The shooter?"

"Yeah," Justine said, her voice unsteady.

He was standing, back illuminated by the Exit sign by the kitchen door, a pistol in one hand and Danisha's wrist in the other. A woman lay sprawled at his feet in a pool of blood.

"It's Alessandro," Justine said.

"The phony Italian producer?"

"The very same."

"Well, I can't say as I'm surprised. Sex trafficking and terror go hand in hand," said Marisol. "Can you ID the victim?"

"Looks like one of the Mossad. A woman."

"I hear another woman screaming. Does he have a hostage?"

"Yup. Danisha. His pregnant fiancé."

"*Aye Dios mío.*"

"I know, right? Oh no." Justine watched in horror as Danisha grabbed Alessandro's hand, the one with the gun. "Oh *hell no, Dani. Leave the gun alone,*" she hissed.

Alessandro released Danisha's wrist to land a violent punch in the center of her face. Justine winced. Danisha collapsed to the floor.

Justine peered cautiously around the leafy tree for a better look. Danisha was on her back, in shock, her face covered in blood.

Scott and Lise could still be alive too. Still reeling from the shock of losing Don, and the guilt of not being able to save him, Justine would do anything to get them all out of this nightmare in one piece.

She had to save *them.*

The last time she'd seen Scott, Lise and Lars they were all together near the bar. She'd start there.

Staying close to the outside wall of the building, Justine crept around to the side entrance, which led to a service hallway lit only by the faint glow of a battery-powered *Exit* signs above a doorway about halfway down. If she remembered the plan of the building correctly, and if the bomb hadn't blown her sense of direction to shreds—these doors opened into the ballroom. She sprinted to the closest one.

The ballroom was only slightly less chaotic than the pool patio. Panicking mobs of entertainment industry elite jammed the main exits. Justine wondered why none of them noticed the signs glowing over the two middle doors on either side of the room.

The stench of vomit and feces stung Justine's nostrils and the din of terrified screams and angry shouts pounded her ears. Bodies littered the floor. As she traversed the room Justine was surprised to notice varying degrees of life and movement in some of the victims.

Near the shattered plate-glass window, a young blond man sobbed over the body of a middle-aged woman in a red silk gown. Both were soaked in blood, but the man looked to be unscathed. The woman's eyes stared up at Justine, registering nothing.

Men and women of varying ages, including waiters and waitresses, were slumped over chairs and tables, shards of china and crystal embedded in their flesh. Silver serving trays were scattered on the floor like Frisbees at a high school picnic and brightly colored pieces of broccoli, carrots, and peppers mingled with bloody slices filet mignon and raw human flesh.

Justine spotted Lars and Lise near the bar, right where she'd left them, far enough from the blast to avoid any immediate fallout. Desperate to get them out of there, she picked up her speed, breathing deeply as Don had taught her to stop herself from retching as she reluctantly and carefully stepped over the wounded and dead in her path.

"Oh Justine, thank God," Lise cried, seeing her daughter. Both she and Lars were dazed, but unharmed. "We didn't know where to go. What the hell is going on?"

"I'm not sure what's going on exactly," Justine yelled over the pandemonium. "But I'll get you out of here. Everything's gonna be okay," she said, absent mindedly running a hand through her wet, wig-flattened hair. But she didn't actually believe her own words; she actually feared that nothing would ever be okay again.

And then she saw Scott. He was so close, not even six feet away, but he didn't see her. If he did he didn't recognize her, even without the wig. His eye was affixed to the viewfinder of his camera.

A new commotion had started on the opposite side of the room. Justine heard a woman screaming something about a gun. She looked towards the sounds of intensifying panic and saw Alessandro holding what looked like a Jericho 941 pistol.

"Get down!" Justine shouted to Lars and Lise. Too shocked to react, they just stared at her. She heard the two shots a split-second apart. The first one hit the back of Lars's head. The second bullet hit Lise, who let out a blood-curdling scream before falling to the floor.

In her earpiece Justine heard a streak of Spanish curse words interspersed with orders and questions. "Lars is dead," Justine told Marisol.

"And Lise?"

Justine was almost too afraid to find out. She didn't know if she had the strength to go on without Lise, and she knew she'd never forgive herself for failing to protect her.

Dropping to her knees, Justine could see that Lise was breathing. "She's alive. Looks like the bullet just grazed her shoulder."

"*Gracias a Dios,*" Marisol sighed.

"I gotta say, I'm having a hard time feeling the God thing right now, Marisol. This place feels like the very bowels of hell."

"Remember your training, *chica.*"

Marisol was right. Justine was in danger of losing control and getting caught up in the madness. She remembered the singular theme that ran through every one of Don's lessons: Pay attention to the details. *All the details.*

"Copy that," Justine said with renewed determination.

She spotted Alessandro, who returned to holding onto Danisha's wrist. He was definitely coming her way. He fired two more shots; two more bodies dropped. The sight of Danisha's tear-streaked face and swollen belly almost stopped Justine's heart.

She looked up to where she'd last seen Scott. He was still there, his eye still glued to his camera. The man was either oblivious to the very real danger surrounding him or simply fearless. Justine knew she'd never want to see the images he captured tonight.

"How many shots is that now?" Marisol asked.

"I counted four, but we don't know how many guns he has or how much ammo. The one he's using now sounds like a forty-five."

"Which he stole from one of the Israelis."

"Right. So what's the upside, how many guns could he possibly have?"

"We don't have an accurate count on the incapacitated agents. Assume the worst and avoid collateral damage."

Justine knew she had to stop Alessandro soon or there was no telling how many people he would kill, but Marisol was right; returning his fire now would draw counter-fire that could easily hit Lise or Scott, not to mention the hundred or so remaining innocent bystanders. Her compact Glock 26, which ordinarily would be her backup weapon for close quarters combat, wasn't the ideal long-distance pistol. It felt tiny, especially in comparison to Alessandro's Jericho.

"I have to get closer to the target," she told Marisol. The Glock had only eleven shots; Justine had to make sure each one counted.

"Justine, if you can move about ten feet forward you can use that woman to shelter you."

"What woman?"

"Straight ahead, lying on her side, in the blue velvet gown."

"She looks dead."

"So she probably won't mind if you use her hip as a rest for your pistol arm."

"And her body as a giant sand bag?"

"This is now a war. You have to use any possible advantage," Marisol scolded. "You want to save Lise? You gotta stop that bastard with a bullet to the brain."

Justine's shooter hand trembled. She knew that indulging in her own fear was a luxury she could ill afford at that moment, so she focused on the prone body of the enormous woman and saw the tactical wisdom of Marisol's advice.

The dead woman's body proved the perfect rest for Justine's pistol as well as a decent barricade to Alessandro's bullets. Breathing heavily, Justine steadied her shooting hand on the woman's ample hip, adjusted her aim for a long shot at Alessandro's head. The dead woman's muscles reflexively twitched just as Justine pressed the trigger and fired.

Her bullet hit the wall just over his head.

Alessandro, who must've heard the bullet's whine, dropped to the ground, pulling Danisha with him. Then, using her body as a shield, he fired two more quick shots at Justine. His bullets missed her but hit two bystanders.

"Fuck," Justine hissed, watching them fall.

"Focus, damn it," Marisol scolded again. "Now, if I'm not mistaken, those were bullets five and six."

"Sounds about right, " Justine responded, peering over her blue-velvet fortification. "Shit, Danisha looks bad. If he kills that baby..."

She watched in shock as Alessandro pulled Danisha into an arm-bar chokehold, then used her as his shield as he walked backwards toward the kitchen. "He's headed for the exit off the kitchen," Justine reported. "We have anyone back there?"

"I'm working on that," Marisol answered. "Is Danisha hit?"

"Not with a bullet, but I'm pretty sure her nose is broken. She's not resisting any more. Alessandro just cleared the kitchen doors, I'm going after him," Justine announced.

She jumped to her bare feet and, trying her damnedest to evade the sharp shards of broken glass strewed about the floor like confetti, quickly zig-zagged her way to the wall. Stopping beside the kitchen doors, she stood dead still and waited for Alessandro to make a move. The door opened a crack. Justine heard three shots, then watched as two men and a woman fell to the floor.

"Bullets number seven, eight, nine," said Marisol.

"So he has either one or two bullets left."

"Unless he stole extra magazines."

"Shit. I think I might've lost him," Justine said. She could barely hear. Her ears were ringing.

Suddenly Justine could hear everything at once; the agonizing screams of victims in the ballroom, the panicked cries of those still trying desperately to find a way out of the death-trap the room had so suddenly become.

She cupped her left hand around her ear. "I think I can hear him. It sounds like he's dragging her."

"I'm coming in," muttered Marisol.

"No," Justine ordered emphatically. "I need you at command and control. Stay there."

"Sorry *chica*, I outrank you now so I get to make the decisions. I'm coming in."

"Fuck it. Where are the *Sparrows?*"

"We just got back on site," said Iya.

"We had to get Alyssa to safety," added Eniko. Justine never thought she'd be so happy to hear their voices.

"I think I might be in over my head here," she admitted. "Lise has been hit. Can one of you go check on her?"

"Iya's taking care of her now," Eniko responded.

"Thank you. Seriously, I owe you."

"Just go kill that snake," Eniko snarled. "And do it right this time."

CHAPTER 61

Justine was overcome with a sudden wave of fury. She wanted to point out that the snake she had neglected to kill months ago in the hills above Palo Alto was already dead, until she remembered that she hadn't been the one to put an end to his misery. Don had taken care of that detail.

Shaking off her bruised ego, she held her Glock securely in both hands and quickly peeked into the small round window of the kitchen door. Alessandro was at the other end of the kitchen now, still holding Danisha. They were not far from the alley door exit. Justine took a breath and charged in. Crouching low, she stayed close to the stainless steel cabinets and stoves, using them for cover.

Two shots hit the swinging door behind her. Justine turned quickly and saw Scott dive for the floor. No blood. He lifted his camera to his face and started taking pictures.

Hiding behind a rolling cart of dishes, Justine had a clear view of Alessandro, who was about ten feet away from her. She could see that the slide of his Jericho was racked back, meaning he was out of ammo. She aimed her Glock directly at Alessandro and said, "Let her go."

"Not a fucking chance, you filthy whore," Alessandro hissed, pulling Danisha around to shield him.

"Don't shoot!" Danisha screamed. "Please. Please? My baby," she was sobbing now. "You'll kill my baby girl."

Alessandro dropped his empty pistol. "I want my lawyer. I know my rights."

"Let go of her," Justine demanded.

"I do that and you shoot me. I don't think so."

"No she won't,' Danisha whimpered. "Justine's not a killer, Alessandro. Please."

Justine aimed her pistol straight at Danisha and took one cautious step forward. "Let her go."

Alessandro's hand darted into the small purse that was miraculously still hanging from Danisha's shoulder.

"What's *that*?" Marisol asked.

"What's *what*? Oh for fuck's sake," Justine said, realizing that the object Alessandro had stashed in Danisha's evening bag was a hand grenade.

She watched him pull the pin and drop it to the floor, then hold the spring-loaded safety in his clenched fist.

"The first dead man's switch," Justine and Marisol said in unison.

Don had warned her that the hired security force would let the VIPs pass through the line, metal detectors be damned. But she never suspected that anyone would consider Danisha a celebrity worthy of such special treatment.

"He must've pulled a few strings to get that grenade through security," Eniko said.

"Well, now he's pulled his final string," said Marisol. "Justine, how far is he from you?"

"About eight feet. I figure that little bomb of his has a lethal radius of fifteen feet and a wounding radius of fifty feet?"

"Sounds about right. You need to get away from there."

"Not a fucking chance. I *need* to shoot this mother fucker."

"You shoot me, I drop the grenade," Alessandro sneered. "You and your pretty brown friend here will be blown straight to hell."

"So will your baby," Justine reminded him.

"You think I care about that? Drop your gun little girl."

Danisha's eyes bulged in terror. "Please Justine, I'm begging you. Do what he says."

Justine held her pistol level. "Step away from him, Danisha," she said slowly, firmly.

"No, please Justine, no. If you shoot him we all die."

"Dani, if you don't break away," Justine said, aiming the pistol at her best friend, "I'll have no choice but to shoot *you*."

Alessandro gaped at Justine. "You don't have the balls to shoot her. She's your best friend, remember?" he said, taunting her.

She saw him clearly now, the façade of his charm had decayed like a dead rat on a hot street. His features were transformed; the sparkle that once illuminated his crystal blue eyes and playboy smile was gone, replaced by the hideous determination of a psychopath.

Justine smiled as she placed her index finger on the trigger.

"*Just try me,*" she said, enunciating every word.

Still shielding himself with Danisha, Alessandro backed slowly toward the exit.

The events of the past four months ran through Justine's brain like the trailer of an action adventure movie. Palo Alto, the fake cop, Scott tied to her bannister, the mountain cabin, Gemma. She had allowed her attacker to live then, and he thanked her by murdering an innocent little girl. Don was lying lifeless outside by the pool. No way was she going to let Alessandro survive this nightmare he'd created.

She took careful aim at the outer edge of Danisha's right thigh and pulled the trigger.

Blood spurted from the wound like a geyser. Danisha screamed, then fell to the floor.

Now, finally exposed, Alessandro looked shocked. Justine raised her Glock and aimed for the spot right between his eyes, and pulled the trigger, killing him instantly.

As the grenade fell from Alessandro's lifeless hand, its safety flew off. Justine knew that she had five seconds to stifle the explosion.

She counted silently, o*ne-thousand-one*, as she leaped over Danisha. *One-thousand-two*, as she grabbed the grenade. *One-thousand-three*, as she thrust the grenade under Alessandro's body. *One-thousand-four*, as she threw herself on top of him.

She squeezed her eyes shut. *One-thousand-five.*

The muffled explosion lifted her, along with Alessandro's corpse, several feet in the air. Time slowed to a crawl as she flew up, up, up. From her vantage point at the apex, Justine surveyed the displayed misery and destruction below; so much suffering, and for what? She floated down, crashing to the floor beside what was left of Alessandro.

Her entire midsection was soaked with blood. She felt for wounds through the tattered silk of her dress and found only a few minor cuts and abrasions.

"Justine, you copy?" she heard Marisol say in between the deafening ringing in her ear.

"I'm good. Looks like 'Sandro here caught the brunt of the shrapnel for us."

"We won't know that until I examine you," Marisol barked. "I bet you're wishing you'd listened to Don and worn the pantsuit."

The adrenaline rush of the thrill must've been wearing off because all of a sudden Justine felt the sting of shrapnel in the skin of her abdomen. "Copy that," she admitted. But she was far more worried about Danisha than she was about her own superficial wounds.

Choking on the stench of the RDX and TNT explosives, Justine could hear Danisha groaning. "Dani!" she screamed over noises real and imagined.

"Here...I'm...here..." Danisha responded, her voice filtered through what felt like a mile of thick fluffy cotton balls.

She crawled towards the sound. "Dani! My ears aren't working too well. Wave something so I can find you."

A frail but beautiful brown hand floated into the air about five feet away. Justine crawled towards it, ignoring the stabbing pain in her gut. She was crying when she reached Danisha, not from pain but from fear.

"You shot me. I can't believe you fucking shot me." Danisha's eyes were closed, but she clearly had enough strength to swear.

Justine holstered her pistol and ripped a ribbon of silk from the hem of her shredded gown. "I made an executive decision," she said as she wrapped the fabric tightly around Danisha's thigh. "You're still losing a lot of blood. This tourniquet will hold it back until I can get you out of here."

"Fuck you and all your fucking executive decisions, Justine."

"That's it, Dani, let it all out. Don't hold back." Justine was laughing now, elated to hear Danisha say anything to her.

"Glad you find this so amusing. You could've killed me and my baby."

"But I didn't. You can sue me later. Right now I have other problems, like three live bombs in the swimming pool. Come, try to sit up. We have to get you and your baby to a hospital."

Outside the exit door Justine saw an elderly man in a wheelchair. "Open the door you dumb bitch!"

Danisha collapsed. Justine struggled to hold on to her.

"Did you hear me?" the man in the wheelchair snapped. "I ordered you to open this door."

His voice sounded like it came straight through his nose. Justine looked directly at him and he returned her look with unmistakable disdain. That did it. She finally snapped.

"I heard you. Even though a fucking grenade just went off less than six inches from my *ears*, I heard you *loud and clear*. And you know what else? I'm not your fucking servant. Fuck you and your fucking wheelchair. This woman is severely wounded, and she's pregnant."

He looked at her dumbfounded as she approached his chair, then screamed as she grabbed the handles and heaved them up, up, dumping the old dude onto the tile floor.

"Yeah, yeah, whatever. Don't give me that incredulous look. You reap what you sow, right?"

She rolled the chair back to Danisha and lifted her into it. "Dani, can you hear me?"

As Danisha's eyes opened Justine could've sworn she saw them smiling. "Did you just dump an old man out of a wheelchair, or did I imagine that?" Danisha asked with a definite chuckle.

"What I do for love, eh?" Justine said as she pulled Danisha and the chair backwards towards the door. The old man let out a few more furious curses as Justine's foot helped to nudge him out of her path. "Stop kvetching. Someone will be by soon to collect you. Just sit tight."

"You know you're going straight to hell, right?" Danisha asked as the door slammed behind them.

"We're just leaving hell!"

Outside, all was bedlam. People ran around in a hyper-panic mode searching for safety. No one seemed to be in charge, no one knew who or what to consider safe. Sirens screamed towards the hotel from every direction. Police squad cars, unmarked detective vehicles and bomb disposal units competed with ambulances and fire trucks for space. The many police men and women already on site either scrambled about aimlessly or huddled in packs, waiting for their supervisors to arrive. Or something. Justine looked out at the traffic on Canon Drive and then Santa Monica Boulevard. Nothing moved. No supervisors would be getting through that mess any time soon. Beverly Hills had become one big parking lot.

She raced Danisha past the line of ambulances to the last one in the queue. "Load her up, please. "

A young paramedic sat waiting in the back of the truck. He gave Danisha a quick once over and said dismissively, "Sorry lady, you gotta wait your turn. We have to do triage first, priority goes to the critically wounded."

"*She's* critical. Pregnant, seven months, with a gunshot wound. She's bleeding out!"

"She doesn't actually look too bad."

Justine un-holstered her pistol and aimed it at the young man's crotch.

"I said load her *up*."

The paramedic blanched. "Right. I'll g-g-get the stretcher," he stuttered.

"I'm not the enemy, you know," Justine told him as she helped him lower the stretcher to the sidewalk.

"You have a gun."

"I also have a friend who will die without medical attention." She re-holstered the Glock and helped him lift Danisha onto a stretcher and into the ambulance. Watching him insert an IV needle into Danisha's arm, Justine wanted to cry.

"Fluids," the paramedic said, his voice shaky, as he attached the tube to an IV bag. . "To augment her blood volume."

"Yes, I understand the reason for IV fluids. I've watched my fair share of ER episodes."

Justine leaned over to stroke Danisha's head. She let her hair, still wet from the falling pool water, cover her face so the paramedic couldn't see the tears in her eyes.

"Um, lady? You, um, you look. I mean, I think I should take a look at your wounds?"

She quickly wiped her eyes with the back of her hand. "It's not my blood. Well, some of it might be, but really, I'm fine." She looked straight into his eyes and stated with genuine sincerity, "I need to get back in there. I'm actually working security tonight."

The young man smiled. "In *that* outfit?"

"Right? It's a long story. Which I'd be happy to tell you one day. Can I trust you to get her to Cedars now? Without me? I promise to make it worth your while."

He took a small yellow Ryder notebook from his breast pocket and handed it to Justine. "Write down your name and number. I will call you as soon as I have news."

Justine quickly scribbled down her information then leaned over and whispered to Danisha, "You're gonna be okay. I'll see you in a few hours."

"Miss Baron, right?" the young man said.

"You get her there fast and you can call me Justine."

"And you can call me Adnan," he said, taking off his jacket. "Here, you might need this. It's getting cold and your, um, dress is kinda wet."

Justine stopped, touched by his sudden display of sympathy. "Why, thank you. I've always depended on the kindness of strangers."

"I find that hard to believe," Adnan said with an easy laugh.

"You're right. I've just always wanted to say that," Justine said, hopping off the tail lift.

She was about to start sprinting back into the hotel when she had a thought. "Hey Adnan," she shouted over the escalating blare of sirens and screams. "Any chance you have an extra stretcher in there?"

CHAPTER 62

Marisol was a master of advanced surveillance. Arriving earlier that afternoon at the Beverly Stanton she commandeered the perfect parking spot; a handicapped space with an unobstructed line-of-sight to the hotel's main and side entrances as well as clear views of its cell phone towers. From that spot her van would serve as the command and control post for Marisol's entire team. From there she saw everything, heard everything, and called the shots like a director on the set of a blockbuster movie. The original plan was for her to stay there and be ready for a quick getaway. But plans change, sometimes suddenly, and Marisol had learned from years of experience to always be ready.

She wanted to abandon her post when she first saw Don through Justine's camera, lying on his back by the ruins of the swimming pool. But she waited, knowing Justine still needed her help with the second suicide bomber. Hearing the sounds of chaos and agony coming from the ballroom, pool deck and kitchen, she knew she couldn't just sit in the van any more. She was preparing her gear, getting ready to join Justine, Iya and Eniko in the battle when she heard the explosion of Alessandro's grenade, and she was on her way to pull Don from the rubble when Justine summoned her.

"Marisol! Where are you and why've you been so quiet?"

"On my way to get Don. Meet me there."

"You mean I finally get to meet you face to face?" Justine said. "Wait, how will I know you?"

"Don't worry. You'll know me, *chica*. Nice work back there with Adnan, by the way."

"Thanks. He gave me the stretcher and the extra gear bag from his rig."

"I saw. Please tell me there's a stethoscope in that bag."

"There's a stethoscope and a portable defibrillator."

"Negative on the defib. Electricity and water, bad idea."

"Good point," Justine conceded, a little disappointed in herself for overlooking that basic law of physics. "We need to get Don out of there, ASAP. The dead woman in the pool still has three unexploded bombs in her."

"I'm well aware of that. I'm trying to revive Don now. I just hope that scarf you tied will hold the dead man's switch in check for now."

Justine met up with Eniko and Iya, who, as was their habit, showed up out of nowhere but then realized they had hacked her communications' GPS. She radioed Marisol.

Even Marisol couldn't keep track of those two by her GPS tracking capabilities. "Welcome back *muchachas*," she greeted them over their radio links.

The dominatrices were wearing somehow stolen, surgical scrubs now, which, along with Justine's paramedic jacket and stretcher gave the three women easy access to the carnage on the other side of the growing barricade of police and FBI agents. The hotel's main entrance was clogged with mobs of people still attempting to get out of the ballroom, while uniformed police tried desperately to impose order on the chaos. A gaggle of TV reporters and paparazzi jostled for advantageous positions and shouted questions at the police, who impatiently pushed them all back.

Around back on the pool patio, Justine found yet another scene of what looked like pure anarchy. Strobe lights flashed as photographers snapped shots of emergency responders attending to the victims scattered across the ground. Spouses and significant others sobbed over bodies of their loved ones.

Don was right where Justine left him, lying face up on the side of the pool, near the deep end. A woman was astride Don performing CPR. With each pump at Don's chest, the woman's gorgeous, long, thick auburn hair swung violently, almost completely covering her face.

"I'll take it from here, ma'am," Justine shouted impatiently.

"*Easy*, girls," Marisol growled at Eniko and Iya as they attempted to lift her off of her patient. "It's me, your team commander."

All three women reacted in unison. "Marisol?"

"You have another team commander I don't know about?" Marisol snapped. "Justine, give me that stethoscope."

Justine handed it to Marisol, "Is he...?" She was as afraid of the question as she was of the answer.

"I couldn't feel a pulse but I started CPR anyway," Marisol said. She placed the drum of the stethoscope on Don's chest and listened with intense focus. "*Gracias a Dios*! I might finally be able to hear a heartbeat through the screams of the chaos."

"None of us will have a heartbeat if those bombs go off," Eniko said, pointing at the dead female jihadist' body, laying face up on a mound of bodies in the half-empty pool.

Marisol suddenly raised a triumphant fist in the air. "He's alive," she declared, then checked her watch again. "It's been nineteen minutes since the explosion, and his heartbeat is getting stronger. He must've put himself into a deep state of unconsciousness."

"What, like a coma?" Justine asked.

"Not exactly. More like Don's version of ninja healing magic. Come, help me get him out of here before Lady Ophelia there detonates," Marisol said as she rolled herself onto the ground.

Justine leaned over to offer Marisol a hand. "Oh my God," she shrieked, seeing her mysterious team commander up close for the first time. "Your legs! Where are your legs?"

"Not sure," Marisol replied calmly. "Parts of them are dust in the wind in Afghanistan." Her arms, shirt and pants were covered in blood from having crawled over the dead and wounded to reach Don. Pushing her palms onto the ground, she swung herself upright onto mid-thigh stumps.

Eniko and Iya smirked. "You knew about this?" Justine asked them, incredulous.

"No," Eniko answered. "We're just not shocked."

"But we are amused, at your reaction," Iya added. "How innocent you are."

"An IED got me three years ago," Marisol explained. "After that, Don kept me from killing myself."

"Oh my God," Justine whispered.

"Skip the pity party," Marisol said, "Our first priority is Don. Then take both of us to my wheelchair!" She pointed to an empty upended wheelchair towards the entrance that had been blocked by the bodies of the victims.

"We'll take care of him," said Eniko.

Marisol watched the *Sparrows* lift Don from the ground and place him onto the stretcher with the care and skill of a crack emergency response team. "He's trembling. Losing body heat. Lay me on top of him, STAT," she commanded.

Eniko and Iya nodded their agreement with Marisol's diagnosis and swiftly scooped her from the ground and lay her face-down onto Don's shivering body. They raced towards Marisol's upended wheelchair. Justine righted it and push Marisol's empty wheelchair behind them as they maneuvered the overloaded stretcher through the crowd of newly arrived paramedics, EMTs and uniformed police officers, towards the closest exit.

CHAPTER 63

The cops had cleared the scene of all uninjured guests, but scores of moaning wounded and silent dead remained, creating a gruesome obstacle course for any stretcher-bearer.

"Who's the CO here?" Marisol yelled at a plainclothes female officer.

A woman in a pantsuit said that she was in charge. Then, unsure who had posed the question, her gaze darted from Eniko to Iya to Justine.

"You need to clear this place immediately," Marisol commanded. "The female jihadist's corpse in the pool has three unexploded bombs implanted in her torso."

"You sure?" The officer, still confused by either the situation in general or the source of this fresh intel as well as the owner of the voice that delivered it, posed her question to Justine.

"We're sure," Justine responded. "I'm the one that got her into the pool. She has plastique explosive in each breast implant."

"And she's not pregnant," Marisol added. "Don't forget that part."

The cop was really confused now. "What the...who the fuck is saying that?" she asked, her eyes still jumping from Eniko to Iya to Justine.

"Does it even fucking matter?" Eniko responded as she navigated towards the exit. Outside, a cordon of police surrounded the building and parking lot. Iya, carrying the front of Don's stretcher, pushed through the throngs of strobe-flashing cameras, vociferous reporters and lines of waiting ambulances.

The driver's door of Marisol's van slid open as her group approached it. Marisol sat up and with surprising agility, grabbed on to the handles over the door opening and swung into the driver's seat. She pushed a button inside and the van's rear doors opened. Iya set her end of Don's stretcher on the rear bumper, hopped in, then pulled as Eniko pushed Don into the van.

"My wheelchair!" ordered Marisol.

"Got it," Justine hollered from the back bay of the van and lifted the chair alongside Don's stretcher.

Eniko climbed in next to Don, "He needs fluids," she said, looking at Don. "You have a med kit back here?"

"Is the Pope Argentinian?" Marisol quipped. "Next to the wheel well. The bag with the red cross?"

"Got it," Iya called out, opening the bag. Eniko attached an IV tube to a saline bag as Iya tied off Don's right arm.

"All set?" Marisol called out to her team, turning the key in the ignition.

Justine closed the rear doors, raced to the front passenger door, opened it then hesitated, "I should go back in there."

"The boob bombs?" Marisol asked.

Justine nodded. "If I don't tighten the scarf around that woman's hand, the detonator could easily go."

"You're right. But you also know that this group uses bombs with multiple detonators. You sure you know what you're doing? LAPD has an excellent bomb squad."

"I'm good," Justine said.

"Wait, take this," Marisol commanded, as she reached into her military bag and tossed a coil of parachute chord to Justine. "It'll hold better than that scarf."

"Good call," Justine said as she closed the door and darted back towards the pool.

CHAPTER 64

If she were being totally honest, Justine would've preferred to climb into Marisol's van and ride off into the safely of the dark night. She probably would've gone anywhere to get away from that goddamned swimming pool. Returning to the chaos of victims and rescuers and un-exploded bombs, Justine was engulfed by a feeling of desperate solitude. She fought the urge to flee and looked to the sky for comfort. Lise had taught her years earlier that she could always find her way by locating the celestial constellations of the Big and Little Dippers and the Hunter, Orion. Ever since then she'd looked to those constellations as a sort of spiritual anchor. Seeing Orion and his belt winking down at her from billions of light years away gave Justine a renewed emotional strength, just as it had when she was a girl at summer camp or a teenager stumbling home from a high school Homecoming party.

The situation at the pool looked even worse than it had just a few moments earlier. Clusters of collapsed bodies rested in silence on the blood-soaked terra cotta tile. Others were draped over the chaise lounges and toppled glass-top tables. A few sat motionless in chairs, some still clutching champagne flutes, their heads slumped forward onto tables covered with blood. They all looked like they'd fallen in mid-conversation, reminding Justine of the ancient figures at Pompeii, preserved forever in the ash of Vesuvius.

The almost empty pool water was blood-red now, a temporary shallow grave for a mound of entangled corpses swept in with the backwash of the first explosion. Justine stepped closer to the edge where she'd last seen the female bomber.

There she was, face-up, enmeshed in a tangle of corpses in torn tuxedoes and tattered gowns. Justine's nostrils flared at the stench of destruction and death. Holding her hand over her mouth and nose, she turned away and fought the urge to vomit.

She'd always craved thrills, exhilaration, a life lived on a somewhat less than—comfortable edge. Now she had to remind herself that she'd come this far relatively unscathed, that if she could just continue to ignore the throbbing sting of her superficial abdominal wounds she could handle this. She told herself to just move on, to consciously block out all horrific sights and sounds and smells. She'd spent months preparing for this kind of mission, now she needed to complete it.

Closing her eyes, Justine focused on clearing her mind of the here and now, mentally transporting herself back to Big Sur with Don. Memories of the place, the light, the smells, enveloped and comforted her like the warm waters of his mineral spring.

Don's lessons on explosives and bomb detonation had lasted the better part of a week. All those details and facts sprang to the forefront of her memory, as accessible as a fifth grade math lesson.

Al Qaeda created the breast implant and womb bombs. Each breast implant could carry up to one pound of Russian Semtex, more than enough explosive to take down a jumbo jet. A womb bomb could carry twenty pounds of explosive and thousands of marble-sized plastic spheres the fragments of which would be hard to detect on X-rays.

If the scarf she'd tied around the dead woman's fist came loose, those three bombs would rip Justine and every other living man and woman within fifty yards to shreds.

She opened her eyes and stood, terrified again, and thought about what Don would do.

Don wouldn't be standing here thinking, that's for damned sure. Don would be balls-deep in that death pool, making sure that the scarf holding the dead man's switch in that poor formerly-deluded and now very dead jihadist woman He would disarm the bombs those psychopaths buried in the very organs that give and nurture life.

Mother-Fuckers!

A new sense of rage propelled her into the grisly mix of the pool. While wading slowly through the shallow, viscous stew of blood, organs, and shit, something grabbed the flesh above the backside of Justine's left hip. Startled—and scared half out of her mind—she shrieked, lost her balance, and fell face down on top of her dead bomber.

"Fuck!" she screamed as she struggled to get back to her feet. The hand was still on her hip, not grabbing of course, just kind of hanging out there like it was claiming territory to settle later. Only when Justine twisted around to push it away did she realize that the hand, though attached to a wrist wearing a still-ticking, diamond-encrusted gold watch, was too dead to grab onto anything but was just entangled in the remnants of Justine's Chanel gown, swirling in the water under her borrowed paramedic's jacket.

Turning back to her task, Justine held her breath and took a closer look at the body that still held three live bombs. The eyes, an exquisite shade of amber even in death, were wide open and staring straight up to the starlit sky.

Struck by the beauty of the killer's eyes, Justine suddenly felt sorry for her. "Did your womb ever hold anything other than death?" she said out loud, as if the woman's dead ears could still hear. "Why did you let them do this to you? You had a brain, you had a purpose, but you chose to swallow their fucking poison propaganda, and for what?"

Justine carefully crawled up the dead woman's body, the bombs pressing into her bloody wounds. She tore open the top of the woman's kaftan. A shiny crescent moon and star pendant hung from a gold chain around the bomber's neck. Thinking about her own gold necklace, the *chai* pendant Lise had given her so many years ago, Justine felt another brief stab of pity. The crescent moon necklace had been a gift from someone, perhaps a husband, a parent, a child. This was once a woman with wishes, hopes, thoughts, emotions, and opinions, just like every other human being here. Now she was nothing more than a hunk of rotting flesh, a repository of more gruesome death and destruction.

There was no way to retie the knot without disturbing the hand, and Justine knew that even the slightest movement could trip the spring-loaded switch and trigger the implanted bombs. Slowly, she placed her palm on the woman's right shoulder, and, carefully feeling for wires she might've missed or any other surprises, she ran her open palm up the length of the dead woman's arm, inch by inch, until she reached the scarf tied around her fist. Then, holding her breath, Justine slowly and carefully wrapped Marisol's twine tightly around the lifeless fist and detonator switch.

Confident in the success of this second attempt, Justine almost allowed herself to breathe a sigh of relieved satisfaction. Until she caught a glimpse, in her peripheral vision, of what looked like the red glow of a blinking LED display between the jihadist's legs.

Timer?

Another detonator.

Numbers. Counting down, *33...32...31...*

Another fucking detonator.

Justine stood up straight. She had only thirty seconds to get as far away from the pool as possible. Nowhere near enough time to disarm the bombs.

Silently counting down the seconds, *29...28...27...*she leapt over bodies and debris as she frantically splashed her way towards the exit.

Passing groups of first responders, she screamed with all the strength she could muster, "There's another bomb. Twenty seconds and counting."

A chorus of confused voices shouted back at her. "Where? What? How?"

Thirteen...twelve...eleven...

Justine tripped over a fallen ice bucket then slid on scattered melting cubes of ice, and landed flat on a half-empty bottle of champagne.

Eight...seven...six...

"Everyone down!" The violence of Justine's scream tore at her vocal chords.

Every man and woman in uniform dropped to the ground.

Three...two...one...

Silence.

A pair of strong hands wrapped around Justine's waist. She turned to see the face of a young man, Hollywood actor handsome, wearing a paramedic's uniform. He lifted her onto his shoulder, and ran towards a grassy knoll near the exit closest to the street, where he laid her down, rolled her onto her belly, and covered her body with his own like a protective shell.

What the fucking fuck?

Images, hundreds of them—maybe even thousands—all illuminated by a veritable aurora borealis of lights and colors, raced through Justine's mind in an instant. A triumvirate of percussion instruments punctuated the glorious *Spectacle du Son et Lumière*.

In one brief shattering moment Justine saw Scott, and Lise, and Danisha—poor Danisha with the baby in her belly and a 9 mm bullet ripping through her thigh. And the woman with the LED chastity belt between her legs. *Our Lady Of Perpetual Detonators.* And the hero paramedic. So tall and broad and strong, like a genial Tom Brady.

Tom Brady is my shell right now. Alternate Universe Tom Brady. He's my man-meat bullet-proof vest. Warm. And breathing. Like me.

In what felt like ages before the fallout of the bomb's fragments descended at two hundred miles an hour, Justine saw bright flashes of light behind her tightly shut eyelids. When she finally opened them she saw thousands and thousands of solid and shattered plastic spheres whipping chaotically throughout the outdoor space like a simulated meteor shower at the Hayden Planetarium. Lightweight and innocuous in isolation, they ganged up now and rained down on survivors and corpses alike like angry bullets, bouncing about in all directions, ripping through any and all flesh loitering in its path.

Suddenly the symphony of destruction came to a halt. The rational part of Justine's psyche reestablished its dominance over the drug-less acid trip she'd just been on. Rolling out from under her man-shell, she sat up and took in the aftermath of the blasts.

"You with EMT?" It was a rhetorical question; the serpent-entwined rod embroidered on his uniform pocket told her everything she needed to know about him.

He nodded, but looked too dazed to speak.

"You okay?" Justine asked him. "Can I check you for injuries? Deep cuts, head trauma?"

He shook his head like he was shaking water from his ear after a cross channel swim. "I'll be okay in a sec." He pushed himself to his feet to survey the scene. "Looks like we were saved by the pool."

"How?" Justine asked, incredulous.

"The concrete shielded us from the worst of the blast," he explained as he helped her to her feet. "How 'bout you, you okay?"

"Yeah. I still can't hear too well."

"Your ears ringing?"

Justine nodded.

"It'll stop, eventually," he said, pressing his palms to his ears.

"You don't look so okay," Justine said. He actually looked like he was about to faint. She took hold of his arm with both her hands to steady him as his eyes clenched tight.

"I...um...bit dizzy..."

"Yeah, I can see that," she said. She saw his back looked like hamburger bleeding through the shreds of his jacket. If he hadn't thrown himself on top of her, Justine would have been shredded instead. Tears finally burst from her eyes because of his sacrifice as she started half carrying and half dragging him towards the line of waiting ambulances.

The second she stepped onto the sidewalk at the front of the hotel, a paramedic carrying a stretcher rushed up to help her.

"Holy shit, Dave! He's still alive?" the paramedic asked Justine.

"Rattled and shredded, but alive, yeah," she responded, relieved. "You know him?"

"He's on my team, yeah," he said, his voice cracking with emotion as he lifted Dave chest down onto the stretcher. Justine carefully turned Dave's head sideways so he could breath.

"The explosion probably shattered his eardrums. That's gotta be what's making him so dizzy. He's also lost a lot of blood." Justine squatted beside the stretcher and gently embraced her now unconscious rescuer. "Thank you, Dave," she whispered, kissing him gently on his cheek. She pulled off her borrowed paramedic's jacket and tucked it around his now shivering body.

"He saved my life," Justine said to Dave's associate, her voice shaky with emotion.

"I gotta get you both to the ER," the paramedic said as he started to push the stretcher away from the hotel. "My rig's right over there. I should check you over as we ride over."

"I'm fine," Justine said.

"No offense, but you don't look at all fine."

She looked down at her body. Alyssa's Chanel gown, soaked with the bloody muck of the pool, hung off Justine's torso in shreds. Her arms, shoulders and chest were covered in scrapes and cuts, grass and mud. "It looks a lot worse than it actually is. Most of this is not my blood," she lied, helping him lift Dave in the stretcher into the back of an ambulance.

CHAPTER 65

Justine ran toward the spot where she'd last seen Marisol's SUV in front of the hotel. As she ran toward it she was temporarily blinded by bright flashing lights. Standing dead still in the parking lot, she shielded her eyes with both hands.

Wheels screeched. A pair of headlights came careening towards her. Justine thought they could belong to an ambulance or police car. Whatever it was, it sure loved playing with its high beams as it accelerated to breakneck speed towards her.

Within seconds it was almost upon her, but it missed her by a matter of inches, then turned sharply, before screeching to a stop.

The rear door lifted open and someone yelled, "Get in!"

Justine recognized Iya's voice. Without the blinding headlights she also recognized Marisol's van. She ran towards the light shining through the lifted rear door and leaped in, landing with a dull thud beside the still unconscious Don and the as yet silent Eniko.

The rear door lowered slowly as the van lurched forward, then turned right on Canon and left on Santa Monica towards the 405 freeway. They rode in silence, just another anonymous vehicle speeding through the night.

"You think anyone's following us?" Justine asked when Marisol stopped at the traffic light at Sepulveda Boulevard.

"I always think someone's following us," Marisol responded impatiently. "So I don't make it easy for them. This rig has four, rotating different license plates, all legit."

Justine gazed out the SUV's darkened rear window, focusing on nothing. Thoughts of Lise and Danisha, alone in the hospital, plagued her. She rested her head on Don's chest and finally allowed herself to cry.

Marisol turned onto the onramp of the northbound freeway and pushed heavy on the gas.

Justine watched numbly as they whizzed past the exit for the Getty museum, the Skirball Cultural Center, The American University of Judaism. Her hand reached reflexively for the *chai* charm on her necklace, which of course she wasn't wearing, and her eyes welled up with a fresh batch of tears.

Suddenly she sat straight up and wiped her eyes with the back of her hand. "Anyone have a burner cell I can use? I need to call Scott."

"Do you know if he even survived?" Eniko asked.

"Right now I know nothing about anything," Justine said.

"Glove compartment," said Marisol. "One of you will have to come up here and get it. I'm driving."

"Thanks for pointing that out," Justine laughed as she climbed into the front seat.

"Don't talk too long," Marisol said. "They can still trace us, so you have three minutes of talk time. No more."

"*Jawohl*," Justine said in her best imitation of a German accent, with a mock salute. "I know the drill. Yank the battery when I'm done."

She took the burner from the glove compartment and waited for it to power on. Her hands trembled as she punched in Scott's number. She almost started to cry when her call went straight to his voice mail, but using the breathing techniques Don had taught her a lifetime ago, managed to steady her emotions.

"I hope you're okay," she said in a soft voice. "Call me back on this number, it'll only work for the next two minutes so check the time stamp."

She snapped the phone closed, crossed her fingers, and waited. Within a matter of seconds the phone vibrated.

"Scott?" she shouted, fumbling with the phone as she tried to answer it. "Please tell me you're okay."

"Jussy? Have you heard the news? I was there! Right smack in the middle of all of it."

"Yes, I heard. I didn't know where you were. Oh my God, Scott," she was full on sobbing now. "You're okay? You weren't hurt?"

"Jussy, it was fucking amazing! I got the most amazing shots, probably the best of my career."

"What are you talking about? Pictures of the explosion? The news says hundreds of people are dead. Is that true?"

"Pictures of a *real* live Wonder Woman. You should have seen her. She killed a guy, dropped him like a bad fucking habit. Turns out the dude was bad, real bad. He was using his girlfriend as a human shield and was shooting everybody until he ran out of ammo. Then he surrendered, dropped his gun and started calling for his lawyer like a fucking coward! Then he pulled a grenade out of his girlfriend's purse!"

Justine was so relieved to hear Scott's voice she almost laughed at his enthusiasm. "What the hell are you talking about? Is the woman okay?" she said, as though this was all news to her.

"Wonder Woman shot her too!"

"Oh my God, no!"

"In the thigh. She then shot him right between his eyes! That caused him to drop the grenade he was holding. I dove for cover after that so I didn't get the rest. Every news agency in the world will want these shots. My agent has already started fielding offers. I'm telling you babe, any one of these pictures is worthy of a Pulitzer. I'm gonna have the Feds on my ass though, they're definitely gonna wanna see these."

"Feds?" Justine asked, suddenly worried.

"That's my agent on the other line. I gotta hop off. Love you."

He hung up before she could respond. Reluctantly Justine pulled the battery from the burner, then slumped in her seat and wept.

"Blow your nose," Marisol commanded, handing over a tissue. "I'm sorry, *querida*. Go ahead and cry. We have at least four hours before you have to pull your shit together."

"He has pictures of me shooting Alessandro and Dani."

"I know, I know. But right now we have more pressing problems to solve, like Don. We have to take care of him."

Justine sat up straight and tried to pull herself together. "Yes. I can do that," she stated with absolute certainty.

"Get off at the next exit and take a left," Iya called out from the back as they merged onto the northbound 101 Freeway.

"Thanks for the advance notice," Marisol snapped, rapidly crossing four lanes of interstate freeway to get to Iya's desired exit ramp. She turned left at the first street, as per instructions, and continued for three blocks, stopping at the first red light.

"You can pull over right here," Iya told her.

"I already pulled over," Marisol snapped, pushing the button to open the rear door.

Eniko and Iya each gave Don a tender kiss on the cheek, murmured something in Ukrainian, and slipped silently through the raised door.

Justine lowered her window. "Hey," she started to call out to the girls, but stopped when she saw their faces on the other side of her door. "Why the hurry, was it something I said?"

Iya looked confused but Eniko smiled. "We have to get to our next assignment. I'm sorry we can't help you take care of Don."

"I understand," Justine responded. It was a lie, of course. She didn't understand why they would leave now, of all times. But she brushed those thoughts aside and reverted to her old corporate self, all business and pragmatic gratitude. "Thanks," she said, fighting back tears again. "You guys really saved my ass. And taught me a lot. I do hope we can, um, continue our relationship."

"We would love that," Iya said without a drop of enthusiasm. Justine wasn't sure if she was being sincere or sarcastic.

"Don't get too attached," Marisol warned as she and Justine watched the two beauties slink off into the darkness.

"Why do you think they just walked away from twenty five million? All they had to do was shoot us, then turn Don in! Irina must have been sacred to them?"

"I don't know much but I do know that nothing is simple."

They continued watching the girls, each with their hair hanging loose over their faces, their heads bowed low as they crossed the street and approached a BMW dealership, empty of security guards but brightly lit. Justine leaned out her window to get a closer look as Iya, always the stronger of the pair, kicked the showroom glass, shattering it.

Alarms blared and strobe lights flashed. Eniko and Iya disappeared into the cavernous showroom and emerged less than thirty seconds later straddling two huge black motorcycles. The engines roared as the bikes sped past the van and headed east. Justine watched, mesmerized as the long platinum strands of their wigs streamed from their helmets like fire from rocket ships.

Marisol, broke Justine's reverie, "Time for us to get the hell outta Dodge."

CHAPTER 66

Most people called it the 101, but the signs all referred to it as the Ventura Freeway. Justine had only passed through Ventura, but never explored it. Everything looked dull and empty in the dark of the winter night; Justine closed her eyes and tried to visualize a beach in Tahiti.

"You look like hell," she heard Marisol say from the seat beside her.

"Funny, I was just there." Justine kept her eyes closed.

"I put your suitcase in the back of the van. You could go change."

Justine sighed and unbuckled her seat belt. "Alrighty then," she said, "If my appearance offends you so much, I shall crawl back to the baggage section and make improvements."

"Don't start twisting my words, *chica*," Marisol responded with a chuckle.

"It's just that I was almost in Tahiti, about to get laid," Justine said, sitting on the floor beside Don's stretcher. She peeled off the shredded Chanel gown stiff with Allesandro's and her blood and inspected the wounds on her torso in the intermittent lights of the freeway. Remembering all the blood and gore that dress had absorbed, she shook her head rapidly in an effort to exorcise those memories.

Marisol called from the front, "There's also a trauma kit back there. Maybe you wanna clean those wounds a little?"

"I wanna clean everything, Marisol. Point me towards the showers please."

"Soon, *mija*, soon."

Justine felt around in the darkness for the trauma kit, which Marisol had placed conveniently right next to Justine's overnight bag. The trauma kit resembled an old fashioned doctor's bag.

"And another Mary Poppins bag," Justine said as she opened it and started pulling out bottles, boxes, and other small packages wrapped in paper. "It's bottomless! All this useful stuff." She placed the items in front of her, waiting for the freeway lights to give her enough illumination to read the labels.

Iodine. Hydrogen Peroxide. Isopropyl alcohol. Gauze pads of various sizes, gauze rolls, medical tape, cotton swabs and bandages (she didn't need any light to identify those). Neosporin, Epinephrine. Medical tape. Syringes. Saline. Exam gloves. Surgical masks. Antiseptic wipes.

She soaked a few gauze pads with peroxide. Dried blood and dirt bubbled as she dabbed the drenched pads over the wounds on her belly. Then she slathered herself with iodine and Neosporin before wrapping her entire torso in the sterile cotton bandages like a mummy.

"Here," Marisol said as she tossed back a plastic container of baby wipes. "To clean your arms and legs."

"I gotta be honest," she called out to Marisol as she opened the container of wipes, "I never thought I'd be so happy to see a tub of baby wipes." She used one to clean the soot and blood off her face, then the rest of the package to wipe down her limbs.

"And drink this," Marisol added, tossing back a small box.

"Mmmm, coconut water."

"You need the electrolytes."

Justine guzzled the liquid down. "I don't think I've ever tasted anything so delicious." As she rifled through her overnight bag to find something to wear.

"Wait, who packed this bag?" she asked, finding nothing in it but the ugly pant suit Don had wanted her to wear to the Oscars.

"I did. You got a problem with that?"

"Seriously? You expect me to put this thing on *now*?"

"Since when have you known me to be a joker? If you'd worn it in the first place you wouldn't be cleaning your wounds right now."

"Fine," Justine grunted, lying down to wriggle herself into the clean gray pants. She struggled to hold back a yelp of pain each time the fabric made contact with her bandages, pushing against the tender torn flesh beneath them. Marisol wasn't completely heartless, she'd also packed a reasonably attractive scoop-neck white cotton t-shirt. Justine slipped the shirt over her head, carefully tucked it into the pants, then dug her hairbrush from the bag and dragged it through her matted hair. Feeling somewhat human again, she made her way back to the front seat.

Marisol glanced over at Justine and smiled. "Now you look like a bodyguard."

"You mean acting like one isn't enough? I think I proved myself tonight, no?"

"You, were fucking awesome. You've got some set of balls on you."

"Um, thanks?"

"It's a compliment, believe me."

"I do, I do. It's just that, well, I didn't have the balls to stop my attacker in Palo Alto when I had the opportunity. Iya told me to do it and because I refused, because I let that bastard live, he was able to kill Gemma, not to mention all those other innocent people at the party tonight. He's also the mother fucker that did this to Don."

"Enough. You wanna worry about something? Worry about tomorrow, not yesterday."

"I know, but…"

"But nothing. You killed the bitch suicide bomber and saved *hundreds* of lives. You saved Danisha *and* her unborn baby. And Alessandro, that *maricon*. The leader of a major terrorist cell and international sex trafficker. You blew his brains out. Don't dwell on your mistakes. Learn from them."

Justine reflected in silence for a moment then said to Marisol, "The suicide bomber. Her eyes. They were the most remarkable amber color, a light golden brown. I can still see the fury in them. It terrified me. She let a bunch of misogynists brainwash her with delusions of paradise in the afterlife. Mass murder in the name of religion, what kind of paradise can that lead to?"

"Hell. That's the only kind of paradise those poor unfortunate souls will find. The women in Afghanistan, the local women I met there, they couldn't believe that I could be a warrior. More than a few told me that I inspired them to join the Afghani army and fight for *their* freedoms," Marisol said, one hand nervously tapping the stumps of her legs. "We all pay a price."

"*You* are a fucking rock-star hero, Marisol," Justine said, resting a hand on the older woman's shoulder.

Marisol allowed herself a tiny smile as she squeezed Justine's hand. "And now I have to train you. You are the future, the next generation. And you've got legs," she laughed.

Justine turned her face to the window. "My life's a mess. I'm a fugitive. Scott will probably expose me to the world. The feds will definitely want to *talk* to me then. Maybe even charge me with Alessandro's murder."

"Want to try calling him again?"

"Who?"

"Scott. Tell him enough to stop him showing those photos to anyone. There's another burner in the center console."

"No, it's too late. He's probably already sold the photos. Anyway, we're probably finished.

"Once he founds out it was me he'll think I'm a cold-hearted bitch. He watched me shoot my best friend!"

"He didn't know what you were up against," Marisol argued. "Look, you'll stay with us for a while. You help me take care of Don, then he and I can protect you."

"Thanks, but I think I should probably turn myself in. Between my lawyers, the FBI and the CIA someone will figure out who Alessandro really was."

"Exactly. Think of the publicity! You'll be a national hero, like Eisenhower. Then you can become a powerful politician, take a run for a seat in the U.S. Senate," Marisol said with exaggerated enthusiasm. Then she calmly mentioned like an afterthought. "You'll also be the number one pin up girl target of every fucking jihadist in the entire world!"

Justine sat in silence.

"Or, you could disappear, become someone completely new, like us."

As they drove in silence, they heard Don moan.

Justine unbuckled her seat belt and climbed to the back of the van to check on him.

She pressed the inside of her wrist to his forehead. "He's losing body heat. He might be going into shock."

"Warm him up!" Marisol shouted.

"How?" Justine screamed, looking around for anything that could help. She found a blanket folded beside the trauma kit and spread it over him.

"The same way I did. Hurry!" She looked back through her rearview mirror. "Get under the blanket with him now. Take off both of your clothes and use your body heat to keep him warm."

Afraid of doing any further damage to Don's traumatized body, she used the scalpel in the emergency kit to cut Don's once elegant suit off of his body. Removing his Spectra Shield vest was much harder. She stripped her own clothes off in a hurry then carefully tucked herself under the blanket, close beside him.

"Not like that, get on top of him. Go!"

It occurred to Justine that this would be the first time she ever took a command position over her teacher. The thought made her uncomfortable, though a large part of her ached to be as close to him as possible.

She carefully lowered herself onto Don's body. Her heart pounded against her ribs making such a ruckus she thought even Marisol could hear it.

All the emotions, feelings, sights, sounds, and smells of the past four months, starting with the night with Scott—the romance, the passion, the love, the sex (!), the fake cop, the attack, the panic room—rushed through her mind, body and soul.

Within seconds the memories overwhelmed her. More than anything she craved the *comfort* of Don's words, his hands, his presence. She wanted desperately to talk to him, to tell him what she was feeling, but she couldn't.

Sobbing into his neck, she thought she felt something stir beneath her. She pressed her wrist to his forehead to gauge his temperature. "He's getting hotter," she announced to Marisol.

Don's lips twitched, then curled into a faint smile. Justine laughed, she couldn't help herself.

"What? Why the laughing?" Marisol asked, looking through her rearview mirror.

"A smile. He actually smiled!" Justine didn't tell Marisol about other signs of life stirring under the blanket.

She ran her hand cautiously down his torso, to his groin, and let it rest—for the first time—on the pole that was tenting his pants. "Guess it's my turn to guard your body now," she whispered, then kissed him gently on the lips.

He stirred. She could've sworn he said something.

"What's happening back there?" Marisol asked.

For a split second Justine looked away from Don to address Marisol. "You heard it too?"

"Yes. He's trying to tell you something."

"Don, I'm here," Justine whispered into his ear. She removed her hand from his erection, which, unlike many of his other muscles, seemed to be fully functional.

"My phone," he said.

"Your phone?"

"Jacket. Top. Left. Inside. Pocket."

Slowly, carefully, Justine rolled off of him and sat on the floor beside his stretcher. She slipped her hand into his jacket to retrieve his buzzing cell phone, then gently placed his thumb on the phone's home button and unlocked its screen. "You have twenty-seven new messages, but they're all in some kind of code. I can't read them."

"I can," he said, sounding a touch stronger.

She held the phone up so he could easily see the screen without having to strain his neck. When he finished reading the first message he nodded, and Justine swiped to the next one, then the next, until he'd read them all.

"Everything okay?" she asked him as she placed his phone back in his inside pocket.

He nodded, then said in a weak, raspy, very un-Don-like voice, "Alessandro had a boss."

"What he say?" Marisol called out.

"Something about Alessandro's boss?"

"Yeah, I was afraid of that. It's a many-headed monster that human trafficking terror organization. We thought Alessandro was only one of those heads. Don, can you hear me?"

"He's nodding," said Justine.

"New intel?" Marisol asked, her voice both loud and serious.

"He's nodding again, and his eyes are open. That's a good sign, right?"

"Yes," said Marisol reassuringly. "We've been through this before, Don and me."

Don and I, Justine wanted to say, but didn't. Don grasped her hand and pulled her close.

"Two weeks," he said quietly into her ear.

"Two weeks? He said two weeks," she told Marisol.

"Got it, Don."

"What's he talking about?" Justine was so confused.

"How much time we have to nurse him back to full strength."

"And then what happens?" asked Justine.

"Then we all go back to work. This party ain't over."

Justine contemplated her options. *Did she have any options?* She'd given Don the three months of work he'd demanded, hadn't she? She didn't have the strength to start counting the weeks, or to think about what to do, where to go, who to be next. Don squeezed her hand again, gently.

She looked at him. His eyes sparkled in the low ambient light, and Justine could've sworn they were smiling. "Okay Don. We'll have you back up to speed in two weeks. But I need you to do me one favor. If I can ever get Danisha to speak to me again I want her to design a new bodyguard pantsuit."

Still holding her hand, Don pulled Justine closer to him like he had something to tell her. She placed her ear close to his lips. "Yes, I'm listening," she said.

"Maybe," he whispered. "Depends on the color."

Justine pulled back to try to read his expression. The sun would be up soon; shades of crimson and orange and violet were creeping into the eastern sky, its amber glow giving her just enough light to make out Don's features. Yes, he was definitely smiling.

When he caught the look on Justine's face, he laughed. It was the first time Justine had ever seen Don laugh.

"In any case," he managed to continue, "Danisha only has three weeks to design and stitch together your pantsuit."

"Three weeks? What happens in three weeks?"

"We..." he began to say, his voice weakening with each breath,

"Yes? We what? I'm right here, I can hear you. Don?"

"We have...another...assignment...Miami...Istanbul..."

TO BE CONTINUED

AUTHOR'S NOTE

Trafficking women and children for sexual exploitation is the fastest growing criminal enterprise in the. Sex trafficking is a lucrative industry making an estimated $99 billion a year.

At least 20.0 million adults and children are bought and sold worldwide into commercial sexual servitude, forced labor and bonded labor.

54% of trafficking victims are trafficked for sexual exploitation.

About 2 million children are exploited every year in the global commercial sex trade.

Women and girls make up 96% of victims of trafficking for sexual exploitation.

ACKNOWLEDGEMENTS

A special thanks to my editor Adrienne Friedberg, my agent Stan Corwin, and to my very creative cover designer Paul Posnick for helping to make this novel a reality, as well as to all of my personal protection teachers, who taught me the "Ways of a Warrior." I also want to acknowledge other people for their insights, expertise, and friendship, Judith Agisim, Allen Baron, Barbara Cohn, Georghe and Linda Chessler, Patricia Cloherty, David Patrick Columbia, Diane Falconer, M.C. Hudson, Barrie Lynn Krich, Polly Hill Landess, Eva Lindner, Daniel Matthews, Maureen Meehan, Kip Morrison, Carol Ostrow, "Pixie," Lisa Rosen, Vered Shalev, Jane Shavel, Phil Simms, Maria Elena Torano, and Richard Weber. And of course, a shout-out to my family—David, Jonathan, Lisa, Natalie, William, Catie, Andrew, Chuck, Ruth, Amir and Yael.